THE VOICE
AND
THE ECHO

B J BULCKLEY

Matador
9 Priory Business Park,
Wistow Road, Kibworth Beauchamp,
Leicestershire. LE8 0RX
Tel: 0116 279 2299
Email: books@troubador.co.uk
Web: www.troubador.co.uk/matador
Twitter: @matadorbooks

ISBN 978 1785890 123

British Library Cataloguing in Publication Data.
A catalogue record for this book is available from the British Library.

Printed and bound by CPI Group (UK) Ltd, Croydon, CR0 4YY
Typeset in 11pt Aldine401 BT by Troubador Publishing Ltd, Leicester, UK

Matador is an imprint of Troubador Publishing Ltd

MIX
Paper from
responsible sources
FSC
www.fsc.org
FSC® C013604

DISCLAIMER

This is a work of fiction. In some limited cases, real individuals and events are referred to in their historical context.

All other names, characters, businesses, places, events and incidents are the products of the author's imagination, and any resemblance to actual persons, living or dead, or actual events is purely coincidental.

If you don't read the newspaper, you are uninformed. If you do read the newspaper, you are misinformed

– Author unknown, but attributed to Mark Twain or Thomas Jefferson

1

MARCUS

Mrs Smart affected what she thought was a scholarly tone.

'Breakfast's at eight and supper's at seven.'

She looked at Marcus over the top of her glasses.

'Oh, yes, Mrs Smart.'

'You'll have to get all of your other meals yourself,' said his landlady, 'except for Sunday. On Sunday, I serve lunch at two. You mustn't be late for any meals.'

'No, Mrs Smart, I won't.'

'Here's a list of dos and don'ts.'

It was typed and filled a whole page of A4. The words of greater significance were in bold capitals.

She read every item out aloud and looked up, waiting for him to nod his compliance at the end of each instruction.

'Jack arrived about an hour ago. He's upstairs. He's already chosen his bed.'

Jack was an eighteen-year-old from Burnley.

'She likes rules, doesn't she?' said Marcus.

'Notes everywhere; there's one in the bog telling us what to do when the flush doesn't work and another about how to put a new bog roll in. It's that stuff you get at school that makes your arse sore.'

Jack was able to imitate all of the accents from *The Goons*.

'It's not been on the radio for years. Where did you learn all the voices?' asked Marcus.

1

'My dad was mad keen. What about you? You a Goons fan?'

'Err, yes.'

Marcus did not much like the show, an aversion inherited from his father, and he had not listened to more than a few minutes. Jack was very enthusiastic about his skill, and he performed excerpts from his repertoire for his new roommate.

I won't survive a week if I get this every night. Perhaps all students of ancient history are like this.

That evening, they made their way to the union bar. The noise was ear-splitting. A fresher engaged Marcus in a conversation on popular music, and Jack wandered off. Marcus listened and spoke sparingly, to avoid giving away his lack of interest and knowledge. As each track played, his acquaintance nodded his head, offering a biography of the singer or the group and an opinion on the song. Marcus assumed the 'The Velvet Underground' was a new form of transport system, located somewhere in America.

It took Marcus twenty minutes to fight his way to the bar for a drink. In the process, beer was spilt over him three times. Thankfully, by the time he had completed his task, the music expert had attached himself to another victim. Without loosening the grip on his new prey, he gratefully accepted the beer Marcus had bought. Marcus went in search of the student newspaper office and stumbled over a young couple, under a stairway nearby, in an advanced state of undress.

'Sorry!'

'Piss off!'

The evening did not improve.

The next morning, Marcus Roache determinedly battled his way through the melee that accompanied the first day of Freshers' Week. Groups of final year students were selling the merits of sub-aqua, anarchism, Christianity and the Druids.

They were surrounded by a throng of freshers. Some, who were clear about their interests, had made their way to a club or society of choice, but most were moving from one stand to the next, overwhelmed by the variety. There were leaflets about visiting bands, trips and social events. Older male students circled, displaying the sham indifference of the predator. One of the benefits of being short was that Marcus circulated below the line of sight of these budding salesmen, and they never made contact with his incisive blue eyes. He struggled to force his way forward.

Although most of the people at university were familiarly white, the accents were alien. Marcus had been taught how to speak 'properly' at school. He was accustomed to talking in southern public school English, and even his grammar school acquaintances had remodelled their vernacular to the appropriate polished standard. Here, the accents were untutored, and he barely understood some of his fellow students. It was worse than being abroad.

Marcus managed to avoid two young women who were grabbing men for a visit to a local brewery. He was navigating a map of the Students' Union, and he bypassed the multitude of societies and clubs on offer. He made his way directly to the student newspaper office and stood at the open door.

He had permitted his thick, straight, black hair to grow in the previous few weeks, but it was still much shorter than that on display in the student newspaper office. Where they were languid and cool, he was restless and uncomfortable. His clothes were what would be expected from someone who had never played pinball, listened to Jimi Hendrix, discussed revolution, or attended a student protest. He was stocky and dressed for Frank Sinatra and Bing Crosby's fifties, not Frank Zappa and David Crosby's sixties. He had never heard of Frank Zappa or David Crosby, but his father had voiced his approval of Sinatra and Bing when he had heard them played on Two-Way Family Favourites on the BBC Light Programme.

Three men and one woman sprawled around a desk strewn with paper. They were discussing the typed and handwritten sheets and moving them around as if playing a board game. Posters, sheets from newspapers, messages, reminders and rude comments were stuck to the walls, door and windows. The writers and the recipients may have understood the messages, but they were incomprehensible to anyone else. Cups, plates and mugs were random occupants of tables, chairs, an upturned waste bin and the windowsill. Circular coffee stains showed the journeys of cups during the previous hours, days or weeks, and there was nothing to indicate that anything had ever been cleaned or tidied. Marcus was spotless and gleaming.

One of the men, dressed in jeans and an armless light-blue athletic vest, turned toward the door. Marcus smiled awkwardly.

'Yeah?' he asked, through a mouth framed by a drooping moustache of impenetrable density. The moustache met sideburns in a black mass of curls. It was impossible to discern the facial contours underneath this tangle. The others, paying Marcus no attention, continued their animated conversation.

'I'm interested in joining *Student Voice* and wondered...?'

'The kettle's somewhere over there, man,' he responded, in an unfamiliar accent. He pointed to a piece of furniture that was covered by papers, a filthy towel, a sheet, two rucksacks and a sleeping bag. Marcus could not see the kettle anywhere.

'The kitchen's down the corridor. Four coffees, two black, and make yourself one.'

'Sorry?' asked Marcus.

Perhaps the moustache was acting as a muffle.

'Down the corridor,' he repeated and pointed.

Then he turned and rejoined the conversation with the others. As he leaned over the table, his athletic vest rode up his back. It revealed a brown leather belt, studded with brass rivets. It was failing to hold up his jeans, hanging loosely from his tall and skinny body. The long, straight, black hair, which adorned his head and caressed his shoulders, fell forward. With a flick of his head, it was back in place.

Marcus hesitated at this unexpected and dismissive response. For an instant, he thought about the attractions of the Druid Society, but *Student Voice* was too important for him to be discouraged by this minor irritation. He remembered what his English teacher had told him. In a cold, quiet, empty classroom, they had been discussing his university options.

'University's an opportunity to reinvent yourself, Roache. Here, you're a spotty, embarrassing teenager with an unpleasant nickname. At university, you've a clean sheet of paper. Rewrite yourself, Roache. Rewrite yourself because you won't have another chance.'

'What do you mean, Sir?'

'At school, you have to conform, obey the rules, fit in with the crowd. Parents pay a lot of money for a decent education, and their children don't want to let them down.'

'I'm on a scholarship.'

'And that brings even more pressure to toe the line. You've had to learn the habits of your betters.'

'I suppose so.'

'Nobody at university will care which school you went to or what your father does. They won't find out unless you tell them. They don't know your politics, the music you like, the books you've read, the friends you've kept or even the stupid things you've said and done. So reinvent yourself. Make yourself who you want to be, Roache.'

'Yes, Sir, I'll do what you say.'

'You don't understand me, do you?'

'No, not really.'

'You will.'

The kitchen was a dingy cupboard underneath the flight of stairs where he had encountered the lovers. The coffee was from a tin, and the milk was sour. The blue mould suggested cheese. He cleaned five cups, threw away the old milk, added fresh from a bottle bought from the student shop and carried back the drinks on a tray he had found and cleaned. He cleared a little space on the table.

'Coffee?'

'Cheers,' replied the moustachioed student, who was, Marcus concluded, speaking in a broad Geordie accent. 'What's your name, man?'

'Marcus.'

'Look, Marcus, we're right busy. We've got to get the paper out for the start of term. We'll be in The Half Moon tonight. See you there if you can make it. OK?'

'Is there anything I can do now? I'm sure I can help. I edited the school magazine, and I know the ropes. I'll have a go at anything.'

'This isn't *the school magazine*,' said the Geordie, mockingly.

The other occupants of the room turned slowly, as one. Marcus's eyes were drawn to a petite girl, who displayed a folk singer's looks and clothes. Her floral smock hung loosely and her jeans clung tight. She nodded a welcome and Marcus responded shyly in her direction. A tall, dark-haired and bearded man offered the smile of a friend. The third man wore, on his long and rectangular face, the serious expression of someone in charge. His short hair and clean-shave were more in-keeping with the fashion Marcus had been accustomed to at school.

'Ignore Dave. He doesn't know what he's on about. Hi, I'm Mike Boddington,' he said, seemingly in a hurry.

Mike removed his right hand from the pocket of a threadbare jacket that attempted a style and differentiation, despite its scruffiness. He offered an outstretched hand, an indication that he was the editor. The handshake was firm but momentary. None of the others volunteered a formal greeting.

Marcus's face betrayed a nervous smile. The five pairs of hands set to work, and the rest of the afternoon passed in a blur.

The Half Moon heaved and swayed with freshers. They had been sold the delights of an organised pub crawl and were about to stagger to the next venue. They were already drunk, and it was only 6.30. Mike, although a slight figure, eased his way skilfully to the bar and Clive cleared a way through the crowd.

Without asking what the others wanted, Mike ordered five pints of bitter. Marcus had never drunk bitter; it was a drink that hinted to him that he had entered the realms of the professional pub-goer. Marcus had not mixed in such company before. At home, he was still under the auspices of his father, whose fuzzy religiosity shunned pubs. The bar staff knew Mike and acknowledged his order, barked across the leaving youngsters. Clive led his entourage to seats in a quieter corner. Mike joined them, and they chatted about their afternoon's work.

'You did alright. We need whatever help we can get,' said Clive Parkhouse to Marcus.

Clive took a sip from his glass and casually, but not very effectively, wiped some of the froth from his dark-brown, straggly beard. He then cleaned the back of his hand, wet with beer, on his jeans. Clive appeared to have allowed the beard to grow because he could not be bothered to shave, rather than for aesthetic reasons.

'Where did you edit this school magazine?' Clive continued.

'In London. It was a way to get some experience. I want to get into journalism, and it'd be great to be involved in *Student Voice*.'

'I think you're already in,' said Clara Tomlin, her blue eyes twinkling as she spoke. 'We need some new blood, Marcus,' she smiled.

'Oh!' was Marcus's surprised response.

'Were you expecting an interview?' laughed Clive.

'Err, no, not really.'

'You'll need to get used to the slant the newspaper takes. It's not a hotbed of revolution, but it's left of centre,' Clive continued.

'You're not,' said Clara, speaking with a soft Metropolitan accent.

'You don't know what I am,' said Clive.

Marcus noticed a smile exchanged between them. Clive combed his dishevelled, shoulder-length hair away from his forehead with his fingers. His clean but battered Wrangler jeans, green shirt and black corduroy safari jacket showed no evidence of coordination or care.

When he spoke, his expression mirrored his mood. His hands moved incessantly to punctuate his sentences. He turned his palms upwards and his warm brown eyes widened with every question. He shrugged to show he was not certain, he grimaced with anger, and he always smiled a welcome. Marcus detected an accent that located Clive somewhere in the Midlands or further North.

'Some sort of fucking airy-fairy liberal,' scoffed Dave Shearman through the Zapata camouflage.

'We're all finishing our Bachelor's or Master's,' interrupted Mike Boddington. He placed his pint on a beer mat. 'And this'll be our last year on the paper.'

'You're not going to interview him, are you, Mike? Clara's already offered him the job,' laughed Clive.

Mike rolled his eyes and continued. 'We need fresh blood. I've only seen you operate for a few hours, and you're quickly picking up what's got to be done.'

'Err, thanks.'

Marcus looked out of the corner of his eye, checking to see whether Clara would really drink all of her pint.

'There's one golden rule,' Mike continued. 'Know your readers, and whatever you think of 'em, don't piss 'em off.'

Mike had a hardly noticeable Yorkshire accent and spoke quickly and confidently. He explained how the paper was structured, how the team managed the workload, the ongoing stories and the deadlines that had to be met. By this time, Clive had bought another round of drinks. Marcus had barely started his first, whilst the others, including Clara, had finished.

'We need to follow up on this canteen story,' said Mike. 'There've been loads of complaints that the quality's getting worse.'

'They're trying to make more money out of the students,' said Dave belligerently. 'It's fuckin' exploitation. We could organise a protest. I don't know… get everybody to take ten per cent off the price.'

'Come on, Dave, get real,' replied Clara quietly and with a hint of exasperation. She shook her head, and wisps of her long, straight, ash-blonde hair fell forward over her shoulders. 'Students just want OK food at reasonable prices. Nobody's going to go to war over it.'

'And don't expect arts undergraduates to be able to do the arithmetic. Deduct ten per cent: you're dreaming,' Clive added.

'What do you think we should do, Clara?' asked Mike.

'Interview a few students and print their comments? Perhaps talk to the catering people?'

'Can you pick it up, Clara? We'll run with it in the next

edition,' said Mike. 'I've heard that The Darbys have cancelled their concert in November. I'm not sure why, but there's no end of rumours.'

'That's a bugger 'cos I quite fancied getting tickets,' said Clive.

'Usual story,' grumbled Dave. 'Now they've hit the big time, the manager's after more money. He'll want bigger venues than the Students' Union. All these revolutionary songs, but when it comes to it, they'll screw their fans. They're no better than all the others.'

'Dave,' asked Mike, sighing audibly, 'will you get round the clubs and societies and pick up the usual activity stuff? I need it by Monday.'

'OK, if that's you want.'

'I'll split it with you,' volunteered Clive.

'I'm off home. I need food,' said Mike. With a mighty gulp, he downed his second beer and turned to Marcus. 'If you fancy it, I've a couple of things you could do.'

'Anything, I'll do anything at all.'

'How'd you like to interview Ents? They've got a list of top acts lined up for the year. They'll want a full spread, and you can pick up the story on The Darbys while you're there.'

'Yes, I'll do it.' Marcus hesitated. 'What's Ents?'

Mike smiled.

'It's short for Entertainments. They organise everything in the Union.'

'Clara and me'll be going too,' added Dave. 'We're moving into our new place.'

The others did not notice Marcus cautiously looking to see if Clara wore a ring. There was just one, on the middle finger of her right hand.

Mike, Clara and Dave left. The freshers had already gone, and Clive and Marcus were on their own. Clive was finishing his second beer, but Marcus was only halfway down his first. Clive eyed Marcus's glass, and Marcus, with a shake of his head, declined the nodded offer of a drink. Clive went to the bar, bought himself another and took his seat opposite the fresher.

'What made you come here, then?' Clive asked.

'It's well away from home.'

'What're you reading?'

'History.'

'You'll have plenty of time for the *Voice* then. It's the same with me. I'm doing Politics. We're not very professional, but it goes on the CV.'

'It seems quite professional to me.'

'It's fun, as far as I'm concerned. I can't imagine what unprofessional looks like if this is professional. Mike's good, when he slows down. He's the manager type, but Dave's just a pseudo-revolutionary who likes to see his opinions in print.'

'He seems like an interesting bloke.'

'Suppose so. Don't let him get you on to politics. He'll bore the arse off you.'

'He's got left-wing views, hasn't he?'

'Yes, but sometimes what he says and what he does are different.'

'Was he annoyed that I'm doing the Ents interview?'

Clive was see-sawing on the rear two legs of the pub stool, balancing on his heels as he spoke, and Marcus wanted to tell him to sit properly.

'*He* expected to do it. Don't worry, he'll get over it. That's Mike for you. He likes to be a decisive leader. He reads these trendy management books and tries to put 'em into practice.'

'Management books?'

'Yes, setting objectives for us. He tells us that what gets measured gets done. We just tell him he's a prat and ignore him. Then he gives up. I don't believe any of that bollocks.'

11

'Maybe there's some sense in it.'

'Maybe. He's political; knows who's who in the university and rubs shoulders with 'em. He's into all that sort of crap. He won't ruffle feathers. Clara's the best writer amongst us. Yes, she's very professional.'

'She doesn't get involved in all the banter, does she?'

'No, but don't let that fool you. She always says her piece, and if we get out of hand, she gives us a bollocking. She knows what the readers want, particularly our female readers.'

'She seems nice.'

'She is.'

'She lives with Dave then?' he asked, quietly.

'Yes. Perfect modern couple, I suppose.'

'Yes, I guess so,' Marcus replied, knowing that back home it would have been viewed as scandalous, not referred to in open conversation and whispered about in disparaging terms.

'You'll spoil my image if you tell anyone that we're expert journalists,' Clive smiled. 'I only got into this by accident. It wasn't part of a planned trajectory into a high-powered media job.'

'Oh.'

'The thought of permanent employment's a bit scary, to be honest. I'm never in bed before midnight or up before midday. I hit Mike's deadlines, usually with seconds to spare, and it pisses him off,' he laughed and almost overbalanced on his chair.

'So, you're going into journalism?' asked Marcus.

'Yes, if I can. I'll apply for jobs in regional papers or radio, probably in the Midlands or the North. I won't go back to Stoke, which is where I grew up, and I don't fancy a move to London where the big jobs are.'

'Why not?'

'It'd be a big commitment. I just want a job to earn some

cash. I'm too young to be getting a career. There's a lot to be said for enjoying life when you're young. My dad left school at fifteen, and he's worked in a factory ever since. There's nothing wrong with that, but he's never known any different. He met my mum at seventeen and married at twenty. I don't think either of them had been out with anyone else before they got hitched. University gives you the chance to do different things. It's ironic, but half the people at this place still seem to want a wife and forty years in a career. It's not for me.'

'What about being an editor?' Marcus asked.

'I don't know whether I'm good enough to be a cub reporter. All I've done is write up a few pieces and a bit of editing.'

'I'd like to edit a national newspaper.'

'That's ambitious.'

'I'm sure I could do it. Any of us could if we wanted to.'

'Hell. You've only just arrived, and you're already planning your takeover of Fleet Street,' smiled Clive. 'I suppose there's nothing wrong with aiming high, but you'll stick out like a sore thumb at this place.'

'I don't mean to sound big-headed. It really is a great opportunity to learn the ropes at university.'

He recalled the advice of his English teacher. Nobody here knew how unsure he was of his views. There was no history stopping him being who he wanted to be, no unpleasant reminders and no embarrassing memories. Without risk, he could test out his ideas with his new friends and react to their responses accordingly. He was beginning to understand what reinventing oneself meant.

I'll bide my time, but I'm on my way. I'll do whatever it takes.

2

CLARA

Clara was born in London and she grew up in the suburbs. Clara's father was a doctor and her mother a nurse. Both were non-practising Catholics. They had met at a field hospital in France following the D-Day landings and had seen first-hand the sacrifices made by soldiers of all ranks and backgrounds. They had proudly voted for Clem Attlee and joined the newly formed NHS.

Clara enjoyed her childhood, and she flourished in the environment created by her parents. Conversation was eclectic, and Clara was encouraged to participate, even from an early age. Home was a sprawling, ramshackle place. Books, newspapers, musical instruments and games were scattered because there was no time in the day to clear up.

Clara asked why she had no brothers or sisters. Her friends all had siblings. Her mother explained that she had been ill after Clara had been born and could not have any more children.

Although there was a clear, unspoken moral code, Clara was encouraged to think, say and do what she wished. Mother and Father would guide her, but generally they trusted Clara to make her own decisions. This had caused no problems until grammar school. At first, Clara had enjoyed the environment, but then she reacted against the strict rules on behaviour and the rigorous academic discipline. As she moved into her early teens, she became disillusioned with her education. She loved reading and writing, questioning and debating, but many lessons seemed stifling and pointless, and some teachers became annoyed by her precociousness.

She was in the top stream and expected to do ten O-Levels. She saw no point in studying Physics or Chemistry; so in the spirit of the upbringing she had enjoyed, she ignored them. Her friends at school began to abandon her, encouraged by their parents. They heard that she had become rebellious, and by the time she sat her O-Levels, she was perceived to be a representative of everything that was bad about the post-war generation. Clara's parents saw the spontaneity and zest drain from their daughter, and they blamed themselves. They thought that perhaps they had been too indulgent and had spoilt her. They realised that criticism would be destructive and told Clara that they would back her, no matter what. Her results were predictable: only six O-Levels, all top grades, in her favoured subjects.

She was unconcerned. She had been encouraged to think for herself and make her own decisions, and this was the outcome. Discussions ensued with the school. They wanted her back to do A-Levels, but the invitation was on their terms. Clara refused and joined the sixth form at one of the new comprehensive schools. Clara began to enjoy school again, and she excelled in her chosen subjects, but she was a different, more circumspect young woman.

Her mother became ill, and Clara blamed herself. Perhaps worrying about Clara was a factor in her mother's decline. Clara was distraught when her mother died. It was at the end of her first year in sixth form, and Clara forced it to the back of her mind by putting all of her efforts into school. She was asked to sit for Cambridge entrance, but the idea of Cambridge evoked memories of her loathed grammar school, and she declined.

Just after she had completed her A-Levels, Clara's father

remarried. Although Clara liked her stepmother, it seemed as if her father had gained a new wife, but she had not acquired a new mother. She no longer felt any attachment to home.

Clara had no idea what to expect of university. She filled in various forms and sent them back, thinking nothing more of it. One of them asked about her interests and what clubs or societies might appeal to her. In her first week, she picked up a message at her hall of residence. It was a scribbled request to make contact with Mike Boddington at the *Student Voice* office. She remembered that she had expressed interest in the student paper, and Mike was following up.

She arrived at the office and cautiously peered round the door, but nobody was inside. As she turned to leave, Mike Boddington and Dave Shearman turned up. They explained that the editor-elect had failed his exams and had been thrown out of university. Mike, a second year student and de facto editor, had managed the first edition of the term almost single-handedly. Mike had recruited Dave and another fresher, Clive Parkhouse, and they needed whatever help they could muster to prepare the next publication. Clara knew nothing about newspapers, but she quickly learned.

Although her new friends shared her politics, she was surprised at their traditional attitudes. She was unrestricted by convention and did whatever she thought was for the best. She never worried about the consequences of her actions, and she was unconcerned with how others might perceive them. She became a catalyst, and over time, their mindsets changed. She moved in with Dave and enjoyed a bond with Clive that Mike could not make out. It was a time of changing social attitudes, and she was in the vanguard.

During the second week of Marcus's first term, Clara and Mike were in the *Student Voice* office, discussing the forthcoming edition.

'Attlee's just died, and we could do an editorial about his legacy. Welfare state, health service, that sort of stuff,' said Mike, rubbing his chin and not sounding convincing. 'What d'you think?'

'Abortion's the big topic at the moment, Mike. Attlee's history, but abortion's current.'

'But it's just a women's issue.'

'I'll pretend you never said that,' she growled. 'It's 1967, Mike, for goodness' sake.'

Marcus burst in and interrupted their conversation. He explained that he had found a discarded cork pinboard outside a seminar room that was being refurbished.

'I could put it up. What do you think?' he asked Clara and Mike.

'OK,' Mike shrugged, uninterested. 'Just get on with it, will you?'

'Sorry. I didn't mean to butt in.'

'It doesn't matter. Whilst you're here, we're looking for an editorial piece. Attlee's just died. I thought perhaps something general on the welfare state. The Abortion Act's going through Parliament, and Clara thinks it's a better story. What d'you reckon?'

'Oh, I don't know. I mean I don't know anything about... about abortion. I could do something on Attlee. Yes, I'll do that if you want.'

'It's OK. I'll do the editorial on abortion,' said Clara.

'Thanks, that's a real help,' replied Mike. 'I know it'll not need editing, and that'll save time.'

Within a day, Marcus had screwed the pinboard to the wall and attached a piece of card that read 'Messages' to the top right-hand side. At first, only Marcus used it, and everyone continued as usual. After a few days, Clara noticed the disappointed look on Marcus's face when Dave stuck some photographs to the wall with Sellotape. She started to use the board.

'Good idea, Marcus,' she told him.

'You can put other stuff up too, you know. Photos, reminders, or information,' he enthused.

Marcus got into the routine of tidying up whenever he had a spare moment. Only Clara realised.

'You like things just so, don't you, Marcus?'

'What do you mean?'

'You know, organised, under control.'

'No, I'm just tidying up.'

She smiled to herself.

Mike, who had read in one of his management books that tidy offices were happy and productive offices, adopted the pinboard a few days later. He gave the impression to visitors that the idea was his own. Clive sensed that change was in the air, and he conformed, without being asked.

Halfway through term, at a meeting to agree the final layout before *Student Voice* went to the printers, they were gathered around the table. Copy was being organised and discussed. Dave arrived late, and he casually dropped a flier onto their work.

'For goodness' sake, Dave, pin that piece of paper on the board. Better still, throw it in the bloody bin,' shouted Mike.

'Sorry, I didn't think it…'

'Just do it. Please, Dave.'

Later that week, Clara arrived early at the office. She was due to attend a tutorial at nine and dropped in on the way. Marcus was on his hands and knees next to a plastic bucket of bubbly water. He was dipping a blue cloth into the froth and squeezing out the excess. After each squeeze, he wiped the coffee table furiously, unaware of her arrival.

'Marcus, what *are* you up to?'

He turned, startled and embarrassed.

'I got in early. I wasn't expecting anyone around. I just

thought I'd clean things up a bit. You don't mind?' he asked nervously.

''Course not.'

'Do you think the others, you know, will they be bothered?'

'They probably won't notice. I'll give you a hand. It's a mess, and I guess we should've done it before now.'

'I was going to clean the kitchen too.'

'I've got a tutorial in a few minutes. If you finish here, I'll do it when I get back.'

Clara put her hand on Marcus's shoulder. He flinched.

'We'll nag the others to keep things tidy.'

Clara returned later that morning, and she began the process of washing up the accumulated crockery. Clive sauntered into the kitchen and stood behind her. Her hands were in the sink, and she had her back to him. For a moment, he leant on the doorframe and admired her. Without looking round, Clara sensed he was there and addressed him.

'What do you want, Clive?'

'You know what I want.'

'Clive!'

'A cup of coffee. Honest, all I want's a cup of coffee.'

'Make yourself useful. Bring the rest of the plates from the office, and take the pile I've washed back to the refectory.'

'What's all this about?'

'We're having a clean up.'

'Are we? Whose idea's that then?'

'It was Marcus's, and I agreed.'

'Is Marcus taking charge then?'

'Could be.'

'I thought so. I'd hate it if he was editor. He's already got you running round after him.'

She turned and splashed him with soapy water.

'Perhaps it's *me* who's taking over.'

'Be serious.'

At lunchtime, the team met to work on the paper. They brought their food from the refectory on plates. Over the following few weeks, Marcus, Clara and Clive cleared up afterwards until, without being asked, Mike did likewise and behaved as if this had always been his routine.

Toward the end of the first term, Mike, Marcus, Clara and Clive finished lunch, took their cups and plates to the kitchen and quickly washed up and dried.

'I'll get Dave's,' offered Marcus.

'No you bloody well won't!' said Clara, angrily.

They returned, but Dave's crockery and cutlery were still scattered across the table. Clara gave Dave a look.

'What's the matter, pet?'

'Dave, I'm not your bloody maid.'

'What?'

'Are you going to tidy up your mess?'

'But I never...'

'Now's a good time to start... pet.'

Dave looked toward the others for support, which he did not get, and they watched him slink out, fully laden, to the kitchen.

It was tradition to have Christmas lunch in the office. Tasks had been allocated, and contributions for the event had been donated. It was noon on the last day before the Christmas break. The *Student Voice* office was clean and tidy, unrecognisable from the day Marcus had first arrived. Clara had laid a festive paper tablecloth and was placing a candle in a narrow-necked vase in the middle. Mike rushed in to talk to her before the others arrived.

He explained that he would be under pressure next term, and he could not devote the necessary time to the paper. He was behind on his dissertation, and his tutor had told him that he must catch up. With exams due at the start of the final term, he realised that the others would become increasingly busy too. This was usually when the best second year student took over. Nobody fitted the bill, just the fresher, Marcus.

'What do you think, Clara?'

'He'll manage it, no problem.'

'Sure? He's only been here a term.'

'He didn't really know what he was doing at first, but he watches, listens and learns quickly. Everything he's done has been great. He's ambitious, sure about himself.'

'You think he's confident?'

'Not with chit-chat, he's not. Sometimes it's hard to make him out, to be honest. Intense, sincere, but not always sensitive.'

'A bit old-fashioned, maybe?'

'Yes, he's shy, especially with women.'

'With you, you mean.'

'He likes to be in control. When he arrived he'd no opinions, but he's picking them up, mainly from Dave. It's a bit odd because they're chalk and cheese.'

'No, he's not like Dave,' laughed Mike.

'Underneath it all, he's a nice enough guy, and he'll soon be able to edit the paper with his eyes closed. He knows he's good and I'd give him his head.'

'What about you and Dave?'

'I don't want to run the show, and Dave couldn't. Leave him to me.'

'Clive?'

'Clive'd be scared stiff if he was given responsibility. Nothing'd get done. I like Clive a lot, you know that, but no.'

'Did I hear my name mentioned?' said Clive, embracing a tangle of foliage and stumbling into the office.

'Yes,' said Mike. 'We were wondering where the hell you'd got to.'

Clive had been instructed to find holly with berries, and he explained how he had succeeded, enduring a few scratches to arms and face, a grazed elbow and a twisted knee. He had also stolen a single sprig of mistletoe from one of the female halls of residence where it had seemed to be redundant. He dangled it over Clara's head, but she pulled away.

'No chance,' she laughed.

'You'll change your mind after a glass of wine.'

Marcus opened a box of crackers and laid them out on the table. Dave had brought beer and wine and was trying to ease a cork from a bottle of white. Mike, as befitted his station, pulled a bottle of port out of a bag.

They laid the table and brought in their Christmas lunches from the refectory. They discussed the next edition of the *Student Voice* as they ate, but Mike made no mention of his conversation with Clara.

Within an hour, the beer and wine were having an effect.

Clara and Dave were seated next to each other, Dave draping an arm around his girlfriend's back and Clara resting her head on his shoulder. Everyone was wearing a paper hat, and Clive had stuck a large piece of cotton wool, ostentatiously, on the bloodiest scratch on his face. Mike was opening the port.

'What're you doing for Christmas, Marcus?' Clive asked.

'Quiet. See my mother and father.'

'Any brothers or sisters?'

'No. We have my aunt, uncle and cousins over for Christmas day, that's all. I'll probably come back straight after New Year. I've got an essay to hand in, and I can research the housing story. I think it's got legs.'

'Me too,' said Mike. 'Housing will always be a big topic for students.'

'I've got a few ideas, and I'll bring my camera from home.'

'Anything particular in mind?'

'Perhaps run a competition for the worst accommodation story. Offer a prize and take photographs of the shittiest slum. What d'you think?'

'Yeah, I like it.'

'Everyone with a crap landlord will be able to relate – a campaign we could run for months, years even.'

'Sounds good, Marcus,' said Mike. 'If you're back early, I'll see you around. We can talk about it.'

'Do you go home for Christmas?' asked Marcus.

'I'll see my mum and my brothers. My dad died in an accident in a foundry when I was a kid. Mum brought us up on her own. We all go back on Christmas Eve, and Mum makes a real effort. It's her day, having the family around.'

Marcus noticed a tremor in his voice. Mike finished pouring port into five plastic cups.

'It's nice,' Mike continued, 'but I'm here for a New Year bash. I've got job interviews too.'

'I thought you'd already got a job,' said Clive.

'Yes, I got an offer in November. It's a local paper, the *Star*, but I'm seeing what else there is out there. Linda's starting teacher training, so I'm stuck in the area for at least another year. What about you, Clive?'

'We have a big family get-together. I meet up with my mates on Christmas Eve. It's a bit of a ritual. Things are changing though. Most of my school mates are married or getting married... or divorced. Just a few of us left. Shame, really.'

'Meeting old girlfriends?' Clara asked.

'They're not old. They're mostly my age. Anyhow, what's wrong with that?' Clive replied.

He feigned annoyance and laughed.

'Any job on the horizon?' she asked.

'Not really been looking too hard. I quite fancy working for a regional paper.'

'Still burstin' with ambition,' said Dave.

'You can talk.'

'That's where you're wrong. I'm going for an interview in Newcastle. It's a management trainee job, working for the council.'

'What about that hair?' Clive asked.

'What about it?'

'Well, you'll need to have it cut.'

'I know that.'

'Who's going to lead the revolution when you sell out?'

'Fuck off.'

'Come on you two, it's Christmas,' said Mike.

'Dave already knows this,' said Clara, 'but I've managed to get a job in London. The letter arrived yesterday.'

'Who with?' asked Mike, excitedly.

'The *Sentinel*.'

'Bloody hell!' shouted Clive. 'That's amazing; a top national. Well done, Clara, well done.'

'I can't believe it myself. They asked to see some of the work I've done for the *Voice*, and that seemed to swing it. I start in August.'

'What about you and Dave?' asked Mike.

'Oh, we'll sort something out,' shrugged Clara.

'Try the port. It'll warm you up,' said Mike, who had poured generous slugs into five plastic cups.

Dave and Clara separated and cups were raised.

'Cheers,' they said in unison. 'Happy Christmas!'

When they had finished eating and cleared up, Clive, Dave and Clara drifted away. Mike asked Marcus to stay. He explained what he had previously discussed with Clara and asked Marcus what he thought about becoming acting editor the following term. Mike said that he would retain overall responsibility for the paper, but Marcus would take charge of day-to-day activity, and Mike would give Marcus some editorial freedom.

'Well, what about it?'

'Yes, of course, yes, I'll do it,' said Marcus excitedly and then in a more controlled voice, 'I'll need your help, Mike, but I'll do it. What about the others?'

'I've cleared it with Clara. I'll sort things with Dave and Clive. Don't mention anything until next term. Congratulations.'

Marcus walked home in a daze. He had done it. He had taken his first big step. OK, Mike was still around, but Marcus would be running the paper. He had hoped, expected even, that his time would come next summer, but this was the best Christmas present ever.

3

MARCUS

Marcus was in a forward-facing seat, next to the window, on the train travelling to London. He was dreading his return home and the mindless routine of the visit of Uncle Kenneth and his family. The choreography and script had been rehearsed for almost ten Christmases, and everyone was word perfect.

He closed his eyes as the train rattled and swayed through the darkness, rain clinging mysteriously in droplets to the window, gradually sliding rearward before being whisked into oblivion by the cold night air. He was daydreaming – precise and vivid recollections, not the wild imagery of dreams.

His thoughts leapt back to the autumn term of his last year at primary school. His mother was explaining that he would be sitting the entrance exam for the local independent school.

'But I want to go to the grammar school. That's where my friends are going. My teacher says I'll get into grammar school.'

'Father thinks it's best for you. The high school is more academic than the grammar school.'

His mother was adamant, and anyhow, his father had made his mind up, and that was the end of it.

'Go and tidy your room up, Marcus, it's a mess,' she said, and he sloped upstairs to his bedroom. Within ten minutes, his already tidy room was pristine, and he felt a little better. His father returned from work. He heard the bass notes of his parents talking and guessed that he was the topic of conversation. His father cleared his throat, a trivial act, usually portending a call downstairs and submission to the regime within the Roache's household.

Whenever anyone asked him how he remembered his father, it was the hacking noise and all that it signified that immediately sprung to mind.

'Marcus, come down here, will you?'

His father and mother had taken their positions in the immaculate front room, Father in his chair and Mother on the settee opposite. No speck of dust had ever been allowed to settle because Mother saw to that, and she patted for Marcus to take his seat next to her, but not too close.

'Mother says you don't want to sit the entrance exam.'

Marcus sat nervously, saying nothing.

'Hmm. You're not going to be a baby about this, are you?'

Marcus remained quiet.

'Come on, speak up. I'm not going to bite.'

'No, I won't be a baby,' he sniffled.

Marcus fixed his stare on the carpet in front of him.

'Good. You need to stiffen up. It's dog-eat-dog out there. You've got to be grown-up about it, young man. Yes?'

'Yes, Father.'

'Hmm. You'll have to do well in the exams because we can't afford to pay, you know. You can do it if you try your best.'

Marcus cried quietly that night and mumbled a prayer to himself.

'How did it go, Marcus?' his father asked, the day he completed the exam.

'I think I did OK.'

'See, nothing to worry about. I knew you'd be fine. You're a bright lad.'

That Christmas was the first time Uncle Kenneth and Auntie Moira were invited for dinner. Marcus's dad, Ernest, announced that Marcus had recently sat the entrance exam. He spoke as if success was a formality. He smiled proudly at Marcus's mother, Brenda, who reciprocated. It was as if the invitation to Ernest's brother had been made with the sole objective of parading Marcus's academic prowess and potential.

In the weeks following his father's Christmas announcement of Marcus's assumed success to Uncle Kenneth, he endured more sleepless nights. Then, midway through the Easter term, his mother proudly waved the letter from the high school under Marcus's nose.

'Father will be *so* pleased,' she said.

For weeks afterwards, Marcus endured the ribbing of his friends who had gained places at the grammar school.

As the train continued toward London, Marcus smiled to himself, as he had done to his mother all those years before. Now it was a smile of satisfaction, but back then it had been a smile of relief.

Marcus turned in the uncomfortable carriage seat, his eyes still closed. Now it was the day of his A-Level results. He was back in his bedroom. His father had just left for work, and like almost every morning since he had completed his exams, Marcus lay on his bed, dredging through the answers he had written. He had kept the green exam question papers in his bedroom. He re-marked his answers and jotted his estimates on scraps of paper, just as he had done fifty times before. If they did not give him the right result, he re-calculated until the totals satisfied him. He considered what he would do should he not get the required results, a daily routine for the last month. The alternative was not what he wanted, but he would make the best of it. Before breakfast, he crumpled the scraps of paper into balls and launched them from his bed into the waste bin, followed by the exam questions.

Marcus finished his breakfast and trudged toward the school, head slightly bowed. Ahead of him, groups of students were making the same journey and talking animatedly. Marcus was deliberately taking a route and walking at a pace that would avoid contact with classmates. His stomach churned at the thought of their excited chatter.

He stopped outside the school gates, collected himself and walked inside, pretending he had not a care in the world. Gowned teachers floated by, some offering congratulations to successful students and expecting gratitude in return, others imparting advice, but Marcus just needed to know.

He collected the envelope and weighed it in his right hand, too light for the portentous message it enclosed. Success and failure would take his life in different directions.

In the main hall, students were sharing their results, shaking hands, slapping backs and loudly congratulating classmates, all flushed with success. Marcus ignored them. He sauntered to the rear of the room, and with his back to the wall, so that nobody could see over his shoulder, he tore open the envelope, his fingers trembling as he unfolded the single sheet of paper.

There was no denying the letters that appeared next to each subject – B, C, D. The grades were not good enough. He read the three letters again, but they did not change.

Out of the corner of his eye, he saw Jeremy McNeice. His ear-to-ear smile seemed almost to have split his head into two.

A friend was asking him if he had achieved his grades.

'Three As,' Jeremy smiled.

'Oxford?'

'Can't wait.'

'And then the BBC?'

'Yep.'

'What about Marcus? Have you seen him? He was hoping for the same, wasn't he?'

Jeremy looked toward Marcus, and they mutually turned away, to avoid each other's gaze. Marcus knew his results would soon be broadcast to everyone in the year. He was aware that McNeice had been eying him and Marcus knew what he was thinking. He knew what they were all thinking.

Marcus remembered the lonely walk homeward along the High Street.

He went into a café called Lena's. He had never been in before. He ordered a coffee and sat at the window, thinking about what he would say to his parents. How would he explain that he would not be going to Oxbridge?

The coffee machine choked and spluttered. Brown stains decorated the Formica tables, and a young man in a T-shirt and jeans, cigarette hanging lazily from the corner of his mouth, fed a jukebox. 'A Whiter Shade of Pale' was playing. He recognised the song, but did not know or care who was singing it. When it was replaced by 'Let's Spend the Night Together', a group of lads cheered as their mate at the jukebox performed a Mick Jagger impersonation. The place was half-empty, and the other customers exuded boredom and disaffection. He felt uncomfortable and picked up the *Daily Mercury* tabloid from the next table. The previous reader had left it with the back page up. The new football season had just started, and the pundits were predicting the outcome. As the minutes passed, Marcus's mood changed. His anger and disappointment started to subside. He put the paper down and began to plot a realistic but ambitious career, one that he had been considering for weeks and one that did not rely on getting into Oxbridge. An older man who had just taken a seat at the next table interrupted his thoughts. He was dressed in dirty working clothes and heavy boots.

'Let's 'ave a quick butcher's if you're done, mate,' he said in a working class London accent, any hint of which was disapproved of at home and eradicated at school.

The man nodded toward the newspaper, and Marcus handed it across without speaking. The newcomer quickly fingered through the pages.

'The usual crap,' he sighed, rapidly scanning the newspaper from front to back before settling on the racing page.

'It's not that bad,' replied Marcus, defensively. 'I wouldn't mind working at a newspaper like the *Mercury*.'

'Better 'n that lot.'

The man jerked a thumb over his shoulder and turned to address them.

'I've known 'em from babies. All on the dole and never done a proper day's graft in their bleedin' lives. They think they're gonna be pop stars. Pop stars, it's a bleedin' larf.'

'You sound like my old man, Norman,' laughed Mick Jagger from the jukebox. 'I don't listen to 'im, neither.'

'P'raps yer should,' Norman shouted back, then turned to face Marcus and whispered. 'Idle git.'

Norman took a large bite from a bacon sandwich, used the back of his hand to wipe ketchup from his mouth and chin and cleaned his hand on the front of his dirty overalls.

'You go for it. Better'n roofin'.'

'Anythin's better'n roofin',' shouted Mick Jagger to his mates.

Norman turned.

'You mean anythin's better'n workin'. Anyhow, keep yer nose out.'

'Piss off,' whispered the young man.

'What's the best paper then?'

'Depends what you want. Everyone at school reads the *Chronicle*.'

THE VOICE AND THE ECHO

'Posh school, is it?' Norman laughed.

'No, no, not really,' Marcus replied. He could not hide his embarrassment.

'I don't know nobody what reads the *Chronicle*. It's the *Echo* or *Mercury* if they read anythin'.'

'They're good papers, honestly,' said Marcus.

'The *Chronicle*'s a bleedin' waste of money. I'd never get through it. I like a bit of sport, news and some gossip, yer know, for a larf.'

Marcus thought better of explaining that he'd wanted to join the BBC.

'In a few years, maybe I could be working at a paper like the *Mercury*,' he said earnestly.

Norman busied himself with his breakfast. Between bites, his forefinger was moving down a list of horses. Marcus was not registering what the other man was doing, absorbed in his own thoughts. He addressed his words to himself, wistfully.

'I suppose I wanted to be like everyone else at school. It's no use wishing things were different, but I can still get to the top.'

'Got a pen?' asked Norman.

Marcus pulled out a Biro and handed it to Norman, who proceeded to underline the names and odds of some of the horses.

'They have this… I don't know how to describe it,' Marcus rambled, 'this sort of charm. It's arrogance, I suppose. They just… expect to succeed.'

Marcus looked at Norman, engrossed in the runners and riders. His mind, which had been focussed on the uncertainties of the future, started to see a route forward. The more he thought, the clearer the map became. His future would be in newspapers. He could never get to the top of a newspaper like the *Chronicle*, but the *Mercury* was a different matter. Norman looked up and saw Marcus smile to himself. Marcus, embarrassed, dropped his gaze. He stood up, turned and walked confidently to the door.

'Enjoy the paper. Keep the Biro.'

Norman looked bemused at the sudden and unexpected departure. Marcus was outside and away before Norman, who had just taken his final mouthful, had swallowed and could speak. The youngsters looked on indifferently.

'Fuck 'em,' Marcus whispered to himself. 'I'll do better than all of 'em, especially Jeremy fucking McNeice.'

The carriage shuddered and Marcus was suddenly aware that the train was stopping. He looked at his watch and realised that he was still over half an hour from London.

He smiled to himself. He really would show McNeice and the rest of them.

4

MARCUS

Marcus was seated on a mattress on the floor, his back wedged into the corner of the room. 'White Rabbit' was playing downstairs, and he recognised the crescendo because he had listened to it at every party he had been to since arriving at university.

Marcus nodded to the beat, mimed the familiar refrain and smiled in apparent agreement with the sentiment. Dave was sprawled alongside him, hardly recognisable from the start of the year. His moustache and sideburns had recovered from a serious trim before Easter, reluctantly undertaken for an interview, but his hair was barely longer than military length. In contrast, although Marcus had never attempted the Zapata style, his hair now conformed to the required length for a student in the late sixties. He was clean-shaven and wearing clothing that would be considered just about cool by his friends and seditious by his parents. He had packed his old casuals away, but he could quickly bring them out for trips home. It was early one Sunday morning in the May of the following year, and students were slowly dispersing from the party. The sun was rising, the room was almost empty, and there was a stale stench in the air. It was emanating from half-empty beer glasses, partly eaten food and the fumes of various smokes and joss sticks.

Marcus, who was half-listening to Dave, had heard the same speech many times.

'We need a fuckin' good shake up in this country. The real thing, you know? Miners, steelworkers, dockers and students, the whole fuckin' lot.'

'Yeah,' Marcus sighed.

'The Labour Party's just a load of Tories in disguise.'

'Too right.'

'Whoever's in government, it's the same crowd running everything. They know fuck all.'

Dave struggled to enunciate the words.

'They want to lock you up if you have a joint, but their kids are smoking and shooting up at university,' Marcus added.

Clive and Clara were talking in the corridor, out of sight. They were almost nose-to-nose. Clive leaned over her shoulder and whispered in her ear.

'Is everything, you know, is everything alright?'

'I'm fine, thank goodness. In the end, everything's worked out OK.'

'Sure?'

'There's no need to worry. There's nothing to keep Dave and me together. Clive, you're a real friend. Thanks for everything. I do love you.'

Clive pulled away.

'You're a tease,' he grinned.

Clara put her hands round Clive's neck, gently pulled him back toward her and kissed him quickly, but affectionately, on the lips. They leaned away, looked each other in the eyes and exchanged warm smiles. Clive stumbled into the room, followed by Clara.

'Planning the next revolution, you two? You've become like Marx and Lenin, Groucho Marx and John Lennon, that is.' said Clive.

'Pish off,' Dave slurred.

Marcus smiled, and Dave continued, unabashed.

'It's alright to screw a choirboy if you're a fuckin' priest but not to hold hands with your boyfriend. I'm not queer myself, you know that.'

'You sure?' asked Clive.

'Fuck off!'

'You still here?' asked Clara. 'You should be in bed, Dave.'

'Is that an offer?'

Clara's glower provided an answer. Dave was in full flow. He had an audience and he would be heard, but the others were not really listening.

'What about the Yanks?'

'Here we go again,' whispered Clive in Clara's ear. Marcus saw him enunciate the words, but Dave continued.

'I was outside the US Embassy in May '65.'

'You just went for the day out, Dave. Haven't you had enough of a rant for one night?' Clive sounded exasperated.

Dave took a deep drag on what looked like mainly cigarette paper. He coughed.

'Roll my next one for me, Marcus. I'm all fuckin' fingers and thumbs.'

'Can't imagine why,' said Clive.

Marcus dutifully did what he was told, making a more professional job of it than Dave, who continued to speak.

'It's our generation, with a proper education: we can make a difference. Right, Marcus?'

'Right.'

'Yeah, man,' said Dave, eyes closed.

'When laws change,' said Marcus, 'people'll have to be more tolerant, like on homosexuality.'

'Good news for you, Dave,' said Clive.

Clara elbowed him in the ribs.

'Very funny,' said Dave.

'Dave's right,' Marcus continued. His voice was earnest

and measured. 'Our generation *can* change things for the better. We'll make it happen.'

'I thought you was a bit of a twat when I first met you, but you're alright, Marcus, you're alright,' said Dave, who was having problems moving from sprawling to sitting. He was aware enough to appreciate his problem.

'I need to get home. My fuckin' head's gone, man.'

Marcus handed him a perfectly rolled cigarette.

'That's the only sensible thing you've said so far,' observed Clive. Again, Clara dug him with her elbow.

'Don't get him going,' she whispered in Clive's ear.

Dave stood, gained his balance and followed his hand, which he slid along the wall. He stumbled to the door and disappeared past Clara.

'Pissed? Stoned?' asked Clive. He leant backward against the wall and slid to the floor next to Marcus. Clara was opposite, thumbs tucked in the front pockets of her jeans.

'Both. I know he goes on a bit.'

'A bit?' asked Clara.

'OK, more than a bit, but he wants to change things. I like talking to him, and he's got good ideas,' replied Marcus.

'What are they then?' she asked.

The question was not neutral.

'Well… ' He paused. 'Dave's against drug criminalisation. I agree with him.'

'Why's he against it?'

'What do you mean?'

'Is it because he thinks drugs are a good thing?'

'No, that'd be stupid.'

'Because he doesn't want to be prosecuted for smoking pot?'

'The law shouldn't interfere if it doesn't harm anybody else. That's what you think too, so what's bugging you, Clara? I thought you and Dave… never mind.'

'University's full of students from middle-class families who turn themselves into socialists, communists, Stalinists and now even Maoists.'

'Are you referring to me?'

'Don't want to stick out like a sore thumb?' she asked.

'Come on, Clara,' said Marcus.

'Most working people would laugh if they heard Dave's revolutionary crap. They just want a little more money and secure jobs. A miner at tonight's party would be shocked, especially if he saw what student grants were being spent on.'

'Things are happening in France. Perhaps the same could happen here.'

'What's happening in France?' asked Clara. 'Students sounding off, waving their little red books, putting up pictures of Che Guevara in their rooms and thinking that they're going to change the world?'

'That's cynical. You don't believe it.'

'Last month, Martin Luther King was murdered,' Clara continued. Her voice was now cool and persuasive. 'That's the reality.'

'French students on the streets aren't going to change anything,' Clive interrupted.

'Don't *you* start,' said Marcus.

'This place is full of students spouting revolution; just cheap talk to fit in,' said Clara. 'They'll end up as solicitors, businessmen, administrators, or teachers. Dave too.'

'You think I'm like that, don't you?'

Marcus's voice was prickly.

'I don't know. You've got a Che poster,' Clara laughed. 'Have you bought a little red book?'

Marcus shook his head

'Anyhow,' said Clive, 'next term you'll be Editor of *Student Voice*. No Mike around. It's your big chance. You've done a great job standing in for him. The paper's become a better read, especially what you've done on bad landlords.'

'Do you mean it?'

'Of course,' said Clive.

'When you're an editor in Fleet Street, you'll be able to put your ideas into practice, won't you?' said Clara.

'You're being sarcastic. You don't think I could run a national tabloid and campaign on stuff like decent housing for students, do you?'

'No I don't,' she said.

'You're wrong.'

'I'm sure you'll get a chance.'

'If I ever get to run a national, it'll be done with no compromise… with objectivity, honesty, integrity. I mean it. There'll be no compromises.'

'I hope you're right, but I won't hold my breath,' concluded Clara.

Marcus continued to argue his case.

'I believe you'll do it, Marcus,' Clive nodded in agreement. 'Most people wouldn't, but you're determined enough. Yes, I believe you will,' he said. 'Anyhow, the beer's getting to me. I need the bog.'

He stood up and staggered through the door, and Clara and Marcus were alone. Clara slid down the wall next to him.

'Sorry, Marcus. I didn't mean to have a go at you. It wasn't personal. I'm a bit uptight at the moment.'

'That's OK. I don't think you're being fair about Dave, though.'

'Probably not. Anyhow, we split over a month ago.'

'Oh!'

'I've got a room on my own for the whole of this term.'

'I'm sorry.'

Clara's shoulder touched Marcus and he tensed.

That's why she had a go about Dave.

'You seemed to get on so well,' he said.

'I suppose living together was convenient for both of us, but Dave's got a girlfriend at the LSE, and she finishes this summer.'

'No!'

'It's been coming for months.'

'I didn't know.'

'Dave's made his decision. He'll be off with her as soon as term finishes, and they'll probably be getting married.'

Clara's voice was detached and resigned. She was gazing straight ahead.

'You've known all the time?'

'Of course, and she does too. I'm his term-time lover, and she gets him for the holidays. He took her to the summer ball last year. I went with a friend, and she realised who I was without even being introduced.'

Clara showed no disappointment or bitterness. Marcus half-turned his head and glanced at her. She was attractive without being stunningly beautiful, but she had an alluring aura of equanimity.

'That's terrible. What a lousy thing to do. He's been cheating on you all this time?'

'No, I've known from the start. I was happy with the arrangement, and so was he, and I'm just as happy it's ending. We're not close any more.'

'I'm sorry.'

'What for? Nobody's died, nobody's hurt. We've had good times, and now it's finished.'

'I'm not used to… I couldn't treat you like that.'

'Have you got a girlfriend at home?'

'No.'

'A good looking bloke like you should find a nice girl.

Let's go. The party's over, literally and metaphorically, I think.'

Clara got to her feet and stood in front of Marcus. She looked down and smiled at him, and then she stretched out her arms and grabbed his hands, resting on his upraised knees. She pulled him to his feet and looked at him with a reassuring smile.

'Don't be sad,' she said. 'There's nothing to be angry about, Marcus.'

Marcus shrugged.

They met Clive downstairs, and Clara led them out of the house and into the street. They were heading in the same direction. Clara put her hand round the waists of the two men and their arms draped over her shoulders. Marcus was embarrassed, but his mind was already focussed on the first edition of the new academic year.

He was determined to prove Clara wrong.

5

MARY

In her first year, Mary Godley had not noticed Marcus around the university. In her second, one of her friends pointed him out, engaged in an animated conversation with another student and scribbling notes on a pad.

'Marcus Roache. He's editor of the *Student Voice*. He took it on last year when he was a fresher,' said Maggie.

They were drinking coffee at a table, outside a row of three lecture theatres. They were recovering from an intense hour on Elizabeth Gaskell. The professor, who had just been recruited from Cambridge, was a small and balding man in his fifties. He had made his entrance in a pinstripe suit and had boomed his introduction in a voice that was so deep that some of his audience had let out suppressed guffaws. The man had looked up from his notes, peered over his black reading glasses and continued as if he had not heard anything.

'That's good going,' Mary replied.

'Yeah, and during the summer holidays, he's been working at a newspaper in London.'

'Ambitious, then?'

'You're not thinking...?'

'He'd be a good catch, wouldn't he?' Mary smiled and nudged Maggie. 'Girlfriend?'

'No, I don't think so. He's not the type; dead shy. He's doing History, and the second year History undergraduates are next door to us all this term. You might bump into him. I met him at a party. I'll introduce you.'

'Look at them,' said Mary, nodding toward two young men. An hour before, they had laughed at the professor, and now they were in animated conversation with him. 'Creeps! I like the name. Marcus sounds strong.'

The following week, Mary and Maggie waited for the History undergraduates to exit their lecture hall. As Marcus walked by, Maggie began to chat with him and introduced Mary, but he was offering short and uninterested responses, and he seemed hardly to notice her. As he was about to retreat to the stairs, Mary pushed him in the direction of refreshments. Marcus, guided from behind through the jostling students, was unnerved by this show of strength. He turned round and, momentarily, looked into the square face of the young woman with the dark-brown hair and healthy cheeks. She had a personality to match her robust figure.

'I need a coffee after that lecture!' she said. 'I'll get you one if you like.'

'I can't be long because I've got to get back to the Students' Union.'

'Oh, if you haven't got time...'

'No, no. Sit down. I'll get them.'

Marcus made his way through the crowd, and Maggie, who had been following at a short distance, came across to join her friend with her thumbs up and an exaggerated smile. Mary shooed her away.

Marcus returned with two plastic cups.

'Going back to the newspaper office?' she asked.

'Yes. We had an experienced team last year. This term, I'm the only one with any know-how, and I've got to crack the whip.'

'Crack the whip?'

'Well, you know, keep on top of things.'

'I like the campaign on student housing.'

Marcus talked enthusiastically about the plans he had for the paper.

'I'm surprised you've any time for study,' she smiled.

'Oh, I squeeze it in. In the long term, the paper's much more use than *this*,' he said, tapping the file holding his most recent essay.

'Going to be a journalist then?'

Mary was watching Marcus intently, but he avoided looking into her penetrating hazel eyes.

'Yes, and what about you?'

'Unless I can find a rich bloke to marry, I'm going into teaching.'

'What?'

'I'm joking.'

'Are you sure? You sound like you mean it.'

'There's nobody with enough money round here. Not free, anyhow.'

'What are you doing tonight?' he asked casually.

Over the following few weeks, Mary managed her time around Marcus's work at the newspaper. Every day, they met in the university coffee bar. Marcus persuaded Mary to see the film *Oh! What a Lovely War* at the university theatre. She was reluctant to go, but he was persuasive.

On the way back to her digs, Marcus expressed his view about the futility of the war and the incompetence of the officers. Mary explained that she had grown up in an army family; her father had fought in the Second World War and her grandfather in the Great War. They had both been officers, and her grandfather, who had been gassed, had never properly recovered.

'They did their best. Nobody could have known that the war would turn into trench warfare.'

'I'm sorry, I didn't realise.'

'There's nothing to be sorry about, Marcus. We've not had to deal with the things our parents and grandparents experienced, and we don't understand. With hindsight, it's easy to criticise. They sacrificed their lives for the things we take for granted. Perhaps we're a spoilt generation.'

Marcus said nothing as they trudged the last few hundred metres. He had his hands in his trouser pockets, and Mary put one hand through the crook in his elbow and clasped her hands together.

'No need to sulk.'

'I'm not sulking.'

'You sure?'

When they reached the gate, Mary turned and kissed him on his lips, a manoeuvre made easier by them being approximately the same height. The kiss was fleeting, and Mary quickly unhooked her arm and clicked open the latch on the gate. She opened the front door and turned. He was watching her, a happy smile on his face.

'Off you go,' she whispered and smiled back.

In the weeks leading up to Christmas, Marcus secretly met with a clerk employed at the university. He worked in administration and provided evidence that the university was assembling confidential files on members of far-left groups, the Students' Union council and other activists.

'You're worried about something, Marcus,' said Mary. They were sipping morning coffee from plastic cups, and Marcus was unusually quiet. He looked around to make sure nobody could hear. He explained that he had been given confidential university documents.

'If the authorities find out, I could get kicked out of university. I'm not sure what to do.'

'Wow!' Mary hesitated. 'Genuine?'

'Yes.'

'Sure?'

'Yes.'

'Take it through the Students' Union. That's what they're there for.'

'But I want to print the story. It's what newspapers should be about. It could make my name.'

'Do a deal. You give them the information, and when they take it up with the university, agree that you print the story straight away.'

'Yes, that's what I was thinking. I can't take the risk of going it alone.'

'Too right.'

He met with members of the Students' Union council in their office and provided them with an outline of the secret files.

'That's not much to go on,' said Geoff, the president. 'What about names? Who's on the list and what level of detail?'

'I need your word before I give you anything. No bullshit. If I give you the specifics, it's on the basis that I launch the story on the front page of the *Voice* the day you meet with the university. No deal, no details.'

'From what you've said, it's just the usual suspects – the Trots and Anarchists,' added Ken, who hoped to be president the following year. 'They'd be on my list,' he laughed.

'Yes or no?' asked Marcus.

'Give us ten minutes,' said Geoff, and Marcus was asked to leave.

It was only two minutes later that he was called back into the office.

'They may ask us to keep things quiet until they've had time to investigate,' said Geoff.

'You'll have to say 'No thanks'. This is too big for them to sweep under the carpet. Whatever you agree with them, I'll publish anyhow, and that'll not put you in a good position, will it?'

'That sounds like a threat,' said Ken.

'This is dynamite! I could take the risk and publish without you. I'm giving you every opportunity to do the right thing, and all I want is for you to treat me fairly.'

'OK,' said Geoff.

Marcus opened a file and pulled out one of a number of sheets of paper with the university logo on the top. It was a file list, and Marcus read the first twenty names. They included four members of the council. There was a short silence.

'I've got a copy of some of the detailed files,' said Marcus. 'It gives affiliations and political allegiances.'

He handed out a few sheets of paper to Geoff, who passed them round.

'Shit,' said Ken. 'Me. What the fuck am I on their list for?'

'You're right, Marcus. This really is dynamite,' said Geoff.

The Students' Union council arranged an emergency meeting with the university authorities. They demanded an explanation and insisted that the university should allow students open access to their records and that no information on individual students' political activity should be kept. The *Student Voice* released a special edition. It explained the reason for the Students' Union council meeting with the university and provided a summary of the meeting and the university's response. It included some of the names on the list, the reaction from the council and an editorial. The story made its way into the national news. An action group formed, but the university did not respond, and tension increased in the weeks up to Christmas. In the following term, students organised protest marches and a sit-in.

6

MARCUS

Marcus's mother was cooking and she had her back to her son, sat at the kitchen table.

'Could my friend, Mary, stay here over Christmas?' Marcus asked in a matter-of-fact way.

'Mary?'

Marcus provided the briefest of details.

'She sounds very nice, Marcus,' said his mother, back still turned. 'I'll have to ask your father. We always have your uncle and aunt over for Christmas dinner.'

'I know.'

'I'm sure it'll be alright.'

Marcus's mother spoke to his father, and everything was agreed and relayed to Marcus by his mother.

On Christmas Eve, Mary drove to London in her mother's Mini Clubman. Marcus's mother had made up a bed in the spare room. Marcus could not remember it ever having been used as a bedroom before. It was a small room, barely large enough for the single bed that was squeezed along one wall. Marcus's father stored box files of official-looking papers on the bedspread, and these had had been stacked in a corner or forced under the bed.

On Christmas Eve afternoon, Marcus took Mary for a walk through the west London suburb where he had grown up. The houses had been built between the wars, typical of most of this part of west London. All of the semi-detached houses, such as the one Marcus's parents had bought just after the war, had been built to a pattern, with three bedrooms and a bathroom upstairs and a kitchen, 'front room' and dining room downstairs. Interspersed amongst the semis, there were a few larger, detached houses with four bedrooms and a garage. Mary had parked her mother's car on the road, directly outside the house and next to Marcus's father's car. The convention, strictly adhered to, was that cars would not be parked outside neighbours' houses, a practice that would not survive the seventies.

Marcus thrust his hands in his pocket, and Mary adopted her customary habit, with an arm looped between his elbow and body and her hands clasped together across her middle.

'What do I call them, you know, your mother and father?'

'I'm not sure.'

'Well, they must have Christian names. What do they call each other?'

'Ernest and Brenda, but you can't call them that.'

'Why not?'

'They'd be embarrassed.'

'You'd be embarrassed, you mean. You should have introduced them by their first names.'

'What?'

'That's what I'll do when you meet mine.'

'Perhaps they'll say something about it.'

'And in the meantime?'

'Don't call them anything. Whatever you do, do *not* use their first names. I'd die.'

Mary sighed, let the matter rest, and they walked in silence for a few minutes.

'Happy memories of growing up here?' Mary enquired.

She looked at Marcus, but he faced resolutely forward.

They continued to walk at the same pace along the quiet suburban street.

'Do you meet up with school friends?'

Marcus continued without speaking.

'Well?' she enquired.

'Have you ever had dreams about school, you know, the one about school exams?' he asked.

Marcus did not break stride.

'No, I don't know what you mean.'

'I have them all the time. Other people do, too. I dream I'm reading my A-level revision notes but taking nothing in. My memory's blank, and I get a feeling of panic. Sometimes I see myself at the exam desk, and I don't understand the questions. It's supposed to be History, but I'm looking at the Physics paper. I'm in the wrong exam.'

'That's weird. Then what?'

'I know I'm in a dream, and I tell myself to wake up.'

'But that's not what happened, is it? You didn't mess up.'

Marcus took his hands out of his pocket, unclasped Mary's and held her left hand in his right. They continued walking.

He told Mary how, in every exam, there had been a time when he had laid his pen on the desk, looked up and watched his classmates busily scribbling. On one occasion, the invigilator had glanced at him, and he had hastily continued with his answer, banishing the thought that he was writing everything he knew about the topic but not answering the question.

'I remember results day. Everything depended on that single slip of paper. Just three letters would determine my future. It's crazy, isn't it? My destiny had already been sealed in the white envelope with my name on it.' He hesitated. 'And I didn't get the grades I expected – I needed.'

'But they're good grades – better than me,' said Mary.

'But not good enough for Oxford or Cambridge.'

'Is that why you're so driven?'

'I left school without speaking to anyone, and I've never met anyone from my class since that day. I'd won a scholarship into their privileged world, but in the end, they enjoyed the last laugh. They'd succeeded, and I'd failed.'

'But you hadn't.'

'They were schoolmates, never friends.' Marcus sighed. 'At that moment, I felt like a gatecrasher at their party.'

'You got in to a good university.'

'In the sixth form, I applied to other universities, just in case I didn't get the grades to sit the Oxbridge entrance exams.'

'And you met me.'

'Yes, I suppose so.'

'Don't sound so pleased,' she laughed.

'Oh, I don't mean it like that.'

'Your grades don't matter anymore. Look how things have turned out.'

'It mattered to my parents. It mattered to me too. All those years of schooling, and on the day of reckoning... I'd fallen short. At the time, I was devastated.'

'Oh, Marcus, you seem so sad.'

'Come on, let's get back.'

Marcus's voice sounded a little more cheerful.

'Marcus, it makes no difference. You've been a success at the *Voice*, and you'll make it to the top in Fleet Street. You can't let it prey on your mind.'

'I need you. You're good for me.'

'You've got me.'

They kissed and turned to walk back.

'What happened when you got home?'

'Mother told me not to worry about it. I was upstairs when my father arrived back from work, and I came down before he

THE VOICE AND THE ECHO

had a chance to call me. I guess I must have sounded pathetic. I said that I had no excuses, and I was sorry. I'd done my best, and we'd got to face up to it. He said that he'd expected me to do better.'

'That was unkind.'

'Mother was trying to hide her disappointment, as she always did. With Mother, the difference between joy and despair is barely noticeable. I knew my father hadn't finished; he'd just *have* to say something memorable. He wouldn't be able to contain himself. I was waiting for him to clear his throat. He whispered that I'd let everyone down.'

'No!'

'It was never talked about again.'

Marcus explained how his parents' lives were cosseted in a blanket of lower-middle-class respectability, eschewing displays of anger. They reluctantly accepted that getting to university, any university, would secure Marcus's future. They took comfort from the knowledge that the benefits of their investment in his upbringing had earned a reward. They would hope that Marcus's status would be consolidated and passed to the next generation, hopefully with a dividend.

Marcus finished and looked at Mary.

'Nobody at university knows. Don't tell anyone. Everyone thinks I've always wanted to be a newspaper man, but it was an accident.'

Uncle Kenneth, Auntie Moira, Jessica and Emily arrived at the Roaches' at noon. Marcus's father offered a sweet and sickly sherry to his guests. Moira helped Marcus's mother in the kitchen, and the others were invited into the front room. Marcus's cousins took seats next to each other on the sofa, and Mary squeezed in next to them. Marcus perched on a high-backed chair, and the two older men took their appointed places in the armchairs.

The daughters were older than Marcus but lived with their parents. Marcus's dad often described the sisters as a little odd and screwed up his face, but he never explained what he meant.

'New neighbours, I see,' said Kenneth, who had seen a middle-aged man he did not recognise, looking out of next door's front window.

'Her husband ran off with his secretary, and she hoofed him out,' said Ernest, rolling his eyes and looking skyward. 'That's her new boyfriend.'

'You mean Jack's run off?' smiled Marcus.

Mary noticed how Marcus's father eyed Marcus sternly.

'How's business?' Ernest asked his brother.

'Good.'

'You're looking well?'

'You too.'

'Moira OK?'

'Yes, bit of sciatica.'

'And the girls?'

'Fine,' replied Kenneth on their behalf.

The discussion between the two drably suited and paunchy brothers continued in this vein, with Ernest prompting and Kenneth smothering the polite chit-chat with a blanket of one-word answers, nods and empty stares, which seemed to bother neither of them.

Marcus's cousins, in almost matching dress suits, began to engage Marcus in a separate conversation about their work. They made out that they held senior posts, although both had changed jobs frequently, with no position appearing to meet their high expectations. Mary indulged them, and Marcus nodded and smiled politely.

Thankfully, Marcus's mother called them through for their meal. The task of devouring the feast did not allow for much conversation, a blessed relief for Marcus and hardly a change for the older men.

'Marcus is doing well at university, isn't he, Brenda?' said Ernest as Christmas pudding was being served.

'Oh, yes, very well. Aren't you, Marcus?'

'I'm Editor of the student newspaper.'

'It's an important job,' said his father.

'Yes, and it helped him get a job at the *Mercury* last summer. Marcus is going to work there again this summer. They've already said that they may offer him a permanent position at the newspaper,' added his mother.

'I thought you wanted to join the BBC,' said Emily.

'I decided it wasn't for me,' said Marcus, glancing at Mary. 'Working at the *Mercury* changed my mind. Anyhow, there's no reason I couldn't become the editor of a national.'

'Oh,' said Kenneth. 'Do you think so?'

'Yes he will,' said Mary. 'He'll get to the top. I've seen him in action.'

Marcus's father looked across the table, his face contorted by an ambiguous, asymmetric half-smile.

Mary beamed back at him and then at Marcus, seated next to her.

'It sounds a bit boring, Marcus, editing a student paper, you know, sitting at a typewriter all day,' said Jessica.

'It's not like that at all,' Marcus replied, shaking his head. 'Most of the time, I'm talking to people, getting stories. It's exciting, it's fun.'

'Really?' Auntie Moira asked. 'Fun?'

Marcus explained the story about the secret list. He told them that it had been on national news, but eyes glazed over. Marcus was becoming irritated and Mary squeezed his leg under the table. The conversation ended.

The relatives left shortly after the Queen's Christmas

message. Marcus and Mary helped his mother clear the table, and when they finished, they joined his father in the front room. Marcus's mother passed round a tin of Roses chocolates. Mary rummaged for the nougat and Marcus chose a hazelnut whirl. He screwed the wrapper into a ball and placed it in the cereal bowl, located on the table expressly for that purpose. Mary followed suit.

'That's about as exciting as it gets,' said Marcus, shortly after his parents had gone to bed.

'Don't you ever discuss, I don't know, music, current affairs, sport?'

'We never have. It's just work, domestic chat, television and tittle-tattle.'

Marcus was already thinking about being back at university.

7

MARY

'There's a meeting about the secret files. It's in lecture room two, at lunchtime tomorrow,' Marcus explained early in February. 'Come along, Mary. It'll be exciting to see history being made.'

'It's not my scene. Some of the students are just looking for a fight.'

'Come and have a look, and then make your mind up.'

Marcus was persuasive, and for the only time in her life, Mary attended a political meeting.

Members of the Students' Union council were lounging behind desks on the stage as Marcus and Mary took their seats near the back of the hall. Mary put her arm around him and refused to get closer to the front. The representatives were all men, mainly older students, with jackets and short hair, a sure sign that they were at the job interview stage of the university production-line process. They were unlikely to accede to any demands from the students that would spoil a good CV.

All of the seats in the lecture hall had been taken. Students were standing in the gangways and crowding at the doors to listen to what was being said. They were younger, louder and more unruly than their representatives.

'It's the usual rent-a-crowd,' Mary whispered, but Marcus ignored her.

Mary recognised the president of the Student's Union. He

got to his feet, moved to the lectern and raised his arms for quiet. He had barely started his introductory remarks when he was interrupted from the floor.

'Don't sell out.'

Then another voice rang out.

'Let's march on the Senate.'

There were cheers.

A verbal thrust and counter-thrust continued for almost an hour. Those on the stage were arguing for further discussion with the university authorities. The students in the hall seemed to represent a variety of interests, but those calling for immediate action drowned them out. It was impossible for anyone to explain their position rationally because of the interruptions and heckling. Although the main complaint was the secret list, other students raised questions about having no say in the running of the university.

Marcus was scribbling on a notepad, a task made difficult by the pushing and shoving. He was oblivious to Mary's discomfort. It was an anarchic scene, and it ended abruptly when the president called for a vote. A group of students, ignoring him, shouted that they would take over the administration block. They shouldered their way out through the doors, chanting and unfurling banners and almost emptying the lecture hall. For a few seconds, there was an eerie silence until the president of the union shrugged his shoulders and said, quietly and apologetically,

'Meeting over, I believe.'

'Democracy in action,' said another in disgust, and he jumped from the stage.

'I'm going to find out what they're doing,' said Marcus, nodding toward the door.

'It's a mob, Marcus. They'll just get into trouble, and they won't achieve anything. They've got no idea what they want.'

'Maybe, but it's news.'

'Do you support them?'

'My job's to report what's going on. It's exhilarating, isn't it, being in the middle of the news whilst it's happening?'

Marcus spent the next few weeks reporting the student occupation, and Mary did not interfere with his work. She went to the *Voice* only once when Marcus was late for coffee. It was during the student occupation, and as she approached the office, she could hear Marcus shouting at another student.

'For fuck sake, Terry, this is no good.'

'No need to get uptight, Marcus. I'll rewrite it.'

'I'll do it myself.'

'Give it here. I said I'll do it, and I will. Calm down, will you?'

The heated exchange continued, and Mary made her way back to the refectory and waited for Marcus. She did not mention what she had heard.

As the end of term approached, the protest petered out, and early in the summer term, the ringleaders were sanctioned. Two were suspended and another sent down. It was all grist to Marcus's mill.

'Come on, Mary. What's he like, then?' asked Maggie, on their way back to their separate digs, one evening in March.

'He's sweet, really sweet.'

'You don't want a bloke who's sweet, love. This is the sixties, not the thirties.'

'There's nothing wrong with being sweet. He's kind, and he cares about me.'

'Do you like him?'

'Yes, I like him a lot.'

'Falling in love?'

'Maggie! That's none of your business.'

'You are. I know these things.'

'You don't know anything.'

'Well has he…?'

'Maggs, just because your idea of fun is… well you know what I mean.'

'It's that boarding school education you've had and your dad, the general.'

'He was a major. Anyhow, I enjoyed boarding school.'

'So, what d'you do, then?'

'Don't laugh, but we talk a lot, and he listens. He may be quiet and a bit shy, but he's got loads of ambition and drive. He's really nice. He pretends he's a leftie, but he's not really. He'll have to keep his views to himself when he meets my family.'

'You mean your dad, the magistrate and Tory councillor?'

'That's not a crime. He's a pillar of the community.'

Marcus and Mary went to the theatre whenever they could, and Mary took him to the opera, in London, over the Easter holiday. She travelled up from Woking and he met her at Waterloo. Afterwards, they went to a pub.

'My mum and dad would like to meet you,' Mary said.

'That sounds serious.'

'Are you serious, Marcus?'

'Of course. We're in love aren't we?'

'Yes, I think we are.'

Things were progressing nicely, and they conducted their relationship with total propriety.

8

MARCUS

Marcus was seated alone in the *Student Voice* office. The room was spotless. There were no dirty mugs, just the one lonely, red one, and Marcus picked it up and gulped down the contents. The room was functional with desk, table and chairs, a filing cabinet, bookcase and shelves. It was to the standard Marcus had set.

It was the summer of his third year. He had finished his finals and was leafing through a pile of back editions, stacked neatly on the desk. He scanned the headlines and then turned each copy face down onto a second pile. His face betrayed a glum mood, punctuated with smiles, as the back copies reminded him of highlights from the time he had been editor. He stopped at a point where the height of the two piles of newspapers indicated that he was almost halfway through his tenure. He smiled at the headline: 'Slum landlord attacks *Voice* editor'.

The door opened, and in walked a younger man.

'Hi, Terry.'

'Reminiscing, Marcus?' he asked.

'Yes. I don't like looking back, but there's some good stuff here.'

'Yes, we've a lot to live up to next year.'

'Remember this one?' asked Marcus.

He pointed at a front cover on the table. Terry leaned over and looked at the headline.

'Of course.'

'It was a great campaign. It still *is* a great campaign,' said Marcus proudly. 'It's what a newspaper *should* be about and how stories *ought* to be written.'

Marcus had started to run articles about poor housing during his first year. By the beginning of his second year, the letters section had been inundated with complaints about substandard accommodation. Marcus had offered a prize – a free night out for two at a Beefeater restaurant for the best accommodation horror story. The incentive of prawn cocktail, steak and chips, Black Forest gâteau and a bottle of Blue Nun had been too tempting, and stories flowed in.

It had been difficult to choose the most horrific story, but he had finally made his selection. He had arranged to meet two medical students who had rented the chosen house, and he had set off early one morning, camera in his pocket.

Cockroaches and mice had infested the house. Rooms had been wet from leaking gutters and missing roof tiles, slugs had trailed crazy patterns across the kitchen table and into cupboards, and sparks had flown whenever the electric fires had been switched on.

As he had been taking photographs in the kitchen, the landlord had burst in. He had started swearing, first at the two students and then at Marcus. He had made a grab for the camera, and Marcus had clicked. The *Student Voice*'s front page had a photograph of the landlord in full lunge pose, his arm blurred, giving the distinct impression of a blow being aimed.

'That's the best photograph – the one of the landlord trying to grab me as I was leaving.'

'Brilliant.'

Marcus turned over the next two pages, all on the same topic. The main piece was an illustrated description of what Marcus had seen at the flat. The story had mirrored the experiences of many students. Some may have laughed at the awfulness of the conditions in their own accommodation, but many had also complained bitterly to their landlords. The paper contained a concocted dialogue with the two students. There had never been a formal interview, but Marcus had expressed their views in quotation marks, as if one had taken place.

Over the following weeks, the *Voice* had published interviews with the university accommodation department about their responsibility for student welfare. Every edition had highlighted further real life examples of squalid housing conditions and quotes from affected students. The story had made the front page of the local newspaper and on the back of that Marcus had been granted interviews with the council's Housing and Health Departments. A campaign had been launched to force the university to assess the suitability of all student accommodation and establish minimum standards on landlords. The campaign was still running.

'Something to feel proud about,' Terry said.

'Yes, I *do* feel proud about it.'

'Can you find the one about students smoking cannabis?' asked Terry.

'Yes, I've just had a look at it. Great photograph of you from behind with a joint in your hand. I hope it doesn't come back to haunt you.'

'There's one of you somewhere, too. Can't imagine why it never got published. Hope you've got the negatives,' Terry laughed.

'Too right, I have.'

'Any pearls of wisdom before you leave?' asked Terry earnestly.

Marcus replied without hesitation.

'Don't print what you want to tell your readers, print what they want to read. Even in a student paper, that's what sells.'

'That's a bit cynical.'

'It's realistic. As soon as you start to write things readers don't want to hear, or they disagree with, you're knackered.'

'How can you be sure what readers want?'

'That's what editors are paid to know.'

'What about attracting new readers?'

'A newspaper's like anything in a shop. The shopper looks at price and appearance.'

'You can't compare a newspaper with, I don't know, a packet of washing powder.'

'Why not? Shoppers go for what's attractive. It could be packaging, colour, or a name they trust. If it's eye-catching, the shopper will consider buying it. They'll never pick up something they don't want, or anything that looks unappealing. It's the same with a paper.'

'But no newspaper looks crap.'

'Most of them do; too many boring headlines.'

'A good headline's not enough.'

'Yes, but you can't get new readers if headlines don't connect with them. It's dead simple. What's inside's got to tell readers what they want to hear and make them laugh, or cry, or shout with anger. Like this,' said Marcus pointing at the headline on student accommodation. 'Make readers feel important, virtuous and right.'

'Do you think you can use a paper to change attitudes?'

'Over time you get a reputation that the readers trust, and that's when you can start to influence people.'

These were not off the cuff remarks because Marcus had tried and tested this formula over three years and knew precisely what worked. The *Voice* had been a blank canvas where he had sketched outlines and applied background paint, but the detail was for another day.

'You've made a bit of a reputation here.'

'Hmm.'

'Are you going back to London?' continued Terry.

'Yes, I've got the promise of a job with the *Mercury* if I want it.'

'The *Mercury*?'

'I'll take any job I can get. I've got to start somewhere. Anyhow, Mary and I are getting married, and we need the money.'

Terry moved across to shake Marcus's hand.

'I've got to go, Marcus. The best of luck. Keep in touch.'

'I will,' said Marcus, knowing that he would not.

This chapter was closed. He had enjoyed running the paper, and it had confirmed his determination to become a newspaper editor.

9

MARCUS

Marcus started work at the *Mercury* that August, and Mary began teacher training in London. They married the following summer, rented a flat in Pinner, and Mary's first teaching job was at a local comprehensive school.

Marcus knew some of his colleagues at the *Mercury* from the two summers he had spent there whilst at university. Back then, although he had been little more than the office boy, he had watched and learned how the newspaper had been constructed. Now, as a trainee, he was given journalistic responsibilities. Most of the staff had worked their way up the pecking order, joining the paper from school, and it was with a degree of contempt that he was referred to as 'University Boy' by some of the journalists. He was destined to jump the queue, and they did not like that. Others kept their opinions to themselves because they suspected that this upstart might someday become the boss.

Whenever someone was required to report on a strike, a work to rule or a factory closure, there would be a shout, accompanied by a laugh.

'Send University Boy!'

He would be summarily despatched to the provinces. Most of them did not relish days away in the grim towns of Wales, Scotland, the Midlands or the North, even on expenses. Party and trade union conferences were a different matter. Here they could hobnob with the movers and shakers, avoiding the attendant misery of dreary working towns. At conferences, hospitality was generous, and expenses were not scrutinised too closely, but University Boy was too junior to attend.

Marcus did not let his colleagues know that he enjoyed his assignments. To Marcus, he was reporting real stories, not the gossip, popular culture and sport that interested them. As for the conference junket, he was uncomfortable making small talk, kowtowing and pretending he was enjoying the limelight when he was not. He was happy with his lot.

It was difficult, at first, adjusting to being the man on the ground. At university, he was directly responsible for everything that went into the *Voice*. At the *Mercury*, he had a small part to play in what was produced each day. His work for the *Mercury* was heavily edited, and he often did not recognise it as his own. Whatever he wrote, the editorial process produced the bias the readership expected. Someday, he would be in charge, and he would do the same. He shrugged his shoulders and ploughed his own furrow.

Marcus was despatched to Yorkshire during the miners' strike of 1972. He was sympathetic toward the miners' cause: inflation was rocketing, miners' wages had fallen behind, and they were, after all, the industrial elite. High risks justified high rewards, and they deserved whatever deal they could get. Perhaps this strike was the start of something more profound, something that would change the status quo for the better.

He drove north in his Ford Anglia. It was early February, a month after the start of the official strike. He left the A1 at Newark and meandered through Nottinghamshire, heading in the direction of the Yorkshire coalfield. At first, he passed through quiet villages of red brick farmhouses and cottages, clustered around the medieval church and the pub. There was an impression of permanence. Whatever the economy, whoever was in power, these villages would remain, slowly changing and evolving. As he drove north and west, the rolling countryside became increasingly scarred by spoil heaps and vast pitheads. They appeared to have been dropped randomly, man-made eyesores, onto pristine countryside. Semi-detached estates were built around the pit and seemed grim and characterless. These villages had one purpose: they provided housing for the miners who had moved here, from all over the country, to work at the pits.

He continued on to the Yorkshire heartland, through Frickley, Grimethorpe, Houghton Main and Manvers. Yorkshire had a more permanent industrial feel. The Dearne Valley was a ribbon of industry and mining, drab towns like Wath and Mexborough running one into the other. These were places that Marcus had not known existed, towns and villages where people lived lives he could not imagine. There were signs of prosperity, new cars on drives and plenty of shoppers on the streets, but he was glad he would not have to raise a family here.

Collieries, power stations and fuel depots were idle. Coal and coke were not moving, and it created an eerie atmosphere. These were places that could only justify their existence if they were active – employment and production gave them a purpose. The picketing he witnessed did not give the impression of an industrial battle to the death. Men in duffle coats congregated around burning pallets in a brazier, joking and chatting. It seemed, here in Yorkshire at least, that the enemy had given in, and the unions had won.

He stopped at Manvers and walked up to the picket. It consisted of only a dozen or so men, all speaking a strong south Yorkshire dialect. Marcus was unaccustomed to hearing the foreshortening of *the*, dropped aitches and the absence of the final 'g', and it took him a few moments to adjust to the extremes of the miners' accents.

'How's it going?' he asked.

'Who're you?' asked one of the men in a surly manner.

'Reporter.'

'I'd guessed. What paper?'

'*Mercury.*'

'Well, you can tell your readers that nowt's movin' till we've got a decent pay rise.'

'What will the union accept?'

'Ted Heath's bollocks'd be a good start!' shouted another man.

They all laughed.

'What we've asked for and nowt else,' the first man replied. 'This country stops if we stop, so Heath better get 'is mind round it, quick. We'll be 'appy when we're back at top of the pay league.'

'How long will you stay out for?'

'Long as it fuckin' takes. Tell 'em that. We're in charge, not Heath. Yes, I mean it. We're in charge,' continued the miner, who had witnessed the surprise Marcus had been unable to hide.

Marcus thought for a moment.

'I guess you're right.'

Heath may have been elected but these industrial warriors were shaping events. The government was a bystander.

'Anyhow I'd rather be up here in't fresh air, than down t'pit,' he added.

'Best of luck,' said Marcus.

'Luck's got nowt to do wiy it, just solidarity!' he shouted.

Evening drew in, and Marcus drove to his hotel in Sheffield. He quickly drafted his storyline and phoned it through to the office. He was told to get to Saltley coke depot, on the outskirts of Birmingham, the next day. The picketing at the depot was becoming increasingly hostile. He headed for the restaurant. It was being refurbished and had limited seating capacity. Marcus looked inside. They had a few seats left and he was shown to a small table, set for two.

'We're running short of space, Sir, and you may be asked to share. Would that be a problem?'

'No, of course not,' said Marcus, untruthfully.

The restaurant quickly filled, and Marcus was in the process of ordering when another diner joined him. He apologised and hoped Marcus did not mind sharing his table. When Marcus said not, he took the seat opposite. He was a middle-aged, balding and paunchy businessman from Birmingham. They made introductions, complained about the inconvenience, and the businessman ordered, barely looking at the menu.

Glynn was chatty and inquisitive. He quickly discovered Marcus's occupation and assignment, explained that he ran a family engineering business and was in Sheffield trying to sort out problems with a supplier. He was travelling back to his factory the following morning.

'Your paper's very hostile toward the miners, isn't it?' said Glynn.

'Yes,' Marcus replied.

'What do you think'll happen with all these strikes? We can't go on like this, can we?'

'The public's behind the strikers.'

Marcus explained what he had seen and heard as he had travelled through the coalfields.

'It's not right though,' said Glynn. 'We voted for the Conservatives, but they can't do any of the things they promised. They've no power.'

'Yes, I suppose you're right.'

'Suppose?'

'No, the country didn't vote for this, but I think the government'll back down. They haven't got the stomach.'

'Somebody needs to stand up to 'em,' said Glynn. 'They won't even negotiate.'

'But haven't the miners got a good case?'

'That's for the miners and their bosses to sort out. The problem is that it's threatening everyone else's livelihood. This claim and the strike's nothing to do with me, but the miners don't care. It's just raw industrial muscle.'

'Yes, I know, but workers' pay needs to keep up with inflation.'

'It's like leapfrog. One group jumps over the next, and everybody else follows. That's what the government's trying to stop. If the miners get this increase, I'll have to give my men the same, and inflation'll keep rising.'

'Is it really as bad as that?' asked Marcus.

'Inflation's driving up costs, and strikes are stopping supplies of materials. It's bringing my business to its knees.'

'You're going out of business?'

'That's why I've been in Sheffield. Suppliers can't deliver what I need because of strikes, working to rule and overtime bans. It's not even as if the steel I'm getting's much cop. I send half of it back 'cos it's so shit.'

'You're kidding.'

'I'll be buying in Germany and Sweden when this is over.'

'That'll put more people out of work in Britain, won't it?'

'If I do nothing, the 400 people who work for me will be out of a job. I tell you what, come and see what I mean. Come and have a look at my factory.'

Marcus put the card that Glynn offered into his wallet.

Marcus and Glynn talked until they had finished their meal, and Glynn offered his apologies and broke to make phone calls. Marcus mulled over the words of the miners.

They knew they were in charge, not the government, and from the opposite side of the fence, Glynn had concurred. Working class empowerment had seemed a good idea at university, but Marcus slept uneasily with the reality.

The following morning, Marcus drove southwards, through Derbyshire and Staffordshire, to Birmingham. The road wound through Hathersage, Bakewell and Ashbourne, all of which showed no sign of the turmoil in the towns and cities. The road swept along the contours, cut suddenly into a valley and arced upward to a summit. It was breathtakingly beautiful, the essence of the British countryside. Marcus passed close to the three spires of Lichfield Cathedral and entered Birmingham through Sutton Coldfield. He parked in Aston, some way from the coking plant, and ambled through the back streets of Nechells. It was a characterless mishmash of narrow streets, wide dual carriageways, motorway construction, housing and industry, all seemingly created with no plan. Modernity, such as the soon-to-be-opened Aston Expressway, gave the impression of being imposed on what was already there.

Marcus did not need directions to the coke depot because he could hear the uproar. The picket had started with just seven men, but many more miners had bolstered the numbers. During the past twenty-four hours, building workers, employees from the nearby carburettor factory, car delivery drivers and union representatives from the big local engineering factories had joined them. Marcus kept his distance, but he could see hundreds of men, possibly more, milling at the entrance. The television cameras were there, and local and national press had taken up vantage points. Marcus stopped a man who was walking away from the picket and asked what had happened that morning.

'There's more pickets arrived, but we can't stop the trucks

getting through. Fuckin' scabs. We're getting all the names, and we'll blacklist 'em. They're on sixty quid a week, and I'm on twenty.'

'How much?'

'Sixty a week. Arthur Scargill's taken charge but there's not enough of us to close the place. We're meeting tonight to decide what next.'

Marcus moved closer to the action. Despite the numbers, the police were managing to keep control and shepherd the trucks through the gate. It looked like the coke depot would remain open. He could make out a man urging and organising the pickets, and he assumed that it was Mr Scargill.

Marcus had not witnessed a mass action before. The atmosphere was tense, threatening to boil over. It was a three-way confrontation between drivers, police and pickets. There was little attempt to persuade or negotiate. Cab doors were banged, threats exchanged, and Marcus could see that some of the men were enjoying the confrontation. The union was trying to enforce its will through the sheer numbers it could assemble. He spoke to more of the strikers, but the police were reluctant to say anything, and he could not get near the leaders of the picket.

As darkness fell, Marcus made his way to the hotel he had booked, checked in, went to his room and picked up the phone by his bedside. His first call was to Mary.

'There's a standoff,' he told her. 'I'm not sure what next.'

'It's been on the telly. It looks dangerous. Be careful.'

'This isn't how to settle disputes. It's just brute force and intimidation. Nobody's talking.'

After calling the office, he tried the number on the business card Glynn had given him. It was a direct line to his office, and his secretary answered. After a brief interrogation, she put him through to a surprised Glynn Knowles, and they arranged to meet at his factory in Darlaston the following morning.

The factory was an imposing building of midland red brick, its walls looming thirty feet high and stained by a century of industrial pollution. Marcus slowed and wound down the car window. The cacophony of heavy industry assaulted his ears. Thumping noises came from a forge in a brick building with a corrugated roof. With each blow, the ground shook. He could hear the staccato rattle of mechanical hammers, and cranes rumbled on their skyline track, manoeuvring steel billets, bars and rods into position.

Cars were parked the length of Knowles's factory, and Marcus drove a hundred metres, halfway along this bastion, to a breach. The entrance was wide enough for two lorries to pass through with ease. Beyond the entrance was an oblong cobbled yard, skirted on all sides by the factory. Marcus could not see inside, but he could hear the crashing, grinding and whirring of heavy machinery. Glynn had asked him to report to security. The uniformed guards found him a parking space and showed him to the office block, which jutted out of the factory walls and into the yard. Glynn met him in an expansive reception from a bygone and more affluent age, with marble pillars and staircase, the latter adorned with a wrought iron balustrade and mahogany handrail. The floor was a pattern of massive, polished granite tiles. The receptionist sat at a grand mahogany desk, and behind her was a painting of the factory in Victorian times.

'Impressive?' asked Glynn.

'Impressive.'

'Knowles and Sons goes back a long way.'

They walked upstairs and into Glynn's palatial office. It was in the same style as the reception area, furnished in mahogany, with pictures of his predecessors on the walls.

'Successful day?' asked Marcus.

'I've been made some promises, but we'll have to see. It's difficult times, and industry's not adjusting to it. Anyhow, you're welcome to look round, but don't put anything in the *Mercury*. I can't afford to upset the unions or customers.

Marcus nodded, and Glynn picked up his phone and ordered tea. Glynn's secretary poured from a silver teapot into Royal Crown Derby cups. They talked about business, particularly the increased competition from Europe and the Far East. When Glynn's dad had run the business, immediately after the war, contracts had been lucrative. Back then, the foreign competition had to rebuild its destroyed manufacturing base, but Glynn was now starting to lose more bids than he was winning. Competitors were automating and buying new machines.

'To be honest, we didn't see it coming. We didn't invest during the good times. Right now, any investor's taking a risk because industrial relations are crap, and there's a climate out there where everybody's out to get what they can.'

At that moment, Glynn's secretary reappeared.

'It's Gary, Mr Knowles. He needs to see you urgently.'

'He's the union convener. You'll have to leave till I've dealt with him.'

Marcus was ushered into the secretary's office. Ten minutes later, he was back with Glynn.

'That's an example of what I've been talking about. There was a meeting last night, addressed by Arthur Scargill. He's demanded an all-out strike to support the picket. He wants workers from all the factories in the area to close Saltley depot.'

'That's miles away.'

'Miners have been to every factory round here. The strike's not official, but the convenor couldn't stop 'em talking to the men. Tomorrow, my lot are marching to Saltley.'

'What'll you do here?'

'Close for at least a day. If I try to cover the absent men, it'll only backfire, and I'll have a work to rule, or worse. We'll make up lost output on overtime, and that'll cost me.'

'One day's not so bad, is it?'

'It's not one day, it's one more day. It'll mean late deliveries, which is routine in the UK, but it's no good abroad. They won't come back if we let 'em down. To be honest, Marcus, if I could find a buyer, I'd piss off to Spain with the missus.'

Glynn showed Marcus around the factory. Men were working at giant machines, cutting, forging, drilling, welding and assembling. Marcus had never seen anything on this scale before. Machines were of a size he had never imagined. It was an intimidating environment. Marcus had had no idea that this was how millions earned their living. Glynn showed pride in the quality of the work and the skills of the men, but when Marcus was leaving, he revealed his true feelings.

'Come and see me next time you're around. Don't wait too long, though.'

'What do you mean?'

'With all these strikes, the militants who're taking over the unions, the whole thing'll collapse, and we'll go down with it.'

'You're exaggerating, aren't you?'

'This country needs someone who'll take 'em on, otherwise we're fucked.'

Marcus nodded.

'Yes, I can see where you're coming from.'

That evening, Marcus read an advert in the *Birmingham Evening Mail*. It asked all trade unionists to down tools and support the Saltley picket. Early the following morning, he arrived at Saltley and positioned himself immediately behind the picket, back to a wall, on a pavement. Marcus, shorter than most of those in front, was straining to see all of the action near the gate. Lorries were still entering and leaving the depot, the police holding back every surge. The picket was larger than the previous day and more determined. Marcus was only twenty metres from the gates when a lorry forced its way inside, despite the pickets pushing forward.

Without any warning, a scuffle broke out. Fists were aimed at policemen who were randomly pulling men from the crowd. As another lorry prepared to leave, the police pushed the pickets from the gate, further and harder than before. The pickets were retreating, and Marcus was unable to resist the pressure, stepping backward until suddenly, with a thump, his shoulders hit the wall, and his head cracked against the bricks. All of the air was forced out of his lungs in a gasp, and he could not breathe. His arms were trapped, and his head was being forced against the wall by the shoulders of a much larger man. He could see nothing other than the man's coat, and he smelt cigarettes and sweat. The man in front pushed himself onto tiptoes, gasping for air, and Marcus sensed his own feet being lifted off the pavement by the upward pressure.

He felt faint and started to slip into unconsciousness. He fought the urge to close his eyes, afraid of the consequences. His mind wandered. Would these be his last thoughts? Would the crumpled coat of the stranger in front provide his last view of the world, and would his body odour be Marcus's last smell? Marcus felt urine trickling down his legs. There was a sickly acid taste in his mouth. He imagined that his mind had left his body, and he was looking down on himself, slipping away.

What a strange way to go.

He lost consciousness. He was dying, dying, dead.

The police were unaware of what was happening at the rear of the crowd. Some of the pickets had sensed the danger and pushed forward. They shouted to their mates, and as suddenly as the squeeze had started, it stopped. There were half a dozen men lying on the road, some with their backs against the wall and a few flat out on the ground. Pickets were leaning over their mates, speaking quickly, in downbeat, nasal Brummie tones, befitting the situation.

'Are y'alright?' said a picket to an injured man leaning against the wall. He groaned, mumbled something about his ribs, nodded and staggered away. Only one of the injured men did not stir.

'Fuckin' 'ell, this one's bad, crushed to death,' said one picket.

''E's pissed 'isself,' said another.

He leaned close to Marcus's face and grabbed his shoulders. There was no movement, no sign of life.

Marcus felt his body being shaken. An unfamiliar voice was talking.

'Are y'alright mucka? Come on, you'll be OK. You must've blacked out.'

Marcus realised that he was on the ground, and a large, round-faced man was leaning over him. He recognised the smell. The pickets had created a small space around him, and a few were looking on.

'Shall I gerr' ambulance?'

Marcus took a few seconds to gather his senses. He remembered where he was and what he had been doing. He became embarrassingly aware of the dampness in his trousers.

'I'm OK,' he said, and with the help of the other man, he got to his feet. He felt a large bump on the back of his head, and then the other man spoke.

'That were a fuckin' crush. It knocked the wind outta me too. It were like being down the Villa. Somebody could've got killed.'

Marcus insisted that he was fine and thanked the man

who had helped. When another vehicle attempted to leave, the pickets surged, and Marcus edged to safety. As he staggered from the melee, two policemen ran directly at him. They had raised truncheons and Marcus, expecting the worst, ducked and turned his back. There was a crack as a truncheon landed on the shoulder of a man nearby, who seemed to have committed no other crime than having been there. Despite his protests, he was hauled to a police van.

Marcus trudged past the rank of TV cameras and reporters, but his way was barred. Snaking in his direction were thousands of Birmingham workers, marching to join the picket, some of over thirty thousand who had walked out of their workplaces in the city. As soon as the union leaders arrived and took charge, the violence stopped, and by the sheer weight of numbers, the police were forced to close the gates. There was a thunderous roar from the pickets, and Arthur Scargill made a megaphone speech to his followers. They were victorious and accepted the call to disperse peacefully.

Unless Saltley was formally closed, a further strike across the whole city was promised, and that evening the employers caved. It was agreed that essential deliveries to hospitals could be made but nothing else, and the picket was reduced to a handful of men. Marcus returned to the hotel to change his clothes and then found a dry cleaner. He would not tell Mary what had happened; she had enough on her plate. Marcus lay on his bed thinking about the events of the day and the near-fatal consequences. His contemplative mood turned to anger.

Marcus called the office with the main story. He described it as mob rule, orchestrated by Arthur Scargill. The pickets, who were contemptuous toward the police, had meekly followed the instructions of their bombastic leader.

That evening, the government announced that the first power cuts were being imposed across the country. It would lead to a three-day week, and over one and a half million workers would soon be laid off. Marcus wondered whether Glynn and his factory would ride out the storm. He was not optimistic. The claims of the strikers may have been justifiable, but not the way they were going about it, and not the collateral damage.

When he saw his report in the following day's paper, he realised that fewer changes than normal had been made because, from the *Mercury*'s point of view, there was little to change in what he had written.

10

MARCUS

Marcus and Mary were together on the settee, Marcus with his arm around his wife, watching the end of *Dad's Army*.

'Rub my neck, Marcus.'

She turned her back, and he rested his hands on her shoulders. He planted two thumbs on her neck and rotated them slowly and gently.

'That's nice. You know we were talking about buying our own place, something a bit bigger. Why not look this summer, Marcus?'

'Yes, we could easily afford the mortgage on a small house. It's best to buy in spring. That's what we said we'd do.'

'Up a bit, yes, just there. It might be better to start looking now.'

'Why the sudden change of mind?'

Mary hesitated.

'You're not... '

'Yes, I think I'm pregnant.'

Marcus stopped the massage, and Mary turned to face him.

'You think?'

'Well I don't know. I've never been pregnant before, you idiot.'

'That's fantastic.' Marcus embraced her. 'I feel... oh, I don't know what to say. I feel so happy.'

He kissed Mary on the lips.

'I'm not positive, and it's very early.'

'I'm sure you're right. Yes, let's move. We'll find a larger place, with three bedrooms.'

'Slow down. We'll only have one income. We can't just dive in feet first.'

'I'll have another pay rise in September, and I'll be getting a promotion too.'

Mary's pregnancy was confirmed, and a house was purchased nearby. Mary devoted her time to creating a new home for the family, enabling Marcus to pursue his career. It was an arrangement that they were both comfortable with, and Giles was born at the end of the year.

It was a period of growing industrial unrest, and Marcus spent much of his time covering events for the *Mercury*. This took him all over the country, and he had an angry exchange on the matter with his boss. He had not wanted to be away because Giles was unwell.

'You've got to go, Marcus,' Mary said. 'Your job's important, and it's all we have to pay the mortgage. Don't upset the *Mercury*. Giles will be fine. Babies get chest infections. A few days on antibiotics and he'll be as right as rain.'

'What about you? Number two's due in a few weeks.'

'I'm army stock, love. Godley women have given birth in worse situations than this when we were running the empire.' She smiled, rubbed the bump and addressed it. 'We're made of stern stuff, aren't we?'

'I don't know what I'd do without you. I'll phone and leave a number where you can contact me if you need to.'

Working long hours became the routine, and although Marcus did not become involved in the evening drinking culture, he was rarely home before eight.

Mary Roache sat down wearily one evening.

'I'd love a cup of tea,' she said.

She had just finished putting the two children to bed, and Marcus was seated on the opposite side of the table from his wife. His fortunes were on the rise. He was now Deputy Political Editor, and this meant that he was expected to attend the annual round of political conferences. The Labour Party was gathering for its 1976 conference in Blackpool, and Marcus was travelling north the following day. He had been reading the *Evening Standard*, and the next day's edition of the *Mercury* lay, unopened, on the table.

'Yes, I'll make one,' replied Marcus. 'You look tired.'

'I am.'

'Perhaps I could have put the children to bed?'

'You've only just got home. I can't force them to stay awake till you get back. If you want to help, you need to get home.'

Marcus was filling the kettle.

'I've got to put the time in. It's not nine to five. I'll try to get back earlier.'

'How many times have you said that?'

'It's not easy.'

'The way things are going, you'll miss your children growing up.'

'If you want to get on, you've got to put in the hours. I'm the breadwinner. My father was no different. I see the children at weekends and some evenings. It's not perfect, I know, but you're here all the time, and that's what's important.'

'Important for you, maybe. Anyhow, do you really want to be like your father?'

'Why not? He may be old-fashioned and stuffy, but he worked hard to make something of himself. His dad was only a butler.'

'Don't I know it? You must have told me a hundred times.'

'Because he bettered himself, it gave me a chance.'

'But your father wasn't close.'

'Children aren't as close to their fathers as their mothers. Fathers have to work. That's why it's important you're at home, like my mother.'

'That's all very well for your mum, because she didn't want to go back to work.'

'You don't know that.'

'I've seen how things work. Nobody dares challenge your father. You were scared of him when you were younger, but you're so like him now.'

'That's ridiculous.'

Mary looked at him and shook her head.

'What's that look all about?'

'Your father says 'I think that blah, blah, blah,' and then he asks if your mother agrees. Once he's made it clear what he thinks, of course she agrees. She wouldn't dare to cross him.'

'He listens.'

'He pretends to listen, and then he makes the decision he'd already settled on. There's no discussion. You've said so yourself. Nobody questions him. You didn't. Everyone just bumbles on.'

'Someone has to make decisions, and that's how it works for them. That's what I have to do at work. If I don't tell people what to do, nothing'd get done. There's a lot to be said for traditional families. Yours wasn't so different.'

'You're the same as your dad. You only listen to me if I agree with you.'

'Not true.'

'You're not listening now. It's you who wants me at home. Anyhow, it'd be good for all of us if you could get back at a reasonable time.'

Marcus was pouring tea into two mugs.

'OK, you've made your point. I'll try to get back earlier.'

Mary raised her eyes skywards.

'I trust you too,' said Marcus, in a conciliatory tone. 'You make all of the important decisions about the family, the home and all of our social arrangements.'

'That's because you don't want to.'

Marcus sat down.

'You like doing it.'

'It keeps my brain from stewing. Don't worry, I'm not going to try to change you. There's no point because you'll just ignore me.'

'You knew what to expect before we married. Anyhow, you're not like me, you know what I mean, you're not ambitious.'

'Yes, but the reality of being at home isn't what I expected. We're starting to lead separate lives. I'm filling the gaps in your life, but you're not doing the same for me and the children.'

'That's a little melodramatic, isn't it?'

Mary shrugged her shoulders.

Marcus packed his case early the following morning and took a seat at the breakfast table, reading the *Mercury*. The children were still in bed.

'You remember I met that businessman, the one with the factory in Birmingham?'

'I think so,' replied Mary, stooped over the cooker in her dressing gown, making breakfast.

'Well, I'm going to see if he's still there. I'm dropping in on my way up to the Labour conference.'

'Have you rung him?'

'I can't get through. It's not a good omen.'

'Don't be late for Blackpool.'

'I'm not looking forward to it,' he sighed.

'The front page of the *Mercury* always seems so depressing,' Mary said, 'with strikes and the economy. The government looks to have lost control.'

Marcus folded the paper and put it in his briefcase.

'Heath was pathetic and weak, and Labour is being taken over by extremists. They're frightened to take on the unions,' said Marcus.

'Seems like the mob's in control.'

'When I was up at Saltley, I saw mob rule first-hand, and it's frightening.'

'Perhaps you'll meet some of your university friends up in Blackpool.'

Marcus thought of his university days and the ideas in vogue back then.

'I hope not.'

'Why?'

'I've moved on since then.'

'You wanted to fit in, didn't you?'

'I suppose so, but some of us have never grown out of it, like Dave Shearman. He'll be an MP soon.'

'I never met him.'

'His sort of opinions, those he sold to me I suppose, are mainstream in the unions and Labour. The country needs strong leaders, and all we've got is weakness.'

Marcus headed north along the M6 past Birmingham, in his Morris Marina. He turned off the motorway and meandered through the Black Country. The factory was still there. He wound down the window, as he had done when he had visited in 1972. The noise he had experienced back then had subsided. He could hear individual sounds of activity from some of the smaller factories, but not the crashing, reverberating and deafening din. There were just a few cars parked on the roadside, and the gate of Glynn Knowles's factory was closed.

There was a sign and an arrow pointing to the security office, and Marcus pulled into a space by the main gate. He sighed and shook his head. A young, skinny, bored-looking man appeared from the gloom. Marcus noticed that the uniform he was wearing was too big. Perhaps his employers did not generally recruit such emaciated men to do security.

'Yes?' the youngster asked.

'When did it close?'

'Last year.'

'What happened?'

'They went bust. Knowles closed the factory, just like that.' He clicked his fingers.

'Nobody left?'

'Just four security men on shift, that's it. Machinery sold to Taiwan or somewhere out that way,' he said, jerking his thumb over his shoulder.

Marcus wondered if he knew where Taiwan was.

'What about Mr Knowles?'

'Majorca, he went to live in Majorca. They reckon it's bostin'. 'Ave you been?'

'No.'

'Not that it did 'im much cop.'

'What do you mean?'

'Died, well, when I say he died, it's all a bit mysterious. Car went off the road, and he were killed.'

'Oh no!'

'Nobody with him, like. Some say he had a heart attack, and some say suicide. Nobody knows because of the fire. Anyhow, it don't make no diff'rence. He's dead and that's it.'

Without another word, Marcus returned to his car and slumped in the driver's seat.

'Fucking hell, fucking, fucking hell,' he whispered, banging his hands on the steering wheel. 'What a shithole this country's become.'

Marcus continued up the M6 to Blackpool where he met

his boss, Ken Lees. They were both booked into rooms in a guesthouse but rendezvoused at the conference venue, The Winter Gardens. Ken had attended the conferences for many years, and he was known, if not liked, by many of the delegates. He socialised effortlessly.

'Stick with me, Marcus. When you get the hang of it, you can have a wander around on your own.'

'OK.'

'Then we'll split so we can cover the conference hall, the fringe meetings and the general chit-chat outside the hall. An old friend's invited me out for dinner tonight,' he winked, 'so you'll have to amuse yourself.'

'That's fine,' said Marcus.

'See that bloke over there,' said Ken nodding, 'he's a complete twat.'

The man was tall, slim, effortless and about Marcus's age.

'He started off in student politics; a Trot. The wanker has never done a day's work in his life. He's trying to get the sitting MP in a safe seat deselected because he's not left-wing enough. Watch it, he's coming over. Best behaviour.'

'Hello, Ken. Still working for that awful rag?'

'Good to see you, Jim. This is Marcus. He's learning the ropes.'

Marcus and Jim exchanged nods.

'I see you're being tipped for high places,' Ken continued.

'Yes, when I get selected.'

'Supporting the motion for further nationalisation?'

'Of course! We've got to work closely with the unions. It's no good being confrontational. Look where it got Ted Heath.'

'What about the falling pound and rising debt?'

'We'll bring in import controls and take over the banks. Anyhow, things aren't as bad as you say. Look Ken, the government can't do anything without union support, and the unions won't support cuts.'

'What about the next election. Will people vote for this stuff?'

'They'll never vote for Thatcher. I've got to go, Ken. It's good to see you and you too, err…'

'Marcus.'

'Yes, Marcus.'

'Good to see you too, Jim,' said Ken.

Ken turned to Marcus.

'He's still the same clueless arsehole. They'll lose the next election, but he couldn't care less, as long as he's elected.'

Marcus nodded his agreement.

They mingled, tried to get people to talk, listened and arranged meetings and interviews.

As the conference progressed, the television and newspapers were reporting the plummeting pound, increasing government debt, rising inflation, industrial unrest and rumours of talks with the IMF.

The chancellor, Dennis Healey, had been absent from the conference, and he arrived to tell the audience that he was negotiating a financial bailout with the IMF. He sounded out of breath and was on stage for just five minutes. He made no attempt to hide the seriousness of the situation. It was the largest bailout any country had agreed, and it would mean that austerity measures, already signed off by the cabinet, would be implemented. There was to be no backtracking. The alternative would be economic meltdown and the election of Mrs Thatcher. As Healey finished and left the stage, Marcus heard cheers around the hall. At least there were some delegates prepared to stand up for the country. Then, as Healey rushed from the conference hall, Marcus saw Jim, part of a small group, booing. Others joined in, but more cheers drowned out the booing.

'What's that all about?' Marcus asked Ken, nodding toward the dissenters.

'Fuck knows,' Ken whispered.

'They don't realise what's happening. As far as they're concerned, it's going to be business as usual.'

'Some of them are too fucking stupid to realise that we're in the shit. Twats, they're all twats.'

Later that evening, the chairman read out the result of a motion to nationalise banks and insurance companies, which was carried by six to one. The *Mercury* made sure that it was the booing and the nationalisation vote that would stick in the national psyche, and that the unions and *militants* were really in charge.

Exactly a week later, Ken Lees and Marcus attended the Conservative Party Conference in Brighton. The format was the same, but everything else seemed different. The delegates were people like him: hard working and aspiring. The mood was uplifting. They openly discussed confronting and defeating the unions that had been manipulating the government for their own ends. There was steel in their voices, and Margaret Thatcher epitomised their spirit. She meant what she said. They would not tinker with the system; they would change it. They would not compromise; they would meet the opposition head-on. She was putting into words what Marcus had begun to think. He recalled Glynn Knowles. Thatcher would rekindle the national spirit. It might be too late for Glynn but not for the country.

It was shortly afterwards that the *Echo* made a first tentative approach. They wanted him to be assistant news editor, and they talked openly about his potential career prospects.

'I'm not sure I'm going to get anywhere, staying at the *Mercury*,' he said to Mary that same evening.

'Why not?'

'There are too many people stuck in their jobs, blocking promotion, and it's dead men's shoes.'

'You've hardly had any time in this new job.'

'I need to move up the ladder faster, and I'll only do that if I get out.'

'I'm sure they'll offer you something. You'll have to talk to them about it. They know you're ambitious.'

'I've just had a direct approach from the *Echo*.'

'Oh, that's what it's all about.'

'I'd have more say about what goes in the paper, but I'd have to follow the editorial line. What do you think?'

'Do you want it? You'd have never considered a paper like the *Echo*, you know, when we first met. You thought it was worse than the *Mercury*.'

'It's a great job: more money and responsibility. It could take me right to the top.'

'It took years to come terms with the *Mercury*.'

'What do you mean?'

'When you started, you were always complaining because everything was rewritten. Not now.'

Mary picked up the copy of the *Mercury* spread across the kitchen table. She turned to an inside page and pointed. 'It's all your own work.'

Marcus was deep in thought. Mary continued.

'When we first met, you were always arguing with my father.'

'Not arguing.'

'Disagreeing then, but you agree on most things, now.'

Marcus hesitated.

'The country's going down the pan. I'm not afraid to admit I got it wrong. I'm not the only one. Most of us were left-wing at university.'

'Wrong? You? You're not ill are you?' Mary smiled.

'Weak leaders, scared of the unions, and Labour frightened to stand up to them. I've seen an honest business go to the wall and nationalised industries become bloated and corrupt. Grammar schools are almost gone, and comprehensives are churning out a generation of mediocre clones. We've become a laughing stock.'

'You had a Road to Damascus experience?'

'No, it's been a slow process, ever since the miners' strike and Saltley depot. I haven't felt comfortable with the way the country's been run, and it's been gnawing away at me.'

'There's nothing to be ashamed of, admitting you were wrong. I've never really understood why you had those views. Your parents are so middle-of-the-road.'

'Perhaps I rebelled against them.'

'You've already decided to accept the job.'

'No, not really.'

'Yes you have. I don't know why you bothered asking me.'

The opportunity was too financially attractive to refuse, and Marcus made a virtue out of necessity. He was one more step nearer his goal.

11

MARCUS

Shortly after taking the new job, Marcus and Mary moved into the quiet village of Blackbourne, in rural Hertfordshire, but within easy reach of the city. He could drive to the nearby station, and the train took him to Old Street, a short walk to the office. Mary enrolled the children in the local primary school and they settled in quickly. The house had previously been owned by an old lady and needed major renovation. For two years, whilst Marcus was establishing himself at the *Echo*, Mary managed a series of builders and tradesmen. They extended, rewired, plumbed and repaired the house. The mortgage stretched them financially, and they completed work when spare cash from Marcus's increasing salary became available.

Marcus was learning a great deal from Ronnie Miles, the news editor. Marcus had been a few weeks in the job when Ronnie leaned over his desk.

'You look knackered, Marcus,' he said.

'Some of the stuff that's coming through, well, it's just crap. They don't seem to know what I want, or they're just not up to it.'

'Look, Marcus. You're a good newspaper man, but you can't let those bastards trample all over you,' he replied, referring to a gaggle of staff leaning over a desk and laughing loudly. 'You're not at university now. You can't debate everything. If you want something doing, just tell 'em to fuckin' do it. If it's still not right, tell 'em again, as many times as is needed, or fire a few of 'em. If there's a balls-up, it's your neck, so make sure none of that shower lets you down.'

'I can't just bawl them out in the office.'

'Yes, you can. As far as I'm concerned, do whatever you fuckin' like. Just get results. Start cracking the whip; show you're in charge. We're not paying that lot to mess around; we're paying 'em to work.'

At the *Mercury*, Marcus had had no responsibility other than to fulfil the reporting tasks he had been assigned, but at the *Echo*, what went into each day's paper bore his stamp. His readers would judge him on what they saw, and he followed Ronnie's advice.

Within weeks, he introduced an early morning meeting, at a time when most of his staff were normally still in bed. He expected everyone to attend. Marcus used the meetings to set the tone for the day. He gave instructions and set deadlines. He swore at anyone who did not give him what he wanted. Those that found the new regime too onerous left of their own accord, or they were encouraged to leave. The harder Marcus drove them, the better the results.

It was the day after the 1979 general election. Marcus had sneaked downstairs from the children's bedrooms. Giles had stayed awake, waiting for his father to return from work.

'He showed me a picture he'd drawn at school. I don't really look like that do I? No neck and massive eyes.'

'There's a newspaper in your hand.'

'Gail was asleep.'

The evening meal was on the table in their newly fitted kitchen. They ate and talked, mainly about the children and school, and then they cleared the table together. Marcus sat down, put his hand under the table and pulled out a copy of the following day's *Echo* from a briefcase. He casually flicked through the pages as he spoke to Mary, still at the sink.

'I know there are a few years yet, but what are the secondary schools like?'

'Quite good.'

'How good's "quite good"?'

'People say they're OK.'

'Which people?'

'Why the sudden interest, Marcus?'

Marcus put the paper on the table.

'I want to make sure they get the best schooling, that's all.'

Mary took a cloth and wiped the table. He lifted his arms as she swished the cloth past him.

'We're in the catchment for Queen Elizabeth,' said Mary. 'It's pretty new, with a thousand or so kids.'

'What sort of kids?'

'What sort of question's that?'

'Are they from the villages, the town or the council estate?'

'Oh, I get it. You don't want the children mixing with the wrong sort.'

Mary smiled and shook her head.

'To be honest, no, I don't.'

'It's a mixture, including the Goldstone Estate. Where's all this snobbery coming from, Marcus?'

'It's not snobbery. You know the reputation of the Goldstone.'

'Queen Elizabeth's the best school around, unless you want to pay. You're the one with the strong views about private education. You're always knocking your school.'

'Well, there are public schools and public schools.'

Mary rolled her eyes as she dropped the cloth into the sink. She returned to the table and sat opposite Marcus.

'I'd never send the children to Harrow or Eton,' he said, 'but what about one of the old grammar schools?'

'Get to the point, Marcus.'

'I don't want the children mixing with council estate kids. I want them to have the best education we can provide.'

'Harrow or Eton is where they'd get the best.'

'OK, I want them to have a good education. I'd rather not put my children at risk.'

'At risk of what? Do you think they'll catch something?'

'You know what I mean.'

'Don't get me wrong, it's you that's had this hang-up about private schools. If we can afford private, I'm all for it. It's *our* children we're talking about.'

'When we had grammar schools, brighter kids had a chance. Now education's pitched at the lowest common denominator.'

'You don't know that, Marcus.'

'Well, what do you think?'

'You're missing the point.'

'What's that then?'

'If you spent more time at home, and if you met the teachers and visited the schools, you'd know what things were really like.'

'I don't want to go over this again.'

'You prefer to be at work than at home. When you started at the *Echo*, you were as miserable as sin. Now, you can't wait to get out of the door in the morning.'

'I enjoy it there. It's exciting. We've started producing quality stuff. I've had to crack a few heads together, but it's been worth it.'

'Yes, I bet you have. They're terrified of you.'

'Maybe some are.'

'It's become a drug, Marcus. You're an addict. You can't see it, but I can.'

'For goodness' sake, stop exaggerating. I try to keep work and home separate.'

'I see what you're like at weekends. You spend hours reading the papers.'

'That's not work. Most people read the papers.'

'Come on! You can't relax, you're miserable. It's only on Sunday evening that you cheer up again.'

'That's not fair. Anyhow, we were talking about the children's education,' said Marcus. 'I don't need to go to the Goldstone Estate to know what sort of people live there. I read the local papers. Would we prefer our children to go to the local comprehensive or an independent school? It's as simple as that.'

'If we can afford it, then I'd prefer an independent school.'

'We'll be able to afford it.'

'You've changed your tune, Marcus.'

'Anyhow, there are scholarships to the old grammar schools. We'll only pay if they don't get a place by right.'

Marcus picked the *Echo* from the table and began reading. 'See what I mean.'

Marcus put the paper down and tapped his index finger on the front-page photograph of the new Prime Minister.

'Things are going to change for the better, Mary.'

'You mean Mrs Thatcher?'

'She's inspiring – no doubts, just certainty.'

'Perhaps she'll sort out the mess we're in.'

'I'm sure she will. We've all got used to bumbling along and inevitable decline, but she's not prepared to go along with it. It's as if the shackles have been removed.'

'You've become what you always were, Marcus.'

'What do you mean?'

'Oh, you're a traditionalist, a conservative, a conformer.'

'A conformer?'

'I wonder what you'd think of Thatcher if you worked at the *Sentinel* with your friend Clara?' she smiled, and Marcus winced.

'Thatcher's just what we need.'

12

MARCUS

Marcus was at his desk early the following Monday. He examined an unopened envelope that had his name on it with suspicion. It was during a lull in the daily frenzy of newsgathering and preparation of copy. It had been addressed to him at the *Echo*.

He fingered the soft, light, pink envelope. There was a bump inside. It suggested more than paper, and he recognised the handwriting but could not recollect the context. The card inside suggested a different era; a time of Laura Ashley dresses, long flowing hair, frayed, faded and patched jeans and carefree and careless attitudes. It was handmade, with broad swishes of watercolour. Dried flowers and seed heads were stuck to the front of the card, and Marcus looked at this creation with suspicion. Like all works of art, the seconds spent by the uninterested onlooker, to view and forget, is a small fraction of the hours required to create. Marcus swung the card open, a door to the past, and he immediately recognised the signature.

'Clara,' he murmured.

It was an invitation to a party at The Marquis of Claremont in West London. He whispered the words written on the invitation.

'Marcus,

Dave (Shearman) is having a get-together at six pm on

THE VOICE AND THE ECHO

Friday, to celebrate his success at the general election. Thought you might like to come. Give me a ring at the *Sentinel* if you can make it. X Clara'

Dave Shearman was one of the few successful new Labour MPs, having been bequeathed a safe seat in his home town. Marcus dropped the card on his desk. He had no intention of going. The *Echo* had campaigned vigorously for Mrs Thatcher, and it had been scathing toward the outgoing Labour government. He did not want to see Clara or Dave.

Ronnie Miles was passing Marcus's desk.

'Talking to yourself, Marcus?'

'You wouldn't believe it, Ronnie. I've been invited to a get-together with Dave Shearman on Friday evening. He's one of the new Labour MPs.'

'I know who he is.'

'I was with him at university. I'm not going. I couldn't bear it.'

'Yes, you are.'

'Sorry?'

'You're a journalist. Get something interesting for the Monday edition.'

Ronnie was serious, and Marcus had no choice.

Clara was out of the office when he phoned, and he left a message accepting the invitation. When he arrived at the pub, the party was in full swing. He edged past a group with garishly pink, purple and orange hair: some were Mohican style and one was bleached white. Studs, chains and pins adorned their faces and leather clothes, and Marcus looked away. A song was being played far too loud, and he heard the words 'YMCA' being repeated. He recognised a few of the bright, fresh faces. Someone nodded at him.

'Hello,' he responded automatically.

Clara had been awaiting his arrival and made her way through the bustle.

'Marcus, you've hardly changed,' she said as she put her arm round him and kissed his cheek.

Marcus blushed at the warmth of the greeting. He had changed in one obvious way. His smartness was conspicuous. It was not a casual smartness. The shine of his shoes showed no compromise and the cut of his suit made no concession to fashion.

'You've not changed either,' he replied, coldly.

Clara's face still had the warmth he remembered, but her features displayed tiredness and her body had developed a matronly roundness. He had never seen her dressed in a skirt suit before.

'I'm glad you came. There's a lot to talk about.'

'Is there?' asked Marcus.

'Dave's over by the bar.'

Marcus looked across but could not see the new Member of Parliament. Clara grabbed his hand and pulled him through the scrum.

'Marcus!' shouted a man he did not recognise, although the intonation seemed familiar. 'Glad you could come.'

Marcus was taken aback when he finally recognised the apparition offering a hand, but he recovered his poise quickly and returned the greeting. Dave's moustache, sideburns and a large proportion of his hair had mysteriously disappeared. Dave did not notice Marcus's momentary loss of poise, and he seemed unaware of his own shortage of hair.

Dave's mane had receded all the way to his ears, forming a straight line across the top of his head between his shortened and trimmed sideburns. Time had not been kind to Dave. The more Marcus tried to look away, the more he was drawn to the mysterious change that had taken place.

'It's good to see you, Dave,' he replied. 'Congratulations.'

'Thanks. I've sort of lost touch with what you're up to.'

Along with his hair, Dave seemed to have mislaid most of the Geordie accent, which had been so important to him at university.

As Marcus explained what he had been doing for the past decade, Clara became involved in a conversation with two of Dave's acolytes. Meanwhile, Dave's eyes flitted between the members of his group. He smiled at them in turn and nodded a greeting to a young woman, newly arrived.

'I'm Assistant News Editor at the *Echo*,' concluded Marcus, irritated at Dave's lack of interest.

'I'd never have thought you'd have ended up working for the enemy,' he laughed. 'What's happened to your Marxist politics, Marcus? You were a bit of a firebrand back then.'

'Never. Anyhow, I've moved on since university. Looks like you have too.'

'I hope I'll be getting some good coverage from you? We'll need all the help we can get,' laughed Dave.

'You'll need a miracle.'

'Come on, Marcus.'

'I'm just telling the truth. You'll be in the wilderness for years. You never know, you might be a Minister when Labour gets back. In the meantime, Thatcher will have sorted the country out.'

'This is supposed to be a fun evening, Marcus. Anyhow, we'll be back after one term. Have you got a drink? I'll order you one.'

Dave turned toward the bar and started to talk to the young woman he had previously acknowledged. This ended Marcus's conversation with him for the evening as Dave became engulfed in his crowd of backslappers and hangers-on. To Marcus, the voices merged into a wall of abhorrent noise. Some were shouting congratulations to Dave, and others sneered uncomplimentary remarks about Marcus and the *Echo*.

There was a commotion at the door, and Marcus thought that a fight had broken out. The music had changed, and the group of youngsters he'd seen as he came through the door were disco-punk dancing in their corner of the pub. Clara Tomlin grabbed his arm and dragged him to a quiet table. She sat next to him so that their bodies almost touched. Marcus edged away.

'I don't know why he surrounds himself with that crowd, but he's always loved an audience,' she said. 'You know what he's like.'

'They act as if Labour'd won. I don't know why they're so jolly. It makes me sick. No contrition, no humility, just the expectation that they'll soon be back in power, but they're in for a shock. How did he get into Labour politics?'

'He was a local activist, then councillor and now MP.'

'So he's a career politician. I'm surprised you kept in touch with him, you know, after university.'

'Why shouldn't I? We've all changed since then. You used to be friends. You even agreed with his politics. What've you been up to?'

Marcus repeated what he had said to Dave, and Clara behaved as if they had been friends for all the intervening years. She encouraged him to speak his mind, and he stated his opinions and experiences stridently and uncompromisingly.

'Wow, Marcus, you've changed your tune.'

'I've seen the real world, Clara. Look at Dave, even he's mainstream Labour now.'

'But you sound like Mrs Thatcher.'

'You don't still believe all of that socialist nonsense, do you?'

'I believe in a fairer society. Is that so bad?'

'Look where it's got us, Clara. We've had IMF bailouts, strikes, inflation and no government prepared to govern.'

'Some countries in the EEC, like Germany, have achieved a fair society *and* prosperity.'

'Don't get me started on Europe, Clara.'

'What do you mean?'

'It's a retirement home for failed politicians.'

'Goodness me, Marcus, why are you so angry?'

'I don't fit in here,' said Marcus.

He had just observed Jeremy McNeice. Marcus had not seen Jeremy since his last day at school but recognised him immediately, hand in hand with a young man.

'Why come then?'

Marcus shrugged and turned away so that Jeremy would not see him.

'Do you want to hear what I've been up to since university?' asked Clara.

Marcus detected a slur in her voice. Clara was drunk. He'd never heard her slur before, even after a few pints of beer. She was as bad as all the others, and Marcus couldn't wait to get away.

'We'll have to do that some other time. I'll be off. Make my apologies to Dave.'

'No, don't go,' Clara pleaded. 'I thought we could catch up.'

'Look, I don't want to bump into Jeremy McNeice.'

Marcus pointed him out to Clara.

'Oh, he's alright,' she said.

'Give me a ring. I have to get back.'

'We've got so much catching up to do, Marcus.'

'It'd have been better if I hadn't come.'

Marcus stood up and was gone. Clara's head dropped, and

she sat disconsolately for a few minutes before joining Dave. She moved to his side and waited for a lull in the conversation.

'Marcus has had to leave.'

'Not Marcus Roache?' asked Jeremy.

'Yes.'

'What in God's name's he doing here? I was at school with him; complete prat.'

Dave looked at Clara and shrugged.

'We both knew him at university,' she said. 'He edited your school magazine, didn't he?'

'No he didn't. I was the editor, and sometimes he helped out.'

'I must have got it wrong,' said Clara.

'He probably didn't want to meet me,' concluded Jeremy. 'He'd a huge chip on his shoulder about the well-off kids. He was on a scholarship: a cold fish. He never seemed to get involved with anything and never made friends.'

'I didn't know he went to an independent school. Who'd have guessed?' said Dave. 'I wonder why he never mentioned it.'

'He didn't get the grades for Oxbridge. He thought he was up to it, but he wasn't. Can I introduce you to my friend, James?'

Clara whispered in Dave's ear.

'You know, he never asked anything about me or Clive or Mike. It's almost as if we didn't exist. He seemed to have come here to…'

Clara stopped because Dave was already talking to James and was paying her no attention.

Marcus provided Ronnie Miles with exactly what he wanted. If there had been a way to reconcile with his past, it had gone.

13

CLIVE

Dave, Clara and Mike left *Student Voice* for careers, whereas Clive found himself a job. This eventuality had been accepted reluctantly and merely to pay for the basic requirements of life. During the September after completing university, he moved to South Yorkshire and joined the *Comet*, a regional newspaper, as a reporter. It was the best occupation for his chosen way of life.

Clive told his friends that work posed too many demands on his time, and he was no longer free to manage his own daily routine. Most of Clive's acquaintances thought that these words were inappropriate because his life had no routine at all, not in the sense of working around fixed points in the day, such as getting up, eating meals and going to bed. They believed that Clive did not manage his time so much as waste it. Clive considered that there were just too many things to do for him to be spending overmuch time working. How could he fit in sport, socialising and all the routine things in life, like sleeping, shopping, cooking and on top of that, go to work?

He had become close to Clara in the final term, but they had drifted apart in the last few weeks. Clive had thought that their relationship might lead somewhere, but Clara had never given any indication of permanence.

He rented a bedroom on the top floor of a house in

Sheffield, sharing a kitchen and living room with two other 'professionals'. One sold toilet rolls, and the other worked in a record shop. The latter seemed to have developed an on-off relationship with the owner and driving force behind the business, and Clive deduced that his role was to cultivate a detailed knowledge of every kind of music, controlling, as he did, the records being played on the turntable. He never appeared to get involved in actually selling anything.

Clive learned how to fit work around his real life, and he developed the ability to hit deadlines by the skin of his teeth. He also cultivated a formidable roll call of local contacts. It was not the normal networking in high places but an intimate social reticulation, with members arranged in his mind by topic and interest, linked by a complex mesh of mutual interests and friendships.

They were not the important movers and shakers who could directly help his upward path to success, but they were little people, usually with interesting stories and minor influence in their limited sphere. They were the ex-footballers who knew of the next transfer, or when the manager was about to be fired. They were the minor union officials who could tell him of an impending strike. They were the middle managers who would leak plans about a factory closure, or the petty public servants in the town hall who would whisper when a major project was about to be shelved or given the go-ahead.

The common factor with all of these people was that they thrived on social relationships, usually oiled by a drink in a local pub. They shared a genuine like for Clive Parkhouse, and they all trusted him. Clive spent a lot of his time in the pub. His contacts introduced him to a world where he got stories that nobody else was aware of, or he picked up a lead before a story became common knowledge. Through that ability, he became a priceless asset to the paper. He specialised in the quirky and the humdrum, but in a style designed to evoke a sense of empathy and recognition in the readers.

Clive's beard, his shoulder length, unkempt hair and his well-worn clothes did not endear him to the establishment. What was bad for personal advancement was ideal for networking in the less lofty circles where news, his sort of news, was to be found. He looked like the people he associated with. His appearance bothered others, but it did not concern Clive. He aspired to a job well done, usually in time, if only just.

Clive was driven by a soaring lack of ambition. He had a ruthless desire not to succeed and not to appear to be succeeding. He had a career plan with no detail, and his compass pointed in no direction, but this was not to be taken for lack of competence, principles or resolve. Everything he did was undertaken with commitment, integrity and thoroughness, for its own sake, not to achieve some goal or step on a career path. He shunned opportunity that compromised his values, and he preferred honest failure to dishonest success. He moved on when he was dissatisfied, not when he saw some golden opportunity. The job at the *Comet* was fine, and he could not think of anything better to do, nothing commensurate with his chosen lifestyle.

It was only a few years after starting at the *Comet* that he became the presenter for a weekly current affairs programme on local radio. He interviewed people who were not in the headlines but had a story to tell, usually linked to local news. It became a popular programme, and Clive became a reluctant minor celebrity. He followed the industrial unrest of the seventies in mining and steelmaking, both in the paper and on the radio, always finding the human angle.

When power cuts hit, he talked to those who were affected. He interviewed old people who could not keep warm and went to bed early, and he quizzed youngsters who used the power cuts as an excuse to do the same, but they had a different aim in mind. He followed Arthur Scargill's flying pickets, preventing pits from operating far from his Yorkshire base. He was in Sheffield during the steel strike of 1980 and outside Hadfields when the police lost control. He witnessed drivers being dragged from their trucks and threatened by strikers, and he interviewed both the drivers and the pickets.

He first considered buying a house when he secured the radio work, but he never got round to it because it meant talking to estate agents and solicitors. He realised that ownership led to the sorts of responsibilities he eschewed, like decorating and buying furniture, carpets and curtains. When would he be able to find a gap in his busy days for that? Work was already taking up too much of his time. Owning a house would absorb even more. He put this commitment off because there were far more important things to be done.

Fortunately, he fell in love.

Clive was routinely arm in arm with an attractive woman. He was in love with each one, without exception. Sometimes he was in love for just days, more often for weeks, and on rare occasions, he was smitten for months. He fell in love with a few women more than once, with a gap of many years between events. Unfortunately, although Clive was superficially attractive to the opposite sex, they found out that his lifestyle was not so alluring.

Any woman was faced with unpredictable work routines. He was unreliable, particularly arriving late at scheduled rendezvous. His social commitments usually included women as peripheral players. He displayed poor communication skills and always had a roving eye for the next opportunity. There was no malice in any of this, just a fervent desire to enjoy life. No split up was acrimonious, no friend ever hurt.

This was different. It was real love. It was a chance meeting at a party. Clive had categorised parties into three types and was explaining his theory to Jennifer, a petite, newly qualified accountant. They were in a crowded, noisy room, and 'Imagine', recently at number one, was playing in the background, but Clive was not listening.

'Type one's for married couples with families. They have friends round for dinner parties. I used to get invited, but not now.'

'I can't stand them,' replied Jennifer. 'It's all the talk about babies, recipes and decorating the house.'

'Dead right, but they used to be like us,' he said and continued with an exaggerated genteel accent. 'Now they're *so* sophisticated,' Clive's voice tailed off, 'and so middle-aged.'

'Yes. I call them chicken brick and fondue parties.'

They laughed, and Clive continued.

'Type two is for ex-students. Most of them invite themselves. Everybody's an academic, ersatz academic, wannabe academic or failed academic.'

'Yeah, I know what you mean. Dress sense nailed firmly in the sixties and awareness of what's interesting, non-existent.'

'Intense conversations about an esoteric hobby, or their thesis,' Clive added.

'But the grass is usually great.'

'Now, the third type of party…'

'You mean like now?' she asked.

'Yes.'

'Unattached, loosely attached and temporarily attached people in their twenties and thirties.'

'Like us?'

'The women come with a partner just for the evening or without a partner at all,' Jennifer flirted.

'The men usually arrive at the end of a long and boozy session in the pub.'

As Clive was talking, he noticed that one of Jennifer's friends had re-entered the room. She had been in the kitchen with another group. He heard someone call her Marie. Clive's glance became an embarrassing stare. She was a beautiful woman, and her effortless grace and casual ability to claim attention intrigued him.

She joined a small group next to Clive. Marie seemed able to control the conversation without imposing herself. Her voice was sympathetic but persuasive, clear and articulate. She was tall and slim, and her long and light brown hair fell over her shoulders and down her back. She wore a dark loose-fitting jacket over a light coloured blouse and tight jeans. Clive felt love at first sight, not like all the other times, but really, love at first sight.

To the annoyance of Jennifer, Clive could not take his eyes off Marie, and she started to fidget at the lack of attention, bridled and walked away to join some of the other girls who had come to the party with her. Marie saw all of this, and her playful green eyes snared him. He turned his head away, self-consciously. Eye contact was habitually a signal to make a move, but he flunked his opportunity. Marie had no such reservations. She took the opportunity of a break in the conversation to shuffle across to Clive. He was standing at the edge of a mixed group, and she hooked his arm in hers and gently edged him away from the others.

'Hello. You're the famous Clive Parkhouse, aren't you?' Her voice was confident and playful.

'Famous?' Clive turned to face her.

'Well, infamous then.'

'Are you poking fun at me?'

'No, no, no. Why'd I do that? One of your friends pointed you out.'

'Oh dear!'

'He was quite complimentary.'

'Only quite? What did he say?'

'Well, he said you were good fun. He told me to be on my guard because you were probably on the lookout. He said you always were.'

'Some friend. It's not much of a compliment,' said Clive, furrowing his brow.

'Anyhow, you don't seem that scary to me,' she said.

'You *are* poking fun at me, aren't you?'

'Yes, you've seen through me,' she laughed. 'I listen to you on the radio. I like the programme.'

'All the ladies say that. I'm not sure any of them mean it.'

'I mean it. Anyhow, I'm Marie.'

'I know. I overheard.'

'Naughty. I saw you looking at me. What were you thinking?'

'I didn't mean to stare.'

'Tell me, what were you thinking?'

'I was thinking… I was thinking that you're a stunning looking woman, but I bet all the men say that.'

'Not all. Sometimes I reckon I can see men's intentions in their eyes.'

'What do you see?'

'Sometimes their thoughts are, well, they're not very honourable. Your look was different.'

Clive hesitated.

'When I said you were beautiful, I didn't mean in a fashion-model sense, not that I'm in any position to pass judgement on fashion, as you can see.'

Marie leant back and looked at him ostentatiously, from head to toe.

'You're right.'

'What I meant to say was that there's something about you, something... alluring, magnetic. I couldn't take my eyes off you.'

Clive paused and shook his head.

'What the hell am I on about? Shit. I'm sorry. I must be embarrassing you. I'm embarrassing myself. I don't normally talk like this.'

Marie leaned forward and pulled his face to hers. Her kiss was deep and passionate. Clive responded, surprised at her action, and captivated.

They talked together, the intensity and closeness of their conversation deterring interruption from others. For a man who was confident with women, Clive felt nervous because for the first time since Clara, this mattered.

Marie taught at a local school. She was a few years younger than Clive was and had moved into the area from Leeds, for a job as a department head. She had found the subjects of his radio show engaging, and she recalled his report about miners with pneumoconiosis and their campaign for compensation. During the steel strike, she'd enjoyed the weekly roundup and interviews with strikers. Marie seemed unimpressed by his celebrity, a pleasant change for Clive, but unsettling.

In the early hours, Clive walked Marie home. They ambled, hands in pockets, talking about nothing in particular. As they approached the door of her flat, Clive dropped back. Marie stopped, turned and walked back toward Clive.

'You want to see me again, don't you?' she said, teasingly.

Clive was nonplussed by the question. It seemed more of a statement. She kissed the fingertips of her right hand and placed them on his lips.

Clive shrugged, appearing coolly uninterested. Marie continued.

'I'd like to see you, but there are a few complications. Let's meet at The Bear on Friday night. You know it, do you?'

'Of course.'

'Half seven. Don't be late.'

She was playful in her tone, and Clive was lost for words. She stepped to her door, turned the key, and in seconds, without looking back, was through and gone. Clive noted the door number, just in case.

That Friday, for once, Clive was on time for a date and had taken a seat before Marie arrived. She swept in, and as he stood up, she grasped the back of his head, pulled it to hers and enveloped Clive's mouth with a long kiss. She asked Clive what he was drinking, refused to allow him to order and bought two drinks: a pint of bitter and a glass of Guinness. The head of the Guinness stuck to her lips as she drank, and she licked it away.

'What a week,' she sighed.

'Good or bad?'

'It's a long story. I don't want to bore you, but one of the reasons I moved here from Leeds was… Well, there's no point beating around the bush. My boyfriend lives here. That's where I went the other evening, to our flat. He was away for the weekend.'

'You live with your boyfriend?'

'I did, but I'm staying with another girl at the moment.'

'So what's happened?'

'Don't worry. It's over, well almost over. I've some stuff to pick up.'

'Just like that?'

'I should've known it wouldn't work right. He wanted a younger version of his mother, to clean, cook, have his children and look after them for a lifetime.'

'You mean you've a problem with that?' smiled Clive.

'Don't push your luck.'

'Sorry.'

'It wasn't me he wanted, but a comfortable future. Anyhow, that's enough about my problems. Let's eat.'

They went to Uncle Sam's Chuck Wagon, and Clive felt as if he was under a spell. He leant across the table and whispered, 'Don't laugh, but it's as if I've known you all my life.'

'Me too, so let's just enjoy it.'

They had eaten and were outside the restaurant when Clive asked, 'What are your plans for tonight?'

'Back to yours?'

Marie's visit was fleeting, but it was long enough. She briefly met Clive's flatmates.

'You can't live in a place like this,' she whispered. 'Your two flatmates, they're…'

'Weird,' said Clive. 'I've got used to them, I suppose.'

'We can't stay here tonight. It's not… I'm trying to be polite… hygienic.'

They managed to book a room at the Hallam Towers.

The following morning, lying in bed, Marie spoke.

'Things are moving fast, Clive. What next?'

'What d'you mean?'

'I can't stay where I am, and I'm not moving in with you, not into that place.'

'Well, I suppose I could move out.'

'Let's find a place somewhere.'

Clive had no desire to argue. It seemed a perfectly natural next step.

'OK.'

'Do you have plans, Clive, you know, things you want to do with your life?'

'I've never made plans,' said Clive. 'I'd like to be happy. It'd be nice to do some good. Is that a plan?'

'That's enough of a plan for me,' she laughed.

Clive looked across, not sure why she should laugh at something so serious.

A few weeks later, they moved into a rented flat near Endcliffe Park.

Their relationship was deeply passionate and fulfilling. They became engaged. It was an engagement by default, with no formal process and no announcement. They were lying in bed when Marie said, 'Do you think we ought to get married?'

'You're not pregnant, are you?' asked Clive.

'No, but I'd like children.'

'Me too. I suppose we'd better get married first.'

'We could do it before Christmas.'

'We've only just met.'

'Cold feet?'

'No.'

'We should look for a house.'

'Lots of bedrooms for all of the kids?'

'Perhaps something a little run-down, to renovate. What are you like at DIY?'

'Fantastic,' said Clive, sarcastically. 'I did woodwork at school.'

'It's something to look forward to, isn't it, having our own house?'

When they told parents, family and friends, they were asked when they had become engaged, so the day when marriage had first been mooted became their retrospective engagement day.

Parents were met, a wedding arranged, a house sought and purchased, a wedding and honeymoon completed, and the married couple moved into their new home on Christmas Eve. They spent Christmas and New Year sleeping on a settee that opened out into a makeshift bed.

Clive spent less time in the pub. There was now a reason to get home, so the amount he drank and the frequency and duration of pub visits reduced. It seemed to him, in retrospect, that he had wasted a lot of time in pubs and at parties, trying to find his next new love. As that was no longer necessary, life was both enjoyable and efficient.

The week the 1984 miners strike started, Marie told Clive that she was pregnant. The baby was due in September and starting a family would make life complete.

14

CLIVE

Mike Boddington had been appointed Editor of the *Comet* in 1980. Clive and Mike got on well, even if Mike had tried to act the manager, something for which he was entirely unsuited. Mike continued to read books on how to manage, but each one appeared to tell a subtly different story, and nobody was clear about the mantra in vogue. He was at his best just telling everyone what he wanted, shouting when he did not get it and gruffly accepting anything that reached the appropriate standard. At least everyone knew where they stood when he was a grumpy bastard.

Clive had followed the prelude to the miners' strike from a distance. Unlike previous skirmishes, which the miners had won hands down, Clive realised that this time it would be a battle if not all-out war. The government had taken on the steel unions and beaten them, and the public mood was changing. The government had brought in Ian McGregor from British Steel, and the intention was to drive through plans to close inefficient pits. The atmosphere had changed. The government was prepared for battle, and the rhetoric was confrontational.

In January 1984, there had been overtime bans and a spate of strikes across the coalfields. In March, the Coal Board announced that Cortonwood pit would close. Shortly afterwards, the miners at Cortonwood walked out. It soon became clear that there was a mood for a national strike. The skirmishes in Yorkshire and across the rest of the country were organised locally, and the Yorkshire miners were waiting for a declaration of war from the National Union of Miners' leader, Arthur Scargill.

Clive was known to many of the miners in South Yorkshire because of his radio programme about miners from the area who were suffering from pneumoconiosis. The interviews with those affected were poignant, drawing a large and positive response from miners and the general public. He had followed up in the newspaper and had helped draft an editorial in the *Comet* as part of a campaign to support the miners' case. It was in the period leading up to the Pneumoconiosis Compensation Act of 1979, and many miners regarded Clive's work as part of the successful campaign for statutory compensation.

Clive thought that it might be a good time to rekindle old friendships. There was a breed, particularly of younger miners, who treated the press as a single, unified and malign force, and Clive needed to be careful who he spoke to and what he said.

Charnley was a good barometer for the feelings of the Yorkshire miners. It was the day after the walkout at Cortonwood, and Clive was driving toward the village. He saw the flashing blue lights of an ambulance in his rear mirror and pulled over. Fearing the worst, he turned on the radio. There were initial reports of an accident underground.

As Clive arrived, a gathering of miners at the gate began to disperse. He was the first journalist on the scene. He parked his car near the entrance to the pit and made his way inside the gates. He quickly confirmed with the deputy manager that there had been one miner killed, trapped under a piece of heavy machinery. He phoned through a report, not naming the miner, whose relatives had not been informed. Later, the regional and national news picked up the story.

He tried to speak to a miner he recognised, who had been on the same shift.

'I've nowt to say, lad. Thank God there were nobody else caught,' he wheezed.

It was late in the afternoon, and he realised that his chance to break the ice had gone. It reminded him that, whatever the rights and wrongs of the forthcoming confrontation, this was what being a miner entailed. There was a daily risk of death and severe injury, or worse, the long-drawn-out agony of miner's lung.

The next day, Charnley stopped work.

The following week, Clive returned to find the gates to the pit blocked. The strike had been made official in Yorkshire, but there was an atmosphere of phoney war. Everyone was waiting for the announcement of a national strike. The picket was noisy and men were jostling, arguing and placating. He recognised Martin Jarman, a miner he had met when he had been researching the pneumoconiosis story.

Jarman was a short and sturdy man in his mid-forties, with a full head of grey hair, a square face and a strong chin. Clive, over six feet tall, towered over him.

Clive had kept his dark beard, and although his hair was shorter than at university, it was still touching his collar. He was in Levis, an open collared shirt and a dark pullover, visible through an unbuttoned duffel coat. This garment had more buttons missing than attached. There was nothing in his dress or demeanour that would have shown an onlooker that he was not a miner, and nothing that would associate him with his trade. His soft hands were deep in his pockets, as if to hide the shameful evidence of his non-manual job. Martin offered a nodded greeting to Clive, respectful but not over friendly. He was being watched by his workmates.

'Good to see you, Martin.'

'Ay up, Clive. Where've you bin? I haven't seen you for a bit.'

The broad accent, which had been difficult for Marcus to understand, was familiar to Clive, and he heard the words as if they were the Queen's English.

'Busy. I'm a married man, and I'm going to be a dad.'

'I never thought you had it in you.'

'I was here last week, you know, when the lad died.'

'Aye, he were only twenty-seven, with a wife and two kids.'

'That's bad.'

'Aye.'

There was a respectful silence before Clive spoke.

'What's going on, Martin?'

'Waiting for the strike to be made official.'

'What's the mood?'

'The lads want to get stuck in, picket every pit that's working and stop any coal moving, same as before.'

'Do you think it'll be as quick as last time?'

'Thatcher'll not make it easy. It'll take a bit longer, but the country stops if we do.'

'When'll the picketing start?'

'That's what they're talking about.' Martin jerked his thumb over his shoulder. 'Some of the lads want to picket Notts before they've voted.'

As Martin and Clive continued to talk about the likely course of the strike, they heard someone shouting excitedly. All the miners turned. A man was running toward them, waving his hands above his head.

'It's official lads. It's a national strike! Arthur's just announced it. It's a fuckin' national strike!'

A cheer went up, and Martin grabbed Clive's hand and shook it vigorously. Clive was taken aback.

'We'll have this government out in no time,' Martin shouted above the cheers.

Then he slapped Clive on the shoulder. Someone in the picket shouted, 'Maggie, Maggie, Maggie! Out! Out! Out!'

It was the first time Clive had heard the refrain. A few others joined the second chant, but the third rendition was a mighty chorus, and Martin and Clive joined in. Miners clenched their fists, punching the air in joy that the national strike had started and in rage toward Margaret Thatcher.

The euphoria quickly turned to calls for action. There were animated discussions, and Martin returned to his workmates. It was as if Arthur Scargill's announcement had released days of pent-up frustration. The men were debating whether they should picket Nottinghamshire pits or not. The younger men were for immediate action, and a hard core broke away and made for their cars. The picket now reassembled in an orderly fashion, and Clive caught Martin's eye. Martin wandered over and spoke quietly.

'I've not said this, but they're off to Harford.'

'Flying pickets?'

'Yes. Notts'll vote to support the strike if they're left alone. Some of the lads are looking for trouble.'

'Thanks, Martin. I'll pop down there and see what's happening.'

'Always on the lookout for trouble yourself, aren't you? I'd better get back.'

Clive left for Harford, just across the county border in Nottinghamshire. It was not long before he realised that he was part of a convoy of miners, all with the same idea. Harford would be busy. When he arrived, he could not get close to the pit gates. Cars were parked on every piece of spare ground. He pulled onto a grass verge outside the village and walked in the direction of the noise.

The milling crowd choked the pit entrance. It was an intimidating show of force. Men who could not be persuaded by the mythology of the picket line would be forced by the weight of numbers. They pushed, shouted, swore and threatened, and surely nobody would cross. Clive caught glimpses of some of the men he had seen at Charnley, but he kept his distance. The police were there in numbers, and they looked in the mood for confrontation. The aggressive intent of both sides frightened Clive, and he moved further away, fearful that a battle would break out. A few minutes later, cars appeared in convoy further up the pit road.

What the hell are they up to? They must be crazy.

The police attempted to form two human barriers, parting the pickets like Moses at the Red Sea. Warily, the cars edged forward into the gap created, but the miners would not cooperate, and some were left in the wake. A few policemen broke ranks to deal with these stragglers. They rounded up a small number, but many escaped. Scuffles and fights broke out. Miners were being smashed on their heads, arms, legs and backs by the police, who were wielding truncheons, and miners were lashing back with fists and feet.

A miner, blood streaming down his face from a gash on his forehead, and caught in a headlock by a policeman, was helped out by mates, who kicked the officer's legs from under him. He let go of his captive and fell to the floor, screaming and grasping his foot, twisted at an unnatural angle. Miners, held back by the blue lines, were trying to force their way through to help their comrades. When it was clear that those being chased would not be apprehended, a cheer rang out. These skirmishes were repeated until the lines weakened, drowning the police in a surge of miners. A roar went up from the pickets when they realised that the way through was blocked.

Clive had never seen anything as violent and out of control

as this. He could sense hatred toward the police amongst many of the pickets and unnecessary ferocity in the response of the police.

The cars became engulfed. Fists smashed on bonnets and boots crashed into doors. Insults and threats were being traded as the cars tried to edge forward, occupants enduring the pickets' mantra.

'Scab, scab, scab, scab, scab!'

The noise was deafening, and Clive could see that the leading car was being pushed from side to side, the petrified driver trying to reason with the men. The crowd was excited, angry and not heeding his words. The lead car's engine revved, and Clive realised that the driver, fearing for his life, was about to accelerate through the pickets. He closed his eyes. The strikers appreciated the implied threat and eased off. In the momentary release of pressure, the police regrouped and pushed back.

The first car edged forward, bumping into miners, and a wing mirror was wrenched off. Suddenly the car was clear. With the others close behind, the convoy surged through the gap. The pickets had lost this battle, but reinforcements were pouring into the village. Within minutes, there was no chance of anyone driving through, and the police made no further attempt to control the picket. Clive was relieved and surprised that nobody had been seriously injured. If this intensity was to continue, people would get hurt, possibly killed.

Clive phoned his report back to the office. The following morning, he picked up the news that a miner had been attacked at his home in Harford. He decided to go to the hospital in Worksop where the miner had been taken and followed the signs to the ward.

A woman in her early thirties and three young children were all seated at the miner's bedside. The woman was facing Clive across the white sheets. She was holding the miner's hand. The children were all girls, aged from about three years old to eight or nine, and they stared in dumb, shocked silence. The man had a cut to his face. It ran horizontally across his right cheekbone and was stitched with black thread. A grotesque swelling had closed his right eye. He seemed to be sedated and was unable to speak in anything more than a whisper, and his wife leaned over and whispered back. Clive kept his distance, standing in the doorway until a nurse arrived. He introduced himself.

'Any chance I can talk to him?' he whispered.

'You're kidding?'

'What injuries has he got?'

'Broken his cheekbone – could have blinded him. We operated this morning.'

'Sounds serious.'

'That's what one well-aimed punch can do. We get this sort of injury after pub brawls.'

'How long will it take to mend?'

'It's uncomfortable now, but he'll recover in a few weeks. He's still a bit drowsy.'

'Thanks.'

'They're waiting to see him,' she said, pointing to three men seated in the corridor. 'Talk to them.'

As she made her way to the bedside, Clive casually walked up to the men in the corridor.

'Hi. Are you his mates?' he asked, nodding in the direction of the door to the ward.

'Yeah. Who are you?' asked the nearest man.

'I'm from the *Comet*.'

'The *Comet*'s a Yorkshire paper, isn't it? We're not talking to no Yorkshire bastards, so piss off.'

'Hold on, this guy's been badly hurt, and I want to report what happened.'

'Haven't you got owt better to do?' asked the second man.

'There's nowt to say,' said the third. 'After his shift, he were followed home by some Yorkshire pickets.'

'Sure?'

'Fuck off. Of course I'm sure.'

The nurse put her head round the door to the ward.

'Quiet please,' she whispered.

'What's the mood?' asked Clive, softly.

'What do you think?' replied the first. 'We're not going to be shat on by these Yorkshire bastards. We're going in today and every other fucking day till we vote. If we vote to work on, we're going in, as long as there's one of us standing.'

'Nobody here'll vote for the strike, nobody, not now! You can put that in the fucking *Comet*,' said the third.

As he left the hospital, Clive mulled over what he had heard. It was a good story, but it would damage Clive's standing with Martin Jarman and the Charnley men.

Clive was not surprised when, a few days later, he heard that the Notts miners had voted against striking. He drove to Charnley to see how the Yorkshiremen would respond. Clive parked his car, stepped out into the biting morning cold and donned the usual duffel coat. He sauntered toward the Charnley picket line, and his cheeks flushed with the chilling north wind. He stopped some distance away.

Martin was facing Clive, his back warmed by a blazing fire made out of pieces of a pallet. He sauntered across to Clive, away from a group of miners talking animatedly. They noticed Clive, and their conversation stopped. They looked suspicious and then turned their backs on him.

'Don't talk to that bastard, Martin, he's with *them*,' one miner shouted over his shoulder.

Martin kept his distance.

'How's things, Martin?' asked Clive.

'That report about the Harford man didn't go down well. I can't talk.'

'I thought it mightn't. I'll keep away.'

'Give it some time.'

Martin turned, started back toward his mates and shouted over his shoulder,

'You need to tidy yer sen up though. Scruffy bugger, you'll not keep your job at the *Comet* looking like that. Get a decent pair of trousers, and buy a proper jacket. Since the strike started, we've been getting a better class of journalist round here, from down south.'

Clive made a cursory downward glance at his jeans and shrugged his agreement. Martin stopped and turned.

'You'll never get on the telly like that.'

'Who wants to?'

'You're a good looking lad. You'd make a star.'

Clive laughed at the thought.

In the early hours of the following morning, Clive arrived at one of a number of police roadblocks that had been set up to prevent pickets from Yorkshire getting to the Nottinghamshire and Derbyshire pits. He witnessed the police secretly taking the registration of every car, and he guessed that this information would be used to identify miners and stop them passing through the filter. These were not local police, but new arrivals from around the country who were being billeted in the area. Many were from London and the Home Counties.

The police at the roadblock set out to create a confrontational atmosphere. There was a standoff, but rather than hold their ground, the police ordered the miners to disperse. When they refused, the police advanced with their truncheons raised, scuffles broke out and miners were singled out and arrested. Those apprehended were bewildered, many resisting because they had committed no offence. The miners seemed unaware that they were playing into their enemies' hands. It was clear that some of the police were enjoying the altercation. Clive later found out that these scenes were being played out along the length of the border between Yorkshire and Nottinghamshire.

Clive showed his credentials and made his way to the Nottinghamshire pit villages. The police were in control, and he could see that the Yorkshiremen had not been able to find a way through. The only pickets were local miners, and there was nothing they could do to prevent a free flow of traffic. He managed to speak to one of the officers from the Met. He made it clear that their job was, 'to protect anyone who wants to cross a picket line'. The balance of power had changed.

Clive drove back to the office where he wrote up his story. Mike read it and called Clive into his office.

'It's a bit political isn't it, Clive? I want a factual report.'

'That's what you've got, Mike.'

'Crap. You say it's all been planned.'

'Yes, it's obvious, I'd have thought.'

'No it's not. The police are just reacting to events.'

'How do you stop every Yorkshire miner from crossing the county border unless you've got a plan?' asked Clive incredulously.

'But you're making out that the miners are being ambushed.'

'Police secretly taking down car registrations at every roadblock and random arrests; what would *you* call it?'

'The police provoking the miners; that's just your opinion.'

'Well, edit it out, but it's true,' said Clive angrily. 'The miners weren't breaking any law, and the police singled out innocent blokes and arrested them. The miners saw it. They know. If you're not prepared to put it in the paper, nobody else will, and it's as if it didn't happen. Is that what you want, Mike?'

'Opinion, Clive.'

'The police are intent on starting trouble, not keeping the peace. The only thing that'll get reported in the nationals is that miners have assaulted policemen and resisted arrest because that's what the police are saying. It's not true.'

'Opinion, you're just seeing one side.'

'Mike, I'm doing a piece on miners' wives for the radio. I've interviewed working miners' wives in Notts as well as Yorkshire.' Clive was pointing at Mike as he spoke. 'That'll not go down well in Yorkshire, but it's factual and balanced, like everything I do. Don't you dare accuse me of bias.'

'Do you want a medal?'

'Come out with me, Mike. I'll show you.'

'Just do your job properly, Clive.'

'No complaints about the story on the injured miner at Harford because that fits, doesn't it?'

'Good story.'

'Are you being leaned on, Mike?'

'Piss off.'

'You are. I can tell by your reaction. There's been some heavy editing in the past few days. It's *your* editing that's political, not my reporting, isn't it?'

'Get out, you twat,' ordered Mike.

'I'm not having you questioning my integrity, Mike. I'm not going to be gagged by you.'

'Get out, you idiot. Nobody's gagging you. My job's to make sure things are reported properly, and that's what I'll keep doing.'

Clive slammed the door as he left.

15

MARCUS

By May, the strike was dominating the news. The outcome seemed in the balance, but the miners were convinced that the newspapers, television and police had aligned themselves behind the government.

Two men walked across the newsroom floor at the *Echo*. The younger man spoke in a whisper. His voice was educated and displayed no regional identity.

'I can't make up stories if they're not there.'

Only a few years before, the younger man would have had to shout above the noise of clattering typewriters and other voices competing to be heard in the open plan newsroom, but the age of the computer had recently been embraced at the *Echo*.

'Don't talk shit,' said the slightly older man.

A few heads were raised. He turned to face the younger man.

'We're here to set the news agenda. The news is what we make it, Simon.'

'Yes, Marcus, I'm...'

'The way you're talking,' Marcus interrupted, 'you'd think that it was hanging from a tree, and we pick it off and give it to the readers for breakfast.'

'I've been doing this job...' was the start of a whispered response.

'If the right story isn't staring you in the face, then find it,' Marcus said, rolling his eyes. 'If nothing fits the bill, organise things, you know, make something out of what's there. I've already thought up the headline I want for tomorrow morning.'

In the office, eyes were downward, but ears were listening as Marcus snapped his opinions and instructions.

'Yes, *I* know what you want, too,' said Simon.

'The news is what we print. If fifty thousand Chinese die in a flood and we don't report it, then it's *not* news. If a man farts at a bus stop and we report it, then it *is*.'

'I'll get on to it right away.'

'Find someone, anyone who's a victim of this strike and get an interview. I'll be back in ten minutes, and I want you here with ideas. I've got a meeting with Sir Clifford.'

The younger journalist, Simon Howman, gave the impression of hiding behind his small, round, wire rim framed glasses. He was a short, neat and dumpy fellow with close-cropped ginger hair, and he seemed to shrink further under Marcus's gaze. His small round face perspired as he scuttled away from the deputy news editor. Marcus was smartly dressed with a sober tie, neatly pressed white shirt tucked into dark trousers and short hair immaculately combed to one side, giving the appearance of a model in a mail order catalogue.

Marcus wasn't sure what to make of Howman. He'd asked Ronnie some months before.

'He's bright,' said Ronnie, 'articulate, a competent journalist, perhaps the best we've got but not great under pressure.'

'Yes, he gets pushed around by the others; never stands up for himself.'

'It's all very well having a first from Cambridge, but this is a newspaper, and Howman thinks we should play by the rules of chivalry.'

'He thinks we're not as smart as he is,' added Marcus. 'Sometimes he needs putting in his place. If he can't take criticism, that's his problem.'

'It's either sink or swim. He'll toughen up or he'll have to go. He knew what to expect when he joined.'

Sir Clifford's PA waved, indicating that Marcus should not be late. Marcus acknowledged her and put on the suit jacket that had been draped over the back of his chair. Checking his watch, he rushed along the edge of the newsroom and turned left and left again to an office marked 'Editor'. The door was open for him to enter. A silver haired and immaculately groomed man in his late fifties was on the telephone and waved, rather imperiously, for Marcus to enter. He was in the same uniform as Marcus, except that his jacket hung from a metal coat stand behind the door. He was embedded in a swivel chair, covered in a well-worn dark fabric. He swung half away as Marcus entered, as if to signal that some confidence was being discussed, but Marcus could hear every word.

It was a large room, white-walled and sparsely furnished and decorated. Sir Clifford was behind a metal framed pine desk facing matching chairs and a settee. The austerity of the office reflected Sir Clifford's character. Marcus mused that it would be a lively place when he was in charge and pictured himself behind the desk. He was jolted out of this daydream when he heard the door close behind him. Ronnie Miles had walked in and positioned himself by the door. There was no greeting.

Another wave of the hand, and Marcus was offered what was usually Ronnie's chair. Marcus looked over his shoulder at his direct superior. Ronnie nodded that Marcus should take the seat offered. It was a remarkable event.

The culture at the *Echo* was defined by its hierarchy. Respect for the pecking order educated every interaction. It dictated who should receive a copy of any memo and who should not. It defined who should be invited for a drink, which colleagues should be sent a Christmas card and whether it was appropriate to return one. Deference was the accepted behaviour when dealing with those one above in the hierarchy and reverence for those two above.

It was a different matter for the gods in their dealings with the mortals. Sir Clifford adopted an avuncular manner with all employees. His editors treated their staff with indifference, disdain and even downright contempt. This was transmitted through the ranks as those nearer the bottom of the organisation copied their betters. It provided a reassuring clarity in relationships, even if it militated against warmth or closeness. It was what Marcus had been used to at home and at school. Somebody was in charge, gave the orders, and others obeyed. Under Ronnie's guidance, Marcus quickly adopted a method suitable for the patterns of behaviour at the *Echo*.

Ronnie had made it clear that Marcus could do whatever he needed to get results, and Marcus had progressively removed all of the dead wood – the drinkers, the idlers, the closet lefties and the womanisers. He had no place for anyone who could not spell or construct a concise sentence, anyone who did not obey and anyone who did not fit the culture. He had personally recruited and promoted all his staff, and they all knew they owed their position to him.

The chair was uncomfortable for a slouch, but not for Marcus. He sat with his fingers clasped together on his lap. Sir Clifford finished his call and swung through forty-five degrees to face the man he had attracted from the *Mercury*.

'Marcus,' he said softly, 'we're going to ramp up the support for Margaret, Mrs Thatcher, that is. It's a once-in-a-lifetime chance to change things, change them for the better.'

Sir Clifford's educated voice delivered a dull monotone.

'Yes, Sir Clifford.'

Sir Clifford was accustomed to giving speeches, and Marcus knew that a minimum of interruption was expected. When Sir Clifford gazed at him, he looked back for an instant, and then he respectfully diverted his own eyes to the carpet until he sensed that Sir Clifford was looking away.

'There's plenty going on in the background, yes, things you need to be aware of. Things that'll help us to get the paper better aligned; things *not* to be repeated. I'm putting my trust in you, Marcus. I know you won't let me down.'

It was difficult to read Sir Clifford's thoughts. His face showed no emotion.

'Thank you, Sir Clifford.'

'I'll be coordinating editorials. I've had informal discussions with ministers. We're going to help the government smash the unions.'

Sir Clifford paused for a moment, hands planted firmly on the top of his desk.

'There's a deal on the table, unwritten, but a deal nonetheless. If Margaret Thatcher wins, we'll take on the print unions, and we'll have government support. Some of our competitors have already decided to move printing out of London, as soon as the miners' strike's over.'

'You're meeting with other newspapers, Sir Clifford?' asked Marcus nervously.

The use of the title was not optional, and Marcus wondered what his wife and children called him. Sir Clifford continued quietly, but the timbre in his voice commanded attention and respect.

'Don't underestimate the amount of planning that's gone into this. It may not have been in any election manifesto but we're part of the second Battle of Britain. McGregor's appointment wasn't an accident. The government wants to break the unions and make an example of the miners. We must ensure that this sort of strike can never happen again.'

'Yes, Sir Clifford.'

'Nothing's been left to chance. The PR people have been working with McGregor, looking after relations with the media. They've made Margaret, how shall I put it, more presentable. You know what I mean: her clothes, hair and a more sympathetic voice. There have been meetings since 1979, involving what I'll call 'interested parties'. It's all about managing the news to support the government and making it impossible for anyone in the media to support the miners. It's a critical few months, Marcus. We've got to do whatever we can.'

'Yes, Sir Clifford. I understand.'

'We don't just want defeat. Margaret wants humiliation, with miners dragging their tails between their legs back to work. The government's *not* going to capitulate. Everything's been planned.'

'Yes, Sir Clifford. I know they've been stockpiling coal and building gas power stations.'

'The job is to rally support for the government and demoralise the miners. Relentless, Marcus, it has to be relentless.'

For a moment, the voice became steely and the fingers clenched into two fists on the desk. Sir Clifford looked Marcus directly in the eye as he spoke.

'What have you got lined up, Marcus?'

Marcus threw a quick glance at Ronnie Miles.

Sir Clifford saw him and, with a show of irritation, gestured Marcus to respond.

'We're working on stories about brave miners going back to work, crossing hostile picket lines and standing up to intimidation. We've just picked up a photograph of a working miner beaten up crossing the picket. You can see his broken nose and a black eye,' Marcus said. His voice was quiet and unemotional.

'That will create the sort of impact I want. Anything gruesome, get it on the front page.'

'We're digging out details about the redundancy terms on the table. People will be amazed at what's on offer. It's a small fortune, and it'll turn more readers against the miners.'

Marcus was not as confident as his quiet assurance suggested. There had been a quiet period, and he did not like waiting for events. He wondered if Sir Clifford felt the same.

'They're getting clever though,' said Marcus. 'Scargill's running a tight ship. The union leaders are keeping most of the hotheads under control.'

'There'll be trouble at Mansfield, mark my words. The police have been told to stand no nonsense. Get a man at the rally, a good operator, someone who can take some rough-and-tumble.'

'Smallman, Sir Clifford; I know that he's brash and loud-mouthed, and it's got him into trouble in the past, but he understands our readers better than any of the others.'

'He's just the man.'

'Yes, Sir Clifford.'

'What about returning miners?'

'We're publishing the daily list of numbers returning to work. It's not many, but it's increasing.'

'The PR people are working on it. They're looking at making the numbers seem, how can I put it... more favourable. Ring them. Ronnie's got the contact details. We need a drip, drip of information so that it saturates the national psyche. What have you got on Scargill?'

'We're trying our hardest. We've spoken to neighbours and ex-colleagues, but they've clammed up.'

'Find something. If not, be creative. Even if there's nothing substantiated, the public are ready to believe any rumour. They hate him. The more bad press we can muster against him, the better. Anything, absolutely anything will do.'

'Yes, Sir Clifford.'

Why's Ronnie keeping quiet? Why's Sir Clifford ignoring him?

'This is a big chance for you, Marcus. I've agreed with Ronnie that you'll take the lead on the strike. There are plenty of opportunities in this company. Make a success of this and doors will open.'

Am I being lined up for something?

'Of course, Sir Clifford.'

'It's your big chance. I want our circulation above the *Globe*. We're a long way off.'

'Yes, Sir Clifford.'

'Make sure you're discreet, Marcus. I've got business with Ronnie, so you'd better get back to work.'

Something's afoot.

Ronnie opened the door, his face betraying no emotion, and he swung it quietly shut when Marcus was out of the room.

Marcus flew back to his desk, and with his index finger, he gestured Simon Howman to follow him.

'Kevin, Stephen, Peter, get over here now,' he shouted.

Four journalists from the news desk joined him. They forced themselves to face Marcus's fiery gaze, when primal instinct was to look downwards. Marcus's demeanour changed the moment he left Sir Clifford's office.

'We've been fannying around on the miners' strike for too long. Sir Clifford's asked me run the coverage of the strike.'

'What about Ronnie?' asked Stephen Glazier.

'That's none of our concern. Just listen to what I'm telling you. Fucking hell.'

'Sorry.'

Marcus explained what Sir Clifford had demanded, showing the discretion required of him.

'I want dirt on Scargill. Every picture of him has got to give a clear message. He's an evil bastard. Have you dug up any scandal yet, Stephen?'

'It's impossible,' he said with a precise and broad Yorkshire accent. He realised his mistake as soon as he had uttered the words. He had started, and reluctantly he had to finish, '...to get anyone to talk.'

Stephen Glazier was a stocky, wide-mouthed and wide-eyed young man with a naturally confident and personable character, epitomised by his cheery expression. His hair had been longer than was acceptable when he had started at the *Echo*, and he had immediately fallen into line with an extreme number one cut, a style also suiting his prematurely receding hairline. His jolly countenance faded with every word.

'Even the scabs won't talk to us. They hate the press, especially us and the *Globe*, more than they hate Scargill,' continued Stephen slowly.

'Impossible? Nothing's impossible. You mean it's difficult. Doing what's difficult is what we expect!' Marcus shouted.

'Yes, Marcus, I meant...'

'You're paid to get whatever the editor needs. OK?'

Marcus finished with a nod of his head. The gesture signified that Stephen had been reprimanded and that he needed to deal with the task at hand.

'For fuck's sake,' Marcus whispered under his breath.

'I'll get on to it,' Stephen confirmed.

'Good.'

Marcus began issuing instructions and offering ideas.

'I need something on the aggression of the pickets, yeah, examples of violence against the police.' Marcus jabbed a finger at Peter Kellock. 'How many miners have been in front of the magistrates?'

'I'll find out.'

'How many charged?'

'I'll get numbers.'

'There's the Mansfield rally coming up. With a bit of luck there'll be some trouble. Kevin, get up there and take a photographer.'

'How is it I get a day in Mansfield? I've heard it's worse than Beirut.'

'Pack for a long stay. I want pictures showing intimidation and fighting. If there isn't any, perhaps you could start something,' Marcus laughed.

'I'm past all of that stuff now,' said Kevin Smallman, a small and slightly built man with deep set eyes and a thin hooked nose. He was in his late twenties and had started at his local paper, straight from school.

'I want stories and pictures that make it impossible for Scargill to win. Peter, we'll have to change the way we report miners returning back to work.'

'What have you got in mind?'

'How about a thermometer gradually rising as more miners go back? Use your imagination.'

'I'll come up with something.'

'I've got a contact you can phone. I want the figures every day, and make sure the numbers go the right way. Simon, get me a victim story. Find someone who's suffered from the strike.'

'I've already started on that.'

'Your job is to make the news. No excuses. Just get on with it.'

16

CLIVE

Clive headed for the miners' rally, driving south and passing the Mansfield exit on the M1. He left the motorway at Annesley and drove through the picturesque villages of Linby and Papplewick. This route took him to the south of Mansfield, and he expected the miners from the Midlands and Wales to arrive from this direction. Mingling with them would give him a feel for the mood in other areas. He passed the main entrance gate to Newstead Abbey, with large houses nestling in woodland on both sides of the road. He entered Mansfield through the wealthier suburbs, and parked near the football ground, on a road of red-bricked terraced houses. The rally was being held in the leisure centre, about half a mile away.

Clive heard, for the first time, the ominous rumble of helicopters circling overhead. He walked down the street and turned left, heading for the town centre. He joined a trickle of miners walking in the same direction. As others joined from side streets, the trickle gradually became a flow. It was hard not to become overwhelmed by the atmosphere.

Coaches were blocking the road, seemingly from every mining town and village in the country. The coaches were full, and banners adorned the windows, each proclaiming the names of the pits represented. Voices were chanting and singing. Even working pits were represented. A tatty standard was raised ahead of him in the snaking crowd. It consisted of felt tip pen scrawled on a dirty sheet and it read:

'Calverton Strikers, Banner Withheld By Scabs.'

Calverton pit was only a few miles south of Mansfield.

A deafening cheer erupted in support of the men holding the makeshift banner. A chant started, accompanied by clenched fists punching the air.

'Maggie, Maggie, Maggie!'

'Out! Out! Out!'

Clive avoided the temptation to take his hands out off his pockets and join the chorus, and he hoped that nobody noticed. He saw two men, easily identified as journalists by the camera one held, being jostled and enduring the insults that were being hurled at them.

'Lying bastards!'

'Tell the truth, you fucking liars!'

'Scum, scum, scum,' chanted a coachload of miners from south Wales. The coach swayed rhythmically from side to side. The mood was boisterous, with an occasional verbal insult thrown at the small number of police on patrol.

'*Sieg Heil, Sieg Heil,*' rang out, accompanied by a Nazi salute.

The police laughed, and so did the perpetrators. It was a curious mixture of good humour and contempt for authority. Clive hoped that no cameras had taken the Nazi salutes, a perfect front page for some of the newspapers. He mentally noted the banners for his report.

It was at about 11.00 in the morning when Clive arrived at the leisure centre. Hundreds of lodge banners were raised above the crowd, each one depicting the name and a colourful representation of a pit and its history. They were rallying points for the miners from each village. Women's support groups had joined, and there were thousands of Socialist Workers party placards, declaring 'Victory to the Miners'. The miners and supporters were crammed into the tight space, and officials were trying to organise them. There was a hubbub as people talked, joked, chanted and argued.

Clive kept to the fringes of the march as it set out, and Arthur Scargill was in the vanguard. It was a warm spring morning, and there was a carnival atmosphere. Locals leaned out of open windows and stood in the doorways of offices and shops on the route. Some were inquisitive, and others were openly supportive. As two young women in low-cut tops leaned out from a first floor window, a group of young men started chanting:

'Get your tits out for the lads!'

There were shouts from the crowd for them to stop, boos, and then a scuffle erupted and quickly subsided. As the march progressed, more police were evident, but they were not in the sort of numbers Clive had witnessed at picket lines. A chant broke out from a group of young miners.

'Piggy, piggy, piggy,'

'Oink, oink, oink,'

Many of the miners laughed at this variation on the 'Maggie' chant. Clive walked along with the marchers, and he picked up a rumour that Arthur Scargill would ask them to join mass pickets that day, closing the working pits in Nottinghamshire.

Someone tapped Clive on his shoulder. It was Martin Jarman.

'Thought it was you, Clive. Pretending you're a miner?'

'Martin, I've been looking out for you. There are more here than I'd imagined.'

'Some say as many as forty thousand.'

'Perhaps twenty.'

'Enough.'

'Getting a bit old for this, Martin? You've seen it all before.'

'With all these cameras, I might get on the telly.'

'For the right reasons, I hope. I'm a bit nervous. I hope there's no trouble. The slightest step out of line, the papers will have a field day. The problem with these cameras is that they seem to encourage trouble.'

'For goodness' sake, Clive, it's going to be a great day out: inspiring speeches and a show of solidarity from the miners.'

'A misleading camera angle or a misjudged quote's all that's needed. The papers have already sided with Thatcher.'

'We're here to show the country we mean business. People need to realise we're strong, despite the scabs. There'll be no trouble.'

'Do you think this'll persuade them to stop work?'

Before he could answer, a youngster tried to sell them *Socialist Worker*. Martin showed him that he already had a copy in his pocket, and they moved on.

'Maybe not, but we have to get the other unions behind us. This'll show 'em we don't mean to quit, and it'll remind the scabs.'

'Remind them what?'

'That every miner relies on his mates. You have to trust the man next to you. Nobody talks about it, but that's how it works underground. It's the same here today. We all know we're in this together. That's what we've got to remind the scabs 'cos they've broken that trust.'

'Good atmosphere, isn't there?'

'Brilliant. I'm looking for my missus. She's behind somewhere. I'll see you later.'

As they ambled forward, men spoke to him as a brother miner. He felt honoured and embarrassed.

'Where you from?' he asked two stocky middle-aged men.

'Merthyr Vale,' said one, his voice a giveaway.

'You?'

'Local. What time did you leave?'

'Up at 3.00. It's worse than being on fuckin' shift. Since the strike, used to seeing daylight, I am,' he laughed.

'It's marvellous, fuckin' marvellous,' said his mate. 'So many folk made it here, they 'ave. I just been talking to a docker, from Liverpool he was, who's come down with mates in a minibus. Can't fuckin' lose, can us?'

The march slowly edged around the town. Clive kept pace with the marchers until they arrived back at the leisure centre. Cameras were already in place for the speeches. It was more than fifteen minutes before those behind Clive reached their destination. As they settled, Arthur Scargill introduced Tony Benn. Benn was measured, logical and clear, never with a joke or a wisecrack. He was careful not to say anything that could be seen to be inciting the crowd.

'He needs to loosen up,' said a Scot next to Clive. 'He could do with a beer or two. So could I,' he added.

Everyone knew that Tony Benn was a teetotaller. When he finished, the crowd respectfully clapped him, and Dennis Skinner MP took the platform. He was passionate and furious, and they loved him. He was a local man, from a nearby pit, and he knew how they felt. He took a fierce swipe at the NCB and the government. The crowd had been respectful and quiet for Benn, but Dennis got them roaring, laughing and cheering. When Arthur Scargill spoke, there were chants of 'Scar-gill, Scar-gill', and at times, he found it difficult to make himself heard. Some lone voices demanded a mass picket that day, but he appeared not to hear.

'That's why there's no police,' said a middle-aged woman with a Yorkshire accent. She was next to Clive and spoke to an older man in front. 'Somebody's done a deal. No police if we don't mass picket.'

'I don't believe it,' he replied.

'We were expecting something. It's all talk and no action.'

'It's been a good day. It shows we mean business.'

Despite the grumbles, the mood as they dispersed was optimistic. Clive thought that the day had gone as well as could be hoped. He headed for a pub to edit the notes for his report back to the paper. He was walking across the flow of people heading for the town centre pubs. He turned down a side street and came across groups of policemen on foot and on horseback. They looked at him suspiciously but said nothing. It was a disconcerting and sinister sight. They would not be necessary, he thought, but they were waiting for something.

He phoned his report through to the office and then started to make his way past the leisure centre, back to the car. Groups of miners were casually sauntering to buses parked nearby. He could see a cluster of miners, two wearing joke police helmets shaped like breasts, taunting the police. They had just emerged from a pub and were swearing loudly. There was a standoff for a few seconds, and then a scuffle in which a few blows were exchanged. Clive cautiously approached the incident. Suddenly a phalanx of police rushed out of a side street and attacked the miners. Within seconds, bottles were flying, and a full-scale battle had erupted.

It seemed to have escalated from a joke to a mass brawl in less than a minute, and innocent bystanders were trapped. Clive turned and retraced his steps to the leisure centre, and he was joined by others who didn't want to become embroiled in the fight. They had almost made it when police on horseback emerged from the leisure centre and charged at them. They were swinging their truncheons to clear a path toward where the fight had broken out.

A man fell under a vicious blow to the head, blood spurting from his wound and spattering his mates. As they helped him, blows rained down from above. The horses snorted, and hooves clattered on the tarmac. Clive ran across the road into a doorway. From his sanctuary, he realised that others had been less fortunate. A mother was wheeling a pushchair toward safety and was accidentally smashed to the ground by a horse, and a young schoolgirl, with her bag across her shoulders, was bundled over by a policeman on foot, unaware of what he'd done.

The schoolgirl, about thirteen or fourteen, was dazed. A young miner saw her and tried to help. Her blouse had been ripped by her bag as it had been torn from her shoulder. She looked down and saw her naked flesh, and the miner, instinctively and innocently, followed her eyes. She pulled the front of her blouse together and started to scream, as if he was the culprit. Her eyes were wild, and she backed away before turning and running. The miner, equally shaken, fled in the direction of the buses.

The impact had thrown the baby, wrapped in thick, pink blankets, out of the pushchair as if a rag doll, and the bundle rolled across the ground, silent. The mother lay still, face down in the road. Clive rushed across, avoiding officers with riot shields who were following the horsemen and grabbing anyone they could. One took a swing, and it delivered a glancing blow to Clive's arm, raised to shield his head.

The baby was quiet, but as Clive picked up the child, it let out a piercing scream. The blankets had cushioned the fall, and the baby seemed unharmed. The mother heard the cry and picked herself up from the floor. She had a lump on her cheek and a split lip. She stood up, wafer-thin, and slowly walked toward him, no words spoken. She stretched out her arms, as if she was pleading for the baby he had stolen from her.

'The baby's fine. Honest, the baby's fine.'

The mother whimpered, but Clive could not understand what she was saying. He handed across the pink bundle. She looked into the baby's screaming face and burst into tears. A miner who had witnessed the same events righted the pushchair. He wheeled it across to the mother, comforted her and escorted mother, with the child in her arms, away from the danger.

Clive left them and walked in the direction of the town centre, but the battle was moving his way. Everything seemed to be happening quicker than real life. Broken bottles and shards of glass littered the floor, and men were brawling. The police were organised, charging at individuals, grabbing who they could and then retreating with their prey. The miners wielded chairs and table legs, and the police used their truncheons. Innocent bystanders were still fleeing, some away from the square, others into shops and doorways, and many were being hit by the police for their troubles. A young Geordie was remonstrating with a policeman who had pinned him to a shop window with his forearm.

'I don't want no trouble, honest. I've done nothing. Just waiting till it's all clear,' he said fearfully.

'If you don't get out, right now, you'll all be arrested.'

'Don't worry, I'll be gone.'

The man was released and ran off toward the leisure centre.

Cameras were whirring on the periphery of the action, and Clive saw a group of miners trying to persuade a television cameraman to film two policemen kicking a young man on the floor. The cameraman wouldn't cooperate.

The youngster had staggered to his feet when a policeman, with a clenched fist, smashed him savagely across his nose. The policeman was restrained by his colleagues, and the victim dropped to the floor with a thud. An ambulanceman, who had just arrived, swore at the policeman.

'You bastard. There was no need for that. He was defenceless. What's your fucking number, you cowardly prick?'

The officer was whisked away. The uncooperative cameraman struggled to hold on to his camera. It was wrenched from him and thrown through a shop window. Clive could see that the injury to the young man was serious and rushed across to help. He arrived at the same time as a gangly young policeman with a similar intention. The ambulanceman took a quick look, moved the man to the recovery position, covered him with a blanket he was carrying and made a small pillow out of another. He spoke authoritatively.

'It's bad. I'll get oxygen and a stretcher. Stay with him, and keep him in this position. I don't want him choking on his blood.'

He looked the policeman in the eye and pointed at him.

'You know what to do.'

He stood up and went to find help, and the youngster groaned. The two men crouched over him, providing protection. The police were not trying to control and contain, they were taking on the miners and using force, the like of which Clive had never seen before. A miner, with blood spattered across his shirt from a deep gash on his forehead, stumbled toward Clive, who offered a hand. Before he reached Clive he was overtaken by three policemen. Two grabbed his arms and started to drag him away. The third smashed the miner across his back and legs with his truncheon. Clive attempted to remonstrate, but the policeman with the truncheon turned round.

'You want some too?'

Clive shook his head and turned to the young officer.

'I'll look after him. I know what to do. You can give a hand to your mates.'

'He's injured, and it's my job to help,' said the policeman.

Clive indicated the walking wounded with a sweep of his arm.

'Don't you think the police have helped enough today?'

The young officer looked directly into Clive's eyes and tried to speak, but no words were uttered. He looked down at the injured man and shook his head in shame.

'Sorry,' said Clive.

It took a few seconds for the policeman to recover his composure.

'I've seen you before,' he said. 'You've been watching the picketing. You're a reporter.'

'Yes.'

'This isn't why I joined the Met.'

'I should hope not.'

'I'm ashamed.'

'Some of your chums should be too.'

'They're looking for trouble.'

'Don't the officers keep them under control?'

'They don't care,'

'Aren't there any rules?'

'I'm not allowed to speak about it.'

'How did it start?' asked Clive.

'I don't know. There was a bit of banter but nothing serious. You've seen it before at the picket. Some of the miners were taunting us, you know, on their way back to the buses. They were drunk, and maybe it was a bit worse than the usual stuff but nothing we couldn't handle. I was trying to calm things down, but some were stoking it up. Suddenly it was mayhem.'

'I saw the same as you. Where did all the mounted police come from?'

'I've said too much already.'

'I've got to ring the office. They'll want to know what's happened. I'll be back in a couple of minutes.'

The policeman nodded. Clive stood up and scribbled into his notebook. He went to four phone boxes before he found one that had not been smashed. He dialled, and within seconds he was giving his report down the phone, using his notes as a prompt. When he had finished, he was asked to hang on and was transferred to Mike Boddington.

Clive returned with an angry demeanour. The young man was on a stretcher, his face covered by a sheet of bloodstained cotton wool. He was conscious, and his half-closed eyes were visible. His blond hair was matted with congealing blood, and he was covered in a blanket. Two ambulancemen were preparing to lift the stretcher.

'What's the matter?' asked the policeman, standing up.

'It's already on the news. It's being called a riot. The miners've been accused of going on a rampage and attacking the police. Most of the injuries reported are policemen.'

'The injured miners'll have all gone home. They'll not go to hospital here and risk arrest, not unless they're as bad as this bloke.'

The injured man was being taken to an ambulance, and the officer glanced at his hands, stained with the miner's blood. He took a handkerchief from a pocket and wiped them clean.

'My editor doesn't think much of what I've submitted. It'll be my name that goes on the front page report but not my words,' said Clive, ruefully.

'It *was* a riot though, wasn't it?'

'Yes, it was. There's no way of getting away from it.'

'The police're being used. We made it into a riot.'

'What's your name?'

'PC Norlick.'

'No, your name,' smiled Clive. 'It's alright. I'm not going to make a complaint.'

'Peter. Peter Norlick.'

Clive ripped a sheet of paper from his notepad. He scribbled on it and handed it to the officer. Nervously, Peter Norlick accepted it and put it in his trouser pocket without looking at the name and phone number. Clive offered his hand. Peter was taken aback but responded. Clive looked directly into the eyes of the policeman. He saw a kind and honest man.

'Give me a ring when you've a spare moment, Peter. We've got things to talk about. This isn't the right time or place.'

'What do you mean?'

'Just give me a ring.'

Peter nodded.

17

MARCUS

Marcus stormed across the newsroom to his desk. It was the afternoon of the Mansfield rally. Ronnie was out of the office, and Marcus was in charge.

'Fucking marvellous. Absolutely fucking marvellous. It couldn't have gone better. Let's have a look,' he shouted.

Photographs were spread across the table. Marcus pushed excitedly between Stephen and Peter, stooped over the evidence from Mansfield. Peter handed him a sheaf of papers.

'It's Kevin's report,' Peter said.

Marcus loved the feel of the paper and the ease with which he could slide the photographs and copy around the table to create the pages.

'Let's see the photos first. We'll fit the story around the best. The theme will be that it's a riot. This miners rally's a godsend. Any photographs of Scargill, Benn or Skinner?'

'We've got them giving their speeches, but we've got nothing during the riot,' said Simon. 'Benn wouldn't go near anything like that, and Scargill's a coward. They left the party before the fun started.'

'This one makes Benn look like a Russian leader at a Red Square parade,' said Stephen Glazier, who had been working diligently to recover his status following his previous, misplaced comments. 'Have a look.'

He handed the photograph to Marcus, who moved it across

the table to where he thought it would fit in the following day's edition.

'Not bad… Not bad, but I need a front-page headline and photograph.'

'This one has got a miner smashing his banner over the policeman's head,' offered Stephen.

'I can see a copper booting a miner in the bollocks, in the background,' laughed Marcus. 'It might offend some of our more squeamish lady readers. I only want to see injured coppers – no miners. We don't want to spoil a good story.'

'This one's better. It's more or less the same photo. A different angle, and we can trim the offending policeman,' said Peter. 'It won't spoil the photo.'

Peter Kellock, tall, slim, quiet and peaceful by nature, was finding the violence of the strike distasteful. His clothes hung from his frame as if purchased a size too big. He was intense in his opinions and Marcus had recruited him because he had seen a younger version of himself in the up-and-coming journalist.

He had enjoyed the same minor public school background, and he had travelled the same route from left to right. However, Peter had remained a passionate defender of tolerance and decent behaviour. Although he could be intensely provocative and opinionated, he was always polite.

He was a man educated for and temperamentally adapted to the days of empire, adamant in his desire to do good deeds and defeat evil. He never doubted the righteousness of his position and the wickedness of his enemies. Good and evil were not, in his eyes, points at two extremes of graded moral behaviour. They were absolutes with a gaping chasm between them, inhabited by creatures writhing in the mire and destined for an eternity in hell, called moral relativists. He was known as Cranky Kellock.

Marcus rummaged through the photos, like someone at a jumble sale with particular garments in mind. He pulled out half a dozen of them and made room on the table. Meticulously, he then laid them out, and the desk began to represent the first pages of the following morning's paper. He skipped through Kevin's report.

'I could have written it from here. The story's so obvious. I want a headline there.'

His finger pointed to a blank spot on the table, and he looked at Peter Kellock, who nodded.

'"Riot",' he said. 'I want just the one word, then chapter and verse on the violence here, here and then over the page... here. It's the miners attacking the police, unprovoked. Use Kevin's report and spice it up. Pick out the photographs of the worst injuries to our brave men in blue. Use this lot,' he said, pointing to the incriminating photographs on the table.

'There are more on the way, yes, plenty to choose from,' said Peter.

'Use the word "unprovoked" as much as you can. Next, along here,' Marcus pointed, 'I want quotes from Scargill, Benn and Skinner. Use anything that implicates them.'

'They're getting wise. They're careful what they say,' said Stephen.

'If you're creative, even the blandest statements can be made to sound extreme. See if you can find any politicians who won't condemn the strike. Get a quote and put it here, below the picture of Benn.'

Marcus was moving photographs on the table, leaving spaces where he wanted the incriminating text.

'Kevin's got some great police quotes. Headline them across here.' Marcus jabbed a finger. 'Then here, the personal account from Kevin, our intrepid reporter on the scene,' he laughed. 'Jazz it up a bit. Kevin would do the same for you.'

Marcus leaned back, surveying the embryo of the next day's paper, and smiled.

'It looks good,' said Simon.

'The wankers. The miners have lost it. They've blown the whole fucking thing,' Marcus said. 'If only we could find something, anything, to pin on that bastard Scargill.'

Peter winced at the language.

'This is what gets the adrenalin going, eh, Peter?'

'Yes.'

'Get everything organised. I'm with Sir Clifford in fifteen minutes, and I want the pictures, headlines and the story for the first three pages ready for then. Move. There's no time to be fannying about.'

Marcus could not help but smile to himself at the irony of Scargill propelling his own career forward, whilst he was doing whatever he could to sink the miners' leader. Today's news may have been exceptional, but Marcus's method was typical of any working day at the *Echo*.

18

CLIVE

Mike and Clive argued almost daily. Monday's report from Mansfield was completely rewritten to match the national mood. On Tuesday and Wednesday, Clive attended local magistrates' courts. Every case he witnessed was the same. Miners, who had no time to organise a defence against coherent and corroborated evidence from the police, were convicted. Any organised mass picket came to be seen as a breach of the peace, and the police and courts acted quickly and vigorously. The police requested restrictive bail conditions, and this curtailed many of the more active strikers. Clive's reports were factual, but they were heavily edited, or they went into the waste bin.

The police were learning how to use the media, feeding stories to them to undermine the strikers. The authorities were creating a climate that encouraged conflict and was intended to isolate the miners who, through their own actions, were unwittingly helping their enemies.

Clive didn't want to worry Marie. She had enough on her plate with the baby. He was emotionally drained when he arrived home and was restless in bed.

'Alright, love?' asked Marie on the Wednesday night after Mansfield.

'Overtired, that's all,' he lied.

Marie knew that something was not right at work, but she didn't push the matter. He would talk soon enough.

Peter Norlick phoned the next day. They arranged to meet in Sheffield that evening, at The Harlequin, a short walk from The Wicker. Clive was already seated in the bar area when Peter Norlick arrived. He looked strange in a T-shirt and jeans. He was well over six feet tall, skinny and with a slight stoop. He spoke with a noticeable West Country burr. Clive bought him a beer, and they both took deep draughts.

'Can I call you Clive?' asked Peter. 'Clive Parkhouse's what you wrote on the scrap of paper.'

'Nobody uses any other name, nothing that's polite.'

'It's a risk, me coming here.'

'There's nothing to worry about.'

'Not for *you*. If anyone finds out where *I* am, I'm in for it.'

'I'll be careful what I say or write. Anyhow, my editor isn't printing anything that's critical of the police.'

Peter hesitated again.

'This aggressive policing has been planned.'

'Planned?'

'Not the detail, but how we deal with public disturbances. We got caught out at Brixton, you know, the riots. Not prepared, not trained. I'd just started in the Met back then.'

'1981?'

'Yes. The streets had been a no go area for years, drug dealing and petty crime, so the top brass decided to flood the streets with police. It was called Operation Swamp: funny, yeah? Stop and search increased, and the locals got pissed off. That's when the riots started. We weren't ready. They took control, and there was looting for a whole night before we got a grip. It was the same in the Toxteth riots.'

'The Scarman Report criticised the police for targeting black kids.'

'That's right. Now we've got these special units that've been trained in new tactics and PSUs.'

'PSUs?'

'Police Support Units. They're in every force; sort of mobile, quick-response teams. So far, they've not been used much. The snatch squad idea's already been tried by the regular police. That's what you've seen at the road blocks and pickets.'

'Yes, they're arresting anyone, aren't they?'

'The idea's to make arrests, grab who they can. It's a chance for some coppers to beat the shit out of the miners.'

'Like they did in Mansfield?' Clive said.

'They weren't PSUs, but they were trying out the tactics. The mounted police break the mob up, and snatch squads go in and make arrests.'

'You say you're trying these new ideas out?'

'We haven't got our act together yet, not coordinating the mounted police, the dogs and the fully equipped PSUs. The tactics are ideal for a pitched battle. Perhaps it's a step too far, but I think we're waiting for the right moment. We're not here to keep the peace; we're here to break the strike. I can't prove it, but it's true. The senior officers are telling us that our job's to protect anyone going to work. They don't want us to be even-handed. They want us to smash the strike.'

'What does the average copper think?'

'Average copper?'

'Like you.'

'We're keeping our heads down. It's not policing we're doing. We wouldn't be allowed to behave like this at home. It's not right. Some coppers feel like me. Perhaps most do. Some of the Met lads are looking for a fight. They hate the locals. After any arrests, they sit down together and make sure their statements corroborate.'

'But that's illegal.'

'It happens all the time. Senior officers just want convictions. They don't care. It's always the word of three or four policemen against one miner,' shrugged Peter.

'The police aren't being challenged in court, and the miners aren't getting justice. It's a conspiracy.'

'Your words, not mine. We've been moved around a bit, but being up here suits some of the lads. I know blokes using the overtime to buy a car or to save for a deposit on a house. Some want the strike to last the year, I'm not kidding, and you wouldn't believe the money we're making.'

Clive shook his head.

'Where are you staying?'

'Disused military bases, village halls, that sort of stuff. I've been billeted outside Grantham, and some of the married lads have got women on the side. We've got spare money, and locals want us to spend it. There's one pub that charges out bedrooms by the hour, you know, for sex.'

'That's rich. Mrs Thatcher's from Grantham, and I'm not sure she'd approve,' Clive muttered. 'I don't think Arthur Scargill would be too happy if he knew that the overtime money you're getting is enough to put a deposit down on a house.'

'It's not good. I'm ashamed, and it's not why I became a policeman.'

'What's next?'

'Orgreave, yes... something's gonna break at Orgreave. They're out to get Scargill too.'

'Who are?'

'Don't know, but it's coming from the top.'

'Another beer?' asked Clive, casually.

'You're not kidding,' said Peter. 'I'll get 'em. I'll spend some of my overtime money,' he laughed.

The conversation drifted through family, football and holidays, and Clive brought the conversation back to the strike.

'You talked about Orgreave. What about the cameras? The police can't step out of line.'

'The PSUs, they'll be careful in front of the television

cameras, but that's not where most of the action happens. Anyhow, it's a piece of piss inciting the miners to break the law. One thing leads to another, you know.'

'Where are you tomorrow?'

'Orgreave, again,' said Peter.

The picketing at Orgreave continued into June, and Clive made regular visits. It was late one evening, and Marie and Clive were washing up after dinner.

'Why so glum, Clive?'

'I've been thinking about the *Comet*.'

'Mike getting heavy with you?'

'The editing's getting worse. I met him again today, and it ended up in another slanging match.'

'What does he want?'

'He says I'm biased, and everyone else can't be wrong.'

'Is he right?'

'No. I've thought it through so many times. The police, media and government are working together.'

'I've noticed a change at school. At first, everyone was with the miners, but the pictures on the telly and the front pages have turned people against them. You think they're going to lose?'

'Scargill's being outmanoeuvred. He thought the government would cave, and he's risked everything on it.'

'There's no chance of a compromise?'

'It's too late. The government won't compromise, and Scargill can't. I've been thinking. If I can't report honestly, then I'm not sure I want to continue working for Mike.'

'Come on Clive, I don't like you looking so downcast. You're going to be a dad soon.'

Clive smiled.

'That's something to look forward to. I'm off to Orgreave tomorrow.'

'Be careful!'

19

CLIVE

Trouble had been brewing at Orgreave for weeks. There had been a major confrontation at the end of May, and Arthur Scargill and many others had been arrested. The National Union of Miners had called for a mass picket, and they were hoping for a good turnout. They expected sufficient numbers to close the site. Scargill had made it clear that he wanted Orgreave to be the turning point in the strike, just as Saltley had been, over a decade before. So far, although the police had made arrests, tension had simmered each day and then died down.

Orgreave epitomised the industrial north. The stench of gas from the coke works hung in the air, and the towering chimneys and gasholders cast a melancholy shadow. The M1 motorway and the Sheffield Parkway ran close by, and there was a continuous din from the passing traffic.

Clive arrived and took a quick walk, first amongst the miners, and then he edged as close as he could to the police. He did this every time he came to Orgreave, hoping to sense the atmosphere. For the first time, there were no female police officers to be seen and only a few women amongst the miners.

Clive took up a position on the north side of the rectangular field where the miners and police were assembling, his back to the road. As he looked south, the main body of police was to his left, and to his right were the miners. They were on slightly higher ground than the police and facing directly across the field toward their adversaries. Behind the miners was a railway line, and it seemed to Clive to be an impenetrable barrier. On both flanks, a few police and dog handlers kept guard. The only exit was along the road behind Clive.

There were more pickets than he had seen before, thousands already in the field and more arriving. Clive was surprised that so many pickets had managed to get to Orgreave. He had not come across any roadblocks on the way in, and some of the miners were talking about how they had been escorted to Orgreave by the police. Clive wondered why because their policy had been to prevent pickets travelling. He was uneasy. It felt as if both sides were looking for a knockout blow after weeks of sparring.

There were as many police as protesters, and Clive recognised some of them, from Peter's description, as Police Support Units. They were identifiable by their helmets and plastic shields. As the number of pickets increased, so the police matched them with ordinary officers without riot gear.

Clive surveyed the scene from his vantage point. It appeared to be a trap, a battleground chosen by the police into which they had corralled the enemy. They were waiting for their moment, but for the time being at least, it was the usual standoff.

On many occasions, Clive had witnessed the preliminary forays when the lorries arrived at the plant to pick up coke. Everything about this day was different. There was the usual chanting, shoving and pickets trying to break the police barrier, but today missiles were thrown, and a policeman was hurt. It was a bad start. The police were deploying a line of shields in front of the miners, and this defence was deflecting the stones. A policeman accepted a round of applause when a stone bounced off a shield, spun into the air, and he caught it in one hand. The pushing was short-lived but intense.

Then, the wall of shields parted, and mounted police trotted through the gap, breaking the line of the protesters and forcing them to flee. The mounted officers used no force, and after the miners had dispersed, they returned to the main ranks. The miners immediately reformed, as if engaged in a military manoeuvre.

Some minutes later, the manoeuvre was repeated, but this time the horsemen were followed by the blue line of police. These foot soldiers moved as one, twenty-five yards toward the miners. It seemed unnecessary and deliberately provocative. Miners picked up bricks and hurled them at the mounted police. After a few minutes, a senior policeman with a loudhailer spoke to the miners. Clive could not make it out.

'What's he saying?' he asked a nearby police dog-handler.

'I think he wants them to move back. I heard him say a hundred yards.'

'What was that about shield squads?'

There was no reply because the dog-handler had edged away and was eying Clive with suspicion. The miners did not heed whatever had been said, and Clive witnessed the tactics Peter Norlick had explained. Mounted police advanced for a third time, with military precision and at a canter, and the short-shielded PSUs jogged behind them. There seemed to be two groups, each sweeping into the panicking miners. The mounted police caused confusion, and the shielded officers were waving their truncheons, hitting protesters and grabbing whomever they could. The police were working to a pattern. They would isolate miners, hit them to the body so that they had to defend themselves and then grab them and haul them away. A few seemed to be enjoying the battle, and they were swinging out at any miner in range, aiming at heads as well as bodies.

As quickly as they had emerged and attacked, the police retreated behind their defensive line, and the miners regrouped. Clive could not understand why they had attacked and then retreated so quickly. It was as if the police were putting their training through a dry run. As Clive had witnessed at Mansfield, this was not containment, but organised and aggressive dispersal.

The miners were angry and later that morning, as the fully laden coke lorries left, the usual pushing and shoving was far more aggressive than had been the norm. It was then that Arthur Scargill appeared and ostentatiously walked along the line of shielded policemen. It was surreal. What was he doing? He seemed to be chattering to the police and reproachfully shaking his head. Was he trying to get arrested again? Was this an attempt to boost the spirits of his men? Clive could not work it out.

There would be no more planned coke movements for many hours, and the miners seemed happy to allow the tension to subside. Many were already beginning to feel the heat of the sun, and some walked up to the road past Clive. They headed to the shops in Orgreave for food and drinks. The thousands of miners that had been there at the start dwindled to just a few hundred. Some were lying in the sun, others were baiting the police, and a few were just chatting. As the morning drew on, most of the police kept their position, protecting the coke plant, fully uniformed in the sweltering heat.

Clive edged nearer to the police line with his notebook out, signifying that he was from the press. He tried to listen to what individual officers were saying. A young constable was berating his superior, and Clive watched them out of the corner of his eye.

'What the fuck's happening, Sarge?' the constable asked. 'We should've grabbed Scargill when we could. I'm boiling hot, hungry, and I need a drink. They're just taking the piss,' he said, looking at a group of miners sunning themselves with drinks in hands. Others had started playing football and were goading the sweltering police.

'It's too late to do anything about Scargill,' was the sergeant's reply, 'but any step out of line and we'll get stuck in. No holds barred as far as I'm concerned. I've had a belly-full too.'

Just then, a lorry tyre rolled down the hill, wobbling before falling on its side, twenty yards from the police. It was an innocuous incident, but it was enough.

'Come on lads, let's go. I've had it with these bastards,' said the young policeman. His superior nodded.

Across the field of battle, other officers had come to the same conclusion. The police reformed their line, and as one, they started to drum on their shields and advanced. Earlier, when the miners and police had been involved in a tense standoff, both parties had avoided all-out war when it seemed the only possible outcome. Now, hours later, a minor provocation sparked a full-scale battle. The mood of the police had changed in the heat of the day.

The ostensible reason for the police being at Orgreave was to prevent pickets from closing the plant. That objective had already been achieved because most of the pickets had drifted away, with few likely to return for the second round of lorry movements. The protesters had failed. There had been some missile throwing before the fateful tyre had been rolled, but it was nothing that could not have been endured. Clive concluded that the police had come with the intention of asserting their dominance over the miners, and as tempers frayed in the heat, the police rank and file had decided to get on with the job. Battle was joined.

The noise of truncheons on shields drew everyone's

attention to the line of police. It advanced remorselessly in the direction of the miners, unprepared for this turn of events. Mounted police and snatch squads now went through their routines in earnest. The few miners who stood their ground were swept up in a flurry of fists, boots and flailing truncheons. They were dragged through the ranks to be taken to police stations and then the courts.

As the miners were forced backward, some realised that their only escape route was down the railway embankment and across the tracks. The majority headed for the spot where Clive had retreated, the road that led to escape across the bridge into Orgreave. It was mass panic. The men who had been sunning themselves were stripped to the waist, and they carried their T-shirts as they fled. Some had bleeding cuts where truncheons had caught them, and others were shouting for mates, unsure where they were. One man turned and saw the police set upon a friend, and he launched himself at them feet first. Clive could not see what happened to the two miners because a human tide was sweeping him toward the bridge.

As they reached the bridge, Clive turned and saw the police in pursuit, picking up stragglers and dragging them away. One man was limping, and his damaged leg was knocked from under him by a truncheon blow below the knee. He screamed as he was dragged to his feet and made to hop back through the lines of policemen. Clive noticed cameras following the events as they unfolded. He felt reassured that they would have evidence to show that the police had engineered the conflict.

Clive crossed over the bridge to the sanctuary of the village. The police, surely, would not enter. They formed a barrier on the village side of the bridge. The access to the coke plant was now completely open to traffic, and the miners were in a fierce mood. Most of them had no idea what had happened, or why the police had attacked. A few decided to get even. They found a scrap yard and began to pelt the police with anything they could lay their hands on.

Clive moved away from the bridge and down the road. Miners were wheeling a scrap car the other way, back toward the police. The bridge was above the level of the retreating miners, who pushed it as close as they could before setting it alight. The miners were subjecting the police to an intense barrage of bricks, stones and pieces of metal. They formed their shields into a protective wall. They had to take action because the miners were out of control, and someone was likely to get seriously hurt. There were two options: they could move either forward or back.

There were only a few hundred protesters when the police surged forward with their short shields, and they easily drove the strikers back. They stopped as soon as the fleeing miners dispersed and then retreated to the bridge. The miners reorganised and hurled whatever was available at the enemy. There were injured police and protesters everywhere. A few lay on the ground, some were limping from the scene, and others nursed bloodied wounds. Debris was scattered on the road and pavement. Clive saw Arthur Scargill being helped from the scene, injured. It was a battle, and each action provoked an escalated response. It had reached the stage where a few of the protagonists were enjoying the mayhem they were creating, and they would only be satisfied when they had inflicted serious injury on the enemy.

Two young strikers were laughing and joking as they knocked down a wall. They grabbed bricks, ran forward and hurled them gleefully at the police before returning to repeat the process. Any control that the miners' leaders had exerted was evaporating, and Clive was scared.

Whilst all this was happening, an ice cream van with the

name 'Rock On Tommy' painted on the side, was doing a roaring trade with the miners. It had been busy all day, encouraged by the boiling weather. The ice cream man had seen no reason to stop just because he was in the middle of a riot. It showed entrepreneurial spirit worthy of the new age. Suddenly, the police had had enough and moved forward along the road, forcing the miners into full retreat. Tommy was surrounded by a sea of blue, and as they seemed less interested than the miners in purchasing his fine ices, he moved off to find better custom.

Clive joined the retreating miners. He heard screams from behind and turned. Some police had broken from the main ranks, seemingly out of control, and they were chasing individual miners and lashing out at them indiscriminately. Clive started to run with a group of miners. As they split, he found himself with one other man, running down an alleyway between houses, followed by two truncheon-wielding policemen. Clive was twenty yards ahead of the police, and the miner was just ahead of him. They came to a garden, and the two fugitives turned in opposite directions. Clive turned right and saw an opening. He entered the dark sanctuary and slammed the door behind him. He leaned back to ensure it was closed and breathed a sigh of relief.

An old woman sat at a table opposite him. She placed a finger to her lips and moved past him to release the door latch, locking them inside. Every movement was completely silent, and the woman smiled and shuffled back to her seat. Clive heard shouting. The police had caught the other man trying to climb the brick wall at the bottom of the garden. He heard the sound of a scuffle and then a solid thwack.

'Where's your mate?' asked a voice in estuary English.

Clive heard no response. There was a thump followed by a groan.

'You heard. Where's your mate?'

'He's not my mate. I never seen him before.'

There was another wallop and a pitiable cry. Clive squirmed. He indicated that he wanted to go out. The woman shook her head. Clive turned so that he could look out of the window. He saw the two officers towering over a man who was huddled in a corner created by the wall and a garden shed. He was in the foetal position, covering his sides with his elbows and his head with his hands. Clive saw blood on his clothes.

One of the officers pulled the miner to his feet. He cowered, and the policeman unleashed a cruel smash across his back.

'I think he's a reporter. For fuck's sake, I don't know him.'

Clive shrugged at the old woman and opened the latch. The two policemen heard the noise and turned. Clive confronted them through the open door. He took a step forward. They had seen him with his notebook over the previous weeks, and they knew who he was. They glanced at each other with resignation and a realisation that this was as far as their interrogation could go. They brushed past him and strode down the alleyway.

The miner refused help and limped, bloodied and scared, back the way he had come, looking left and right before he made his escape. Cautiously, Clive returned to the street. Mounted police were patrolling. A protester had been thrown across a car bonnet and was being hit by a policeman. He fell to the floor, and the officer dragged him by one foot across the bridge.

Along the road, by a bus stop, a young woman was kneeling beside an injured man. He was lying on the pavement and appeared to be seriously hurt. She stood up, trying to attract the attention of a nearby policeman. She had her back to a mounted officer, charging with a raised truncheon. Clive shouted as the policeman aimed a blow at her head. At the last moment, she was hauled out of the reach of her assailant by another man, and the truncheon missed by an inch. Clive heard the whirr of a motor-driven camera. A photographer had caught the moment, and he retreated, happy with the day's work. Clive waited until the coast was clear and walked to his car. He was back in the office half an hour later and filed his report for the evening edition.

After about half an hour, Mike Boddington called from his office door. Ominously, he asked Clive to close it behind him, and Clive watched Mike make his way to his desk. Mike, as usual, wore a jacket and casual trousers, with a loosely fitted tie and undone top button to his shirt.

Mike would never tell his reporters how to dress. He believed himself assertive in a laid-back sort of way, and his casual appearance was how he expressed this position. Nobody other than Mike wore a jacket or tie. The jacket draped loosely over his thin frame, and his shirt billowed from his waist. As Mike turned, Clive noticed that his belt was in the last notch, the benchmark Mike had set himself. His gaunt features and concave cheeks made his eyes seem larger than they were. Although no sportsman, he was obsessively fit. He spoke with authority, the virtue that had sustained his career.

'Clive, what's all this crap you've written? It's got to stop. You're taking sides, and it's the wrong side too.'

'That's bollocks!' Clive shouted.

'Don't raise your voice at me. You're not on the picket line with your mates.'

'I've written what happened, Mike.'

'Not according to everyone else.'

'I can't speak for them. Have you ever thought that it's them taking sides, not me?'

'The BBC, they're taking sides, are they?'

'They're running with the tide.'

'The police, they're making it up too?'

'They're provoking, and the miners are reacting.'

'Why's everyone seeing it the other way round, Clive?'

Mike and Clive had adopted adversarial poses on opposite sides of Mike's desk. Everyone in the newsroom could hear them.

'Ask them. The truth doesn't suit some people. *They* might believe what the police tell them, but I don't.'

'They're professional journalists, Clive. They're not going to be fooled.'

'Everything's being managed by the police and government.'

'You've got this thing about Mrs Thatcher. You're not thinking straight.'

'That's shit. It's not reporting we're getting from these so-called journalists, it's fucking propaganda.'

'Don't talk like that to me. Just because everyone else sees things differently, it doesn't make them dishonest.'

Mike started pacing angrily behind his desk.

'Who's pulling the strings, Mike? Anyone who doesn't toe the line's being nailed. People are too frightened to speak out.'

Both men were now shouting.

'Hold on, Clive. Nobody's stopping me printing what I want.'

'Sure about that, are you?'

'You need to question your own motives, not mine. You've got too close to the miners.'

'That is the most...'

'Look at what's coming through on Reuters,' Mike interrupted. 'Look at the television reports.'

Mike turned on the video. He rewound the tape and played the footage.

For a few minutes, the combatants were silent.

'That's not what happened,' Clive said. 'What you've just shown isn't the real sequence of events. It's been edited. Stop the video!'

Mike sighed.

'Rewind it for a minute.'

The machine whirred. The scene at Orgreave was replayed.

'I can't believe this. It's exactly what I've been talking about. This bit just now,' he pointed, 'it happened later, and the action coming up, yes, fast forward, right here, happened first, and there's nothing about what happened in Orgreave village, where the police lost it.'

'What the hell are you on about?'

'The clip shows miners attacking the police first. Then it shows the police responding... just here. See?' said Clive excitedly. 'It's been cut to make out that the police charge was as a response to the hand-to-hand fighting. It was the other way round. The fighting started after the police charged. It's a load of crap.'

'Come on, Clive, you're not thinking straight.'

'I'm not saying that the pickets are angels, but this is a pack of lies. The editing's put the blame for the battle on the miners.'

'So everyone else is lying, and you're telling the truth.'

'Well, Mike, I know I'm a bit old-fashioned, but I thought telling the truth was what journalism's about,' said Clive sarcastically. 'Anyhow, what you've got on here is only half the story. When the police swept through Orgreave, they attacked anyone, I mean anyone, standing in their way. Isn't that worth reporting?'

'Well, nobody else saw it, did they?'

'Yes, they did. The police, the miners, locals, and there were photographers. What photographs have you got?'

'Look, Clive, you're clutching at straws.'

'I just want you to see what really happened.'

'Nobody's stopping you reporting the facts.'

'That's not true. You're stopping me.'

'No, I'm trying to get you in tune to reality.'

'Reality, whose reality, Mike? I'm reporting what's actually happening, not the crap being fed to us by the police and most of the media.'

Mike sighed.

'I'm not letting this paper become the mouthpiece for your politics, Clive. It's as simple as that. It's your choice.'

'You're censoring me then?'

'Don't talk shit. It's not censorship. You just need to be more accommodating toward the paper's editorial line.'

'Accommodating? What sort of doubletalk is that? You're editing what I'm writing into half-truths and lies. It's propaganda, Mike. You're printing propaganda!'

'Clive!'

'It's the owners, isn't it? You know what I'm saying's right, but you're frightened of the owners, and you want to keep your job. Fuck you, Mike, fuck this shitty paper, fuck you all!'

Clive stormed out of the office. He drove to Charnley to judge the reaction to the Orgreave clash. Martin Jarman signed him in at the Welfare. Over a drink, Clive told Martin what he had seen that morning. As he spoke, miners gathered and listened to the detail. Some of them had been there and nodded agreement. He explained how the confrontation had escalated in the village.

'Now you know what it's really like,' said a voice Clive did not recognise.

'I've known that right from the start, but I was scared.'

Martin asked him what was going into the newspaper.

'I've resigned, or I've been fired.' Clive shrugged. 'It's one or the other. I'm not sure which. My editor doesn't like what

I'm writing, I'm not prepared to change, and so we've come to the end of the line, I'm afraid. I'm swimming against the tide. I'll be looking for a job down the pit at the end of this,' he smiled.

'Not at Charnley,' laughed Martin. 'Nobody here'd have you, you lazy bastard.'

'Mind you, that'd change if he gets a round in,' shouted another miner.

A baby due and income severely curtailed, Clive's mood was sombre as he drove home. He feared for his future.

Later that evening, as Mike sorted through a pile of photographs on his desk, he turned over a picture of a woman, holding her hand up to protect herself from the swinging arm of a mounted policeman. She was in the main street at Orgreave. He turned it face down and sighed.

'What now, Clive?' asked Marie.

She seemed unconcerned, considering that Clive had just told her that he had resigned. Clive was on the settee, and she was lying on her back, head on his lap. He was stroking her hair. They had eaten, and Clive had explained why he had decided to leave the *Comet*.

'I feel bad about finishing so acrimoniously with the *Comet*, but on the other hand, I'm so excited about the baby,' said Clive, and he leaned over and rubbed the baby-bump.

'How are you going to earn a crust, Clive?'

'I don't know, but perhaps it's the right time to make a complete break.'

'That sounds a bit dramatic.'

'We could move south. That's where all the big jobs are.'

'Clive, you're not interested in *big* jobs, are you?'

'No, it's not me, is it? I like it too much here. I could get out of the newspaper business and go into radio or even television.'

'That sounds exciting. Is it what you want?'

'Yes, I'd like to give it a go. Today's a sort of watershed. I don't just mean leaving the newspaper, but I suppose… I don't know how to explain.'

'Career change?'

'Yes, it's that, but I feel like I'm a deserter. There's a lot happening, you know, with the police and the newspapers and the authorities. It's a Faustian pact. Perhaps, if I was really determined, I could do something, but I know I haven't got the stamina for it.'

'Don't say that.'

'Nobody'll back me. Anyhow, perhaps I'm wrong, like Mike says.'

'Clive, love, you know you're not wrong. No regrets now because you've done your best.'

20

MARCUS

The *Echo* had picked up the early reports about Orgreave. At first, the confrontation had not seemed much more serious than on other days. Marcus and Peter Kellock were discussing the potential stories for the day at Marcus's desk.

'It's a phoney war,' said Marcus. 'Scargill's pissing in the wind. He's losing the support of the other unions.'

'More pits are opening, but there's still lots of intimidation.'

'Not enough police at the pickets.'

'The numbers back at work are increasing. I've got the figures here,' said Kellock.

'Thatcher will make sure that McGregor doesn't negotiate, so there's no way the talks with Scargill can go anywhere.'

'If she doesn't cave in, the strike's going to crumble.'

'The only problem is that stories are drying up,' said Marcus, anxiously.

'It's the same for everybody.'

'The *Globe*'s doing better than us with sales.'

A young man walked up to the desk and nervously addressed Marcus.

'There's more information coming through about the set-to at Orgreave. It's not the usual stuff.'

Marcus nodded, and the youngster turned and disappeared.

'We'll pick up what's happening at Orgreave in a minute,' he said. 'Peter, I need more on the breakdown of law and order. A general piece, but use the photos from the Mansfield riot and Scargill's arrest at Orgreave, the other day.'

The phone rang, and Marcus picked it up. He listened, asked the person on the other end to hang on and put his hand over the mouthpiece.

'Kevin's on the phone. He says that there's been a massive pitched battle at Orgreave. Scargill's involved, and he's been hurt.'

'Bad?'

'Badly enough to cause him pain, I hope, but not so bad he'll get any sympathy.'

Marcus flicked a switch so that the conversation was relayed through a microphone.

'Kevin, you're on the mic,' said Marcus. 'What's happening?'

The young man returned and whispered into Peter's ear.

'Pictures are coming through,' said Peter. 'I'll go and have a closer look.'

Excitedly, Kevin reported the events he had witnessed. As Kevin was finishing, Peter returned.

'It sounds like you've had a lively day,' said Marcus. 'I've got Peter here. Let's decide how we're going to pull this together. Can you hear us?'

'Yes, loud and clear.'

'The pictures coming through are confusing,' said Peter. 'It's hard to tell how it kicked it off and I'm not sure who's doing what. We'll have the BBC claiming police brutality, and the police'll end up on the defensive.'

'OK Kevin, send an eyewitness account of what happened. I don't want any doubt that this was started by the miners and that the police responded to protect the coke works. Get the gist of it down here double-quick, and we'll edit it,' Marcus said.

'OK, I'll get on with it,' replied Kevin.

'I'll organise the photographs to support the story,' said Peter.

'I want quotes from the police about provocation, Kevin. I'm sure someone up there will tell you what you want to hear. If not, you know, use your creativity. Get numbers of arrests and likely charges and injuries to the police.'

'Riot and unlawful assembly, I've heard,' said Kevin.

Later in the afternoon, Marcus was organising pieces of paper on his desk. He smiled at Simon, Stephen and Peter.

'Fabulous stuff, and I love this photo,' Marcus chuckled. He fingered a photograph where a picket, with a police helmet on his head, was trying to escape at full tilt from the owner. 'How many policemen injured?'

'Kevin says about seventy,' said Simon.

'Great! Make it over a hundred,' said Marcus.

'They're going to charge them with riot,' added Simon.

Marcus was thumbing through a pile of photographs. One showed a policeman, his arm raised, holding a truncheon and about to hit a protester lying defenceless on the ground. The protester was trying to protect his head with his arm, and his face was covered with blood. Marcus ripped it up.

'I want the front six pages ready in an hour. Put the eyewitness account from Kevin on the front page and the "Riot" headline. Kevin's getting us a police angle. You should know how to organise this stuff by now.'

'Yes,' was the chorus.

'Sir Clifford's working on the editorial,' continued Marcus. 'Peter's got a feature on crime and he links it nicely to the strike. Fill the gaps with the best of this lot.'

Marcus pointed to the photographs on the desk.

'We'll sort out the shots that show the police being attacked,' said Peter. 'I can't see anything with Scargill.'

'Capture the mood – a country under threat. Stephen, get the number of returning miners updated. I want the total so far, as well as the figure for today.'

'I don't think the numbers are accurate,' Stephen replied.

'Are they too high or too low?'

'Too high, because they're being massaged by the Coal Board.'

'Whatever number they give you, prefix it with the words "at least". I saw a photo with pickets throwing stones at a bus going into a pit. It was in Wales, I think.'

'I've got it here,' said Stephen.

'Put it on page two.'

'I've seen some great photos of returning miners going through the pickets,' Stephen added.

'Save that for later in the week.'

'Do you want numbers on redundancy payments?' asked Stephen.

'Yes. It's the taxpayer who pays. Our readers will never get a handout like that,' said Marcus. 'They'll go spare.'

Thoughts were fired at the team in a scattergun way. The acolytes knew not to interrupt the flow unless necessary. He stopped, put his hands on his hips and nodded.

'It's coming together nicely. The pressure we're creating is starting to make the BBC much more favourable toward the government. Let's make it impossible for anyone other than left-wing lunatics to support Scargill.' Marcus paused. 'Create an atmosphere where even the Labour Party and trade unions won't back the miners.'

There was a break for thought.

'Peter, could you get me a list of high profile Labourites who are with Scargill? I need some quotes.'

There was a hiatus, and then Marcus continued.

'We can keep this pot boiling up to party conference time.'

Rub of the chin.

'Did Scargill really get hurt?'

'Yes,' said Simon.

'He's a twat. We still need to dig the dirt. Tail him and talk to neighbours, ex-colleagues, anyone. The one thing we haven't got is the skeleton in that bastard's cupboard. I don't care how much, or who you have to pay, just don't get caught.'

'I'll see what we can find,' said Simon Howman.

'What's this on Greenham Common, Simon? No hanging around, the rest of you.'

Simon was left on his own with Marcus.

'Well,' said Simon, 'the protesters at Greenham Common, who were cleared out in April, have all returned.'

'Yes, I know. They're mainly lesbians and dropouts, by all accounts.'

'There's a woman called Emma Gladwin, one of those who have been there from the start. She's just been arrested. She's camped there with her daughter.'

'Name's not familiar.'

'Her daughter's school age, about thirteen, I think. Anyhow, cannabis was found on the mother, and the daughter's name is Becky... Becky Shearman.'

'You're kidding, aren't you? You mean Dave Shearman's daughter?'

'Yes.'

'I knew him at university,' Marcus replied.

His right hand rubbed his chin contemplatively.

'Well, it gets juicier. Becky *is* Dave Shearman's daughter and this Emma *was* his first wife. They got divorced some years ago, and Shearman hasn't seen Becky since. Anyhow, Emma's girlfriend's sleeping in the same tent.'

'Girlfriend? Shearman married a lesbian?' Marcus laughed.

'He had a series of affairs during the divorce. He's now

remarried to a social worker. We could headline a Greenham story and link Shearman at the same time.'

'Careful!' said Marcus. 'Don't overstep the mark. I wouldn't want to harm the child. What's Shearman up to now? I've lost track.'

'He's keeping quiet at the moment, but he's in the shadow cabinet, sponsored by the National Union of Miners. We could jog memories about Shearman's womanising past and his sponsorship.'

'I'm serious about the child. She can't help what her parents have been up to, and we've got the courts to consider. I'll think about it. I've got to go. I'm meeting with Sir Clifford in three minutes,' he said, glancing at his watch.

Marcus put on his jacket and made his way to Sir Clifford's office, checking the time as he walked.

I wonder if I'll find out what's been going on. Sir Clifford's up to something.

Punctuality was critical. Earliness and lateness were sins of equal gravity. The door was ajar, awaiting his arrival. He knocked, was beckoned in and Sir Clifford waved him to shut the door. He looked around and could not see Ronnie anywhere. He had never been in the room alone with Sir Clifford. Marcus put his hands by his side, then behind his back and finally he clasped them loosely in front. He wasn't invited to sit down and stood at the opposite side of the desk to the editor, who prowled, hands behind his back and head slightly bent, seemingly weighed down by the cares of the world.

'Well, Marcus, how are things going?' Sir Clifford asked quietly.

'I'm not sure what to say, Sir Clifford.'

'How do you think you're getting on? Are you doing a good job?'

Marcus hesitated.

'Come on, Marcus, I haven't got all day. Tell me what you think.'

'I think I'm doing a good job. Ronnie would be able to give you a better idea.'

Marcus could not hide his embarrassment.

'I don't want Ronnie's view, I want yours.'

'I reckon the *Echo*'s doing the best coverage of the strike,' he said confidently. 'The *Globe*'s blatant in its anti-miner stance, but we're more persuasive. It's hitting the right buttons with the readers and, I hope, with the government.'

Sir Clifford hesitated.

'Mmm, yes, I think you're doing a fine job. I see you as the future of the *Echo*.'

Marcus exhaled deeply. Sir Clifford was walking away as he spoke, and Marcus strained to hear what he said. Sir Clifford turned and stalked back.

'Ronnie Miles has had to go home today. He'll be leaving us. He's nearing retirement age, and he hasn't been a well man of late. He has a dicky heart, you know, so it's the best thing for everyone concerned.'

'I'm sorry.'

'Yes, yes, yes; I'm sure you are.'

Sir Clifford waved his hands impatiently and continued.

'I had been considering moving you straight into his job, but you need a little more time. I'll be appointing Barry Halstead from the *Mercury* to take over from Ronnie, and I intend to appoint you News Editor of the *Sunday Echo*. I know it's all a little sudden, but it's how these things often happen. Anyhow, that's my decision.'

Sir Clifford had stopped pacing as he said these words, as if for dramatic purpose, but he enunciated his words in a monotone, and the effect was lost.

'It's an opportunity for you to put your mark on the paper, Marcus. If you get it right, you have a bright future here. None of us will be around forever, and you need to show me you're the right man for a bigger job.'

Sir Clifford turned.

'What do you think?'

'Thank you, Sir. Thank you, Sir Clifford. I wasn't expecting it. It's a fantastic opportunity, and I won't let you down.'

Sir Clifford turned his back, as if he was offended or embarrassed by Marcus's obvious pleasure.

'No, you won't let me down, or at least you had better not,' said Sir Clifford, looking over his shoulder and speaking in a manner that did not promise tolerance of anything short of absolute success.

'When do I start?' asked Marcus excitedly.

'July. I need you here until Barry arrives. Simon will take over from you when you leave. Barry wants him in your job. I know Simon needs to toughen up, but Barry thinks he's got the brains and the potential. He has one chance to make a go of it, and it's Barry's call. You can tell Simon whenever you want. I'll be announcing Ronnie's retirement and your departure later today.'

Sir Clifford turned to face Marcus, expecting him to leave. Marcus stood his ground.

'I'd like your advice, Sir Clifford. We've a story about Dave Shearman's ex-wife and daughter. They're at Greenham Common. The daughter's a juvenile, about thirteen, but not attending school. Mother's living with her daughter and another woman, in a tent. The two adults are lesbians, and the mother's been caught with cannabis. I knew Shearman from university. The issue is the girl.'

'Are there any court proceedings?'

'No. Well not yet anyway'

'You say that you knew Shearman. Has he anything on you?'

'No, Sir. Well, we may have been together in a room where cannabis was smoked, but nothing else. We've got some dirt on Shearman's womanising and his pro-miner stance. He's sponsored by the NUM. We'd want to use the lot.'

'What do you think?'

'I'm reluctant to run it. It's the girl. We're family people at the *Echo* and so are our readers.'

'Run it. We're a family newspaper but not this type of family. Make that clear. They aren't our kind. It's the sort of story where things come out of the woodwork.'

Sir Clifford did not offer his hand for a congratulatory handshake, or to signify acceptance that a deal had been done. Marcus had never made physical contact with Sir Clifford and had never seen him shake the hand of any of his staff. As he left, Marcus put his hands behind his back, clasped together, as if he was trying to prevent them from taking precipitate and unwanted unilateral action.

Marcus made his way back to his office and immediately gave the go-ahead to run the Shearman article.

21

MARCUS

The following week, the *Echo* told Shearman that it was about to break the story, and he was asked if he had any comments. Shearman tried to make contact on the morning before the story broke. He was told that Marcus was out. He phoned three more times that day. On the final occasion, Peter was at Marcus's desk and picked up the phone.

'Is Marcus there?'

'Who's that?'

'What the fuck does that matter? I know he's standing next to you, so tell him that if he doesn't take this call I'll ring him at home. I'll call round tonight if I have to.'

'It's Shearman again,' said Peter Kellock, hand over the mouthpiece.

Peter told Marcus what Shearman had said, and Marcus grabbed the phone and ushered Peter away.

'Hello, Marcus Roache here.'

'Hello, Marcus. Been trying to avoid me?'

'Why should I do that, Dave? It's good to hear from you. What can I do?' replied Marcus affably.

'Come on, don't act innocent with me. You're the assistant news editor. You know what news you're printing. It's the story in tomorrow's *Echo*, about my ex-wife at Greenham Common. This guy Howman will make life difficult for Becky. I need to talk to you about it.'

183

'I'm busy, Dave. I haven't got the time.'

'Perhaps I could share a few snippets with you, you know, off the record. Come on.'

'You'd better make it worth my while.'

They agreed to meet at a bar in Ealing at 7.00.

The chit-chat was perfunctory, and the conversation quickly moved to university days and their erstwhile friends.

'I see Clara occasionally,' said Dave. 'She's doing very well at the *Sentinel*.'

'I've only met her once since university – that evening in the pub, with you, after the election.'

'Clive's been in contact. He wants to do a radio interview with me. It'll be good to bump into him after all these years.'

'He's got a job in radio has he?'

'Yes, local radio, and I'm told he's quite a celebrity.'

'I didn't think he was ambitious.'

'He isn't, but he's probably good at the job. He's got the charisma, I suppose. Not like the rest of us.'

'Hmm. Look, Dave, I haven't got long. What do you want, and what have you got for me?'

'Can you get Howman to back off?'

'I'll need something juicy, and I can't promise.'

'My divorce was acrimonious. Emma tried to keep me away from Becky, and then went to live with this other woman. I'm trying to build bridges. Emma's been stopping access, and the *Echo* mentioning Becky and raking up my past, it will screw things up.'

'Greenham Common's a live issue, and it'd be dereliction of duty not to report it. It's impossible to do the feature without mentioning you and your daughter. She's a big part of it because she's not at school.'

'Are you planning any more?'

'We've got some stuff for later in the week.'

'What *stuff*?'

Marcus hesitated. He took a deep breath.

'We're going to name some of your ex-girlfriends and print what they have to say.'

'That's got nothing to do with the Greenham story. It's my private life. It'll ruin any chance of access to Becky.'

'It's getting a bit late to stop the ball rolling.'

'I'm not the only man who's had a failed marriage. Why are you trawling this up? You're just trying to fuck things up for me!'

'I'm getting the impression that you're more bothered about protecting yourself than looking after your daughter,' said Marcus calmly.

'No, that's not true. Anything you publish will hurt innocent people, especially my daughter.'

'You've got nothing for me, have you? I won't stop the story, Dave. You can't blame Simon for…'

'Call your bloodhounds off!'

'Being angry and aggressive isn't helping.'

'You'd be angry if it was you!'

Marcus continued to speak quietly.

'But it's not me. I wouldn't have got into this position. Do you think your daughter should be camped at Greenham Common? We're doing this in her best interests. She should be at school, shouldn't she, Dave?'

'Looking after her interests? That's bollocks. You're looking after your circulation. All we are is a fucking story.'

'Why shouldn't the voters know about your colourful lifestyle? I remember what you were like at university.'

'University, you're going to bring up university? I remember what you were like too. Don't forget.'

'I wonder how many more skeletons you've got in the cupboard.'

Dave glared at Marcus, who continued.

'Have I hit a raw nerve?'

'Fuck off, you slime ball.'

Marcus watched Dave storm out of the bar.

I don't know why I was so worried about meeting Dave. He's just a selfish and self-absorbed fool. Why did I ever think he had something worth listening to? He deserves what's coming.

'Simon, Simon,' he shouted across the newsroom when he returned.

Simon rushed across.

'Shearman's got something to hide. Find out what it is. No holds barred with that bastard, and no expense spared. Do whatever it takes.'

'Whatever?'

'You heard.'

22

DAVE

Later that evening, Clara phoned Dave and asked if he would be prepared to provide any unattributed comments on the strike. They met at a café near Old Street early the following morning.

'It's politically very delicate,' he said, shaking his head despondently. 'Labour politicians are reluctant to speak out.'

'The government have got the media toeing the line. It's a lonely battle,' Clara sighed. 'Thatcher's working the press and the police, like puppets. They're undermining the NUM, and Scargill's powerless. It's impossible to put across a balanced case because you're shouted down as an extremist.'

Dave detected a slight tremor in her voice.

'You OK?'

'Fine.'

'We're off the record, aren't we?'

'Of course.'

'Everyone in the party knows that Thatcher's outmanoeuvring us. I'm a sponsored MP, and I have to stick up for the miners, but the party's split. Kinnock, Hattersley and the rest of the Labour leadership are shit scared. They don't want the strike to undermine the party. We're doing OK in the opinion polls, but this could ruin our chances at the next election.'

'What's the likelihood of Labour supporting the NUM?'

'Zilch. Kinnock thinks Scargill's misjudged the mood of the country and is in this for himself. There's no love lost.'

'But Labour Party members are behind Scargill.'

'Maybe, but Kinnock and Hattersley know that what appeals to the membership isn't what wins elections.'

'What about you, Dave?'

'I'm between a rock and a hard place. I think Scargill's gone too far, but I'd never say that publically.'

'I'm not optimistic.'

'I see our old mate, Marcus, is in the vanguard for Thatcher,' said Dave. 'He's a two-faced bastard. I wish I had a photo of him smoking pot.'

'He's probably thinking the same about you.'

'The miners hate the press. They think they're a pack of lying bastards. They hate the police too.'

'I'm not surprised.'

'Last week, Clive Parkhouse rang me.'

'Clive?'

'He's asked me to do an interview on a radio programme he hosts. He also works for a local rag in Yorkshire, and his boss is Mike Parkhouse. He's been reporting the strike, and Clive says that Mike's editing his copy because he doesn't want to upset the owners. That's why I'm being invited on the radio, so I can't be censored.'

'Censored!'

'That's how Clive describes it.'

'Same old Clive. Give him my love.'

'Same old Mike – keeping the establishment sweet.'

'What's Clive up to? Still single?'

'No, he's married and soon to be a dad.'

'I'm so happy for him. How's Becky?'

'Emma hasn't let me near her since we split.'

Dave coughed and then sniffed. He told Clara about the story in the *Echo*.

'Sorry,' said Clara and rested her hand on his, which was on the table. 'How could he do such a thing? Isn't he bothered about you and Becky?'

'It's a story, and he won't let old times get in the way. How's Lucy?' he asked.

'Fine,' replied Clara.

Dave phoned Clive the following day. Clive reassured him that it would be a sympathetic interview, and the date was agreed. Dave was nervous, but the interview ran smoothly, and they went for a beer when the programme finished. The pub was quiet as the two men walked in.

'Good show today,' the landlord said to Clive.

'I've brought my guest in to meet you. Dennis, this is Dave Shearman. Dave, this is Dennis, the worst landlord in Sheffield.'

'Pleased to meet you, Mr Shearman. I enjoyed the show. You've gotta kick Thatcher out at the next election.'

'Thanks, we'll do our best.'

'Good interview, Dave,' said Clive when they were seated. 'You came across well. It'll do no harm to your standing in the party.'

'Thanks.'

'You were very slick, very professional; nothing like the bullshitter I knew at university,' he laughed.

'You too,' Dave replied and then took the first sip of his pint, 'holding down two jobs when I thought you'd never get one.'

'Seriously, it was just the sort of stuff listeners like, particularly the stories of the hardships in families and small communities. It gets audiences to understand that the strike affects thousands of ordinary people across the country. It isn't just Scargill against Thatcher and McGregor.'

'On the phone, you said that Mike's censoring you.'

'Perhaps that's a bit extreme, but he'd been stopping me giving a balanced picture.'

Clive described to Dave his experiences of the picketing, the police reaction and the press coverage.

'Anyhow, that's all in the past,' he said and explained the circumstances in which he had parted company with the newspaper. 'Mike's having his arm twisted,' he concluded.

'Thatcher's changing the way politics works. It's a propaganda war,' said Dave, 'and the only way to get into power and hold onto it is to manage the media. It's sad, but it's true.'

'You used to be the man with high principles. Politicians could change things, you said.'

'Perhaps we can, but it's money and support in the press that win elections. We're not helping ourselves because we're making it too easy to be portrayed as militants, and the public are buying it. The stream of hostile propaganda is turning the public against miners and unions in general. We've got to get better at managing news than Thatcher.'

'I don't like that idea at all, Dave; managing news.'

Dave defended his position, and Clive argued that when politicians had a good case and sound ideas, the public would vote for them. The argument remained unresolved.

'Do you ever see any of our old mates from university?' asked Clive.

'I met Marcus a few years ago and again recently. He's a fucking turncoat.'

'I read the hatchet job the *Echo*'s just done on you.'

Dave explained the circumstances and his recent meeting with Marcus.

'My daughter, Becky,' Dave cleared his throat, 'I don't see her. What Marcus has done means I'll never get access to her. It's not good, Clive. Don't let it happen to you.'

'I didn't realise that Marcus was behind it.'

'He's become a Thatcherite.'

'I always thought his politics at university were more about fitting in than conviction.'

Dave told Clive of his earlier meeting with Marcus in 1979.

'He kept it quiet about the private school, didn't he?' said Dave. 'Anyhow, it seems that his conversion to socialism was temporary.'

'I'm not surprised. Clara thought his politics were skin-deep too.'

'I bump into Clara occasionally, mainly in a professional capacity.'

'Oh! How is Clara? Married?'

'No, she's still single and she'll stay that way, I guess. She asked me to give you her love.'

'Same old Clara.'

23

CLIVE

That evening, Clive got a call from Peter Norlick. The conversation was short because Clive explained that he had left the newspaper. He told Peter to keep in contact.

The following week, Clive met with the radio station's programme controller and managing director. They were completing a review of the schedules, and Clive made a series of proposals. He suggested developing a daily morning programme and linking it to an evening roundup, adopting the same quirky style that he had used in his weekly show. Clive convinced the managing director that it would boost ratings. It would require more investment in reporting, to gather the right local interest stories, which would be added to the general news and comment. It was a risk, but they agreed to give it a trial run. It turned out to be an excellent decision, and the local radio station took him onto their full-time staff.

It was not intentional, but he saw less of his previous circle of contacts. He devoted his time to radio work and to Marie. Despite what Marie had said, he felt guilty that he should thrive whilst others were suffering, but he was too busy to linger on negative thoughts for long.

Chloe was born in September, right on time, and Clive launched himself into fatherhood. Chloe prospered, and so did Clive and Marie.

Clive was enjoying the job at the radio station. He got to

work at 9.00 in the morning and returned at lunchtime. He was able to be with Marie and Chloe during the afternoon, returning to work for the evening roundup. Marie put Chloe to bed, usually before Clive returned at 7.00.

The house they had bought required major renovation. Despite their best intentions, they had only dabbled with a little decoration and had completed the baby's bedroom just before Chloe was born. They decided that they should start in earnest on the rest of the house.

'Right, Clive, where do we begin?' asked Marie, one evening.

It was early in December. Chloe was into a routine, and Marie had more time on her hands. Her mind had been active, planning their future. They had eaten and washed up, and Marie had laid two A4 notepads and two pencils on the same side of the kitchen table. There were two glasses of red wine on beer mats and a bowl of salted nuts. They sat like schoolchildren in class.

Clive raised his hand.

'Please, Miss, may I go to the toilet,' he joked.

Marie glared.

'It's serious, Clive. We've both got a bit of time. We can get most things done in the house before we try for number two.'

'Even if we try for number two tonight?'

'Concentrate.'

'Where do we start?'

'We have to consider the money. We'll be short till I get back to work, so we'll do what we can ourselves. I can do stripping, painting, making curtains, that sort of stuff.'

'I'm not totally useless either.'

'I know,' she mocked and put her arm round him. 'Not *totally*.'

The electrics were fine, she told him. She had had an

electrician in to check. The heating was OK, but the boiler needed replacing.

'It's something we've got to do because old boilers are dangerous and inefficient. I've transferred our savings into our current account to pay for it. I've got quotes, and the boiler man's in next week.'

'Everything seems in control. Do you need me?'

'Clive!'

'What about Chloe? She's a full-time job.'

'She's a darling. It's tiring, but she sleeps a lot.'

'That's not what you say at two in the morning.'

'When she starts to sleep through the night, she'll take up more time in the day, but we'll get more sleep. Anyhow, arranging things isn't so tiring.'

'So what needs doing?'

'The guttering needs repairing, and some of the pebbledash is breaking off. All the windows are sound.'

'Somebody else you got in?'

'Yes. He's sending a quote. It's too wet right now, and it'll have to wait until spring. We've just enough money for that. We can do the garden in the summer. What I suggest is this.'

Marie picked up her pencil and wrote down a list of every room in the house. She left a gap between each line to itemise what they needed to do. She asked Clive what he thought, and there was little to disagree with. The biggest expense would be the kitchen and bathroom. By the time they went to bed, they had a plan for the next two years, room by room.

'I suppose that if you didn't take charge, nothing would get done,' he said as they made their way upstairs.

'Shush. You'll wake Chloe.'

'I mean it,' he added as he shut the bedroom door. 'I don't mind.'

'We're a good team.'

194

Clive found that he had time to do everything. Marie was up at seven in the morning, and Clive rose with her. After breakfast, they did the washing up together, and he tidied the bedroom and loaded the washing machine before he left for work. It became a pleasure, not a chore.

Over the months, they stripped and painted windows, walls and ceilings. Clive bought tools he had remembered using at school and recalled some of the skills that he had been taught. Where there were gaps in his knowledge, he bought DIY books. When others in the road found out what Clive and Marie were doing, they offered guidance and help. It was not long before they sought his advice, which he offered with the self-assurance of a professional. Neighbours knew local craftsmen who would do jobs at short notice and at competitive prices. He found a thriving alternative economy, based on self-help, barter and favours offered and repaid. It was the type of out-of-the-ordinary system that Clive was happy to endorse.

One evening, they were decorating the living room.

'Let's look what's behind there, Clive.'

He had levered a piece of plywood away from a fireplace surround.

'Oh, yes, it's got the original fireplace and cast iron grate,' Marie said. 'Look at those tiles. Why did they cover them up? You can buy stuff to shine the cast iron too. I'll do that next week.'

'We can't have carpet with an open fire, can we?'

Marie put her arm round Clive's waist.

'We'll have to strip the floor and seal it.'

'We?'

'Well, you know what I mean, and you did such a brilliant job of the stairs and hallway.'

'You always get your own way.'

'If you're not happy with it…'

'It's fine.'

'D'you mean it?'

'Of course I do. You've got an eye for design and detail, and you always pick the right fabric and colour. I'm pleased with what we've done so far.'

Nothing was too much for Clive. Carpets were lifted and floorboards revealed. Dark lacquer was removed, and exposed wood was sanded and sealed. Upstairs, new carpets were laid, a bathroom fitted, curtains made and furniture bought. When the inside of the house had been completed, Marie talked about having friends round for a dinner party. Clive gulped and then explained his classification system. Only 'type ones' were invited.

In the spring, the back garden was dug, grass sown and vegetables planted. Clive had never imagined the pleasure to be gained from watching things grow. In the summer evenings, he sat on a garden bench, beer in hand, amazed by his own good fortune. Marie would wave from the kitchen, and if Chloe was asleep, would join him with a glass of wine.

At first, the money was tight, but after a couple of years, they could afford a holiday together in Spain. At about the same time, they decided to try for another child. A second pregnancy did not happen as planned. At first, it was not a matter of concern, and they made light of it. Marie looked in books and magazines and worked out when she would be most fertile, but still nothing happened. Then Marie started making excuses, and she did not seem to enjoy sex anymore. Clive began to worry.

'Perhaps we need to get advice,' he said one evening. It was a few months before Chloe's fifth birthday.

'Stop making mountains out of molehills.'

'Well, do you want another baby?'

'If it happens, it happens.'

'That's a change. When we first got married, you were keen to have a large family.'

'Well, I'm not now!'

'No need to shout.'

'Well, stop being so aggravating.'

'Why can't we talk about it?'

'We talk about it all the time.'

'Yes, but not finding out what's wrong.'

'I'm not having a doctor prodding me around if that's what you think. Go and see if the problem's with you.'

'Let's go together.'

'No.'

'You're being stubborn and irrational.'

'No, I'm not,'

'And irritating.'

She's not telling me everything.

These conversations recurred, and Marie refused to budge. Reluctantly, Clive stopped talking about this prohibited subject.

24

MARIE

Marie returned to work in September 1989, the same time that Chloe started at primary school. Marie found that working was exhausting. In the evenings, Clive got into the routine of cooking, but Marie did not seem to enjoy his food.

Marie had been back at work for a few weeks. Chloe was upstairs in her bedroom, and Clive and Marie were in the living room, watching television. Marie was at one end of the settee, legs along its length and feet rested on Clive's lap.

'You look shattered,' said Clive, massaging Marie's feet. 'If it's too much, you'll have to stop. You're not eating well, either.'

'I'm fine. It'll get easier when I'm in the routine. Stop nagging.'

'I'm not nagging, I'm concerned.'

Marie moved to get more comfortable.

'You couldn't get me some paracetamol for my backache.'

'You've had this backache for months now, and the painkillers aren't doing any good. You need to have it looked at.'

'Just get the paracetamol and some water. If it doesn't get any better, I'll go to the doctor.'

At first, Marie blamed the wooden chairs at school for

her pain and the stress of work for her tiredness. By October, Marie's numbing back pain had worsened. Even the strongest non-prescription painkillers did not alleviate it. As soon as Marie started bleeding, she arranged an appointment with the doctor. She told Clive that she was seeing him about her backache.

The doctor completed a thorough examination.

'You'll need to see a specialist. There's nothing to worry about. It's not likely to be anything serious,' she said.

Marie wondered what the doctor had meant. She was being deliberately vague. Marie prepared her response for Clive, who was bound to ask how it went. She repeated what the doctor had said.

The first hospital doctor conducted a general examination, followed by tests. Nothing was conclusive, and she went back for a second appointment, which was with a gynaecologist. He examined her, asked detailed questions about her sexual history and immediately booked another appointment for the following week. None of the doctors seemed anxious about her back. They were looking elsewhere.

'What did the doctors say?' asked Clive casually.

'Just routine tests.'

The tests may have been routine for the doctors and nurses, but they were not routine for Marie.

'So what sort of doctor was it? Did you see a back specialist?'

'It was just a doctor.'

'That doesn't make sense. He must work in some department or other.'

'He's a gynaecologist. It's probably something gynaecological. Look, I don't like talking about women's problems, so stop going on about it.'

'Marie,' Clive pleaded, 'We used to talk about everything.'

'Not this, we don't. I'm back next week, and I'll find out more.'

She saw the gynaecologist first thing in the morning, and he sent her for further tests and x-rays. She had become known by a few of the staff, who engaged her in chat, but she was not in the mood. Marie started to think that it was all part of the softening up; preparing her for the knockout blow that she knew was coming.

Why are gynaecologists always men?

She was invited into the consulting room by a middle-aged nurse.

And why are the nurses women?

The gynaecologist was a short, thin and middle-aged man. He started talking about the test results, but Marie was not listening. She was preparing herself for bad news, and her mind was wandering.

What about Chloe? How do I tell Clive? I can't face Mum and Dad.

Then she tried to force herself to think optimistic thoughts, but it did not work. She knew that there was not going to be a positive outcome. She visualised families boarding trains for concentration camps. They pretended they did not know. They even convinced themselves that it was for the better, but in the end, it made no difference what they thought.

The doctor did not seem aware that she was not paying attention, but perhaps he was used to it. She had been on the ropes for five minutes when the knockout punch hit her.

'I'm afraid, Mrs Parkhouse,' the doctor said in a deep monotone, 'that you have cervical cancer.'

She felt like telling the fool that she knew, but the blow knocked all the breath from her lungs. He explained the possible treatments, and Marie tried to concentrate on what he was saying. Then he said something about secondary tumours. There was nothing they could do. She was falling to the canvas, but the blows were still raining in. Was there anything she wanted to ask? She was floored. His words were devoid of meaning, so she did not have any questions. He asked her whether she had understood. It was almost a taunt. She sat motionless and did not reply. She just wanted this to stop.

The room was silent, and then she asked, 'When will I die?'

Her mouth was dry, and she croaked her words.

'It's very advanced, Mrs Parkhouse. It is not possible to be sure. It will be a matter of months.'

Marie walked for two hours and arrived home in the middle of the afternoon. She had arranged for a neighbour to pick Chloe up from school, and she dropped Chloe off and hoped everything had gone well. That afternoon, Clive was at a meeting with the programme controller. He would be home after his evening roundup had finished.

'Are you alright, Mum?' asked Chloe when she had finished her tea.

'Yes. Go and play in your room.'

Chloe could see that her mum was upset, but she did as she was told.

Marie was upstairs when Clive arrived back, and he called her. Marie came down and took a seat at the kitchen table. Clive was making a cup of tea and had his back turned.

'It'll be a minute,' he croaked.

Please don't turn round, Clive. I can't bear to see the pain in your face.

'It's cancer, Clive,' she blurted. 'I'm barely forty, and I've got cervical cancer.'

Clive, who had been pouring milk into two mugs, froze. He closed his eyes and mumbled.

'God, no.'

Slowly, he put the milk jug down.

'It's too late. They can't do anything. What about Chloe? What about you? I've got so much to live for. It's not fair. It's just not fair.'

Marie began crying.

Clive turned, walked across the kitchen and sat next to her. His jaw had dropped vacantly open. He held her cold hand. Her body shivered with each wretched sob.

'I want to say something positive, but there isn't anything; nothing to console you, nothing optimistic, nothing, nothing.'

Clive was about to speak, but she eased her hand from his grip and put it across his gaping mouth.

'Don't talk, Clive. I know you want to, but just let me alone.'

Clive did as he was asked. He avoided talking about Marie's illness to her. He took over all domestic chores, and he organised his work so that he could provide Marie with everything she needed. She stopped teaching. Clive took Chloe to school before he went to work, and he picked her up in the afternoon. In the evenings, Clive and Marie shared a bottle of wine together. It seemed to ease the pain and the tension for both of them, but Marie refused to talk about her cancer.

It was late November, just after Clive had dropped Chloe off after school. He had gone back to work, and Chloe was scribbling on a piece of paper.

'Why have you stopped teaching, Mum?' Chloe asked.

'I'm not well.'

'Is it your back?'

'No, not really.'

'What is it then?'

'It's something in my tummy.'

'When will it be better?'

'I don't know. It may take a while.'

Chloe looked up at her mum, who was fighting back tears. Chloe hesitated, thinking.

'It's alright, Mum. Me and Dad'll look after you, till you get better.'

Marie leaned over and hugged Chloe.

'I know you will, love. I know you will.'

Marie told school and friends that she had stopped working because of her bad back. As Marie became weaker, Clive worked harder. Late one evening, with Christmas approaching, Marie and Clive were watching television in the living room. Marie was on the settee and Clive in the armchair. She sensed that Clive was watching her, not the screen.

'You OK, Clive?'

'Fine.'

'You're not. Something's up.'

He hesitated.

'Come on,' she urged.

'We have to talk, Marie, we just have to talk,' he pleaded. 'I can't go on like this. It's killing me; the silence is claustrophobic. It's wearing me down. You have to share it, for you, for us.'

'Come here, Clive,'

She beckoned him, and he sat next to her on the settee.

'I'm sorry. I know, I know,' she said.

She put her arm round him and pulled him close.

'Clive, it'll be my last Christmas. I want you and Chloe to remember sharing it with me. I don't want anyone to know until afterwards. Not parents, friends, family, work, nobody. Whatever happens, this fucking cancer won't get me before Christmas; fucking, fucking, fucking cancer. See, there, I said the word.'

'What word was that, "fucking" or "cancer"?'

They laughed because Marie rarely swore. The use of the dreaded 'c' word somehow lifted the burden. Then they cried.

Arms intertwined they held each other tight and sobbed. She told him about the events leading up to the diagnosis.

'I'm sorry, Clive. I'm sorry for lying.'

'You haven't lied; you've just not told me everything.'

'It's much worse than that, Clive. I've known for a while, and I could have done something.'

'Don't say that.'

'I had problems some years ago, before we met. It wasn't cancer but serious problems; a virus. It was from sex, and I had quite a few boyfriends.'

'Please Marie, please.'

Clive wiped away the tears from his cheeks with the back of his hand.

'I have to tell you now. Doctors weren't sure of the link back then, but they said it could cause cancer later on. I knew the signs, but I ignored them. I didn't want to tell you before we got married, and now it's too late. I pretended I was being honest with you, but I wasn't.'

'Shush. Please don't criticise yourself, please.'

Clive never again used the word *cancer* to Marie. It was as if the saying of the word was a tacit acceptance of the disease and its inevitable outcome, and he could not bring himself to do that. Marie started to use the word because she had to accept it and because if she accepted the course it would take, she would fill every day, brimful and overflowing. She organised her personal effects, putting photographs and jewellery in boxes. She gave Clive instructions about what Chloe should have and when. It would be her legacy.

By the time Christmas arrived, Clive could see the first significant outward signs of her illness, particularly loss of colour and weight. Marie put all her dwindling energy into making Christmas a time to remember. She bought a camera, and Clive took endless photographs.

Marie's mum and dad came for Christmas dinner, and Clive's parents joined them for Boxing Day. Marie's mum said that she looked a little drawn, but Marie brushed her off with a white lie. In January, Marie phoned her mum and told her. Her mum phoned Marie's sister, and the house was flooded with her family. Clive explained to his parents that the family visits were a stressful time for Marie, and they paid just one visit. As Chloe, Clive, and Marie waved his parents goodbye, Chloe turned to her mum.

'Why is everyone coming to visit? They never used to.'

Clive closed the door, and Marie took Chloe by the hand and led her to the living room. She sat down and Chloe cuddled up to her. Clive sat opposite, in the armchair.

'It's because… It's because they won't be able to see me soon.'

'Why?'

Clive could not bear to listen and started to get up.

'Don't go, Clive, please.'

Clive sat back.

'Because I'm not going to get better.'

There was a short hiatus before each question.

'You're always going to be poorly?'

'No, Chloe. I'm going to be poorly, and then I won't be here.'

'Are you going to hospital?'

'You remember your Uncle Philip?'

'He died, didn't he?'

'Yes, he died. He went to heaven.'

'Are you going to heaven, Mum?'

'Yes, I'm going to heaven.'

'Where's heaven?'

'Oh, I don't know. Somewhere in the sky, I think.'

'Will I see you again?'

'No, but you can remember me. You must remember me, Chloe. Will you promise?'

'Cross my heart,' said Chloe making the sign. 'I don't want you to go.'

'I don't want to go either.'

Chloe was thoughtful for a few seconds before Marie gave her a squeeze.

'Not so hard, Mum, you're bony.'

'Go to your bedroom and play.'

Chloe went to the door and looked at her mum in a new light.

'Off you go,' said Marie.

Clive got up and sat next to his wife.

'That was… wonderful. You're a beautiful woman. I do love you so.'

'I had to tell her as best I could, Clive. You need to explain things properly when she's older.'

Chloe did not fully understand what was happening, and she asked her mum questions over the next few days. Being an irreligious family, the notion of heaven was not something that they had discussed before. It took a while to explain that there were not any visiting hours. It was impossible to explain the concept of *forever*.

25

CLIVE

After Christmas, Marie's deterioration was rapid because the cancer had spread to her lungs. She became bedridden, and Clive took time off work to care for her. Nurses provided pain relief and support. Marie now took only one glass from the bottle they had shared equally only weeks before. At first, Clive left the bottle unfinished, but as Marie became weaker, the bottle was emptied. Clive could not endure the sight of her physical deterioration, and the drink gave him the valour that was not there by nature.

Clive sat with her whenever he could. Sometimes, they said nothing, and he was careful not to force her to talk when she did not want to. She whispered to him early one evening.

'Clive, sometimes I wish it was all over.'

'No, Marie.'

'We can't stop what's happening. I'm not in pain because the nurses are doing a good job, but I can't bear the upset I'm causing you and Chloe.'

'No, you're not.'

'I can see it in your eyes. I want you and Chloe to remember me, but not like this. The longer it lasts, the more painful the memories. You've to get on with your lives.'

Clive held her cold hands. They were skin and bone. He had run out of things to say. Their lives had been optimistic and forward-looking, but Marie had no future, and he could not find words of comfort.

'Can I come in?' shouted Chloe from outside the bedroom. 'I'm ready for bed.'

'OK,' said Clive. 'Hands, face, teeth, all clean?'

She rushed in, held out her hands and bared her teeth as evidence.

'Story, Mum?'

'I'm too tired, love.'

'I'll read to you both,' said Clive.

'Can you get *The Worst Witch*, Dad?'

'OK. *The Worst Witch* it is.'

Clive fetched the book, and when he returned, Chloe had snuggled under the duvet, next to her mum. He could see that Marie was exhausted, and by the time he had read the first two pages, she had fallen asleep. Clive beckoned Chloe to get out of the bed, but she shook her head, and Clive left them together. He went downstairs to eat, and when he came back, they were both asleep. He switched the light off, lifted Chloe back to her own bed, and neither Chloe nor Marie woke.

Marie caught pneumonia. The remorseless cancer sucked the strength from her body, and she had nothing left to fight. Marie's spirit faltered, and Clive knew that she had decided not to resist any longer. The nurses told Clive that the end was near, and Marie slipped in and out of consciousness. Clive and Chloe stayed at her side. Clive held Marie's hand. It felt cold, but that was how it had felt for months. Occasionally, she twitched as she dozed, and Clive gave a tender squeeze. Her breathing was so feeble that is was impossible to tell the moment that she died. The nurse, who was at the bedside with them, felt for a pulse and nodded at Clive.

'We can leave Mum now, Chloe. There's nothing more we can do.'

Chloe leant over her mother and kissed her cheek. She bit her bottom lip and silently walked out and into her own bedroom. The nurse left, and Clive kissed the same spot.

'I'll never stop loving you,' he whispered.

It was the end of winter, and Clive found it impossible to find any comfort in his darling wife's death. The preparations for the funeral diverted his attention for a few days, but Chloe and Clive barely spoke. He heard her sob in her room, and he tried to console her, but there was nothing he could do except let her cry herself to sleep. He felt helpless.

Condolence cards crashed through the letterbox. They talked of 'going to a better place' or 'one more star in the sky'. Clive squirmed and piled them one on top of another, face down, on the kitchen table.

'They don't get it,' he mumbled to himself. 'It's just a nasty, unforgiving death for someone who didn't deserve it. No half-thought-through cliché is going to change that.'

Before the funeral, he picked up the cards and threw them in the dustbin.

Marie's parents tried to help, but they were as distraught as Clive and Chloe, and neither he nor Chloe wanted company.

Every weekday, Clive made Chloe a packed lunch, took her to school and then went straight to work. He picked her up in the afternoon and made her tea. He employed a childminder, and she looked after Chloe until he arrived home in the evening.

Clive and Chloe missed Marie most at meals and bedtime. Marie had enjoyed Chloe's company in the kitchen. Chloe would chatter excitedly, unable to hide her pleasure at some new experience, or she would ask her mum to look at something she had drawn or scribbled. Clive would sit at the table and moan about work or politics, and Marie would sympathise or provoke. Marie had been the catalyst, and they became aware of the space in their lives that she had filled.

The more Clive tried to fill the gap, the more they were both aware of what was missing. Mealtime conversations became stilted and finally almost stopped. Clive immersed himself in cooking, and they both ate in silence.

Bedtime had been a battle when Marie was alive. Chloe would try to delay the moment, not because she was not tired, but because it had been a challenge to think up a new ruse to buy extra minutes downstairs. Marie had usually read a story and then, as Chloe had got a little older, the task had been shared with Clive if he had managed to get home in time.

Although Chloe liked the childminder, a jolly woman in her sixties who liked to be called Auntie Sheila, she always waited for her dad to put her to bed. Clive read her a story, and they had a cuddle, but the ordered regime with Auntie Sheila was no substitute for the chaos Chloe had enjoyed with her mum. The house became a quieter, more ordered and less fun place.

For a while, he stopped drinking wine at home because it reminded him of those last weeks of Marie's life, but after his morning stint at the radio station, he would find reasons to spend occasional lunchtimes at the pub. There was usually someone celebrating something; a birthday, an engagement, or a birth. At home, there were constant reminders of Marie, but at the pub, he could forget. Where the others had one drink, Clive began to have two and gradually, over the months, the lunchtime pub visit became the routine it had been before he had met Marie.

Weekends were precious for Clive and Chloe. They tidied

the house and shopped together. They had lunch out, went to the cinema, walked to the park, and Clive took her to her friends, or they came to visit Chloe. What struck Clive was Chloe's growing ability to adapt to events compared to his own lack of resilience. She appeared to be gradually coming to terms with her mother's death.

Clive never let on to her the void he felt. In the evenings, the loneliness seemed to drain his body of life. He saw visions of his love, first in all vitality and then pallid in death. Every object in the house had an association with her. With every draw of the curtains she had sewn, every push on a door she had painted, or meal from a plate she had chosen, there was a reminder of what was lost forever. He hoped that Chloe never had the same thoughts.

Drinking at lunchtime eased the daytime hours, but it did not help the evenings when Chloe was asleep. These were the hours when Clive and Marie had enjoyed each other's company. It was when they had talked, argued, laughed and even played like children together. In the evenings, he started to take an extra glass of red wine. The more he drank to banish these thoughts, the more he needed to drink. At lunchtime, drink was a social habit; in the evenings, it was out of loneliness.

For the first few months, Clive and Chloe were close. Chloe was dependent on her dad. He was a provider, and he filled some of the gap left by her mum. At first, Clive was mother and father in their depleted family. Slowly, as she grew older and his drinking increased, Chloe took over some of her mother's role for herself.

By the following winter, an empty wine bottle crashed into the dustbin most evenings. On the anniversary of Marie's death, having dropped Chloe off at school, Clive returned to the house. The date was not marked on the diary, never discussed with Chloe, or with anyone at work, but Clive felt the fear of Damocles, with just a single hair holding the mighty sword suspended above him. His hands were shaking, and his mind was focussed on a dark image of Marie lying dead in their marital bed. He forced himself to think other thoughts, but the morbid image returned.

Clive had so much to say, so much to unburden, but no one to talk to. He started to whisper to Marie, as if she was seated opposite him, still alive, smiling and sympathetic. He talked about the times they had shared and how he missed her. Less than half an hour later, a wine bottle dropped into the bin. Before his morning programme started, the programme controller sensed that Clive had been drinking. He knew that Clive took an occasional drink, they all did, but he had never come into work like this.

'Are you alright, Clive?' he asked.

''Course I'm alright,' was the hostile and untruthful answer.

'Look, I'm only asking. I know you've had a hard time recently.'

Clive lunged forward and jabbed his finger against the controller's shirtfront. The controller could smell the alcohol on Clive's breath.

'You don't know anything, you arsehole. I can do this show with my eyes shut. Let's get on with it.'

The controller reminded Clive of the interviewees. There were three guests that day, a police inspector who had walked from Land's End to John o' Groats for charity, a steel worker who had lost his job and was emigrating to New Zealand to work on a sheep farm and a local schoolgirl from a working class family, who had won a scholarship to an American university.

'It's sensitive, Clive. Just because he's a copper, you don't have to have a go at him about the Hillsborough Stadium disaster.'

'I know my job.'

The programme started with the usual roundup of local news. The first guest was introduced, and the controller realised that Clive was slurring. The policeman seemed unaware and responded to the questions about his month-long trip for about five minutes.

'What about the charity? Did you consider donating to the Hillsborough victims?'

'My God!' said the controller. 'What's he asking that for?'

'No, no, it's going to a cancer charity. I've supported it for years.'

The policeman was beginning to realise that something was amiss.

'I just thought, you know, you might,' he hesitated, 'because the police must take some blame, for the deaths,' another hesitation. 'You might think it would be a good gessure, gesture to make,' he slurred.

'I'm sorry but that's not true. The police...'

'But it is, isn't it? The report on the disaster said police evidence was evasive. That's a eupha, a eupherism, a euphemism, I think.'

Clive smiled at his inability to enunciate the word.

'I've come on the programme to talk about my walk, not Hillsborough.'

The first complaints had already started to arrive from listeners who realised that Clive was inebriated.

'You were there, weren't you, at Hillsborough? A lot of people from Liverpool think the police mishandled the sishuation, and thas why so many fans died,' Clive slurred.

The police inspector attempted a diplomatic answer but Clive would not let him speak.

More listeners, who were expecting a leisurely chat about a charity walk, phoned in. Telephone lines became jammed. The programme controller was gesticulating to Clive, unaware of the impression he was giving, to calm down. The police inspector was indicating that he would leave, and that they should stop the programme.

'The police tried to blame innocent fans. That's true, isn't it?'

'I'm not taking more of this hostile questioning...'

By this time, the managing director had ordered the programme to be stopped. The sound was turned off, to end embarrassment for the police officer, the management and the listeners. There was a brief apology, and Musak was played until the next programme started.

The controller and managing director burst into the studio.

'What the hell do you think you're doing?' shouted Clive.

'What do you think *you're* doing?' replied the controller.

Clive was almost dragged by the managing director into his office, in full view of the fuming policeman.

'Get your hands off me,' Clive shouted.

'What the hell are you playing at? You're bloody pissed, aren't you?' said the managing director.

'I'm not pissed. I've had a drink but I'm not pissed.'

'You've had a drink? It's not even lunchtime and you've had a drink. What the hell's up with you? I can't have you working here. You've had long enough to get over your domestic problem.'

'Domestic problem! Marie wasn't a fucking domestic problem, you prick. Marie was my wife. How dare you talk about her like that.'

'I didn't mean to... I'm sorry.'

'Sorry? You're sorry?'

'If you need some more time, that's fine. Perhaps you could take some leave. Take a break, but don't come to work drunk.'

'If I want a drink, then I'll have one. I don't need your advice, your fucking job or this two-bit radio station.'

'That's your choice, Clive.'

Clive stormed out and was in the pub all afternoon. He noticed that Dennis was uncommunicative, and he guessed why. He went straight from the pub to pick Chloe up. She did not kiss her dad before bed because he smelt so strongly, a smell that made her feel sick.

She lay on her bed listening to the music being playing downstairs. It was the same song, 'Love Minus Zero/No Limit', repeated time after time. She did not understand what all of the words meant, and she was unaware that Bob Dylan had penned them, but she knew that they had been written about her mother because Chloe and her dad always thought about her when they were alone. The wind rattled the window and the rain drummed against the panes. She began to mime the now familiar words to herself. She saw her mother, watching through her bedroom window, and she cried herself quietly to sleep.

That evening, there was a formal complaint to the radio station from the police, and extracts from the interview received national newspaper coverage, but Clive was unaware.

26

CLIVE

The next morning, Chloe got herself out of bed and poured cereal into her bowl. Her dad was still asleep. She knocked quietly on his door, and he stirred.

'It's breakfast time, Dad.'

She half-filled her dad's cereal bowl and left it on the table. Clive staggered downstairs, dressing himself on the way. He was buttoning up a shirt and tucking it into his trousers. He had nothing on his feet. He filled the kettle for a cup of coffee. His hair was dishevelled, and he scratched it vigorously with both hands. Chloe had taken an open bottle of milk from the fridge. She dribbled a little into her bowl and began eating.

'Could I have a dippy egg, Dad?' she asked.

Without speaking, Clive boiled water and then lowered the egg on a spoon. He made his coffee and sat down opposite his daughter as she finished her cereal.

'Is it time, Dad?' she asked.

'Another minute,' he croaked, looking at his watch.

'Are you poorly, Dad, like Mum?'

'No, I'm not poorly, love. I'm…'

Clive was holding back his tears.

'It's all right, Dad.'

'I'm just very, very sad.'

'I'm sad too. I still miss Mum.'

Her bottom lip trembled as she tried to be brave.

'I miss her giving me cuddles. I dream of her,' she continued. 'I dream of her nearly every night. I don't want her to be sad about us, Dad. I want her to be happy.'

'Me too,' said Clive, and he got up from the table and sat next to Chloe. He hugged her tightly.

'I'm not as good as your mum at this, am I?'

'No, but it's nice. Don't let go yet.'

The water bubbled over onto the hotplate and hissed. Clive rushed across, lifted out the egg on a spoon and dropped it into a chicken-shaped eggcup. He buttered a slice of bread and cut it into soldiers. Chloe propped up her head with her left hand as she ate her egg. Clive knew what she was thinking, and he was thinking about Marie too.

Clive opened the door to take Chloe to school and was startled by the flash of cameras and a group of reporters shouting questions. He saw a television camera pointing at him and said nothing as he pushed past the melee with his frightened daughter. He fled too speedily for his pursuers, and he left Chloe at the school gate.

The incident did not pass unnoticed. As well as featuring on local television, he was news in all of the tabloids, with unflattering photographs and moralising text, which did not improve his standing in local pubs. He noted that Marcus Roache's paper was particularly vitriolic.

Clara Tomlin wrote to him, a beautiful and sympathetic letter, enclosed in a handmade card. Clara had obviously gone out of her way to find out the full story. She left a home number to phone and a promise of work contacts if necessary. He placed the card on the mantelpiece and proudly read it to Chloe that evening.

Over the next few months, the balance of power shifted further. Chloe started to look after herself and later, in small ways, her dad. She got herself up every morning and made her own breakfast. She placed the packed lunch, which her dad had made the previous evening and put in the fridge, into her Postman Pat lunchbox. She made her way to school, tagging along with the mothers of her friends, and she came home in the evenings with them. She enjoyed school and preferred it to being at home. Auntie Sheila was no longer required.

Clive made tea and Chloe helped. Clive would not let her use the cooker. He read to her most evenings after she had got herself ready for bed. She cleaned and tidied her own room as best she knew how, and although Clive occasionally pulled out the vacuum cleaner, the house became untidy and dirty. Sometimes, when the sink was full, Chloe would fill it with hot water, and Clive would guiltily wash up and dry, with help from Chloe.

She dragged her dad round the supermarket. Chloe picked the food for her lunchbox, and she made sure her dad put what they needed for the week in his trolley. He always bought wine.

Some evenings, she went round to her new friend Nasim's house. Nasim's mother always asked Chloe to check that it was OK with her dad. Chloe went inside through the unlocked back door. Clive always said that it was fine and told Chloe what time she had to be back. Occasionally, if he was upstairs or listening to music, she pretended that she had spoken to him, and with make-believe approval, quietly shut the door behind herself.

It was fifteen months after Marie had died, and Clive had spent all of the family savings. He had no income, and even with benefits, he began to get into debt. He argued with the bank manager, who refused an overdraft or loan. It was a shock, and for a few weeks, he did not drink at all. It was a struggle, but he started to feel better.

Marie's birthday came and went. Chloe wrote her mum a card and put it on the mantelpiece. When Clive saw it, the memories flooded back, and his sobriety ebbed away. That lunchtime, Clive went to the pub, The Clash thumping out in the background. He remembered the first time he had heard 'Should I Stay or Should I Go'. Marie and Clive had been to watch them at The Fair Deal Hall in Brixton in 1982. They had just married and Marie had wanted to see a band she loved.

It seemed to Clive to be an insult to use one of her favourite songs in an advert for jeans. At first, Dennis was indulgent toward Clive, allowing him a little credit, but he had no work and could not pay off his debts.

'I'm sorry, Clive, 'cos you're a good mate, and I don't like seeing you like this, but I've got a business to run, and I can't keep funding your boozing. You need to find a job and get busy. You're always welcome if you pay your way.'

Clive nodded ruefully. He said nothing, backed away from the bar, turned and left. At every pub he visited, he told customers that drink was the answer to his troubles, not the source of them. Soon, pub after pub refused to serve him because he drove custom away by attempting to cadge beer. Some publicans told him they did not want to be associated with a man who had disgraced himself on TV and had appeared, for the wrong reasons, on the front pages of every tabloid.

He started to sell things to pay for essentials. He sold personal possessions and then household valuables, such as ornaments and pictures. One lunchtime, just over two years after Marie had told him she had cancer, he had no money in his pocket and went upstairs to his bedroom. He opened Marie's chest of drawers. During her last months, Marie had spent much of her time collecting her treasures, and this was where she had placed them.

He knew that he was violating a sacred place. It had been forbidden territory throughout their marriage. He had never opened the top drawer, but he knew of the cardboard shoebox at the back. This was where Marie's private possessions were stored. He left the box in the open drawer. Beside it was her jewellery case. He pulled it out and sat on the bed, placing it beside him on the duvet. Marie had told him that there were things inside for Chloe when she grew up.

The case was leather, and a brass key was in the lock. He turned it and lifted the lid. There were items of jewellery he had never seen. He fingered the bracelets, brooches and chains and the engagement and wedding rings he had bought. They had not fitted her when she was ill because her fingers had become emaciated, and they had rubbed and made her knuckles sore. She had put them carefully in her jewellery box, ready for Chloe. These items were in a tray, which he removed. Beneath the tray, it was empty, except for an envelope. The envelope had one word on the front of it.

'CHLOE.'

It was a letter from Marie to her daughter, which Clive had been told to give her when she was sixteen. He had promised not to open it.

There was no food in the house, and he was desperate for a drink. He pocketed a gold bracelet and left the rest of the contents on his bed. The bracelet raised enough money for lunch, with some to spare. Clive did not consider any consequences. He had only the need for food and drink on his mind.

27

CHLOE

Clive had forgotten that Chloe would be home early that afternoon so that she could get ready for the school nativity play. She was an angel, and she had rehearsed nightly to sing two hymns, as part of the chorus. She arrived back from school and went to look for him.

The bedroom door was ajar, and she saw the open jewellery case. The jewellery attracted her attention, and when she got closer, she saw the envelope with her name on it. She was not sure who had written the letter, but it was addressed to her, and she presumed that it was from her mother.

She knew that the jewellery case was intended for her, and she guessed why her father had opened it. She fingered the jewellery guiltily, but with the warm feeling that her mother had worn all of the items. She wanted to touch every one and feel them adorn her, as they had her mother, but she knew that her father would work his way through them until they were all gone. She could not let him do it. She put the letter into the case and closed the lid on all its contents. It was her very own Pandora's Box.

She was about to go back into her room with the prize when she saw the drawer almost fully open. She guessed that it was where her mother had hidden the jewellery case. She went to shut it, as if it would somehow hide the secret that she had taken the case, but she saw the cardboard shoebox. She picked it gently out of the drawer and placed it on the bed next to the jewellery case. She lifted the lid. On the top of a pile of belongings was a picture of her mum and dad, hand in hand. They were much younger, and her dad looked much happier. She was attracted to the picture and carefully picked it up.

Underneath the picture was a letter addressed to her mum and other photographs, documents, postcards and letters. She took the case and the box back to her room and hid the jewellery under her bed. The box was what was important. She delicately fingered through it, picking out the photographs of her mother. She laid them out on her My Little Pony duvet cover, putting everything else in a pile next to the shoebox.

She placed the photographs in chronological order, and Chloe began to see herself in the photographs of her mum. Her mum was beautiful. Chloe picked up a pink mirror from her bedroom table and looked at herself and then at her mum. They had the same green eyes and long, straight, light brown hair. Chloe was slim like her mother but with a paler complexion.

She covered her duvet with photographs, and knelt on the floor at the side of the bed, scanning them with interest, joy and pride. The pictures of her mum started when she was a baby, on the top left of the bed, and the most recent were on the bottom right.

Minutes after having completed the organisation of the photographs, she heard her dad arrive back from the pub. He rushed upstairs to the toilet. He then went into the bedroom, and when he saw the still-open drawer, remembered what he had done earlier that day. He immediately realised that the jewellery case and the cardboard box had gone.

He calmly looked under the bed and then, wildly, everywhere in the bedroom. Suddenly the value of the jewellery was unimportant. The only things that mattered were the letter from Marie to Chloe and the promise he had made to Marie.

He became frantic. He rushed onto the landing and noticed that Chloe's light was shining from underneath her door. He remembered that she was in the nativity play that evening. She would be home early from school, and he had promised to take her. He realised where the box and case were. Chloe was rapidly tidying the photos when her dad knocked.

'Can I come in?'

'Yes,' was the reluctant reply.

Chloe had her back to the bed, facing her dad as he entered. She had cleared the bed of evidence.

'Hello, Chloe. I forgot you'd be back early,' he said nonchalantly.

'Hello, Dad,' was the sheepish reply.

'We need to get you ready for tonight. I left some things on my bed. You haven't picked them up have you?'

'What was it, Dad?'

'You know, Chloe. Mum's things,' he said indifferently.

'They were for me. Mum said that they were for me.'

Chloe was speaking with a determination in her voice, which took her father by surprise. It was Marie talking.

'But you weren't to have them until you're older. I'll keep things safe until then.'

'No, Dad.'

'What do you mean? You give everything back to me, now,' said Clive with a raised voice.

'I know what you'll do, Dad. You can't have any of it.'

'I'm your father, and you'll do what you're told!'

'She's my mum and I won't give it back. It was meant for me. You'll sell the jewellery. I won't let you!'

'How dare you! I'd never do such a thing,' he blustered.

Then Clive remembered what he had already done. He

put his right hand across his mouth, as if to stop himself telling another lie. He turned, walked back into his bedroom and slammed the door shut.

Chloe pulled the case and box from under her bed and put them on the duvet. She opened the box and sorted through the photographs, her mother's kind eyes watching her. She selected one of her mother when she was about eighteen and then closed the box. She quietly opened her door, and she could hear her dad sobbing in his bedroom. She guessed he was angry with her but could not understand why it made him cry.

She held the jewellery case in her left hand and wedged the box between her left elbow and her side, so that her right hand was free to knock on the door. She turned the doorknob and entered. Her dad turned and sat up on the side of the bed, facing her. He roughly cleared the tears from his reddened face.

Chloe walked across the room, box now transferred to her right hand and case in the left and handed them to her dad. He stretched out his arms to accept the gifts. In her right hand, there was also the single photograph.

'Can I keep this one, Dad?' Chloe asked sheepishly.

'Of course you can.'

Clive put the boxes to his left and lifted Chloe under her armpits, to sit at his right hand side. She could smell the stench of alcohol on his breath. He looked into the jewellery case and could see the unopened letter. He took it out and closed the lid.

'The letter's for you when you get a little older. Mum asked me to keep it safe. I've done a bad thing today, Chloe,' said Clive, sniffling and looking sideways and down at her. She stared forward.

'I've sold a piece of your mum's jewellery, to go to the

pub. I'd no right. I'll buy it back. I've been such a terrible dad, Chloe.'

'No you haven't. You're just very sad. I'm sad too. I don't think it'll last forever. My friend Nasim hasn't got a dad. He says that it was horrible at first, but he's got over it. It took a long time, and he still thinks of him, but it doesn't make him sad any more. It made his mum ill. She had to go to a special doctor, but she's better now. I don't think we'll ever forget Mum, but we'll get over being sad.'

Clive burst into a flood of tears. Chloe was unsure what to do, so she grabbed her dad's hand and held it between both of hers. He seemed unaware of what she had done. As his crying subsided, Chloe let go of his hand, sat on her dad's knee and put her arm around his neck.

'You keep the jewellery, Chloe. It's all for you. I'll keep the letter. I'll be a better dad to you. I promise, I will.'

They hugged for a few minutes more.

'You need to get ready for tonight. It's a big evening for you.'

'I'm just an angel, Dad.'

Clive laughed.

'Yes, you are.'

'It's not funny. It's from the Bible.'

'I've got to pop out. I won't be long.'

Chloe put the jewellery case under her arm, and Clive went downstairs and picked up a large brass carriage clock from the mantelpiece. It was unwieldy, but it might be worth a few days' drinking, and he needed a drink. From the top of the stairs, Chloe saw him put it under his coat, and she feared the worst. She went into her room with the jewellery case and put it carefully on her bed.

28

CLIVE

In twenty minutes, he was back. He rushed upstairs and knocked on Chloe's door. She opened it, timidly. He walked across to the bed and carefully placed the missing piece of jewellery into the open case. He left without speaking, had a shave, and soon they were on their way to school. It was the last time he wore a beard. He had promised to be a better father, and this was to be his statement of intent.

Mothers and children were shoaling in the school playground, and Clive kept his distance and made no eye contact. He had not attended this school ritual for many months and his absence had been noticed and talked about. The children carried the costumes, which they would put on in the classroom, in plastic bags. There was an air of excitement. Chloe found her friend Nasim, who was with his mother. She smiled in a friendly way at Clive and then walked across and spoke in a gentle Yorkshire accent. Night was closing in, and Clive could not see her clearly. She was a small and slim woman, with a scarf wrapped over her head and around her neck.

'You're Chloe's father?'

'Yes. You're Nasim's mother?'

'Yes. They've been friends for ages, but we seem to have avoided each other.'

'I'm very busy,' Clive said, and then he thought for a moment. 'No... that's just an excuse. I'm Clive.'

'I used to listen to you on the radio. I'm Ameera.'

'Hello.'

'It's shortened to Amee. You can call me Amee if you want,' she said shyly.

'Which do you prefer?'

'Ameera.'

'Thanks for having Chloe over, Ameera.'

'She's no bother. It's good for Nas to have a friend to play with, and they get on well.'

There was a call from a teacher, and the children rushed to their class. Ameera explained that she was helping and followed them inside. The school play was a resounding success and Chloe was tired but happy from her exertions. Clive walked home with Ameera and the two children, talking about the nativity play.

The following day Clive took Chloe to school in the morning and picked her up in the afternoon. He convinced himself that the other mothers were talking about him. Ameera was there in the evening, waiting for the children to come out of school. She was a little younger than Clive; late thirties, he thought. She was plain looking, with a warm smile. She wore a silk scarf, partly covering her hair, and a long dark skirt could be seen below her knee-length, blue winter coat. She walked across to speak to him. He was aware of the stares that followed her route across the playground. She smiled, and Clive smiled back.

The first shrill shouts of children leaving school cut the air, and Ameera turned to see the two friends rush headlong out of the main entrance toward their parents. Chloe launched herself, and Clive caught her in mid-air and held her. Chloe inhaled the soapy and clean smell, untainted by alcohol and kissed him on the cheek. The jump and kiss were from happier times. Nasim looked enviously at the flying leap and mid-air catch but turned away at the sight of the kiss.

'Hello. I'm Clive,' he said, and Nasim shyly presented his hand, in response to the one offered by Clive.

Nasim was a thin boy, shorter than Chloe and quiet.

'You're Nasim, aren't you?'

'Yes.'

Nasim responded to a shout from Chloe, who had jumped down and was off up the pavement.

Over the following weeks, Clive developed a routine, walking Chloe to school and bringing her back in the evening. At first, Ameera was the only mother to talk to him.

'Are the other mums frightened of my reputation?' asked Clive.

'No. I'm sure they all know about the interview on the radio,' said Ameera, 'but it's not that. It's difficult for them, you being the only dad, and they aren't sure what to say. They'll get used to you.'

Gradually, the mothers 'adopted' him as the only single father in the group. After breakfast, Chloe would look out of the window and shout when Ameera and Nasim were passing. Clive and Chloe would join them, and others met them on the way. Although he felt awkward at first, it became a schedule that he enjoyed, but he did not mention Marie.

He started to get up before Chloe, to make breakfast. He made perfunctory attempts to clean and tidy the house. By lunchtime each day, he was trying to persuade himself that he did not need a drink. To take his mind off alcohol and to take himself away from opportunity, he would walk up the Mayfield valley, along Porter Clough and out of sight of any pub. Over the weeks, the walk became a pleasure.

He arranged another meeting with the bank manager. Clive convinced him that he had stopped drinking and would be able to find work within a few months. Clive was encouraged to sell Marie's car to raise cash, and on that basis the bank manager allowed him an overdraft, which he would review in six months. This would enable him to pay his outstanding bills, and if frugal, the spare cash would provide him with a few months' breathing space. Marie's car was parked in the garage, and Clive could not bring himself to drive it. He advertised it and sold it privately to a buyer who came to the house, reversed the car out of the garage, inspected it and offered him a fair price. Once the money had been cleared, the buyer picked the car up, and Clive breathed a sigh of relief.

The routine of walking to and from school encouraged him to stay sober. He did not want to embarrass himself, Chloe or any of the mothers. On most days, he walked the last hundred yards home with Ameera, and they talked. The conversations were never about themselves. After Christmas, Ameera invited Chloe to her house on a number of occasions, and Clive decided it was only fair to reciprocate.

'Tomorrow, Nasim can come to ours if he wants.'

'Are you sure?'

'I'll make them tea. What does he like?'

'He'll eat whatever Chloe eats.'

'That'll make it easy.'

'I'll help… perhaps not.'

Ameera was flustered.

'It's all right. I'll make them tea, and we can have a cuppa.'

'I was thinking that we've not long met, and I've invited myself round your house.'

'I'll not tell if you don't,' Clive smiled. Smiling was not something he had done very often recently, and it felt good. 'Tomorrow evening after school?'

Clive wondered what he'd let himself in for. What would Ameera think when she saw the mess in the house? Everyone

at Chloe's school would find out. What a stupid mistake! Clive
told Chloe about the invitation and reassured her that things
would be OK.

'I know they will, Dad,' she said.

Chloe told her dad what Nasim liked to eat. Chloe made
sure that they had enough bread in the bread bin, and Clive
went to the corner shop and bought Alphabetti Spaghetti.
That evening, after he had read Chloe a story, she rubbed his
shaven chin and smiled.

'I think it's getting more... more like it used to be.'

'Yes, I think it is.'

'Do you think Mrs Karim's nice?'

Clive had not thought about the matter, and not wishing
to annoy Chloe, he nonchalantly said, 'Yes, she seems very...
yes, very pleasant.'

'I do too.'

Clive resolved to pay Mrs Karim more attention.

He slept badly. He was anxious to make a good impression
and got up early to give the house a top-to-bottom clean.
Making breakfast, cleaning, tidying and shopping absorbed all
of his time that day, and he missed his customary walk. He
counted the days and realised that it was now more than a
month since he had taken a drink. It was not easy.

He spoke to Nasim on the way back from school.

'We've got your favourite for tea.'

Nasim's forehead wrinkled, mystified that Chloe's dad
should know what his favourite tea was when he did not know
himself. The walk home was slow. The children ran off in
various directions, playing games with their friends, and they
had to be rounded up. The mothers peeled off to their own
homes, one at a time. Chloe and Nasim skipped ahead, and
Clive and Ameera were alone.

'How long have you lived here?' Clive asked.

'A few months.'

'I've been here about ten years, I suppose. Where were you before?'

'It's a bit complicated.'

'Oh.'

'I had to sell our other house in Dore. My husband died a while ago, and the money ran out. I've just started back at work, part-time.'

'I'm sorry.'

Ameera shrugged.

'What do you do?' Clive asked.

'I'm a doctor.'

'Nearby?'

'Yes, it's a small practice where I can fit work in with school. It's a bit of a rush, but I enjoy it, and I need the money.'

'Nasim's a nice lad. It's good that they've made friends.'

They had arrived at Clive's house, and he opened the front gate. It was a detached building, built between the wars. The pebbledash upper half was painted cream and the lower was brick, with a bright red door and shiny white window frames. Although Clive and Marie had completely refurbished and modernised the house, an overgrown and untended front garden, weeds pushing between the paving slabs and one garage door not closing fully indicated lack of recent attention.

'Come in,' said Clive. 'We can have a chat.'

At that moment the two youngsters, who had run around the next corner, reappeared. Clive opened the door, and they all traipsed into the kitchen. Chloe noticed her dad's efforts to clean and tidy, and she smiled her appreciation. Ameera and Nas assumed it was the norm. Clive served tea, and the children ate quickly and went upstairs to play. Clive cleared the table and started the washing up. He would not let Ameera help. She sat at the kitchen table.

'Your wife died recently, didn't she?'

Clive did not answer.

'I'm sorry. I didn't... I didn't mean to be so direct.'

'No, no, no. It's... it's OK.'

Clive gathered his thoughts. He was leaning over the kitchen sink and did not turn to face Ameera when he replied.

'Yes. It's been tough on Chloe. I've not been the best dad.'

'But it's been tough on you too. You need time.'

'Two years. I'm sorry.' Clive hesitated. 'I don't know what to say. My mind is suddenly full of memories. I'm... I'm not thinking straight.'

'I was hopeless for the first couple of years, too.'

'It's the first time... the first time I've spoken about her since she died.'

'Don't talk about it just now, not until you want to. Sit down and listen.'

Clive sat opposite, and Ameera continued.

'Perhaps we have a lot in common. When Saajid died I... I lost my motivation. I had everything and it was taken away. I felt lonely, and I had nobody to talk to, you know, about what happened.'

'You must have had friends or family?'

'Yes, but nobody close enough to confide in. It's difficult...'

Ameera hesitated, and Clive gave her time to continue.

'I grew up close to my mother. She's a loner, and perhaps I'm a bit like her. We haven't spoken for years. We fell out over Saaj, and my mother and stepfather disowned me. I had to return to work to pay the bills, and my colleagues at the surgery helped me back to normality.'

'How long ago was it that your husband died?'

'It's over three years. Nas was very young. I don't think he really understood, and I'm not sure how much he remembers of his dad.'

'It must be difficult for him.'

'I don't know if it's better or worse not having memories.'

'What did your husband do?'

'He was a trader. He imported carpets and rugs, from Pakistan, Afghanistan and Iran. Saajid loved the risks, and even the birth of Nas couldn't change that.'

'It sounds exciting.'

'He was killed on the Afghan/Pakistan border. I never found out the details.'

Ameera stopped, as if to picture her husband. She took a deep breath and sighed.

'It must have been tough,' said Clive

'His passport was returned by an uncle in Pakistan, along with a wallet and a photo of the family he always carried. I looked out for him for months, in the street, on the bus, whenever anyone knocked, expecting a phone call. For all that time, I'm sure I was a bad mum.'

'Now who's being hard on themselves?'

'It's a beautiful house,' said Ameera, admiring the bright and modern kitchen.

'That was Marie. I've no idea about style, but it came naturally to her. She was into wooden floors, light furnishings and bright airy colours. I'm a bit old-fashioned myself.'

'She had good taste.'

Clive said nothing, and there was a long silence.

'I'm sorry, I keep putting my foot in it,' said Ameera.

'No, it's me.'

Clive hesitated again.

'There's no rush,' said Ameera.

'She was a beautiful woman,' Clive croaked. His eyes watered, and he dropped his head. 'We were so in love.'

Ameera waited for him to continue, but he could not speak.

'Have you got a picture?' she asked

Clive fetched a framed photograph from the hall but said nothing.

'You're right, very beautiful.'

'I was so lucky.'

'What do you do now you've left the radio station?'

'Nothing, except feel sorry for myself. Oh, and I got into the habit of drinking too much.'

'You've had to deal with a lot, but life hasn't come to an end. You can get back working again, I'm sure.'

'I have to because we need the money.'

'You were the best show on the radio.'

'Thanks.'

'I found it hard, starting work again, but I'm glad I did. It stops me thinking too much about the past. Life's got more bearable.'

'I'm in a rut.'

'Something's happened in the last month because you've suddenly reappeared, and Chloe's got a new lease of life.'

'I haven't had a drink for weeks. You *are* right; I've got to get working. I don't think anyone will let me into a studio again, but I could go back to reporting. That's how I started. The radio work began as a way of earning a little more money and boosting my ego.'

'You're running yourself down again. You're not like that.'

'How do you know what I'm like?'

'I know. I used to listen to you, every day when I was low.'

'I probably made things worse.'

He felt the warm pleasure of his laugh.

'No. I could tell you were a good man. You listened, you encouraged guests and the show wasn't just about you. Your personality shone through. Why not try the same sort of thing?'

'Honestly, nobody would have me. I've got people in the newspapers I could contact.'

'Ring them up.'

'I could do some freelance work. Maybe I've got a book or two in me? I don't know,' he sighed. 'Perhaps I've forgotten how to work.'

'You'll be alright once you start. It's like riding a bike. You never forget. It's the routine that's important. It stops you finding time to do all the bad things. You know; the things you need to avoid.'

'You mean the booze.'

'I didn't mean to…'

'It's OK.'

'I'm quite happy to have Chloe around in the evenings if you need time to get yourself started, or if you have to work late. She's no bother.'

'Why are you doing this, for goodness' sake?'

'Why not? It keeps me busy. It helps Nas. It might even help you. We single parents need to stick together, don't we? We're an oppressed minority,' she smiled and thumped the table theatrically. 'Mind you, I don't think we fit the stereotype.'

'Thanks. I might take you up on your offer. I'll probably have to go to London to get work. I've friends from university days who owe me a favour.'

Clive explained how he had worked on the university newspaper and then moved from the local paper to radio. The conversation drifted imperceptibly to his life with Marie and then about life without her. It was painful, but Ameera listened with smiles and knowing nods. She asked questions only when Clive stopped, and she waited patiently when he stumbled for words.

He spoke about Marie's death and his drinking. He admitted that he had sold possessions for food and drink and told her of the shame he felt. He could not look Ameera in the eye, and his voice dropped to a dull monotone.

'We all do things we regret when we're really down, you know. I'd got no family to rely on, and I thought about ending my life… and Nasim's too. I nearly did, more than once,' she whispered.

'I never felt like that.'

'I couldn't bear being alive, and I couldn't bear the thought of him having no mother or father. I didn't have the courage to do it. As a doctor, I'd plenty of opportunities.'

'Do that to your child, that's, well it's…'

'I know, a mother killing a child is evil, but that's not how I saw it.'

She was speaking so quietly that Clive could barely hear her.

'What made you think like that?'

'I was doing the only thing I could do to avoid two ruined lives. If I wasn't such a coward, I don't know, perhaps I could have gone through with it.'

'But you didn't, did you?'

'But I could have. I was so close, believe me.'

Clive was shocked. At first, she had seemed such a straightforward woman, but now he did not know what to make of Ameera. It was many weeks later that she explained the full story.

29

AMEERA

Ameera's father had been in Burma during the war, fighting in the British Army, and he had lost many of his friends in the conflict. He had been trained as an engineer, and before the war, he had worked on the railways. He was a Muslim in a Hindu area. When Hindus murdered his brother and family, he decided to move to Rawalpindi. He saw partition as a disaster and took the first opportunity to emigrate from Pakistan to Britain.

He was single when he arrived in the UK in 1949, and with his training, he quickly found work. He returned to Pakistan three years later to get married, and brought his young bride back to England with him. He spoke English, but his wife's first language was Urdu. She learned rudimentary English, understood reasonably when she had to, but Urdu was the only language she spoke at home, and she insisted that Ameera should do the same. Her father held down a regular job on the railways and bought a small semi-detached house in York.

'Ameera, turn that noise down,' her mother yelled in Urdu.

'It's not a noise; it's T Rex,' she shouted back in English.

'Off!' shouted her father, Ali, also in English. 'Ameera, come down now, please.'

He was not a Marc Bolan fan. She silently mimicked him, tapped the 'Stop' button on her cassette recorder, and her room was silent.

Ameera was dressed in jeans and a smock. Her black hair was cut to shoulder length. Her mother, Noor, did not like her casual dress and, almost daily, asked her to cover her head. Ameera refused.

Ali was standing in the living room, and Noor was sitting. Her father had adopted what Ameera called his 'military pose'. He was a small and thin man, straight-backed, with his hands clasped behind him. His chin jutted and he looked down his nose. Ameera thought that he was pompous. She stood opposite him, hands in pockets, defiantly.

'What's the matter, Father?'

'Mother and I don't like you mixing with that girl, you know, Sharon.'

'Why not? She's my best friend.'

He glanced back at her, and Noor stared downwards, her eyes fixed on a spot on the ornate rug in the middle of the room.

'For a start, I don't like that short skirt, showing her legs like that.'

'She's got nice legs. It's the fashion.'

'Don't be insolent; nice legs. What sort of talk is that? She shouldn't be showing herself. It didn't used to be like this. Back home, the wives and daughters behaved like ladies. The English used to set standards, but it's all gone downhill since then. Yes, and everyone knew their place. That included daughters who knew not to be rude to their fathers. Anyhow, she's a bad influence. I don't want her round here.'

'I'm sixteen, Father. I choose my own friends. If she can't come here, I'll just go to her house. Her mum and dad are friendly, not like you.'

'See, you don't respect your own father. Hang round with girls like her, and you won't get to university.'

'That's rubbish. She'll get straight As. She's cleverer than me.'

'I don't want you dressing like that.'

'I wouldn't wear a short skirt, not to please you, but because I don't want to. Anyhow,' she added, 'it wouldn't suit me.'

'See, you don't want to please me, or your mother.'

'I don't want to upset you, either, but I'm not going to be told what I can or can't do. I'm old enough to make my own mind up.'

'You're not. You're a sixteen-year-old girl.'

'What's being a girl got to do with it?' Ameera shouted at her father. 'I'm not going to do what you say, *just because I'm a girl.*'

'But I care about you, and I want you to do well.'

'You like me being clever, so you can boast at work.'

'Don't talk to me like that!'

'I am not going to let you bully me. I can't wait to get out of here, I just can't wait.'

Ameera stormed upstairs and slammed her door shut. The disagreement with her father was similar to many conversations over the previous months and many more that would be repeated until Ameera left for university.

Ever since Ameera could remember, Ameera's mother had talked to Ameera about her life in Pakistan. She had made no friends in York and had only Ameera to talk to. Ameera knew her mother had been depressed and ill after having given birth, and that she could not have any more children. Noor's heart was in Rawalpindi.

It was a shock to Ameera when her father died suddenly. He was only in his fifties. Ameera was in her first term studying medicine in London. During the Easter holiday, her mother started talking about returning to Pakistan.

'Your grandmother is very ill, and I have to go home,' said Noor. 'I want to see her before she dies.'

Her grandmother had visited when Ameera had been in her first year at secondary school. Ameera remembered it as the only time her mother had looked happy.

'We should both go this summer,' Noor continued.

'What about my summer job? I've got to save up for next term.'

'Just a few weeks. It's not much to ask. It'll be at the end of the summer holiday.'

'You're right. I didn't mean to be selfish. A few weeks in Pakistan would be a break, and I would like to see Nani too.'

The flights were booked. One evening, at the start of the summer holiday, Noor and Ameera were in the kitchen together.

'I want to move back to Pakistan. You know I'm not happy here, Ameera,' Noor said, in Urdu.

'You mean, leave England for good?'

'Perhaps you'll like Pakistan. They need doctors. I don't know. Living here isn't what I want.'

'I'm not going to work in Pakistan. I've got a life here in England. I'm English.'

'OK, OK. I'm not happy in England. Now you're at university, I've got nothing to do and nobody to talk to.'

'But you were never happy before. You were always arguing with father.'

'Ameera!'

'It's true.'

'Stop it.'

'Look, I'll get back to York, whenever I can. When I graduate, I'll probably move nearby.'

'But I'm lonely now. It'll get even worse when you start working in a hospital full-time. I have your father's life insurance and his pension. Then there's the house to sell and mortgage to pay off. That'll leave me some spare cash. I'll be well off back home – better off than here. I don't know what to do because I want to be near you, but I can't live in England anymore.'

'You could stay in York until I finish.'

Ameera's mother dropped her head into cupped hands and cried. Ameera hugged her and began to cry with her.

'You move to Pakistan, Mother. Next year, I'll find somewhere in London to stay permanently. I'm an adult.'

'But you're a woman on your own, in London, and I don't like that at all. In your first year, you were in student accommodation, but not next term. Perhaps I'll have enough money to buy a small flat in London for you.'

'No.'

'Don't you understand? There's no way out for me. I hate it here, but I can't leave you on your own. You'll enjoy Pakistan. There are people I'd like you to meet. They…'

'What people?'

'Friends and family,' she continued, in Urdu.

'English. Speak in English.'

'I might remarry. I am not so old. There is a man.'

'What man?'

'His wife died two years ago. I haven't met him.'

'Who is he? What does he do?'

'He is high up in the bank. His name is Parvez. I have a photograph. Here, look.'

Ameera glanced at the black and white photograph of a smiling, moustachioed, middle-aged face.

'He is a religious man, not like your father.'

'Not like you.'

'Mother, I'd be very happy for you to marry this man and for you to live in Pakistan if that's what you want, but my future's here.'

At the end of summer, mother and daughter boarded a plane to Pakistan. They took their two centre seats. Her mother had a Pakistani woman of a similar age next to her, and they were soon engrossed in conversation in Urdu. Ameera smiled at this transformation in her mother, and they had not even taken off. A man, who was quite a few years older than Ameera, sat next to her. He smiled and then started to read a magazine. Ameera was reading a book.

Not long after they had taken off, he turned to her.

'Visiting family?' he asked.

'Yes, I'm with my mother. We're visiting my grandmother, and we're staying with my great aunt. It's my first trip to Pakistan.'

'It'll be a culture shock.'

He had a hint of a public school accent, something Ameera had never heard in a Pakistani man. She assumed, by his looks, that he was Pakistani.

'I know.'

'Where are you staying?'

'Rawalpindi.'

Ameera explained that she had just finished her first year at medical school in London. He was travelling back to Pakistan. He also lived in London. He was sourcing stock for his trading company. Saajid seemed so different from the other Pakistanis Ameera had met – dashing, fun and exciting. He told her he was thirty, but there did not seem to be an age difference to her.

Ameera's mother became aware of the man talking to her daughter and elbowed Ameera in the ribs, but they continued non-stop. Ameera told Saajid about her family background, the recent death of her father, her mother's possible remarriage, and she explained that her mother was likely to remain in Pakistan. Noor started to nudge her daughter and told her that she should not be speaking to him.

'We're not in Pakistan yet, Mother.'

'I can't hear what you're saying over the engine noise.'

'I know.'

The conversation continued unabated. A couple of hours into the flight, Ameera went to stretch her legs. When she returned, Saaj was sitting in Noor's seat, with Noor next to him, and Ameera was forced to sit in the aisle seat.

Noor was in fierce conversation with Saajid in Urdu. She was asking if he had no shame, and she told him he should not be talking to a young girl he did not know. The woman on the other side of Saajid nodded her agreement. Ameera tried to speak, but she was told by her mother not to interrupt. Saajid just smiled, apologised politely and shrugged his shoulders. Ameera was embarrassed, but she did not want to make a fuss in front of the other passengers and sat where she was told. As they disembarked, Noor kept herself between the two, but Ameera asked Saajid to get her bag out of the locker. As he passed it to her, she pressed a slip of paper into his hand. She had scribbled her address on it, a foolish thing to do, and she immediately regretted it. What would he think of her?

Noor and Ameera stayed at the house of Ameera's great aunt, just outside Rawalpindi. The beauty of Pakistan was astonishing, but Ameera found the culture of the extended family and religious observance was claustrophobic. At home, they were not religious and they had no family nearby. Ameera chose her friends and never socialised with older people. In Pakistan, she was introduced to friends and relations she had not met before, and who seemed to know everything about her.

The main topic of conversation was Nani's health, and because Ameera had learned Urdu from her mother, she could pick up the gist of the discussion. Nani was frail and bedridden and did not seem to recognise her granddaughter at first.

Noor and Ameera met Parvez, a quiet and undemonstrative man, who spoke good English. After only a few days, Noor and Parvez announced that they would marry early in January, and Ameera said that she was very happy for them. Plans were agreed, and Noor would return to England to sell the house. She would move to Pakistan at the end of the year, and Ameera would fly out for the wedding after Christmas.

The family engaged in numerous conversations about Ameera. She must not be left to fend for herself in London. Surely, a marriage could be arranged, in Pakistan or in England. Ameera felt uncomfortable about being discussed in this way, and she told her mother that she would take the next plane home unless it stopped. Her mother said it was just idle chatter, meant nothing and tried to persuade her to stay a little longer, but Ameera knew where that could lead.

Saajid was rarely out of Ameera's mind.

Noor only allowed Ameera out with an escort, which she hated. She had taken to walking in the walled garden of her great aunt's house, always in her bright and cool shalwar kameez. It was the day before her return, a blistering hot afternoon, and over the clamour in the street, she heard a shout. It was from the other side of the wall. She stopped in her tracks and listened. Was someone calling her name? She must be mistaken. Then, much nearer, someone repeated her name. She turned, but there was nobody in the garden.

'Here, I'm here,' but she still could not see where the ethereal voice was coming from.

'I'm on your left. Look, on the wall, behind the tree.'

She saw a face peering into the garden. It was resting between two arms, which were flat on the top of the wall. As soon as he realised Ameera had seen him, the hands pulled the body upward, and Saajid appeared.

'Come on, quick. There's nobody looking. There's no time.'

Without any thought or discussion, Ameera walked boldly through the front gate and followed Saajid to his car.

They drove to Daman-e-Koh.

'What are you doing here?' she asked in the car.

'I thought we'd finish the conversation your mother interrupted. Then there's the small matter of the address you pressed in my hand.'

'That was stupid. I don't know what I was doing.'

Ameera explained that her mother and Parvez would be getting married. She told him of the emotional pressure she felt she was under. The words flowed in a torrent, and Saajid let her speak. Saajid parked the car, and from high on the hill, they viewed the beauty of Islamabad, Rawalpindi and the plain below.

They sat side by side on a bench. She told him that she felt embarrassed that she had said so much to a total stranger.

'What about you? Where've you been?' she asked

'Peshawar. I have a contact who sells me Afghan rugs, and then I went across the border to Jalalabad. That's in Afghanistan, on the hippie route to India. I'm the only Pakistani hippie in the world,' Saajid laughed.

He described a magical place, and Ameera was mesmerised.

'But the Russians are in Afghanistan. It's dangerous.'

'Yes, but I know my way around. They'll never get their hands on me. Anyhow, I had important business.'

'What's that then?'

'Ah, wouldn't you like to know,' he teased.

He spent much of his time on the border between Pakistan

and Afghanistan. It was a frontier that was unrecognised by locals. Ameera fell in love in those few minutes. Saaj was an exciting and uncluttered man. He was tall and thin with a mischievous smile. He gave the impression that anything was doable if you wanted it enough. His accent, an odd mix of public school English with a hint of middle class Pakistani, sounded noble to Ameera.

'I was worried about you. I can have you smuggled back to England in a hurry if you need me to. I've got bigger packages than you back to London,' he laughed.

'What!'

'It's a joke, honest it is.'

'I don't believe you.'

'Which bit?'

'Oh, that you were worried about me. You could be up to anything. Are you married?'

'No, but I've no evil intentions. I'm almost old enough to be your father,' he laughed. 'You've got a future in England. If you got to know me, I'd only fuck it up for you,' he said.

'Really, there's no need for that sort of language!'

'Sorry. Look, whatever your mother does, you've got to finish your studying.'

'I'm going to, don't worry. Mother's afraid of leaving me on my own in England. I have no family there, and she thinks I'm going to be led astray, whatever she means by that. Last term, I was in a hall of residence and shared a room with another girl. Mother was happy with that, especially as we are both medics. All students have to move out during the second year, and we're renting another shared room. It seems ideal, but my roommate's new boyfriend wants to move in with her. After Christmas, I may be able to move into a house with some other medical students, but mother is horrified that things are so easy going. She thought accommodation would be, I don't know, like a nunnery. Mother doesn't trust me and she doesn't trust men, as you've already found out.'

'She's got a point. I'd be worried about you too. It would be better if you had long term accommodation and shared with friends you know and trust.'

'But, at the moment, I've got no alternative, and I am not getting hitched!'

'OK, OK. You've got your passport haven't you?'

'Yes.'

'And tickets?'

'I'm leaving for England tomorrow night.'

'Make sure you catch that plane.'

'I will,' Ameera replied.

'Coming back here works for some people, but it won't work for you.'

'Why are you telling me all this? Are you after a wife?'

'Of course I'm after a wife, stupid. You might even do, when you're a bit older and meatier.'

He laughed at her, as if he was her older brother.

'Seriously, you're a beautiful young woman,' he said, 'but you should go to university, enjoy yourself and get qualified.'

'What about you?'

'I'm building my business and I've got to spend a lot of my time here, making the right connections. We can keep in touch if you like. I've a sister in London, and if you need a contact, I know she'd be happy to meet you.'

Saaj gave her his details and his sister's. He told Ameera to stay in touch.

When Saaj's car pulled up outside the house in Rawalpindi, Ameera had been away for more than three hours. She got out and casually sauntered through the garden and into the house. It was turmoil, and her mother was frantic. She lied about where she had been. She said that she had needed to walk, and her mother shouted angrily because she had not told anyone, and she had been out on her own. Her mother tried to persuade her to stay a little longer, but Ameera refused.

That evening, she packed and spent the next day around the house with her bedridden Nani and walking in the garden. It was a night departure, and a cousin arrived in the evening to take her to the airport. It was a tearful farewell because she and her grandmother knew they would never see each other again. Noor and Parvez came to the airport to see her off. They were caught in traffic and were running late, and there was a perfunctory farewell. Ameera checked in, watched her baggage disappear and felt a tug on her sleeve. She turned to see Saaj, a broad smile on his face.

'I thought I'd make sure that my cargo was in order,' he said. 'You're late and I feared the worst.'

'What? My mother might have seen you. She would recognise you.'

'I'm careful. I have to be in my job.'

They only had minutes, and Saaj explained that he had arranged for his sister to meet Ameera at Heathrow and drive her to Kings Cross station. He said that she might be able to help Ameera with accommodation. They clasped hands tightly, and Ameera made her way to departures. Ameera's cousin had parked up and been sent back by Noor to check that Ameera had made her flight. He did not know what to make of it.

30

AMEERA

Ameera was tired after her journey, and Saaj's sister, Aisha, persuaded her to stay overnight. They immediately struck up a rapport. Aisha was a GP in Shoreditch, and she and her husband, Nick, owned a small house near Victoria Park. They had two young children, aged five and seven. Ameera slept in the attic that night: it had been converted to a small flat.

The following morning, Aisha said that Saaj had made contact and had explained Ameera's personal situation. Aisha and Nick were looking for a tenant for the flat – someone they could trust because access to the attic was through the main house. Aisha had discussed it with Nick, and they had agreed that Ameera was welcome to stay with them, on a permanent basis, until she finished university. It would be as helpful to them as it would be for Ameera. Ameera explained that she was sharing a rented room for the coming term, but it would be possible to get out of the commitment.

'What about Saajid?' Ameera asked.

'I hardly ever see him.'

'He doesn't stay here, does he?'

'No, of course not. He knows your situation. He wants to help, and so do I. There's no ulterior motive, Ameera. Your mother wants to know you're safe in London. I can write to her, tell her I'm a young Asian doctor, and that I will be like an older sister. That's what your mother wants to hear. It will give her peace of mind. There's no need to involve Saaj in this at all.'

Aisha suggested that Ameera should stay another night. She could look around the area, and it might help her make up her mind. Aisha gave Ameera a spare house key, took the children to school and then drove to work. The flat was perfect, and Aisha loved the area. It was a warm day, and she walked along the Regents Canal, crossed the Mile End Road and made her way to the house with the room she had agreed to share. Her roommate and boyfriend were in bed, not expecting a visitor. After the embarrassment had subsided, they agreed that the boyfriend would pay Ameera's share of the rent, and she would not move in. That evening, Ameera accepted Aisha's offer and agreed to move into the flat the following week, for the start of term. Ameera caught the train back to York.

Noor arrived back in York a week later. It was early in the evening, and Ameera had already packed for her return to London the following day. Ameera was excited about her mother's return; she could give her the good news about permanent and 'respectable' accommodation and present the letter from Aisha. Barely had Noor closed the door when she confronted Ameera.

'You met the man on the plane, didn't you?' Noor shouted.

'What?'

'Who was the man you spoke to at the airport? Your cousin saw him. It was the same man you met on the plane. It was, wasn't it?'

'Yes, yes it was. So what?'

'That's who you were with when you disappeared, wasn't it?

'Yes.'

'You lied about where you'd gone.'

'I'm sorry. I didn't want to upset anyone.'

'You lied. How did he find you?'

Ameera explained what had happened. Noor started crying when she realised that Ameera had instigated the meeting with Saaj.

'Are you going to marry this man?'

'No, I'm not.'

'Then you will not see him again?'

'I can't promise that.'

'What's that letter in your hand? Is it from him?'

'No, it's from… It doesn't matter.'

'Let me see it.'

Noor made a grab and tore it from her daughter's grasp. There was a small corner of envelope left in Ameera's hand. Noor started to read.

'Who is this woman? How did you meet her? She's something to do with your man-friend. You're plotting against me, aren't you?'

'No, no, no. You've got it all wrong.'

Ameera explained who she was, parrying repeated interruptions from her furious mother, who continued reading as Ameera spoke.

'You cannot stay with this woman. She's his sister.'

'I'm sorry that it's all happened like this. I know it's my fault, but I *am* staying with Aisha. It's the best thing I can do. I will be safe, and she can be a friend.

'The whole family knows about *him*,' she said.

'There's nothing to know.'

'This has brought shame. Your father was right about you. I was too soft.'

'He made your life a misery, and mine. I've made my mind up.'

'And mine, too.'

Ameera turned her back and rushed upstairs to her bedroom. She did not sleep that night. The following morning, Ameera explained that Saajid was a friend, and there was nothing more than that.

'We don't know anything about him. You didn't tell us.'

'I'm sorry. I should have, and I was wrong, but I'm nearly twenty and it's my life.'

'What do you think they're saying back home?'

'I don't know. You'll have to explain to them. There's nothing going on between me and Saajid.'

'Parvez might not marry me if he finds out.'

'He's never met Saajid or his sister.'

'He never will.'

Ameera tried to reason with her mother, but she would not listen. Ameera put her bags in the hallway and said a tearful goodbye to her mother.

'You've made your choice, Ameera.'

'I'll write every week. I'll see you at the wedding.'

'No!'

'Mother.'

'I mean it.'

She wrote regularly to her mother in York until the new owners of the house returned all of the letters. Then she wrote to her mother at her great aunt's address in Pakistan, asking about the wedding, but her mother never replied. Later, she found out that Parvez tore up the letters, and he forbade any attempt to contact her. Ameera nurtured a deep hatred for him.

Saaj only appeared at his sister's house once that year. He kept aloof from Ameera, especially in front of Aisha. He lived in East London but travelled extensively. Ameera stayed with Aisha during her holidays and began to see Saaj more regularly. He told her that he had fallen in love during the plane flight but had not wanted to press the issue because of the circumstances. They decided to marry when Ameera had qualified. Ameera wrote to her mother and invited her back for the ceremony, but she did not reply.

She told Saaj how angry she was with herself that the rift with her mother had been caused by her own dishonesty and how sad that it seemed irreconcilable. Saaj convinced Ameera that, whatever she had done, Noor and Parvez would have forbidden Ameera to contact him or his sister. Ameera would have had to choose. He had split acrimoniously from his own family when he had refused to practise the faith and adopted a western lifestyle. He had accepted his fate as a price worth paying, but Ameera wished things could have been different. They married at a registry office, and Ameera took her first post in London.

Unexpectedly, a job offer came up in Sheffield. It was working in a practice with two girls Ameera had studied with at university. They were starting a surgery in a part of the town with a growing Asian population. Saaj said that she must take the job, and they moved to Yorkshire. Saaj spent a lot of time travelling to London, where most of his customers were, and abroad. He was making good money, and they bought a beautiful house in Dore. When Nas was born, everything seemed perfect.

Ameera went back to Pakistan with Nas and Saaj, but Parvez refused to see them. Her mother came to their hotel to see her grandson, without Parvez knowing. She would not touch Nasim or speak to Saajid, and Ameera cried. Ameera had not seen Noor since.

31

CLIVE

Over the weeks, a mutually beneficial working relationship developed. Clive and Ameera shared the duties of escorting children to school and sometimes cooking for them in the evenings. It was also the start of Clive's return to a more normal life. That meant getting work and dealing with his lingering craving for alcohol.

Clive contacted Clara Tomlin and asked if there was any possibility of employment. He also tried to phone Marcus, but he never got past his secretary. Then he wrote and received no reply.

He travelled to London and met Clara at a coffee shop in Soho. He recognised her as soon as he entered. She stood up and hugged him.

'Clive, you look fantastic. It's good to see you.'

'You too, Clara. You've hardly changed.'

'Oh, I wouldn't say that.'

'We've a lot of catching up to do.'

Clara was smartly but casually dressed, and her demeanour was as warm and empathetic as ever. A furrowed brow and the implications inherent in 'I *do* know how you feel' suggested that she had her own troubles to contend with. Clive noticed that Clara had hooked a walking stick over the back of her chair, and her speech seemed slightly slurred. He observed that her hands were shaking, and her right leg was tapping rhythmically on the tiled floor. When she saw him looking, she placed her hands out of sight on her knees. She said nothing of her symptoms to Clive, and he felt too embarrassed to ask.

She revealed little about herself, nothing more than Clive already knew. She was unmarried and lived on her own. Clara knew, from the newspapers and TV, of Marie's death and the background to his dismissal from the radio station. She wanted to discover what Clive had been doing since university and turned the conversation away from herself, whenever it strayed in that direction. Clive thought how typical of Clara it was.

She explained that she had arranged for someone from the BBC to join her. He was involved in producing documentaries and needed experienced journalists to work for him on a contract basis. His name was Jeremy McNeice, and Clive would be able to work freelance. When Jeremy arrived, Clara made introductions and then left for another appointment. She used the stick and walked as if she was stiff and arthritic.

'Give me a ring, Clive, whenever you want.'

Clive didn't get the impression that she meant it. She was helping him for old times' sake, and because she was the lovely, caring and thoughtful Clara he'd remembered, even though the affection and closeness of those last few weeks at university had gone. Jeremy promised to make contact with Clive. He said that he had a TV project in the offing, and Clive might fit the bill.

Clive made his way to the *Echo* offices and asked the receptionist if he could speak to Marcus. She told him that he would need to make an appointment. He explained that it was urgent and persuaded her to put him through on the internal phone. Marcus's secretary asked Clive to wait, and it was enough time for her to ask Marcus if he wanted to speak to Clive and for him to decline.

'He's not available,' was the reply.

Clive withdrew gracefully, suspecting that Marcus would never employ someone with his reputation. He had, after all, a readership to satisfy, and Clive was not quite the sort of person who would appeal to *Echo* readers.

Clive had not consumed alcohol since before Christmas, but he realised that opportunity and temptation would present themselves when he was back in work. Ameera put him in touch with a colleague who was able to offer advice and direct him to a self-help group, and they supported him during the first few months of abstinence. He quickly learned how to deal with situations where drink was readily available.

The freelance work started slowly. His first assignment was a TV programme for the BBC, which dealt with the growth of AIDS amongst heterosexuals. It was broadcast a year after his first meeting with Jeremy. Jeremy asked him to do a documentary on the rise of the BNP in Tower Hamlets, screened the following year. Soon after, they were planning another about the miners' strike and its impact on villages in the North, the Midlands and Wales. Jeremy McNeice was proving a valuable contact and was quickly becoming a friend.

Home life developed a settled routine. It was a practical arrangement as far as Clive was concerned. Nas and Chloe were inseparable. When Clive had to work away, the burden fell on Ameera, and Clive reciprocated when he was between assignments. Ameera became Clive's best friend. Arrangements seemed to suit Ameera too, although Clive never asked her.

Shortly after the BNP programme had been televised, he received a phone call from Peter Norlick. Peter was now an

Inspector of Police. He would not say what the call was about, and they agreed to meet. Peter insisted that Clive should tell nobody about the meeting. Clive phoned Ameera at work.

'I'm off to Leeds to meet an old acquaintance,' he said.

'Work or pleasure?'

'It's work. I'm meeting someone I've not seen for years. I'm not sure what time I'll be back. I was wondering if you'd pick Chloe up from school. Could she have tea at yours?'

'No bother.'

'I'll be home before ten. I'll ring if there's a problem. I've got to rush because I don't want to miss the train.'

'Clive, there's no problem. It'd be nice if we…' Clive had put the phone down before she could finish the sentence. 'Clive, why… oh, never mind,' she whispered to herself.

It was early evening when Clive walked through the door of a pub in a Leeds backstreet. Peter was in civilian clothes and was seated in a dark and quiet corner of the pub. He had put on a little weight, and his hair had started to recede. He acknowledged Clive, offered a handshake and invited him to sit opposite.

'It's good to see you after so many years,' said Peter.

'You too.'

'Are you having a drink?'

'You know about my drinking then?'

'You were on the news and in some of the papers. I didn't get the full story.'

'Orange juice is fine.'

Peter went to the bar and returned with drinks.

'Well,' said Clive, 'I might as well clear the air. I had a bit of a rough time, drinking heavily and a few other things, but I'm over it now. End of story.'

'Sorry. Not a good start, eh.'

'Forget it. I didn't mean to be so touchy.'

'I've seen your investigative stuff on the telly, and I know you're a straight bloke. That's all that matters to me. I've got a story, and it's dynamite. I'm not sure how to deal with it, and I could do with some help. I need to know if you're interested. If anyone finds out, it could be the end of my career, and you're the only bloke I trust.'

'Well, give me a clue.'

Peter told Clive how, after the strike, he had become disillusioned by the attitudes of many of his colleagues in the Met. He was based at a police station in East London, and some of the officers had engendered a culture of aggression and violence toward minor criminals. In particular, they targeted drunks, drug takers and petty thieves. Officers concocted crimes and drafted corroborative statements to incriminate those they took a dislike to, particularly blacks.

'I saw assaults by officers during arrests, and I made a formal complaint. Everything in confidence, but within days it was circulating in the locker room.'

'That must've been hell.'

'I got verbals and cold-shouldered.'

'I'm not that surprised, Peter.'

'They closed ranks, and my complaint went nowhere. Things were getting worse, not better. Locker room chat was… well it was terrible, you know, racist. If you were black, you were guilty of something.'

'The Met *do* have a bit of a reputation.'

'Domestics were never investigated, and bad policing was covered up. It got to the stage where I had to get out and start again. I took a promotion that brought me here.'

Peter explained that he had enjoyed working in Leeds and had been seconded to Manchester and then Grinderton where he joined a team investigating drug gangs. There had been a successful outcome, but he had encountered levels of racism in Grinderton that he had not seen before, even in London.

'It was the sort of stuff you reported in your programme on the BNP.'

'What about the senior officers?'

'Most accepted it. Officers were told to curb their language in front of outsiders like me, that's all.'

'What was policing like on the streets?'

'Black guys routinely stopped, just because they were black. Crimes against blacks and Asians ignored.'

'What did you do?'

'I spoke to my boss and was shunted straight back to Leeds. That was over a year ago.'

'But, as you said, it's over a year ago.'

'Yes, but it's still going on, and there are lots of people out there who've been affected.'

'Police victims often don't go down well with the TV audiences. Viewers think they've an axe to grind and take the side of the police. I'd need something concrete to make a story that'll work.'

'A few weeks ago, I was back in Grinderton, giving evidence in court. I met a young officer who'd just come out of training academy. That's where they're picking it up. He was reeling off the same sort of garbage, and it seems the trainers are allowing it and even spouting this racist crap themselves.'

'For the telly, I'll still need visual evidence.'

'Could you get someone through recruitment and into training? What about a hidden camera. Can it be done?'

'Maybe, but it'll take time. We could spend a lot of effort and achieve nothing, and we'd have to get up-front money from the broadcaster. I'd have to convince them there's a good chance of a result... I need to think about it. I'll talk to my contacts.'

'How long will it take?'

'I'll have to get someone interested, then a few months to find an actor to do it and time to get him through the police recruitment process. It's hard to say… in total, a year, probably more. Getting an actor with a credible background, that'll not be easy because the police are bound to do checks. You can leave all of that to me. I'll need to contact you, to tell you if it's a goer or not.'

'No, we can't talk again. If anyone finds out, that'd be the end for me.'

'So, how will you know what's happening?'

'I won't. As far as I'm concerned, we mustn't have any more contact. I have to keep clear of any suspicion. That's why I rang you from a public phone box, but there'll be no more calls. We need to leave separately. I'm not prepared to take any risks.'

'That's a bit melodramatic, isn't it?'

'No, not at all. I've already nailed my colours to the mast at work, and if this story gets in the news, they'll suspect me. No telephone calls. No contact.'

'You mean phones could be tapped?'

'Yes.'

'Who'd do that?'

'The police if they think there's a leak. It'd be a disciplinary matter if I got caught.'

'Police tapping a policeman?'

'The police have links with private detectives. They'll do the dirty work, legally or not. They're generally ex-coppers who've left under a cloud, but they've kept their pensions intact.'

'How common's that, then?'

'It happens all the time. You boys in the press don't help. The nationals have regular contact with ex-coppers and send them on paid commissions, or they promise to pay for stories and leads. There's contact, all the time, between press, police and private investigators. You must know that.'

'You're the only policeman I've had a private conversation with.'

'If the police suspect I've spoken to you, things'll get nasty. Colleagues will sell stuff to the papers about me or you.'

'Such as?'

'The drinking, that'll be dragged up. The *Echo* threatened to expose a mate of mine who was having an affair with a policewoman. He had his arm twisted to provide information about a footballer who'd been questioned about drugs and under-age sex.'

'That's blackmail.'

'Yes, and once it's happened, the policeman can't get off the hook. You're a newspaperman. I'm surprised you don't know.'

'I hear stories but…' Clive shrugged.

'Look, Clive, no contact. I'll have to watch every step from now on, and I can't afford any slip-ups. Neither can you.'

'OK.'

'Don't mention me to anyone, especially not by phone. If anything comes of this, assume every conversation's being listened to. I only met you for a few minutes all those years ago, but I'm talking to you now because I trust you. Don't let me down… please.'

'I won't.'

32

CLIVE

It was 9.30 when Clive came to collect Chloe. He did not ring the doorbell and walked to the back door, which he knew would be open. He heard the television through the wide-open living room door, glanced at Ameera, Chloe and Nasim as he went by, and went to put the kettle on. They had all seen him slink past the door, and Ameera got out of her seat and followed him, quietly.

'Let's listen at the door?' giggled Chloe.

'No.'

'You know your mum fancies my dad something rotten.'

'Stop it.'

'Straight. How is it we know and he doesn't?'

'You've been watching too much *Neighbours*.'

'Your mum'll have had enough if he don't do something soon. You won't be able to come round. See how you like that!'

Ameera walked up behind Clive, who was washing a mug at the kitchen sink. He did not notice her. She was about to put her arms round his waist when he suddenly turned.

'You frightened me,' he gasped. 'I didn't notice you.'

He walked past her, oblivious of her action, to get tea from the cupboard.

'Cuppa?'

'Yes.'

They sat opposite each other, facing their mugs of tea.

'Why didn't you join the family?'

'I didn't want to disturb you. I needed a drink.'

'Successful evening?'

Clive explained what had happened in the vaguest terms he could. He did not mention his contact by name, or the police force concerned. Ameera did not push him.

'Have you had a good evening?' he asked, finishing the last of his drink.

'It was a traditional evening in, yes, very English. We played Junior Scrabble but they're getting too old for that and then a card game. I can't remember what it's called. It's a sort of whist. You should have been here. Yes, we've become like a proper family.'

Ameera looked for a reaction, but Clive had not registered her comment, thinking only about his evening in Leeds. Ameera started to move her hand across the table, but he was unaware. As he leaned across to pick up her empty mug, he inadvertently brushed her fingers.

'Sorry.'

'That's OK,' Ameera sighed.

'Apologies for the short notice tonight,' he said, walking across to the kitchen sink and turning on the taps. 'We could set up a token system if you like, you know, to make sure the childminding evens out.'

'Yes, that would be a *great* idea.'

Ameera sighed, shook her head and sneaked back to the children.

Clive wondered why she had been acting so oddly, creeping up behind him, and that last comment, what was all that about? She was a lovely woman, but she behaved strangely sometimes.

'How's Dad?' asked Chloe.

'Usual,' was the bored reply.

The children glanced at each other and sighed. It was the sigh of parents who needed to take their children in hand.

They were watching *Children's Hospital* on TV. It was from Sheffield.

'I was born there,' said Chloe.

'Looks like they've recovered,' said Nas.

Chloe hit him with a cushion. Nas retaliated, and Ameera slapped his wrist. He stopped without a murmur.

The next day, Jeremy McNeice phoned. He was enthusiastic about Clive's proposition, and gave it the go-ahead. It took four months to recruit a young actor, Graham Knott, who applied to join the police, passed his interview and commenced his training. He was fully equipped with a hidden camera. The results of the filming were instant. The words 'Paki' and 'Nigger' were smattered in day-to-day conversation by trainers and trainees. Shortly after he had finished his training, Graham was posted to Grinderton.

One evening, shortly after Graham had started on the beat in Grinderton, Jeremy and Clive met in London. Clive ran through the evidence already on film. At some stage, they needed to pull Graham, edit the footage and schedule the programme. For every hour that the camera ran, only minutes were useable.

Clive proposed that they work with what they already had, but Jeremy said he would like more evidence. Jeremy wanted to be able to show that the problem was widespread and substantiate it on the beat and in the locker room. Graham was getting edgy. He was riding his luck and taking bigger risks. They agreed that Clive would tell Graham to continue filming for a few weeks more.

As Clive and Jeremy were speaking, Delroy Adams was lying on a pavement in Grinderton, bloody, cold and weary.

33

LUCY

It had seemed like any other evening on a dull street in the northern town of Grinderton. A siren blared in the distance. It was rapidly getting closer, urgent and attention seeking and brakes screeched. The police car pulled up suddenly. A gory, glistening trail splattered the pavement for a hundred yards. It started at a bus shelter and stopped abruptly by two young men.

Delroy Adams was lying in a pool of his own blood, oozing from the flesh immediately below his ribcage. He was stretched out on his back, eyes open, muttering to another black youngster. Delroy's friend leaned over, and his head was almost touching the victim's face, trying to hear the faint, whispered words. Delroy was shivering. The blood, which was draining the life from the youngster, dribbled wantonly over the edge of the pavement and into the gutter.

Peel Street was a wide main road, cars going by every few seconds. A few passers-by were on the other side of the road. They were all white-faced. None of them spoke, and none of them made to cross the colour bar that extended across the carriageway. A man was rounding a corner further up the road. He was walking a dog. As the police arrived, he turned, looked back and watched events for a few minutes. It was a gloomy evening, lit only by a flickering single streetlight, which seemed unsure whether it was day or night. The boy who was kneeling over his friend was sobbing as Delroy's voice got fainter.

'Armstrong, Armstrong. You there, Armstrong?'

'Yeah, Del. I'm 'ere.'

'It's cold, Armstrong. I'm feelin' real cold.'

Armstrong had left bloodstained handprints on the T-shirt of his friend, and he winced at the sight. The kneeling youngster grabbed Delroy's shoulders.

'You'll be OK. Just 'ang on Del. You'll be OK. The police is here. They'll know what to do. Just 'ang on man, 'ang on...'

He spoke these words as a mantra, in a hushed voice, repeating himself, as if his own concentration would keep his friend alive.

Just after 9.00 the following morning, Lucy Kwame jumped off the first train from London. She had received the phone call about the murder the previous evening and was up at 4.30 to catch the train north. She had been in bed when the phone had rung. She had mumbled to Victor that she might be away overnight, but she could not throw this opportunity of a story.

He had told her that it was fine, and he would get Emily to school in the morning. She had written a note for Victor before she left, giving instructions, but had immediately ripped it up and binned it.

She was purposeful in her stride as she headed for Grinderton station taxi rank, her small travelling bag over her shoulder. She gave the taxi driver the address, and he looked quizzically at her but said nothing. The police had cordoned off a small rectangular area of pavement and roadside. Police cars and vans were parked further down the road. There were chalk marks on the pavement, and a few officers were inspecting the footpath, gutters and the bus stop. She identified herself and spoke to the solitary officer who appeared to be guarding the crime scene. He looked her up and down and saw a petite, young woman in her mid to late twenties. She had strawberry blonde hair and pale, freckled skin. She wore tight jeans and a blue duffle jacket, and she radiated a casual confidence.

'What happened, Officer?'

Lucy spoke with an estuary accent and a hint of a lisp.

'Black lad killed. Knifed and bled to death just there,' he said, pointing to the pavement where the dried blood was still in evidence. Lucy could see a single wreath leaning against a lamppost.

'Got the weapon?'

'No knife, no witnesses yet, except one other lad. He's not helping. He's protecting himself, I think.'

'So he's a suspect?'

'What do you think? He says that it was an unprovoked attack, but I don't believe him. There's always a reason, and it's usually drugs. Black gangs deal round here, and there were other black lads seen running away.'

'Is he in custody?'

'He's at the police station. There'll be a statement later this morning.'

'It's a busy road, and there's a bus stop over there. There must be witnesses.'

The policeman shrugged.

'Have your enquiries picked up anything?'

The same response.

'Any passers-by?'

'Dunno.'

'Is there a door to door?'

The officer shrugged again.

'So there's no evidence?'

'It's not the first time we've had a stabbing over drugs.'

Lucy concluded that it was likely to be a short visit. It

seemed like just another gang murder over drugs. She had plenty of time to attend the police briefing and make her way home. She was about to turn away.

'How old was the victim?'

'He was still at school. Sixteen or seventeen, I guess.'

'So young.'

'That's when they start round here. Thirteen and fourteen even.'

Lucy ambled toward the police station. She was expecting a buzz of reporters and cameramen, but there was nobody but the desk sergeant. She asked him if there was any information on the killing and was told that a statement would be issued at noon.

'Can't you tell me *anything*, Sergeant?'

'We've one lad being questioned.'

'Is he a suspect?'

'Can't say.'

'Anyone else?'

'Sorry.'

'What about enquiries on the streets? I couldn't see much going on when I was out and about this morning.'

'You'll have to wait until the press briefing.'

Lucy went to a nearby bakery. It had a coffee shop at the rear. She picked up the local newspaper, which had been left on the seat next to her. As she sipped her coffee, she read about the plans to pedestrianise the town centre, reports of a spate of robberies from newsagents' shops, the closure of an engineering company with the loss of 300 jobs and pictures from a local fundraising event. A middle-aged white woman, laden with two full, plastic, Tesco shopping bags, staggered into the café. Lucy and the woman exchanged smiles.

'Terrible, that killing on Peel Street,' she said to the woman serving.

'Been in here. Nice lad. Who'd do a thing like that?'

'That gang from Broxley, they done it.'

'No, the police said it were black lads fighting each other over drugs.'

'I'm telling you, it were that gang from Broxley.'

'How d'you know?'

'My next door neighbour were at the bus stop. He seen it. They all seen it. White lads chased 'im down and stabbed him.'

'I don't believe it. Tea, love?'

'Yes,' she hesitated, looking at the display, 'and a Danish. Yes, that one there.'

Lucy walked straight back to Peel Street. A middle-aged man with pale skin and unkempt hair was standing in a doorway, metres from the bus stop. It seemed as if he had just emerged from bed, and he had the bleary-eyed look of the morning after. He was talking to a much older woman. She was leaning on the doorframe of the adjacent house. She glanced up the road and then went back inside, leaving the door open. Casually and confidently, Lucy approached him. She could smell cigarette smoke on his clothes.

'Did you see what happened yesterday evening?' she asked.

'No.'

'Oh.'

'I heard it though,' he continued in an accent familiar to viewers of *Coronation Street*.

'What did you hear?'

'Lads calling names. Not nice.'

'What names?'

'Like "Nigger, nigger, what you doing 'ere, nigger?" and "Come on, coon, give it a go". That sort of shit.'

'Didn't you see anything?'

'No. I heard the shouting, and when I got to the window, I saw the white lads run off down there. The police car went past them, coming the other way,' he said, pointing at a road off Peel Street and almost opposite his front door, 'and the black kid were staggering over that way.' He pointed up Peel Street. 'There were a queue at the bus stop opposite. They must have seen it all, and there were a bloke walking a dog.'

'Are you sure?'

''Course he's sure.'

The woman had re-emerged from next door. She had a cigarette drooping languidly from the left corner of her mouth, and her left eye was half-closed. The cigarette bobbed up and down as she spoke, the ash clinging miraculously to the unburnt end of the cigarette.

'I heard 'em too. Everyone round here knows 'em and where they're from. They're always in trouble.'

'Have the police spoken to you?'

'Nah, they're useless.'

'The lads, do you know any of their names?'

'Who are you, anyway?' the man asked suspiciously.

'I'm a reporter.'

'Don't get me involved in this. It's bad enough living here without getting on the wrong side of the Broxley mob. I've said nothin'.'

With that, the man abruptly stepped back and slammed the door. The neighbour looked Lucy up and down contemptuously through the grey haze before returning to her tasks inside, leaving the door open.

'Yes, everyone round here knows where they're from, but nobody'll say,' she added from inside before she punctuated the conversation with the full stop of a slammed door.

Lucy walked along Peel Street, a road lined with red-bricked terraces. It was a mixed area of houses and shops, typical of the edge of town. The shops were an assortment of laundrettes, off-licences, hairdressers, convenience stores and fast food outlets. Many shop windows were boarded up. Doors led upstairs to flats, lawyers' offices and dentists' surgeries. Free newspapers and circulars bulged from letterboxes, indicating that some houses were unoccupied, and graffiti garishly adorned many walls with random clashes of colour.

The front doors of the terraced houses opened directly onto the pavement. Many had been converted to multi-occupancy, and the street, which had probably been thriving in its industrial heyday, had the uncared-for appearance of an area in decline.

She wondered what had gone through the young man's mind as he lay on the pavement. Did he realise he was dying? It was not an immediate death, and it was not the death of an old person, expected or planned. Delroy must have known. Were his final moments full of regret, or longing? Did he fight death until the last gasp? It made Lucy shudder. Vile murder is so mundane. It happens. It's gone. It would leave no trace on this street but it would scar the lives of so many.

She continued to the end of the street, turned to the left and walked back through a park that was to the rear of the houses fronting Peel Street. By 12.00, there was a small gathering at the police station, reporters from local and national newspapers and two television crews. They were ushered into a large rectangular room where two investigating officers were already seated at a single desk. Members of the press were invited to find a place on metal-framed chairs arranged in three rows, either side of a central aisle. The policemen introduced themselves as Assistant Chief Constable Curry and Detective Superintendent Walther. The ACC, referring to his notes, spoke in a dreary monotone.

'You'll have heard that a young man was found late yesterday evening in South Grinderton. He had been seriously injured and was bleeding from what appears to be a stab wound. He died at the scene. His parents have been informed. His name was Delroy Adams and he was sixteen years old. So far, we've one witness who was present when the offence was committed. He's being questioned. Let me hand you over to DS Walther.'

DS Walther spoke with the same indifference in his voice.

'As many of you know there've been a number of violent assaults in the area recently, and there's a turf war between rival gangs in South Grinderton. However, we're following all lines of enquiry at this stage. Forensics has been over the crime scene, and an autopsy is being carried out. There appears to be at least one deep knife wound on the victim, below the ribcage, and there's evidence of other blows to the head and possibly other knife wounds. We're appealing for witnesses and there's a number to ring. Any information will be treated in the strictest confidence. Any questions?'

Lucy Kwame put her hand up, but a TV reporter accompanied by a cameraman stood up. She reluctantly conceded to him.

'What's the name of the man in custody? How old is he, and is he a suspect?'

'I can't answer at this stage,' replied the ACC.

'Who reported the stabbing, and how long was it before the police arrived?' asked the same man.

'We received a 999 phone call from the crime scene, and a police patrol car got to Peel Street about five minutes later. By the time we arrived, there were just the two lads and a few onlookers,' replied DS Walther.

The reporter continued to hold the stage.

'Has a weapon been found?'

'No, not yet,' Walther said.

'Have you any idea who did it and the motive for the attack?'

'It may be drugs, or gangs, or both, or a fight that got out of hand,' said Walther.

'What about the others who witnessed what happened?' Lucy interrupted, impatiently. 'Have you identified who was at the scene and interviewed any of them?'

The ACC nodded for the DS to answer.

'Enquiries are ongoing,' he said.

'Yes, I'm sure, but have you identified witnesses?'

The ACC coughed but said nothing. The DS was not going to get help from his boss.

'We're not sure if anybody saw the stabbing. Nobody else has been interviewed.'

'There was a queue of people waiting for a bus who'll have seen what happened. Have you got their names?' she asked. Lucy could not hide her exasperation.

'I'm sorry, but we can't provide any further operational information at this stage,' said ACC Curry. He looked at her disapprovingly, but Lucy Kwame continued.

'He was killed on a main road.'

There was an embarrassing silence. Then ACC Curry spoke.

'That's all the information we can provide at the moment. Thank you.'

The two men stood up.

'Did any of your men see a gang running away? They'd have had blood on their clothes and the weapon.'

'We've given you all the information we have at present,' said the ACC.

The two officers edged out from behind the table.

'Were reinforcements called in to identify potential suspects or witnesses?'

The two police officers were making their way through a side door as Lucy Kwame fired another question.

'Are you aware that a gang of *white* youths was involved? They've been in trouble before. You'll know the names.'

They were at the door.

'DS Walther, have you been to the crime scene?'

'Do either of you give a damn?' she mumbled to herself.

The room was a silent witness as Lucy Kwame stormed through the back door and out of the police station. She contacted the *Sentinel* from a phone box outside. She asked to speak to Clara Tomlin.

'Hi.'

'Hello, Lucy. How are you getting on?'

'Fine, Mum.'

34

LUCY

Lucy sighed.

'I'm not sure what's going on here. I've no idea how to handle it. When I arrived this morning there were just a few policemen cleaning up. It didn't seem like a crime scene investigation.'

'What do you mean?'

'Well, nobody knew what to do. There was nobody in charge.'

'What have the police said?'

'I went to the briefing, and they don't seem to have followed basic procedures. They couldn't even answer straightforward questions. I don't think they've started a proper investigation.'

'They must have done something, surely?'

Lucy explained what she had heard at the briefing.

'They've already decided that the murdered boy's a gang member, and he's involved in drugs, and they're not too interested in finding the murderer. I'm sure it was racist,' said Lucy.

'Why do you think that?'

'A local said he heard a gang shouting racist taunts at the lads.'

'Is that the story?'

'Everyone else will cover it as a gang murder – headlines

for a day or two and then forgotten. Yes. It's a racist murder. I'm sure of it.'

'If you're right, why haven't the police picked it up?'

'They're completely incompetent, but it's mainly because the boy's black. If it had been a white kid in west London, killed by a black gang, there'd be police and reporters crawling all over the place.'

'Get the report in. Don't give too many clues to the other papers, particularly the locals. Some can be pretty hot on these things. Then, do some more digging.'

'Where should I start, Mum?'

'Try family, friends and school. Keep close to the police.

'It's too late. I've already upset them.'

'Well, try to build bridges.'

'It's really frustrating. Even on the street, people don't want to talk, especially to a reporter.'

'And a woman, from the south. When will you be home?'

'I'll think I'll stay overnight and get back sometime tomorrow.'

'Victor's looking after Emily?'

'Yes.'

'I'll pop round this evening, on the way home. I'll give him a hand.'

'Mum, he's perfectly capable.'

She knew what Victor would be up to whilst she was away. He would tidy up the mess that Lucy always trailed behind her; clothes taken from the wardrobe, tried on and not put back, piles ready for washing, cutlery, crockery and pots in a dirty sink, books and CDs parked on every empty space in the living room and toys scattered across Emily's room. Everything would be tidy and spotless, and a visit from Mum would be welcome, but unnecessary, from a practical point of view.

'I know, but I haven't seen Emily since the weekend.'

'I've got to go now, Mum. Tell Victor I'll ring tonight.'

'Bye, Lucy.'

Lucy wandered slowly back to the crime scene, deep in thought. She was on the opposite side of the road to the police. She recognised DS Walther, who was talking intently to one of the policemen. He was making some effort, at last.

She took the side street the gang had fled down. It was, like Peel Street, of red-bricked Victorian terraced houses with black slated roofs. It was neat but not affluent. Cars were parked along much of the length of the road. After ten minutes' walking, she walked into a newsagents shop. It had metal bars the full length of the windows and a second outer door, fully opened and made out of galvanised steel. She asked the shopkeeper for directions to the Broxley estate. It was two streets up and to the left, and she could not miss it.

The shopkeeper was right that she could not miss it. It was an anachronism. The part of the town she had just walked through had roads that met at right angles or followed a contour, canal or railway line. All the arteries led somewhere, perhaps somewhere better. The houses were of uniform height and simplicity of design. They were sturdy and gave the impression of solidarity.

Broxley had been dropped into the here-and-now from another time and place. Perhaps it had been a bombed area of town or a factory had been torn down. What had been put in its place did not belong. The estate had been designed out of context. Grey and faded pastel tiles hung from the upper walls. Where it could be seen beneath the harsh scrawls of graffiti, the brickwork was blue/grey. Lucy could discern some of the words, which shouted their ugly racism.

On some of the buildings, white-painted wood panelling adorned the walls, breaking the drab monotony of the bricks, but the paint was peeling or gone, revealing dullness beneath. Roofs were flat, and low-rise angular blocks of four or five storeys scarred the skyline. They were set around grass rectangles, which were a mockery to the countryside. Roads did not go from A to B. Instead, they ended up in cul-de-sacs or crescents, and journeys often finished where they had started, like many of the lives played out here.

Lucy stopped to collect her thoughts. She knew that what she was looking for was here, but she was not sure what to do next. She could always ask the next passer-by, 'Do you know who killed Delroy Adams?' She did not think that was wise, and it would be unlikely to elicit a positive response. To her right, about two hundred metres along the main street into the estate, was a row of shops. She could see that one of them was a café, and she was hungry. As she made her way, she passed two young men. They were in T-shirts and jeans, working under the bonnet of a car. She noticed the tattooed union flag and bloodied daggers. They stopped their work as she walked by.

'Nice arse, love.'

She continued, not looking back.

'I'd give her one,' shouted the other, and they both burst out laughing.

Lucy quickened her step.

The Red Rose café was small and almost empty. Two older couples and a pair of younger men in overalls sat at three separate tables, finishing their lunches. Lucy ordered scrambled eggs on toast and a mug of tea. A middle-aged, kindly looking woman was serving, and another, perhaps a sister, busied herself in the kitchen. Before Lucy sat down, the woman who was serving cleaned the table. She picked up the condiments in the chubby fingers of her left hand, and worked a blue cloth over the table with the right. Lucy could smell the disinfectant.

The two young workmen were talking in hushed voices. They were at a table on the other side of the central aisle that ran the length of the café, one table nearer the serving counter than she was. She glanced over the back of one and could see the face of the other.

'He said they just laced into 'em,' said the one facing her.

The man with his back to her gave an unintelligible response and made a stabbing movement with the knife in his right hand.

The other looked her way, and she carefully pretended to remove something from her bag, which was on the seat next to her, as if their conversation was of no interest and to avoid catching his eye.

'There weren't even a fight,' he continued. 'They reckon the black kid didn't run, the stupid bastard. You know they're fucking crazy, them Broxley lads. I tell you, they need locking up, but nobody dare say nothin'. They're brutal, man.'

The other spoke, but Lucy could not hear what he said. His mate replied.

'They'll get away with it. They reckon that... you know,' the man facing her said, rubbing his thumb across his fingers, indicating money was involved. 'You'd have thought the police'd be crawling all over the place, wouldn't you?'

The tea arrived and the two men were temporarily blocked from view, and then Lucy's lunch was served. The man facing her was watching her out of the corner of his eye, perhaps sensing that Lucy was eavesdropping. He put a finger to his lips and nodded in Lucy's direction, and his friend got the message. Their conversation moved on, and she tucked into her meal. They were first to leave the café. Only one person had subsequently entered, and he sat at the window with a coffee, studying the outside world. Lucy went to the till to pay.

'I needed that,' she said.

'That'll keep you goin' till teatime.'

'Did I hear the lads say someone's been killed?' she asked, innocently.

'Not here love. It were last night, up on Peel Street. Terrible. A gang of lads. We've got some bad uns round here and lots of good uns too. There's all sorts of rumours. Whenever there's trouble, it's the same names.'

'Seems like everyone knows who did it,' said Lucy, rummaging nonchalantly for change.

'What d'you think? They've been bragging about it to their mates.'

Lucy handed over the exact amount. 'I guess the police will get them.'

'No chance.'

'Well, if everyone knows who did it…?'

'Nobody round here'll talk. They don't grass. They daren't.'

The woman in the kitchen cleared her throat. More than enough had already been said, and a few seconds later, a group of young lads swaggered into the café, and the women went silent. Lucy turned to the door, tumbling the change into her purse and casually looking up at the five young men as she made her exit past them.

'Thanks,' she said, turning to the serving counter and giving herself time to memorise the faces of the youths.

'See you, love,' the waitress replied, and Lucy was quickly out the door.

Lucy could see the two mechanics and quietly crossed the road. She was past them before they realised, and it was with relief that she made her way to the main road and retraced her steps back to the murder scene.

It was shortly after 3.30 when she reached Peel Street, and a small group of youngsters had already assembled. There were around a dozen boys and girls in total. They were about sixteen years old, and all but two were black. A single policeman was guarding the cordoned off area, and he was allowing a young black girl to place a tightly gripped spray of flowers on the pavement. There was a card with a message attached. The youngsters made no sound. They huddled in a single group, heads bowed, embarrassed and unsure what to do.

As she laid the wreath, the girl inside the cordon said something in a whisper. It was as if she was speaking directly to Delroy on their behalf. She turned and joined her friends, who stood in silence. Lucy, who was observing the scene from a distance, walked slowly toward the group as it started to break. She drew level with the wreath and stopped to whisper the words to herself:

'To Delroy. Our friend. We will miss you and we won't forget.'

She turned and casually walked up to the girl who had laid the flowers.

'They're beautiful,' Lucy said, nodding toward their memorial. 'So is the message.'

The girl seemed embarrassed, and her friends looked at Lucy with surprise and consternation.

'I'm sorry. It's such an awful tragedy,' she continued.

'Not as sorry as us. He never hurt nobody. Why would they wanna kill 'im?'

'You went to school with him?'

'Yes.'

'Which school?'

'The Rivers. What's it to you?'

'I'm from a newspaper. I'm trying to find out what happened.'

'It were that white gang from Broxley,' shouted one of the young men. 'They chased me and Kelvin last month. We was well scared, but we was too quick for 'em. Everybody knows who they are.'

'If you know them, tell the police. There's one here, or go down to the police station.'

'What for?' asked the young man. His eyes blazed and his voice trembled. 'I told 'em the time they went for me, and the pigs never even took my name. They couldn't care less. The police know who they are, they know, trust me.'

'They should've saved Delroy but they couldn't be arsed,' another shouted, so that the policeman could hear him. 'They didn't do nothin' to help him. They was more bothered 'bout arresting Armstrong. I seen it. They think that Armstrong done it. Armstrong's his best mate. The police? You're kiddin'. Don't talk to me about the fuckin' police.'

'I seen it too,' said another.

'Tell the police. It's the only way to get them locked up.'

Another teenager spoke. He was tall and skinny and was at the back of the group that had formed a semi-circle in front of Lucy.

'Don't go there, lady. We know what the police done to Armstrong, and they'll do the same to us. He's still bein' held by the pigs. He was tryin' to help Delroy.'

'Some of us've been in a bit of trouble with the police. Nothin' serious, you know, but warnin's,' said the girl quietly.

'There's no way the police'll listen to us. We live here. We know what it's like.'

'Eventually the police will work out what happened. You're more likely to be believed if you come forward now. Come on, it's your chance to get them locked up,' implored Lucy.

'You don't get it, d'you?' said the girl. 'Where *you* come from, that may be true. Not in Grinderton. The police won't never believe he were murdered by white kids.'

'How many times you been stopped and searched on the streets, Mrs White Woman?' sneered the tall, skinny youth. 'They think it's blacks doin' everythin'. If I go to the police, I'm a suspect. That's how it is on the streets. We know 'cos we see it every day.'

'You can speak to me. I'm not the police. I'm a reporter. I believe you.'

'It's no good gettin' arsey with us,' said the girl.

There were shakes of the head, and the group turned and dispersed. The girl shrugged and followed. Lucy sighed.

Fifteen minutes later, she arrived at The Rivers Comprehensive School. A TV van was parked outside, and she followed a young cameraman who seemed to know where to go. It was a flat-roofed, white-boarded, single-storey building, built in the sixties but with the signs of decay of a school much older.

They entered a courtyard where the headmaster was standing with a script in his hands, preparing to speak. The cameraman was setting up, and adjustments were being made to the technology and the main participant's tie. There was a cry of 'Ready?' and the head spoke. It was a touching eulogy, and Lucy was left in no doubt that Delroy was a model pupil. He was from a humble background, planning to go to university to read law. Lucy recognised some of the faces from the press briefing earlier in the day. The media questions were based on the assumption that this was just another gang murder, and by tomorrow, the country would believe the same.

35

MARCUS

It was 6.30 in the morning, and Marcus had already digested the contents of the other dailies, now neatly stacked on the kitchen chair beside him. He had just been on the phone to the office and was sipping coffee from a plain white cup. More than a decade had passed since the 1984 miners' strike and his promotion to the *Sunday Echo*. Marcus had achieved his ambition. It was not the *Mercury*, which he had dreamed of all those years ago, but Editor of the *Echo* was the greater prize.

Mary was nibbling at a slice of toast, smothered with marmalade she had made the previous year. Marcus still had the same mail order catalogue smartness and dress, although he had filled out a little, and there was some tightness around the waistline. His black hair was flecked with grey, and most of Mary's hair had turned silver. Mary was in a long, white towelling robe, and as soon as Marcus would leave for work, she would have a shower and prepare for school. She repeated this routine on the three days she taught at St Stephen. The children had both finished university and settled into work, and Marcus had reluctantly accepted this change to the daily schedule.

Mary had been active as a parent at the private school that both of their children had attended and had become friendly with the headteacher. They had paid for Giles, but

Gail had earned a scholarship. Mary had accepted that Giles was not particularly academic, but Marcus had blamed the poor teaching he had received at the state primary school. It was part of the 'dumbing-down' of education he attributed to trendy teaching methods and comprehensive education. Gail was studious, single-minded and hard working, and she had sailed through the entrance exam.

Mary had not applied for the job. The head had found out that she was a qualified English teacher and had offered her the post without an interview, something not unusual for those in her circle. Giles had parachuted into his first job in the city after Mary's discrete lobbying of a governor at St Stephen.

'I am getting a bit of aggro at school,' she said. 'Comments about the *Echo*.'

'What are they saying?'

'One of the English teachers mentioned she had met up with some lesbian friends. She said that they had been threatened on the Tube because they were holding hands.'

'She's not a lesbian, is she?'

'I've no idea. It's not been a topic of discussion. Anyhow, she made a remark about how the press vilify gay people. Others chipped in, and one of the history teachers mentioned the *Echo* in unflattering terms. He said it was racist and homophobic.'

'Did you put them straight?'

'A few of the staff know that I'm the wife of the editor, and they tried to move the conversation on. They were embarrassed, and I guess, behind my back, everyone's been told, but there's a bit of an atmosphere.'

'How do people like that get to hold jobs in a school like St Stephen?'

'Because they're good teachers. It's not a problem, and it'll blow over. Why do they think so badly of the *Echo*?'

'What we say is what people are thinking. That's why we sell more newspapers than the broadsheets. Some people don't like that.'

'Is the paper racist?'

'No, it's not, but we don't buy into all this multicultural crap or the race relations industry. There's a difference between tolerating different cultures and promoting them. The country has stepped over the line, and we point that out. It's a British paper for British people, and we're all proud of it. There is nothing wrong with that.'

'I suppose not.'

'I'd have thought that a private school would have weeded these types out. That's what I'd have done.'

'No laws or rules have been broken.'

'The law's making it harder to get rid of troublemakers.'

'Hmm. I do wish there was less of the celebrity stuff in the paper.'

'It sells. The paper is not meant to appeal to you and me. I'm judged by my readers. Have you heard of Becky Shearman?'

'She's a pop singer. She's married to a footballer, isn't she?'

'Yes, she's a celebrity; Dave Shearman's daughter. She seems to have left her youngster at home alone when she's been out clubbing. It's a public interest story and it'll be in tomorrow's *Echo*. So, to be honest, she deserves all the criticism she gets.'

'If that's what she's done, then I guess you're right.'

An hour later, Marcus was in his office at the *Echo*. He had already phoned his staff from home to prepare them for the meeting. He had met with Barry Halstead to share views about the key elements of news that day and the possibilities for the next day's paper.

He had opened the ritual of the daily morning meeting a

few minutes earlier. It was a set piece, a continuation from Sir Clifford's era, which had ended with Sir Clifford's retirement some years before.

The office had been redecorated, pictures of his predecessors hung on the wall and modern furniture purchased. Marcus had acquired a large, oblong table, which had been located centrally in the room. It could seat up to sixteen, and fifteen chairs had been bought from the same catalogue. Marcus had dragged the swivel chair from his desk and had spread himself and his papers at the head of the table. It gave the impression that the top third of the table was his, and he was poised to move forward to capture the rest of the stage. His senior members of staff sat around the bottom two-thirds of the table. Marcus looked happy in his hegemony.

'Well, Barry. How do you think we should handle the latest Becky Shearman story?' Marcus asked.

Barry Halstead sat to the right of Marcus. Barry was tall and stooped-shouldered, and he hunched over his notebook and assorted papers, like a vulture over its prey. His skull had a wide, flat area at the rear, as if it had been hit by a great weight that had caused his nose, mouth, eyes, chin and ears forward. His rim of hair was cut short, and polished pale skin gleamed in a circle on the top of his head.

'Kevin and a photographer have been tracking her after a tip off. We're the only ones on the case. She's walked out on her husband and is living in... where is it?' said the news editor, hesitating as he rummaged through his papers. 'Yes, a flat in the East End. Her husband's the footballer, Danny McFeeney. She's been leaving her daughter alone and going out till the early morning, you know, getting blitzed.'

'Tip off from where?'

'Let's just say that someone in the police owes Kevin a

favour. It cost us, but we have to pay the market rate. There's a premium for exclusivity.'

'I didn't hear that.'

'Anyhow, last night she was out with a rapper. We did a spread on her in the celeb section two years ago. That was when she was on the up. It was glitzy stuff for women readers. Difficult background, but she's worked hard, to her credit. Dave Shearman, her dad, split from her mum when Becky was young.'

'She was at Greenham Common,' said Marcus.

'I've got pictures of Becky at music school and when she released her first single. She's been on the slide, and Noreen's done a piece about her putting on weight and letting herself go a bit. We covered her twice last month.'

'Remind me,' Marcus said.

Barry shuffled his papers and turned the leaves of his notebook.

'We got a photo of her in town, a drink in her hand. There was another story about how much she spent on a party. I can't remember the cost, but I'll dig it out. She's been seen with this rapper, called Razer. He's got form for drugs,' said Barry.

'We need better photos! The ones I've seen are too bland for the story I want.'

Marcus had been quiet when the meeting had started, but his voice had become progressively louder. He leaned back in his chair, hands clasped behind his ears.

'Kevin, you're losing your touch,' he said. 'Better photograph, and get more on the *Home Alone* kid. Dig up some stuff on the rapper. You know the angle. Dan, what's the story on McFeeney?' Marcus asked, nodding toward the sports editor. 'Front page and back page would be perfect.'

'Big game at the weekend, so there could be a good follow-up on Monday if they don't win,' Dan replied.

'Come on, I want something for today. How will this affect morale in the team? That's not a question because it'll have an adverse affect, won't it? Get quotes.'

'There's been a rumour about Becky Shearman having it off with one of the other players,' said Dan. 'I'll follow it up. I'm sure we'll be able to get a few unattributed comments from bitchy football wives and girlfriends.'

'That's more like it, for goodness' sake!' exclaimed Marcus, whirling his swivel chair through ninety degrees and jumping to his feet.

'I'd like Noreen to do another celebrity piece on her. Get her in here. It'd be good to land something on her father too. Shearman leaves daughter who goes off the rails. Family values, that sort of stuff. We'll see what Noreen's got. There's dirt out there if we can find it,' said Marcus, his words launched at a furious rate.

Noreen Parfitte was summoned, and she explained more about Becky Shearman's past. She reminded Marcus that Becky had a younger stepsister who had been convicted, some years before, for drugs offences. The father was not known, but it was not Shearman.

'Shearman's ex has another kid when she was supposed to be a lesbian,' said Barry. 'Call me old-fashioned, but...'

'Nothing surprises me about this crowd. Noreen, get details. Perhaps we major on the drugs? What about the rapper? He's been convicted, hasn't he?'

'Yes, he's been done for possession.'

'Make all the connections. Organise it to press the right buttons for our readers.'

Marcus stopped and paused. Barry and the other members of the team were making notes.

'We ought to tie into the debate in Parliament on drugs. Let's do a two-page feature,' Marcus said, nodding at Stephen, seated next to Kevin Smallman.

'The message is that Parliament doesn't care, so I want a photograph of an empty chamber. Something from the archive will do. Nobody will know. Get the facts on MPs in favour of legalising cannabis. If I remember rightly, Shearman's one, so dig up what you can. Peter can pick it up. He's supposed to be our legal expert, isn't he? I haven't seen him this morning. Could somebody grab him?' Marcus said, referring to Peter Kellock.

'He's looking into a murder,' Barry muttered.

'Doesn't ring a bell.'

Barry skimmed through sheets of paper. He explained that a boy had been killed by a gang on the streets of Grinderton. Marcus wondered why he had not recalled it.

'What was his name?' Marcus demanded.

'A kid called Delroy Adams.'

'Delroy?'

'Yes.'

'Oh, I remember now. Get the stupid twat in here!'

There was a suppressed laugh from the others around the table.

'What do we know about these girls who've disappeared in Barringham?'

'They were out roller-skating, and they missed the late bus home,' said Barry. 'They've not been seen since.'

'How old?'

'Both ten.'

'Family?'

'Our sort of people, I think.'

'Photos?'

Barry handed him a file of photos, which Marcus spread across the table and browsed. He fingered the photographs showing the two girls with their families. He thought about how he would have felt if it had happened to one of his children when they were at the same age. He visualised a limp young body lying in a field and saw a face he recognised. He shuddered, coughed and concentrated on the task in hand.

'They're lovely children.' Marcus's voice trembled. 'Parents look respectable too. I want a sympathetic story. Check out the background. No skeletons in cupboards. We won't get interviews with the parents, but find out what friends and neighbours have got to say. I want a human-interest angle. What are the children like? What hobbies, sports, school interests? It'll make a poignant story, and we can keep the readers hooked for however long it takes to find them.'

'Who do you want on it?' asked Barry.

'I know you're doing the Shearman story, but I'd like you to run with this as well, Kevin. You'll need someone else working with you.'

The meeting continued for half an hour to a routine that repeated itself every day. The main story for the following morning was usually some aspect of the news that would emerge during the morning meeting, and Marcus never failed to concentrate the energy of his team on a small number of headlines.

Marcus's lieutenants returned to the large open plan office. They started the process of gathering, organising, orchestrating, manipulating and creating the themes for the following day.

36

KEVIN

Steve Gordon, Kevin's dependable photographer, had been following Becky Shearman for three days. He was adopting a tried and trusted formula. Although Steve disliked Kevin, he respected him because Kevin got the leads, and Steve could focus on being in the right place at the right time. Kevin knew all the bent coppers and somehow got the payments through on expenses.

Becky had been tracked down to a flat in Dalston. It was in a large, Victorian, terraced house, recently converted into separate flats and accessed through a single door. The day before, Steve had managed to get within inches of Becky's face with his camera. He caught her as she was about to jump into a taxi, but the picture was blurred. Being the only member of the paparazzi on the case was unusual, and the exclusivity of any photos made this a potentially lucrative pitch. He had hung around unobtrusively and had snapped a photograph of her arriving back in a large American sports car, at 2.00 in the morning. He had managed to get a snatched shot of the driver, who had not expected him to be there. On close inspection, he had realised that it was the rapper, Razer. The photograph was not clear enough to be printable.

He had tried to interview neighbours. Only one, the man from the flat above, was prepared to speak. Kevin had ascertained from him that there was a baby inside the flat because he had heard it crying. The man did not know any of his neighbours because the other flats were all on short-term rental. He had said that drugs were everywhere, and the area had been overrun by foreigners and was going down the drain.

There had been a number of visitors to the flats, but they had refused to say anything to the press. One particular woman had told him to 'Piss off you fucking scumbag!' which he had not taken as an insult, merely typical everyday conversation in his line of work.

Kevin and Steve were determined not to miss the moment when Becky came out, and they were waiting on the doorstep. Kevin was planning to confront Becky and had arrived at her flat straight from the morning meeting. He was sure that he would be able to provoke a reaction because he always did. He could not stay beyond 1.00 because of the work required to pull together the story on the missing girls, and he was getting anxious. Finally, at about 12.30, Becky Shearman appeared at the front door. Kevin stopped her in her tracks, and Steve clicked away.

'Is it true that you've left your husband, Becky?'

'That's none of your business. Anyhow, who are you?'

Becky spoke tersely and eyed the two men with suspicion. Kevin was below her, on the bottom of a short flight of steps, and Steve, just above Kevin, was pointing upwards to get his photographs.

'Where's your daughter, Becky?'

'What's that to you? You're not Social Services; you're just a pathetic newspaper reporter. Get out the way.'

Becky's voice betrayed her growing anger.

'How much are you drinking at home?'

'Get stuffed!'

'Are you leaving your daughter alone whilst you're out at nightclubs with Razer?'

Becky combed a hand backward through her straggling, long, dark hair. It revealed a pale and tired face. Her cinnamon eyes blazed.

'I've not been out with him. He's been kind enough to drive me home, that's all.'

As Kevin was talking, Becky rummaged in her bag for a cigarette. She lit it shakily and inexpertly, put it to her mouth and drew deeply.

'I'm having a difficult time, and he's been a real friend, you know, helping me out. I'm going to the supermarket, so if you'd please get out of the way.'

'I'm sure he's been a friend,' said Kevin, sarcastically. 'How's he been...?' Kevin hesitated and then smiled. 'How's he been *helping you out*, then?'

'What's that supposed to mean, you shit?'

'So, who's looking after your daughter?'

'That's nothing to do with you. You can fuck off, you slime ball. Keep out my personal affairs.'

'Can I take it you agree with Mr Razer's lyric, *'Beat that bitch'*, Becky?'

'You don't understand the song, you arsehole; don't pretend you do. I told you to get out my way,' she shouted and swung her handbag at the photographer, and the shutter clicked repeatedly.

Kevin and Steve nodded to each other. The two men followed Becky down the street, firing questions at her, which she refused to answer. Kevin smiled at Steve.

'Get the photos on my desk as soon as you can. See you later.'

Three people peeked out from the window of Becky's flat. Two were middle-aged women, and the third was a little girl, below school age.

'Enough of hide-and-seek. Those horrid men have gone.

Let's go to the park,' said the woman nearest the window. The little girl grasped her hand tightly. Emma Gladwin and her partner had been too scared to leave the flat since the press had arrived.

'That *would* be nice, Granny.'

37

MARCUS

During the late morning and early afternoon, the paper was taking shape on the desks in the main office. Marcus leaned over a frightened, young sub-editor at a computer screen.

'That's not what I meant. Fucking listen.'

'But I thought you said…'

'Don't tell me what I said! I know what I told you. I want that photograph here and a fucking headline that makes the point, not this limp-wristed shit!' he yelled. 'It's me that gets judged on what goes in the paper, so get it right.'

Marcus did not see the young man drop his head into his hands in exhausted and fearful resignation. He got up and wandered from the office to the male toilet. He found an empty cubicle and sat on the seat lid, eyes glazed, forehead sweating and hands trembling.

Marcus charged to another desk and looked over the shoulder of an older man. 'That's great!' he shouted, throwing his hands skywards. 'At least *somebody* in this place knows what I want.' He then spoke quietly. 'How about moving this, then insert a paragraph on her father? There's to be no doubt that her dad's the Labourite Shearman.'

Marcus scribbled some suggestions for a headline on a piece of paper. The reporter smiled and set to the task, inspired by the encouragement. The sub-editor returned from the toilet. He whispered to a colleague at the next desk.

'I wrote down what he said, word-for-word. He's changed his mind and expects me to know. He's a fucking unpredictable tyrant. Short-arsed bastard looks like Napoleon and acts like him too. Every day, he picks on somebody for no reason.'

'Never question him, and don't let him hear you complain.'

'But it was an hour's work. Doesn't he realise the disruption he's causing?'

'I doubt it, and as he keeps telling us, all he cares about is editing the best paper in the country; the paper with the fastest increasing sales. It's his way of keeping everyone on their toes. He thinks that if *we* get the dosh, *he* gets the pound of flesh. He must rate you because he recruited you.'

'How do you keep up the pace?'

'If you don't, you're fired because Marcus'll think you're lazy or incompetent. Don't worry; you'll get the hang of it.'

Marcus continued his blitzkrieg. It was mid-afternoon when he reconvened his team back in the main office.

'Let's see what you've got.'

Barry had already spread typed papers and photographs on the table. Marcus recognised much of it as the work he had inspired over the previous hours.

'The Grinderton killing's not what we thought this morning,' said Barry. 'We've prepared a few column inches. Peter?'

'It was a boy doing his A-levels and hoping to get into Cambridge to read Law. He was stabbed to death. The police haven't released details.'

'Photo of the kid?'

'It's there, on the table.'

Marcus found the picture and paused for a moment.

'What's his background?'

'Parents are West Indians. Mother's a nurse and father drives a bus. I don't think there's anything on the boy or the family. He's got brothers and one of them may have been in trouble with the police, but nothing serious. He was with another lad. The police arrested him, but it's not clear why. We've not got a name.'

'Is he the suspect?'

'The police seem to think it was a gang fight.'

Marcus stroked his chin and thought.

'For the moment, one paragraph will do. It won't sell an extra newspaper to make anything of the story, but let's see how things develop. What about the two missing girls?'

'The police are doing the usual search, but there are no clues yet. They've issued more up-to-date photographs,' said Kevin.

'Parents?'

'What we thought; decent middle class and no skeletons. Dads are management types, and both mothers are housewives. The police have started a search. Locals are helping. Reading between the lines, it doesn't sound good. It's not often that children turn up alive after a day missing.'

'Put the faces on the front page,' said Marcus. 'We need a headline. You've got the family story on the inside page. That's fine.'

'There's plenty on the children, from friends and teachers,' Kevin replied enthusiastically.

'Then on page three, something about the search and how the local community's pulling together,' Marcus added, picking up photographs from the table. 'These are all good, so pick out the best. Got anything else, Kevin?'

'I've drafted a swipe at our so-called justice system in my column,' Kevin said. 'I've had a big mailbag from prison officers after last week's editorial on lenient sentencing. They're all saying that prison's become a doddle. I've got quotes and examples of soft punishment for serious crimes.'

'It'll help the Home Secretary. He says he wants tougher justice,' said Marcus.

'I've had letters from victims,' said Kevin. 'There's one case of GBH where the offender was out of prison in less than two years and attacked a pensioner in her house. There's a murderer who was released early and then killed his girlfriend. The family want the death penalty reintroduced.'

'Facts and figures?'

'Over the past ten years, there have been over twenty cases of murderers who've been released and murdered again. I'll remind everyone that dead people don't commit murder. It'll make the liberals choke on their organic muesli tomorrow morning.'

Marcus smiled.

'This is Noreen's masterpiece,' Marcus said as he pointed out a column headed, 'Slags, fags and bags'.

Underneath the heading was a picture of Becky Shearman, cigarette dangling from the corner of her mouth. She was swinging her handbag at the unseen photographer. The bag was inches from the camera, and the photograph beautifully captured the speed of the trajectory.

Kevin explained how he had provoked the reaction, and Noreen enlightened them on the methods she had used to get other celebrities to dish the dirt on Becky Shearman. The men all smiled, except Peter, who had a low opinion of the sort of celebrity bashing that Noreen produced to order.

'Kevin's been rummaging in the dustbins and found empty bottles of gin, and from the date of the last collection, he's worked out she's been drinking two a day,' said Barry. 'The baby's been heard crying at night, so it really is a *Home Alone* story. It'll go here.' Barry pointed to the spot, and Marcus nodded.

Barry continued. 'We've dug out some old stuff on this

rapper and repackaged it. In the sports section we've developed the story about Danny McFeeney. Will he or won't he play at the weekend? The manager says that he'll play, and if he does and plays badly, there'll be a good follow-up story.'

The paper was taking shape, as it always did, and the troops dispersed to their various tasks. Marcus picked up a list of names that had been put on his desk and a file of CVs.

'What's this?' he shouted through his office door.

A middle-aged woman entered.

'It's the shortlist for the job in Features,' she said. 'Personnel dropped it in.'

'Get Tony from personnel, now.'

'It was Janet who dropped it off.'

'I want to see Tony, not Janet.'

Tony knocked on the open door a couple of minutes later.

'Shut the door. Two of the women on this shortlist need removing. One's married. She's twenty-seven, and she'll probably be having kids. The older one has two youngsters at school. She'll not be able to put in the hours we need. Tell Janet to sort it out. She's not going to have kids too, is she?'

'I think she's a lesbian.'

'What! You've recruited a lesbian?'

'I didn't recruit her *because* she was a lesbian, Marcus. Sexual orientation isn't a standard interview question.'

'Couldn't you tell?'

'Well, she didn't fit any of the stereotypes.'

'Don't get clever with me.'

Tony turned and left the office, rolling his eyes.

'Arsehole,' whispered Marcus.

38

MARCUS

Early the following morning, Marcus passed Barry and made his way, at speed, into his office. He waved Barry to follow him.

'It *is* murder then!' Marcus shouted.

'The bodies have been found in woods about twenty miles away,' said Barry. 'The police haven't given details yet, and there's a statement due at midday.'

Marcus picked up the photographs of the two children, which he had left on his desk from the previous day.

'I want our readers to cry and then to get angry.'

Marcus's voice croaked involuntarily. He put the pictures face down on the desk and addressed Barry.

'Get together whatever you can on the two youngsters. We can replay some of yesterday's stuff, but I need more.'

'Kevin's down there, trying to find out if the police have any leads. They're being very cagey, but if they're on to something, Kevin's the best man to find out.'

'Keep this simmering until the police make progress. Is it true that the local force is short of men?'

'Yes.'

'Get some numbers.'

'Peter's trawling for them at the moment,' said Barry.

'Readers get angry when we tell them there are not enough police on the beat and too many of them harassing motorists.'

'Especially if they've just received a speeding ticket.'

'And too many administrators. Peter can get figures on that, too.'

'Have you seen the *Sentinel* piece on the Grinderton murder, Marcus? It's from someone called Kwame.'

Barry pronounced the surname Kwaym.

'What sort of name's that? Kwame? Kwame?' Marcus repeated, using the same pronunciation. 'I read the report, but I didn't register the name. I should have.'

'It's spelt K W A M E.'

'That's Kwar May,' said Marcus.

'No medals for guessing why she's on the case; got a chip on her shoulder. She's saying it's a racist murder, and the police have failed to investigate properly. She's implying that they're racist, too.'

'I heard the chief constable being interviewed on the radio this morning. They must have picked it up from the *Sentinel*. The BBC and the *Sentinel* might as well be the same organisation.'

'Yeah, the interview was biased. The BBC had it in for him,' Barry agreed.

'Undermanned police force being accused of racism by some fucking privileged twat from the BBC who lives in the leafy suburbs. We'll stick up for the police.'

'What I'd like to do, Marcus, is to link all the stories into a law and order campaign. There's an election coming up, and we can highlight politicians' views.'

'Make sure you include Shearman.'

'I've got Peter trawling for quotes from MPs. People will read 'em in the context of these murders. We can do an opinion poll on capital punishment and sentences for violent crime. We know what the outcome is bound to be.'

'Yes, I like that. No politician wants to be seen to be soft on crime when there's an election.'

'Whoever gets elected, we'll hold 'em to account.'

'That's great, Barry. Just get on with it. I'd like to pin something on the BBC too. Can we do some digging on Jeremy McNeice? He's behind some of the anti-police stuff, and he's a friend of Shearman.'

'I'll check what we've got on him.'

'I know he's a homosexual, so he's bound to have some baggage. No holds barred, and no expense spared.'

'You know what it'll mean. The people with that sort of information don't come cheap.'

'I don't want to know. Just get on with it.'

'We've got more on the Becky Shearman story,' said Barry.

'That woman's priceless.'

'Dave Shearman's asked the press to back off his daughter, to give her a chance to sort her life out. Noreen's already on to it.'

'What's the angle?'

'She thought about headlining it with "Hypocrite". She has a picture of Shearman and a double column about him being an absent father when she was going off the rails. We could mention his support for the miners and drugs decriminalisation. We'll dig out what we can.'

'There's a rumour going round that Shearman will be a junior Minister in the Labour government after the next election,' said Marcus.

'God help us all!'

'Get the message across that New Labour means the likes of Shearman in government. Over the next few months we'll have to manage the news carefully; disgust at Tory sleaze but remind our readers what Labour will bring.'

Later that day, Marcus and Barry were discussing the detailed layout for the following morning's newspaper. They were in the main office, studying a computer screen and pieces of paper that were strewn across the desk where the embryonic newspaper was emerging.

'The girls' murder story's good,' said Marcus. 'I like the headline and great pictures of the two girls.' Marcus moved his hands across the table and fingered a sheet of copy. 'This is great. Is it true that Barringham had a record number of speeding fines last year?'

'Honest, we've got the numbers,' said Barry.

'We could do something along the lines of "too much time hounding motorists and too little chasing criminals". There's no mileage in the Grinderton murder,' he continued, picking up the copy and putting it to one side. 'If it's drugs, then our readers won't care who's been killed. If it's racist, to be honest, they won't be much bothered, either.'

'We've managed to piece together a story on Jeremy McNeice,' said Barry. 'We've put it in the Gossip Column, and there's a great picture of him, which sets the tone. He's arm in arm with his boyfriend.'

'I've never liked the man. I was at school with him. He's bright and from a wealthy family. He can't help that, but he's the sort that looks down his nose at the *Echo* and its readers.'

'He doesn't mind flaunting that he's a queer, either.'

'What gets me is that toffs like him have taken over public life, and there's nothing more distasteful to snobs than tradesmen like us. Anything more on Shearman?'

'Noreen's stitched together highlights from Shearman's past, and there's a picture of his ex-wife being bundled into a police van at Greenham. There's plenty to choose from.'

'What was she done for?'

'She was never charged.'

'Pity.'

'No need to tell the readers,' shrugged Barry, 'and anyhow, the picture tells the story.'

'We've still not pinned anything on Shearman about his private life. I bet he's got skeletons in the cupboard. Get Simon in here.'

Barry called across to Simon's desk.

'Just before I went to the *Sunday Echo*, I asked you to dig the dirt on Shearman. He had a string of women when he left his first wife. Are there any children out there that look like our man?' he laughed.

'Surprisingly, he seems to have kept a clean sheet. The marriage ended when his ex-wife defended one of the Greenham women in a court case. They took a shine to each other and shacked up. All very sudden, and she took her daughter with her.'

'I heard he was chasing other women when he was married,' said Marcus.

'Yes, but not before they'd split up.'

'Married women?'

'No. We've published a few kiss and tell stories; nothing much really. It was a messy divorce because of the child, and the mother kept Shearman away. He met his second wife whilst all this was happening, at a Labour Party Conference.'

'What's he been up to since?'

'They've been married for years, ten or more I'd say, with no rumours at all,' said Simon. 'He knows that anything out of line could cost him a job in a Labour government.'

'You surprise me, Simon, you really surprise me. There's something fishy. My instincts tell me that there's something out there.'

'We've paid detectives and police contacts to dig the dirt, and they've been told to do whatever's necessary. You know what that means: telephones, DVLA, medical records, friends and neighbours, the lot. We've a file of confidential stuff, but we've nothing to pin him with. It's cost us a fortune!'

'Do whatever it takes, Simon, do whatever it takes.'

'There's a letter just arrived from Becky Shearman's mother,' said Barry. 'She says that Becky's never left her daughter alone. Whenever Becky's been out, she and a friend have been looking after the child.'

'The two lesbians?'

'Yes. She says the empty bottles were cleared out from a cupboard and were there when Becky moved in. They've asked us to leave Becky alone.'

39

DAVE

The day after the *Echo* story broke, Becky returned to her empty flat. Her mother and daughter had gone out for the afternoon, and she had been to the supermarket. As she fumbled the key into the lock of the front door, she heard footsteps and then a sympathetic voice.

'Hello, Becky. You look like you could do with a hand, love.'

A palm rested on her clenched fist, directed the key into the lock and persuaded it to turn.

'Oh, Dad, Dad, please help me,' she sobbed.

Ten minutes later, Dave and Becky sat opposite each other at the kitchen table, sipping from mugs. Becky was tearful, and Dave tentatively reached across and held her free hand, which felt cold. She did not resist, and Dave put his mug down and took her hand between both of his.

'It's so long since I've seen you, and it's been very painful,' he said.

'You can't stay because they'll be back.'

'I know, but I want to make up with you and Emma. We can't live separate lives forever.'

They talked about Becky's marriage problems. She was distraught that the papers had misrepresented her, and it felt that her life had imploded. Becky looked at her watch.

'You must go.'

'If you promise.'

'What?'

'That we can meet up once a week. Let's try for a month, and see how it goes. I want to help. I want to be a father. Please.'

Becky looked across at her dad.

'OK,' she blurted.

The *Echo* contacted Emma Gladwin's mother and sister. Emma's mother burst into tears, upset by the unsympathetic reference to Emma's sexuality. Emma Gladwin rang the *Echo* to complain, and she was handed over to Kevin Smallman. He enjoyed his brief conversation with Ms Gladwin, which was terminated by the 'lezzer', as Kevin referred to her.

'Mind you I'd prefer watching two lezzers to two queers,' he opined to nodded agreement.

40

LUCY

Lucy was out of bed at 7.00. She turned on the radio and did not have to wait long. The news referred to her *Sentinel* report. The BBC had asked for a comment from the police, who had promised an interview later that morning. It did not seem much, but it was the first time she had gained any recognition.

She had stayed the night in a small hotel. The only paper in the breakfast room was the *Echo*. She leafed through it and saw a brief reference to the murder on an inside page. She dashed out to the nearby corner shop for a copy of the *Sentinel*. There it was, on page two, below a report on two missing girls. Her words had been heavily edited, particularly her accusations about police blunders, but the implications were clear. The police were failing to take this killing seriously, and there was a racial motive.

'Black teenager killed in gang attack' was the headline. Underneath she could see her name, the first time it had appeared in the *Sentinel*. She whispered to herself and smiled.

'Lucy Kwame – Grinderton.'

She took the paper back to the hotel and re-read the report four times.

The story may have been as bitter as her coffee, but the fact that she was being recognised for her work was the sweetener. Her travelling bag was already packed and under the breakfast table. She immediately returned to the scene of the murder, and the change from the previous day was remarkable.

Police vehicles and constables swamped the crime scene. Plain clothes and uniformed police were like mice looking for food, scurrying from door to door, tapping, waiting, turning and then on to the next house. Sometimes a door opened, and following quick shakes of heads, the police officers turned and moved on.

Better late than never.

There was to be another press briefing at noon, and she was aiming to catch the 2.00 train. She had all morning to find out whatever she could about the murderers and took the road toward the Broxley estate.

A car pulled up alongside, and a man leaned over the passenger seat and wound down the window. Lucy was hesitant, but the voice was gentle and friendly.

'Lucy? You're Lucy Kwame, aren't you? I'm a fellow reporter. Could we have a chat?'

Lucy stopped, rested her right arm on the top of the car and looked inside. She recognised the face but could not recall the name. The man was in his late forties. He was clean-shaven, and there was a suggestion of grey in a full head of dark-brown hair. He wore a pullover and jeans.

'I'm Clive Parkhouse.'

'Hello, Mr Parkhouse. I recognise you from the telly.'

'Clive. Call me Clive. Fancy a coffee?'

'What do you want?'

'I may be able to help you.'

'There's nothing you've got that I want, is there?'

'How do you know that? Let's talk.'

Lucy looked Clive in the eye and hesitated for a few seconds.

'OK. I must be mad.'

'Jump in.'

'I know a place. I've a busy day, and I haven't got much time. I'm back to London this afternoon.'

Lucy directed Clive to the café on the Broxley estate where she had been the day before.

'How do you know this place?' he asked.

'I'm a regular. They treat me like family.'

'Oh, hello love,' said the woman behind the counter as they both entered. Her voice was nervous.

'Hello again. How're you?'

'I'm not so bad. Look, you're the lady from the newspaper what caused the bother at the police station, aren't you?'

'How do you know about that?'

Lucy reached the counter, Clive immediately behind her. The café had no other customers.

'You two'd better leave.'

'Come on, chill out. We just want a coffee.'

'It's for your own good,' she implored. 'I'm not tellin' you nothin'. Bugger off before anyone finds out you're here.'

'Those kids that came in. They're the ones aren't they?'

'Off,' she pleaded, 'I've got a life to live and a business to run.'

She waved her hand to shoo the two of them away. Lucy stood her ground, but Clive gripped her wrist. He nodded for them to leave, and she reluctantly acquiesced. As they slammed the car doors shut, four of the five youths that Lucy had seen the previous day crossed the road in front of them. Clive and Lucy had been spotted going into the café, and the word had got round. The moment Clive turned the ignition, they charged at the car from 150 yards away.

Clive crashed the gear lever forward and swung the car in a half circle, and two wheels crunched over the opposite kerb. The young men were within feet of the car as it lurched forward. A solid boot smashed into the side, and Clive saw hatred in the eyes of the teenager who had launched the blow. He was, for an instant, pulling at the wing mirror as Clive accelerated away. There was another thud as a fist landed on the boot lid, and then they were clear.

'Can I choose where we have the coffee?' laughed Clive. 'Did you forget to leave a tip yesterday?'

Lucy was shaking, uncontrollably.

'Sorry,' she whimpered. 'In that split second, I thought of Delroy and how he must have died. The crazed looks in their eyes, d'you know what I mean?'

'I saw it too, but you can't be sure they did it.'

'It was them. Everyone on the estate seems to know. The only people who've no clue are the police.'

'Sure?'

'Sure.'

41

GRAHAM

Graham Knott made sure he was the first to arrive for his shift at the police station in Grinderton. It was early afternoon on the day following Delroy Adams's murder, and Graham had hidden the camera in his shoulder bag. He was expecting a reaction to the murder. The previous night he had planned what he was going to do. He went to his locker at the far end of the locker room and placed his bag on the bench, the hidden camera facing back toward the door. He knew who was on shift that afternoon and where they would change into their uniforms. He calculated precisely where to train the camera to get the best view. The locker room was dark. He turned on all the lights, which was necessary for the camera to be effective.

He worried about two things: being found out and messing up the filming. He had already had one scare. In a coffee break during his months of training, the other recruits had played a game of rugby with his bag, and he had thought his cover would be blown. He had survived, but the camera had been damaged. He'd become increasingly professional with the camera, working out the angles, the light and the sound, but he wasn't in control of what the subjects would say or do, and their movements would often upset his plans. He had learned to get involved in the banter because it forced his colleagues to face him, but he could not encourage racist language because that would jeopardise the integrity of the documentary.

It was only a few minutes after he had set up when Peter Smythe arrived, followed closely by Darren Wyllee and Allan Blackstone. It was Darren Wyllee who would be in the centre of the shot, but the camera would also catch glimpses of the others.

'Watcha, Graham,' said Peter Smythe.

'Hi, Peter.'

Peter and Graham patrolled on foot in the town centre. Darren and Allan shared a police patrol car. They were planning where they would have supper that evening and were opening their lockers as Graham spoke.

'What's the news on the murder, Darren?'

'Fuck knows. Gangs fighting again. A drug dealer's been stabbed. Nobody upstairs seems too fussed about it.'

Darren stood further back than usual and was partly obscured by Allan. Graham pretended to rummage in his bag and moved it into a better spot. He made all his movements seem normal, but he was aware that the bag was now in an unnatural position, balanced precariously on the bench. He hoped it was not too obvious because Allan was looking his way

'I heard it was a school kid,' said Peter.

'One less drug dealer on the streets. They're dealing at the school gates, these niggers. They deserve what they get,' said Darren.

'Come on, Darren,' said Allan, looking suspiciously at Graham, the new boy.

'I mean it. Who gives us most of the gip? Who's dealing drugs? Who is it standing on street corners? I'm just telling the truth.'

'Suppose so,' conceded Allan.

Peter glanced at Graham, shrugged and said nothing.

'Anyhow, I'll tell you what's gonna happen,' Darren

continued. 'We'll put half the station on the case, nobody'll tell us anything and it'll be an unsolved murder. Oh and then we'll get blamed for it by the niggers. We've got better things to do.'

'Get changed,' said Peter to Graham, who was seated next to his shoulder bag. Graham started to put on his uniform, keeping clear of his bag, and the conversation meandered off the subject.

Allan and Darren left first, and Peter nodded in the direction of the showers, indicating that Graham should check if anyone was there. Graham shook his head.

'Not everyone's like that pillock, you know. OK, there may be a few, but most of us are regular guys. Don't pay him any attention.'

'Why doesn't anyone, you know, talk to somebody about him?'

'Dunno. Most coppers wouldn't know who to talk to or what to say. There's a few top brass like him too. They could mess things up for you; you know, promotion. The police force isn't the sort of place where you grass on your mates.'

When Graham finished his shift, he hung around the police station for a while, trying to find out what was happening on the murder case. There was a casual atmosphere surrounding the investigation, and he had few problems getting useful details, particularly about Armstrong Delaney.

When he arrived home that evening, he played the film he had made and gasped at its quality and significance. He had captured everything, and most of the dialogue was head-on to the camera. He decided he would go through the same routine the following day. He phoned Clive from a public box, and told him what he had. The film would be in the usual place, to be collected the next morning. He also told Clive that Armstrong Delaney, who had been in custody, would be released on the morning after next. The police had been granted one more day to question him, but they were not hopeful of getting anything useful. Graham had found out that Delaney had left his parents home some months before and was living with a cousin. His parents and his school did not know where he was staying. He provided Clive with the address he had given the police and where he would be lying low when he was released.

'Make sure you use the information carefully. I'm still a copper and Delaney's only sixteen.'

'It's been on the news all day,' said Allan in the locker room, the following afternoon. 'Upstairs, they're running around like headless chickens.'

'Who *is* this woman Kwame?' asked Darren. 'One nigger woman spreads a load of lies, and all hell's let loose.'

'It's 'cos of the news,' said Peter. 'The brass are frightened 'cos it's on the radio and the telly.'

'They've cancelled all leave,' said Allan. 'That's fucked up my week in Scarborough.'

He slammed his locker door shut.

'They're interviewing everyone involved,' said Peter. 'They've got a PR firm in too. Let's be honest, they made a balls-up of the crime scene, and we're coming across as amateurs. Basic procedures weren't followed.'

'I've heard they gave no first aid,' said Allan.

'For fuck's sake, whose side you on?' said Darren sharply. 'OK, so we didn't follow all the rules, but it's a drug-dealing coon getting what he deserves.'

'We don't know that,' said Peter.

'Black gangs in a fight. Get real,' said Darren.

'This lad's brother's been in trouble,' said Allan. 'No smoke without fire.'

'You wait and see,' shouted someone from the showers,

'When they find out it was a fight over drugs, it'll blow over soon enough.'

'This reporter says it's a white gang. She means the Broxley mob,' said Peter.

'So what?' the disembodied voice shouted. 'White gang fights black gang. It's like fucking chess,' he laughed. 'Yes, and we pick up the pieces.'

'Kwame, what sort of name's that?' said Darren. 'What's she poking her nose in here for? It's none of her fucking business, and she should piss off where she came from.'

'Shit,' shouted the voice, 'I've forgotten my towel.'

A head peered around the corner.

'Lend us your towel, Graham. Come on, you've got one in your bag.'

He leaned over and grabbed one end of Graham's bag, and Graham grabbed the other. The policeman, completely naked, was laughing as he pulled Graham and his bag toward the showers. He was trying to unzip it as he pulled, and it was half open.

'What the fuck you got in here, Knotty?'

'Let go, you idiot.'

The other man pulled a single trainer out of the bag and dropped it on the floor. His arm was quickly up to the elbow and his eyes opened wide in amazement as he pulled out a pair of clean boxer shorts.

'Nice,' he said.

The boxers fell to the floor as his hand began to rummage again. Suddenly, he slipped and fell hard onto his backside, and his colleagues roared with laughter. The fallen policeman picked himself up and started to dry his rear and his groin, ostentatiously, with the boxers.

'Keep 'em,' said Graham. 'They suit you.'

Graham packed his bag into the locker, sighing with relief.

Clive had devised an elaborate scheme for getting the film from Graham, who was living in a flat. His car was in a secure underground car park. The BBC had provided Clive with a contact who worked for a local radio station, and he had a spare set of keys for the flat and the car. At 7.00 in the morning, on his way to work, he picked up the film, which Graham had put under the front seat of the car. He brought it to the radio station where Clive viewed it. Clive was not disappointed because the film was exactly what Jeremy wanted. Clive had heard the BBC's coverage on the radio and read Lucy Kwame in the *Sentinel*. He realised that the more she needled the police, the more reaction he would get. He had heard from Jeremy McNeice that the *Sentinel* had contacted the BBC about the story, which was why it had been given extensive coverage on the news. It was in Clive's interest that Lucy stayed on the case and Graham obtained more footage.

42

CLIVE

Clive found a free table at a café in the High Street and bought drinks. As soon as he sat down, Lucy confronted him.

'It wasn't an accident that you bumped into me, was it?'

'No, I was trying to find you, and I guessed you might be at the crime scene. It's been an exciting and mysterious few minutes, I have to say. I read your piece in the *Sentinel*, and it seems like you're onto something.'

'You still haven't said why you stopped me in the street.'

'We've some mutual interests.' Clive paused. 'I'm working in Grinderton too, investigating the local police force.'

'You want something, don't you?'

'I've some information that could benefit you. In twenty-four hours you've stirred up a hornets' nest,' Clive said quietly. 'I'm researching a story for television.'

'And?'

'It's confidential, so I can't say too much, but we're both onto the same thing.'

'What are we both onto?'

'Racist attitudes in the police, for example.'

Lucy hesitated. 'You still haven't told me what you want. To be honest, I'm more bothered about making the most out of *my* story than benefitting you.'

'Look, I don't want any information from you. The

longer you can keep the story running and uncover police incompetence, the better for me. It's as simple as that.'

'So, what is it you're up to?'

'Confidential.'

'You can trust me.'

'I've obtained evidence on film about levels of racism that's… well, it's barely believable. You're just seeing the tip of the iceberg on the street. It's much worse behind the thin blue line.'

'I'd worked that out from the way they've gone about the investigation. It's more than just a few mistakes.'

'What d'you mean?'

'You're fishing, aren't you?'

'Me?'

'I'm still not sure I trust you. Perhaps you're trying to steal my story.'

'And jeopardise my own? I'd be mad,' said Clive. 'Anyhow, I've already given you enough to blow what I'm doing.'

'How do I know that you've got anything? How do I know that what you've told me is true? Anyhow, everything you've said's too vague.'

'You spoke to Clara Tomlin, last night. She phoned the BBC to get the story a high profile in the morning news. Jeremy McNeice, my contact at the BBC, told me. I work for him as a freelancer. You can talk to Jeremy if you want to. Clara's done a great job because the BBC's pushing the story. I suppose, in a roundabout way, we're already working together.'

'Clara?'

'I know Clara from university. She introduced me to Jeremy. Jeremy hasn't spoken to Clara about what I'm doing, and you mustn't say anything, not yet anyhow. Call Jeremy. I'll give you the number.'

Lucy hesitated.

'How well do you know Clara Tomlin?'

'We were on the student newspaper. We graduated at the same time. Everyone's made it, except me,' he grinned.

'You've done alright.'

'Not as well as the others. There's Clara, at the *Sentinel*, Dave Shearman, who'll be a Minister in the next government and Mike Boddington, who became Editor of a regional newspaper at thirty. Then there's Marcus Roache, who runs the *Echo*.'

'Marcus Roache?'

'Yes, he took over the reins when we left university. If you need time to make some calls, that's fine by me. What do you say?'

Lucy hesitated.

'I could tell you where you can find the lad who was with Delroy Adams when he died,' Clive offered. 'I've got his name. I've got an address too. You could talk to him.'

'He's still being questioned.'

'He'll be out tomorrow morning, first thing.'

'I won't need you to find him, will I?'

'He'll be going into hiding. I know where, but you don't.'

'Hmm.'

'Look, Lucy, I think you should talk to Delroy Adams's friend. Get his angle on the knifing and what the police did when they arrived.'

Clive got out a piece of paper from his trouser pocket.

'His name's Armstrong Delaney. Write this address down. It's Delaney's cousin's house. Delaney *will* be there.'

Lucy scribbled the address.

'Thanks, Clive. Thanks a lot.'

'Get what you can in the *Sentinel*. It'll get a reaction, and that'll help me. That's all I want. Keep the story bubbling.'

'I was going to follow up in Broxley, but I can't do that now,' said Lucy. 'Everyone, I mean just about everyone, knows who did it, except the police. The killers have even bragged about it.'

'No need to go back because you've got the story already. What happened today's the story: the gang, the fear, the intimidation of potential witnesses.'

'It's a pity I got no photographs. Perhaps I should buy a video camera and go back and ask for a replay.' Lucy paused and looked at Clive. 'Joke!'

'There's the racial motive for the attack, and the police are incompetent and prejudiced. The *Sentinel* should major on that. I'm sure you'll get something from Armstrong Delaney.'

'I reckon that Delroy Adams could've been saved if the police had acted professionally,' said Lucy.

'You're right that the police didn't do enough to save his life. I'm sure they'll be trying to cover it up.'

'How d'you know?'

'I can't tell you. You could ask the police for an interview.'

'I'm not exactly flavour of the month.'

'Persuade them it's better to do an interview than for you to do a negative story with a "No comment" statement from them. "No comment" implies that they've got something to hide.'

'I don't know that I've got the bottle.'

'Oh, you have. The police are getting PR advice, so they might be told that it's best to talk. You'll need to handle Armstrong Delaney carefully. He'll probably not want to say anything.'

'I'm surprised that nobody from the local press is taking more interest. It's just their sort of story.'

'Too few reporters left to do the legwork, I'm afraid. Try

to track down Adams's friends. The best place for that is the crime scene. That's where friends always hang out.'

'I've already done that. Yesterday afternoon, I met them on Peel Street, but I'll go back this afternoon. They don't trust anyone white. It's frustrating. They hate the police.'

'Go to the police briefing. Don't make too much of a fuss, but find out anything you can. Don't give any clues about what I'm doing.'

'Don't worry.'

Lucy stopped for a moment's consideration.

'Why are you being so helpful?'

'You're just starting out. You remind me of what it was like back then, or perhaps what I was like back then.' Clive smiled. 'I trust me, so I trust you. Anyhow it's you that's helping me, isn't it?'

'Give me your contact number. This is my card,' said Lucy.

Clive pulled out a wallet from the inside pocket of his jacket. It bulged with receipts, banknotes and cards. He flicked through the tattered leather, but despite shuffling and removing the contents, he could not find what he was looking for. Lucy pointed at his lap. A crumpled piece of card, which had fallen from his pocket as he had rummaged, had lain there for almost a minute. Lucy had not told him because she wanted to enjoy the embarrassment. She was disappointed because Clive showed no discomfiture and handed it to her with a hearty 'Thanks'.

They completed the exchange of details and went their separate ways. Clive phoned Jeremy McNeice and explained what he had done. It was the first time that Clive had heard Jeremy raise his voice in anger. Clive reassured him.

'I hope you're right about her, Clive. *You* can tell Graham.'

'I hope I'm right too because she could mess this up for everybody, including Graham, if she's indiscrete.'

Clive headed for a rendezvous with his informer.

43

LUCY

The press briefing was at noon, and there were fewer people than the day before, just local press and radio and a solitary regional television crew. The story, as far as the national newspapers were concerned, was over. Cautiously, ACC Curry and DS Walther entered the room, and Walther looked nervously around the depleted audience. He caught Lucy's eye and looked downward. Curry opened the briefing, reading from a script.

'Good morning. I can update you on the investigations surrounding the death of Delroy Adams. I'll be brief. This was a brutal attack on a young black man. There were a number of wounds, but the specific cause of death was two knife wounds to the abdomen. We're questioning a young teenager who was with Adams at the time. It's proving quite difficult to obtain a consistent and clear description of what happened as the boy's been traumatised by the events. From what we have pieced together from his account and house-to-house enquiries, there were two groups of youngsters. A fight broke out, and Delroy Adams was fatally stabbed.'

He looked up, expecting a challenge, and then continued.

'We don't know why the fight started, but there appears to have been words exchanged between the two gangs. We're trying to establish exactly who was at the scene. So far, this hasn't proved easy. We've found no murder weapon, but it's bladed and at least nine inches in length. We're pursuing a number of specific lines of enquiry, and we would appeal for any witnesses to the attack to come forward. I will provide you with a phone number that we would like you to publish. In particular, we're aware that there were a number of people at the bus stop opposite. They will have seen what happened. Calls will be treated with utmost confidence. Any questions?'

The reporters looked Lucy's way, expecting her to take the initiative, but she shook her head.

'Is the young man in custody a suspect?' asked a reporter to her right.

'Nothing's being ruled in or out,' said ACC Curry.

'Well, is it true that a gang of white youths was involved in the incident, and they attacked the black boys at the bus stop?' he continued.

'That's one of the possibilities that we're investigating.'

'If that's the case, could this have been a racially motivated attack?'

'It's a possibility.'

ACC Curry looked across to DS Walther for support, and Walther reluctantly spoke.

'In incidents like this, words get shouted, but we don't know what started the argument between these two gangs.'

'You have used the word "gangs",' the reporter continued. 'Are you saying that Delroy Adams was in a gang?'

'I don't... I mean we don't have any evidence, but we have to pursue every possibility. There's always a reason for violence of this sort.'

'Did the police give the boy first aid?'

'I'm not able to confirm that at this stage.'

A much older reporter interjected. 'What sort of lad was Delroy Adams?'

'He's never been in trouble with the police,' said DS Walther.

Lucy left the room with the questions still being asked. There was nothing new in the case, just more evidence that the police were refusing to accept that the motive for the killing was racial.

Lucy bought a roll from a small sandwich shop and went to the station to check later train times home. There was one at 4.40. It would give her time to return to Peel Street. Lucy phoned Victor to confirm her arrival time, and then she contacted the *Sentinel*.

Peel Street was back to normal. She felt uncomfortable. The street had no right to become so mundane so quickly. The only reminder of what had happened was a bedraggled spray of flowers on the pavement.

Within a few minutes, the girl who had laid the flowers walked purposefully in Lucy's direction. She was alone, and she held a school bag in her arms in front of her, as if cradling a baby. She looked at Lucy but continued past her with a determined stride. She arrived at the tribute to her friend. It had fallen to the floor, and she leaned it back against the wall. She stood for a moment and then walked to where Lucy was standing.

'I guessed you'd be back,' she said. 'I want justice for Del. I don't want 'em to get off, just 'cos they're white. Del never done nobody no harm. The lads what ran off won't go to the police.'

'Why not?'

'They're frightened what might happen. They say that they was attacked for no reason but they was black. The police're never gonna catch the killers 'cos they won't listen to the truth. I seen what you wrote in the paper. I showed 'em. If you promise you won't tell the police 'bout who you're meetin' and where, I can get 'em, some of 'em, to talk to you. They don't want nothin' to do with the police.'

'Of course I won't tell the police, but I have to print what they say.'

'They don't like you. They don't trust you.'

'But I'm only trying to help.'

'That don't matter. You're white. You're from the newspapers. People like you done nothin' for us. Papers tell lies.'

'You *can* trust me,' said Lucy.

'Nobody round here trusts you; not the police, the kids, the grownups, nobody.'

'You do.'

'Huh. I can see what you get outta this, white journalist woman, but I don't see nothin' for us. You don't talk to the police, that's all.'

'OK.'

'Sweet.'

'Armstrong Delaney's got to be there.'

'He's bein' held by the police, you know?'

'He'll be out tomorrow.'

'How you sure of that?'

'It's my job to find out.'

'He won't talk.'

'Look, I know he'll be at his cousin's place. I've got the address. Let's meet there.'

She showed the girl the piece of paper with the address.

'How you know that too?'

'I told you, it's my job. I'll meet them there.'

'You're smart. Next Monday after school, at four. Be alone, and you tell nobody, right?'

'I have to tell my boss. I can't just come up here from London without a reason. I won't tell him who I'm seeing, or where, just that I'm meeting witnesses.'

'OK. Monday... right? Ring the bell and give your name,

Mrs Lucy *Kwame*,' she said, emphasising the surname with a hint of a smile.

'What's *your* name?'

The girl turned abruptly and crossed the road. Lucy took one more look at the flowers. It reminded her of a visit to a First World War battlefield when she was about eight years old. Clara's father, who was seriously ill and had only a few months to live, had asked Clara to find and photograph her grandfather's headstone. Her father had been born during the First World War, but her grandfather had been killed in Picardy before he ever had the chance to see his son.

They had been on their way back home from a holiday in France, and Clara had first taken Lucy to the ploughed fields where the battles had been fought and her great-grandfather had died. She could not comprehend that it had once been a place where so many had been slaughtered.

She remembered how she had then been taken to the nearby military cemetery. She had seen the rows of headstones, which seemed like a patterned carpet, stretching forever in all directions. Soldiers did not die in rows, she had thought. It was as if people wanted to tidy up the mess and make it more palatable.

They had gone to her great-grandfather's grave and laid flowers. Lucy remembered that she had not understood when this killing had happened and why. Her lifespan had been a sequence of well-ordered events that she could recall in minute detail, but everything before her birth had been a jumble of unrelated dates. She had guessed that the Second World War was after the First, but one year seemed a long time to her, and sixty years was inconceivable.

She had seen the name, George Edward Tomlin, and the date he died. He was twenty-one when he was killed.

'Is this where my dad's buried too?'

'No, Lucy. Your father isn't dead. It's your great-granddad who died here. That's Granddad Tomlin's dad.'

'Where's my dad then, Mum?'

'He's got a young family of his own. He lives in England.'

Lucy's mum had been so matter-of-fact.

'So I'm part of his family, too?'

'Yes, you are. Your father married someone else. He's got his own children, but we're happy on our own, aren't we?'

'Yes but it would be nice to have a dad too. You've got a dad. Does my dad live near to us? Can we go and visit him?'

She remembered that her mum had turned away. She had tidied her own life, but had left Lucy's in a muddle. The subject of her father was avoided, not through lack of interest on Lucy's part, but because it upset her mother so.

44

CLIVE

Clive met Graham on the outskirts of Manchester, at a café where they had rendezvoused on previous occasions. He told Clive how the *Sentinel* report had caused a change in approach by the senior officers and a hardening of attitudes from some of the rank and file.

'I just need a bit more time, Graham. We'll broadcast later in the month. I've met Lucy Kwame. With a bit of luck, the *Sentinel*'s going to keep the story alive, and you can pick up the reaction.'

Clive told him what he had agreed with Lucy.

'It's a risk, isn't it, talking to her? We said we'd keep this tight. Have you told Jeremy?' said Graham, annoyed.

'It's a risk, yes, and I've just spoken to Jeremy. He's a bit flustered, but he'll calm down. She may be young and inexperienced, but she'll do the right thing. Anyhow, she doesn't know about you or how we're getting the filming done. She'll be the catalyst for getting the footage we need.'

'I hope you're right. The funny thing is, I've enjoyed it on the beat. Most of the lads are OK and doing a good job. Deal with the bastards, and it'd be a great place to work. If I can't get acting jobs, I might sign up,' he smiled.

They left the café separately, and Clive phoned Ameera at the surgery.

'Ameera, I may be a little late tonight. Chloe's got the key, but could you just check on her on your way home? I'll leave her a message on the home phone.'

Clive arrived back at 6.00. Chloe and Nas were watching television in the living room, and Ameera was in the kitchen, clearing away the dishes from the children's meal and washing up.

'What are *you* doing here?' asked Clive. 'I didn't expect you to cook for her.'

'Well it's as easy to do tea for two as for one. I've cooked for us as well.'

'Oh! Thanks. I wasn't expecting a treat. I smell something spicy.'

'Don't sit down. I've done a proper chicken karai with cashews. It's almost ready, and the naan'll be done in a jiffy. Go and freshen up, and it'll be on the table when you're down. Then you can wash up,' she smiled.

Clive could smell the food from the upstairs bathroom and was soon back in the kitchen where Ameera was pouring a glass of Gewürztraminer. The food steamed on the plate, and they hardly spoke a word as they ate. Clive wiped the plate with the last piece of naan and sat back in his seat as Ameera finished her meal.

'That was fantastic. You're a really great cook, Ameera.'

'Thank you,' she said coyly.

Clive did not notice her embarrassment and launched straight into the developments in Grinderton. He could not hide his excitement, but Ameera was not listening. Clive was unaware at first, but then he realised.

'You're not paying attention.'

'*You* haven't been paying attention for… well I don't know how long for.' She hesitated. 'How long have we known each other now?'

'Four or five years, I guess. Time flies, doesn't it? I haven't really thought about it.'

'That's the problem, you haven't thought about it. Well, in that time, we've shared our children, our food, our houses and our kitchens, as well as day trips to the seaside, our cars and our time.'

'I suppose you're right,' he replied. 'Where's this conversation going?'

'There's only one thing left that we haven't shared, isn't there?'

'Oh, what's that?'

'Well, think on it for a few minutes. I'll do the washing up, if you clear the table.'

Clive shook his head. He studied her from behind as she allowed the hot water to pour into the sink. She turned and smiled.

'Any ideas?'

He delivered the plates to the sink. Then he coughed, as if to signal his approach. She had her hands in the hot water and he moved his whole body close behind hers. He had never touched her with intent, but now his hands rested gently and cautiously on her thighs.

'Is this what you mean?'

'Hmm.'

She removed her wet hands from the sink, put them on top of his and guided them slowly up her sides. She said nothing as his hands reached her breasts and then down the front of her body. He remembered the feeling and the soft smell.

'What if the children...?'

'Let's go,' she whispered.

'When?'

'Now.'

'Where?'

'To my house.'

'Your dad's helping me with that light that needs fixing,'

shouted Ameera to Nas. 'Won't be long. What are you watching?'

'*Pride and Prejudice.*'

'Isn't this a bit of a rush?' whispered Clive.

'How many years do you need?'

Ameera was gentle and understanding.

'I can see in your eyes what you're thinking, but it doesn't matter. We can't forget what we once loved, neither of us.'

She told him she loved him. It was the heartfelt words of a mature woman who knew what love was – to find, to possess and to lose.

'That was beautiful,' she said. 'It'll get better. Practice makes perfect,' she smiled.

'I think I love you, too,' said Clive.

When they returned, Chloe and Nas were in the living room, seeming not to have moved.

'I've videoed it for you,' said Chloe to Ameera and nudging Nas with her elbow, she added, ''cos your mum thinks Colin Firth's a dream.'

'Oh, for goodness' sake,' he sighed. 'There's no action. It's so boring.'

'Time for home,' said Ameera, and the two youngsters, approaching their teens, got up from the settee.

Ameera looked at Clive and smiled. Clive responded for the first time. Chloe saw the exchange.

Nas and his mother left, and Chloe sat at the kitchen table as Clive sipped the last of his wine.

'Ameera's nice, isn't she?'

'Yes, she's very nice.'

Chloe smiled contentedly to herself.

45

LUCY

The following Monday, Lucy jumped on the afternoon train to Grinderton. In her case, she had a copy of the second report, which had appeared in the *Sentinel* the previous week. The local media – newspapers, television and radio – had followed up the story, and two nationals had done single paragraphs, but only the *Sentinel* had reported in any depth. She pulled out the paper. The headline was 'Progress on Grinderton murder hindered by police blunders'.

Lucy smiled to herself as she re-read the article, which was unequivocal in its criticism of the police and the racist nature of the attack. On the same day, there had been a paragraph in the Leader Column, headlined 'Racist Attitudes'. It contrasted the way that the Barringham and Grinderton murders had been covered by the press and investigated by the police.

Lucy re-read the reports and then pulled out a copy of *OK!*, which entertained her for the rest of the journey.

Lucy arrived at a large Victorian town house, converted to flats, just off Peel Street and half a mile further out of town than the murder scene. She was confronted by a display of eight doorbells, and she selected the third from the bottom and rang it. She could hear no ring and waited for twenty seconds. She wondered whether it was working. Was she being ignored? She was about to ring again when there was a click and a voice from a small speaker beneath the bells.

'Yeh?'

'It's Lucy, Lucy Kwame.'

'On your own?'

'Yes.'

'OK.'

Then silence. Lucy nervously looked around. There were passers-by, but they paid her no attention.

She heard footsteps and the rattle of the door opening.

'Come on in, then,' ordered an ethereal voice. The owner was already climbing the first flight of stairs as she peered inside. 'Shut the door,' said the man, now on the landing, his back to her.

He disappeared, and she heard footsteps ascending a second flight. She followed the sound and arrived at a half-open door on the second floor.

'Hello,' she said at the door, then pushed it open and stepped across the threshold.

It was a small room and had a single unmade bed along the far wall, beneath the only window. There was a mattress on the floor, wedged into the corner, making an L shape with the bed. The room seemed to be half of a larger one that had been split. She could make out the semi-circle of a ceiling moulding, which disappeared into a room next door, and she imagined the grand chandelier that might have once hung there. The curtains were drawn and a single wall lamp, without a shade, provided the only light.

There were four young men in the room. They were all black. Two were lying across the bed, and she guessed they were Delroy's friends who had escaped from the Broxley gang. Another stretched out on the mattress, feet on the floor, and Lucy speculated that he was Armstrong Delaney. The fourth man, who had opened the door, was older than the other three and was leaning against the wall to her right.

Lucy assumed he was the cousin. The three younger men seemed nervous.

'I'm Lucy,' she said.

No response.

'I want justice for Delroy. I'll do what I can to get it,' she continued.

The two men on the bed glanced at each other.

'Which of you is Armstrong Delaney?'

The two on the bed looked across to the youngster on the mattress and said nothing.

Lucy addressed the young man on the mattress.

'Armstrong, I'm trying to help. I can't promise anything, but at least I can get the real story told. I know what happened. I know the gang from Broxley killed Delroy.'

'He don't want to speak to nobody,' said the older man. 'He's seen too much, know what I mean? The police let his friend die and then accuse him of bein' in a gang fight. He won't talk to nobody. Them white boys'd kill us as soon as look at us, if they had half a chance. I know you don't believe me, but we gotta keep our heads down.'

'I *do* believe you. Come on, I'm trying to help, but you've got to help yourselves.'

There was a hint of anger in her voice.

'Talk to Mark,' he said, pointing at one of the young men on the bed, 'and Darren,' indicating the other. 'They'll tell you what they seen.'

She looked across, and Darren spoke quietly.

'We was on our way home from town 'cos, like, we're all in the sixth form together. We was walkin' up Peel Street when them white lads come round the corner. We said nothin' but they started shoutin' at us, callin' us "nigger" and stuff like that. This one lad was givin' us the come-on. Know what I mean, with the hands, wavin' us forward, like this, you know.'

He made a beckoning movement with his palms upwards in front of him, moving his fingers back and forth.

'He was shoutin' "Come on then niggers. If you're so hard, come on, give it a go." We walked up Peel Street to get away from 'em, but they followed. I know what's up their sleeves. I see knives, straight. Delroy didn't see what they was carryin'. No, he didn't see.'

Mark interrupted. 'I shouted to leg it, and we all ran, but Del and Armstrong just kept walkin'. They didn't run. God, they didn't run. Armstrong grabbed at Del as them lads crossed the road, but Del just keeps walkin'. Man, he just keeps goin'. He don't pay 'em no bother.'

His voice was loud and becoming increasingly excited.

'We'd stopped down the road. The white lads was close to 'em, close as you, then Armstrong ran. Nobody'd said nothin', nothin', nothin'. Then they just smashed into Del, and I saw two of them use their knives. We seen Del go down, and we ran.' Mark dropped his head and was on the verge of tears. 'They was laughin' and cheerin', and we fuckin' ran,' he mumbled.

'Did you see their faces?' asked Lucy.

'It were the gang from up Broxley. Everybody knows 'em,' said Darren.

'The police drove past. They must've seen 'em, too,' mumbled Armstrong from the mattress. 'They fuckin' know who done it. The coppers know 'em. They're bastards, the fuckin' police. They could've saved Del. They didn't care a shit. They just left Del to die. They know first aid. They know what to do, but they done nothin'.'

'Did you see their faces?' asked Lucy.

'No 'cos it's getting dark, and I legged it. The cops... they kept askin' me what we done. They wasn't interested in them white bastards. We was just walkin' home, but they don't believe me. They done nothin' for Del, nothin'. He should be alive now.'

'Why didn't Delroy run?'

'I dunno. Why should he? What's he done wrong, 'cept he's black.'

'What did the police do?'

'I was talkin' to Del, real close, but he couldn't hear. This copper asks me what I'm doin' and I say Del needs help. The copper keeps askin' what happened, and I keep tellin' him Del needs help. "Help him, help him, stop the blood, please stop the blood. You're the police, for fuck's sake. Help him".'

Armstrong was shouting, just as he had that day on the street. His voice dropped as he continued.

'This one copper pulls me away, and Del's askin' for me, so I tries to push him off, but the copper grabs me again and takes me to the police car. The other copper's looking at Del, but he don't know what to do. He sees all the blood and he's just fuckin' lookin'. He's got blood on his hand and he's like, like starin' at it.'

Armstrong shook his head as he relived the moments.

'He should've done something but he never tried.'

'Why not?'

'I dunno. Scared, or he don't know what to do. It's like he don't want to touch Del, a black kid, blood and all. Then he says Del's dead and I'm shoutin' 'cos I wanna see my friend, and I'm fightin', and the copper's got my hand up my back and… I don't wanna talk no more about it.'

'What happened in the police station, Armstrong?'

'I told 'em it was a gang from Broxley. We know 'em. It's the same lads every time.'

'If the police put them in front of you, on an identity parade, could you identify them?'

'I dunno.'

'Have the police asked you that?'

'I dunno. No. I can't remember what they said. They just wanted me to tell 'em it was a gang fight. Drugs, they kept askin' about drugs. They didn't want the truth. I don't want to talk to you no more.'

Armstrong was mumbling down the front of his T-shirt. Lucy could barely hear him.

'Look, I believe everything you've said, all of you. I'll do what I can to get these murderers brought to justice, but I can't promise anything.'

'We don't want no trouble. Nobody must know we spoke to you,' said Mark, nervously.

'I won't report your names but, if it's OK, I'll publish the gist of what you've told me. I'll ask questions of the police in my newspaper.'

'Sweet,' said Mark.

'The best way of getting these murderers to court is to go to the police, and tell them everything you know,' said Lucy to Darren and Mark.

'I'll do anythin' to get them into prison, anythin', but I ain't going to the police,' said Darren. 'Not after how they treated Del and Armstrong.'

'Look, things'll never change unless *you* make them,' said Lucy, pointing a finger at them. 'You could put these racists behind bars if you wanted to.'

'You don't know nothin',' said Darren.

'Are any of you on the phone?'

There were shakes of the head.

'This is my number if you want to get hold of me. If I'm not in, leave a message. It might be a bit of a giveaway reading the *Sentinel* round here, but the local paper will pick up the story and run with it, I'll make sure of that. Is there anything else?'

More shakes of the head.

'OK. I'm back to London. Best of luck.'

None of the young men replied.

She went through the door and reached the top of the stair. A hand grabbed her wrist, and she turned, startled. The cousin put a finger to his lips and spoke in a hushed voice.

'Look, miss journalist lady, Armstrong ain't going to do no identity parade. There's no point gettin' angry.'

'I'm frustrated.'

'No, you angry. The boy's blown. His mind's gone. This killin's got to him real bad. He don't trust the police. He's scared by what the police done. You do what you gotta do without him. The other boys, well they may change their minds. Wait and see. We're gonna keep our heads down till all this blows over. It's not safe round here with them bastards from Broxley.'

He let her go and moved his finger back to his lips. Lucy had promised to do what she could, but perhaps it was already too late to get justice.

46

CLIVE

That evening, back in Sheffield, Ameera and Clive had left the two children at Ameera's house, doing their homework. They went to an Italian restaurant together. It was the first time they had been out without the children.

'After, you know, after what's happened,' Clive squirmed, 'where does it leave us?'

Ameera leaned across and wiped a dribble of sauce from Clive's mouth with her napkin.

'Well, where do you want it to leave us?' asked Ameera, bluntly.

'That's not fair. You've answered a question with a question.'

'Just tell me what you want, Clive. I need to know. What did it mean to you?'

'This is getting a bit heavy, isn't it?'

'No, it's not. We're two adults. We've both been married. We know what it's all about, don't we? Just tell me what you want.'

'I'm a middle-aged man who's been lucky enough to have got a second chance… a chance to rebuild my life, I suppose. Bloody hell, that sounds a bit melodramatic.' Embarrassed, Clive looked down at the food on his plate. 'I'd like to make that life with you, Chloe and Nas, as a family I suppose, but I'm frightened.'

'Frightened of what?'

'I'm frightened you'll say "no", and I'm more frightened that if you say "yes", I'll let you down.'

'Clive!'

'I'm frightened about getting hurt again because I didn't handle the last time so well. I know I can be... well, to be honest, weak. I think I love you, Ameera, but I don't want to make things difficult for you.'

'How can you make things any more difficult? It's been torture in this... this sort of limbo-land. I've wanted to touch you and hold you, but you've not been ready. I've loved you almost since we first met.'

'I didn't realise.'

'You weren't looking.'

'I never saw it because I was thinking about myself. After Marie died I was weak, pathetic. I didn't trust myself, well, not enough to get close to anyone.'

'You're not weak. You're strong, strong inside. You've turned your life round. With some people it takes a long time for wounds to heal. That doesn't make you any less of a person. I needed you, to make love with you, more than anything I can explain, and I want it to be part of my life. Is that what you want?' asked Ameera.

'Yes.'

'Sure?'

'Yes, but I'm not clear where we go from here. We could just continue on as we are, I suppose'.

'We could, or get married, or live together. What do *you* want?'

'Hold on. What do I want? That's putting me on the spot. What about you?'

'I want to live with you,' said Ameera. 'I want to make our two families into one. I don't care about getting married, but we could ask the kids what they think.'

'I'm a bit old to get married. I'm pushing fifty. What about religion? I'm a Catholic and you're a Muslim. We couldn't get married in church.'

'Oh, come on, Clive. You're not a Catholic. When did you last go to church? You're not religious, and me neither. Our children haven't been raised that way. We could marry at a register office. Let's ask Nas and Chloe.'

'Are you sure you want to get married?'

'I'm sure. Are you?'

'I'll need a new suit.'

'Not just a suit. If the children want us to get married, we'll do it properly. I need some new clothes too. It feels like a bit of shopping could be on the agenda. Let's go to Meadowhall. We can enjoy a day out, and we'll take the children.'

'You did say, "Enjoy", didn't you?'

Clive worked tirelessly over the following few weeks and spent many hours in London, editing the film and developing a cohesive story with Jeremy. The BBC prepared a trailer to stimulate interest. Lucy wrote three follow-up articles, and the hidden camera caught individual officers expressing increased hostility toward her, particularly when it became more widely known that she was white.

It was time to release the programme on the unsuspecting public.

47

LUCY

It was late when Lucy arrived home from Grinderton. She had a copy of the following morning's paper in her hand, which she had picked up at work, on her way back from the station. She gave a shouted whisper.

'I'm back.'

'There's tea in the pot, Lucy,' was the equally muted response.

Emily had been put to bed hours before, and Victor was drinking tea at the kitchen table. He looked up, and Lucy spread the newspaper in front of him. She leaned over him proudly as he scanned the front page, her hands on his broad shoulders. The main headline was about government sleaze, but underneath it read:

'Racism and incompetence in police enquiry.'

Victor studied the article and turned to page two where the story continued.

"The police investigation into the Grinderton murder has ground to a halt. Police spokesmen have indicated that they have no reliable leads. They believe that the crime resulted from a fight between two gangs, although they say there has been conflicting evidence from members of the public. The *Sentinel* has interviewed a number of witnesses. They have all given the same story.

A small group of black boys, returning from Grinderton town centre, encountered a gang of white youths who shouted racist taunts at them. The black boys said nothing and continued to walk home. The white gang challenged them, and one of the boys, Delroy Adams, was overpowered as he walked away, beaten and stabbed. He was left to stagger and fall on the pavement where his friend, Armstrong Delaney, tried to help.

The police arrived, passing the retreating white gang as they escaped. Delaney was manhandled into a police car as a suspect, and no first aid was given to Delroy Adams, who died on the street shortly after. The crime scene was not sealed, witnesses at a bus stop across the road not identified, and nothing was done to arrest the fleeing gang. The police and local residents know the gang members, who are from the Broxley Estate. Yesterday, the *Sentinel* put these accusations to the police, and they have declined to comment. The *Sentinel* has also offered to provide them with the information it has gathered. So far, they have not taken up the offer.

As a result of the police incompetence, friends fear it is becoming increasingly unlikely that anyone will be brought to justice."

He finished, turned and smiled at Lucy. It was all her work, with minimal editing.

'You must be proud. It was the same for me when I first arrived here from Nigeria as a kid. People assume that if you're black, you're a problem.'

Lucy sat next to Victor, who spoke ruefully of his own experiences.

'I don't feel good about what I'm doing. I know I should, but I don't.'

'Why?'

'The kids won't help me and won't help themselves. They think I'm more interested in the story than in them, and that'll be their lasting memory. In a way, they're right. But for the story I'd have never got involved, and I feel I've cheated them.'

'You've done what you can.'

'I know, but they are so alienated from society, they refuse to help themselves. That's really frustrating. If everyone had cooperated, we could have nailed the killers and exposed the police.'

Victor put his arm round her waist.

'Victor, I've found out a few other things whilst I've been away. They're about Mother… and me, possibly.'

Victor was still looking at the *Sentinel*.

'Sorry… I wasn't listening.'

'You know the guy I've been working with, Clive Parkhouse,' she said.

'Yes.'

'I've not said much about him, but he knew my mother at university.'

'Have you told her?'

'No. They worked on the university newspaper together, with Dave Shearman and Marcus Roache.'

'The names are familiar, but…'

'Shearman's an MP; Roache is Editor at the *Echo*.'

'Has your mother ever mentioned it?'

'No.'

'That's a bit odd, but why would she?'

'I don't know, but I've got a feeling about it. Perhaps it's something to do with my father. Don't mention anything to her.'

'Mum's the word.'

'That's not funny. There's something about him. Clive Parkhouse is the sort of person mum would like, I mean *really like*. Perhaps I'm making something out of nothing. I've not mentioned Clara being my mum to Clive. He's no idea.'

'You don't think your mother and Parkhouse…?'

'I'm going to try to find out.'

The investigation in Grinderton slowed to a halt. The trail had gone cold, and nobody on the Broxley estate was prepared to talk because the white gang had created a climate of fear. There were rumours that the father of one of the gang had close connections with the police. The police made tentative efforts to trace Delroy's friends, but the black population had lost faith in the police enquiry and refused to cooperate.

Although Lucy had kept the story alive, reporting the lack of progress on the case, she became increasingly disillusioned that her efforts were leading nowhere and that only the *Sentinel* was running the story. It was as if there was a conspiracy of silence.

It was three weeks after they had met in Grinderton that Clive rang Lucy at work. He gave Lucy a full description of the undercover film.

'The programme will be on television next week. The BBC wants to get it on air whilst the Adams murder is still in people's minds.'

'That's great. None of the other papers have shown any interest.'

'There's an intro which talks about the mishandling of the Delroy Adams murder. Then a few short bursts from the hidden camera. They were shot immediately after the murder, and quite a few bits are bleeped out. You're not flavour of the month. After that we've got the earlier clips taken during training.'

'Bleeped out... I can live with that.'

'We'd like to include an interview with you too. It would be good if you could get something in the *Sentinel* before the programme. It'll help both stories. Clara Tomlin will know what to do. Speak to her because she's on the ball, and she can discuss the best approach with Jeremy McNeice. Now we're ready to roll, you can tell her whatever she needs to know.'

Lucy arranged to see her mother that evening. They sat across the coffee table, engaged in small talk. Without any segue, Lucy addressed her.

'I've met someone you know, someone from university.'

Lucy was watching her mum's facial expression.

'Oh. Oh really. Who's that then?' she replied.

'Clive Parkhouse.'

'Oh, Clive,' said Clara.

It was obvious to Lucy that Jeremy McNeice had told her nothing about Clive's investigation. Lucy described her meeting with Clive.

'Does he know I'm your mother?'

'No.'

'Will you tell him?'

'I wasn't going to. Do you want me to?'

'No, no, it's best you say nothing.'

Lucy explained the format of Clive's forthcoming programme.

'He wants a brief interview with me and for us to run something in the *Sentinel*, something to keep the story going.'

'What's the latest on the police investigation?'

'At last, they've realised who murdered Delroy and why, but they've no corroborative evidence. Nobody from the bus stop has come forward. Delroy's mates couldn't identify the murderers and won't talk to the police. Armstrong Delaney's so shaken up by it all he doesn't trust anyone, and he's an unreliable witness.'

'The police've botched the whole thing, haven't they?'

'They're trying like hell to cover it up. They know everyone in the gang, but they've got no proof; nothing to make a prosecution stick. They've never recovered from the foul-up at the start.'

'Then that's what you have to say in the *Sentinel*. The investigation floundered because of the assumptions the police made about the black teenagers. Emphasise the racial element, to link into Clive's programme. Draft something, and I'll agree the timing between Jeremy McNeice and the *Sentinel*.'

Lucy nodded.

'Mother, why have you never talked about your friends at university?'

'Why should I? This investigation will help your career, you know.'

'They're people in the news, or people making the news. Dave Shearman and Marcus Roache were both on the student newspaper when you were there. I'd have thought you'd have mentioned them.'

'It's not important. I've moved on. I'll talk to Jeremy tomorrow.'

'Have you met any of them since university?'

'I've bumped into all of them, through work.'

'What was it like at university? What were they like?'

'It was a long time ago. There's nothing much to say.'

'Mother, I'd like to know.'

'There's nothing to know.'

'I need to…'

'No, you *don't*.'

'What are you frightened about. What don't you want me to find out? My father?'

Clara turned her head away, and her refusal to make eye contact ended the conversation, which Lucy skilfully steered back to the minutiae of daily life. She could see that her mother's legs had started to shake uncontrollably and she felt guilty that she was the cause. Her mother's health was deteriorating.

The following week, Clara joined Victor and Lucy, to watch Clive's exposé.

Clara did not notice that Lucy was watching her mother as she was viewing the television.

48

CLIVE

The following morning, Jeremy McNeice phoned Clive. There had been a fierce response to the programme, and a wide spectrum of views had been expressed. The BBC had received complaints of anti-police bias from the Police Federation, Association of Chief Police Officers, individual police officers and members of the public. Some viewers had expressed the view that there was nothing particularly exceptional in the police behaviour, and they could not understand the fuss. The police had merely been responding to the reality of black crime.

However, as the day wore on, the most common reaction, and that of commentators and politicians, was one was of amazement and shock at the attitudes exposed, and there were demands for action. There was the promise of questions in Parliament. The tabloids were largely silent.

Meanwhile, a warrant had been issued for Graham Knott's arrest. He had resigned from the police the previous week. The charge was related to him being paid as a policeman whilst working for the BBC. The BBC had foreseen this possibility, and all of Graham's earnings had been banked and returned to the police the previous day. Graham would hand himself in later that morning.

Clive had started to write his book on the Grinderton case weeks before and had spent most of his spare time completing the work. He had added the final chapter, which covered the reaction to the TV programme, and it was published shortly after.

Clive and Lucy arranged to meet at a café in Shepherd's Bush. Clive was in London for the day, invited as a guest on a radio show where his book was being reviewed. Lucy was running half an hour late, and Clive was glancing through a novel as she entered the café. He did not see her at first, but she greeted him from the bar as she ordered a drink. He closed the book, and she pulled up the chair opposite him.

'Good book?' she asked.

'Crap. I'm on the Jonathan York radio show this afternoon, and the two books being reviewed are mine and this pile of garbage by Kevin Smallman.'

'Best of luck. How are things with you?'

'Good, thanks. The programme has gone down well, and it's opening doors. And you?'

Lucy expressed her mounting frustration at the lack of action following the BBC and *Sentinel* exposures, but Clive explained that this was often the way. Although an investigation into the police handling of the murder had been announced, Lucy was sure nobody would be brought to justice because of the botched investigation.

'I imagined there'd be much more of a public outcry,' she said, 'but it's all gone quiet. Nobody seems to care.'

'People *do* care, but we're in the news business, not politics. After every news event, another story breaks, and things move on. Newspapers have to fill their pages, and they're always looking for the next story.'

'I know that,' said Lucy, tetchily, 'but there's a wall of silence. The public's not aware racism is a problem because the media's largely ignoring it. What's not printed is more revealing than what is.'

Clive told Lucy about his own experiences during the miners' strike and his realisation that parts of the press were tacitly, and sometimes explicitly, promoting the cause of powerful interests. It was, in his view, a deliberate and successful attempt to move the centre of political debate.

'You're painting a gloomy picture.'

'That's the disappointment that comes with age,' he smiled.

'You're not that old.'

'There are wealthy people controlling all parts of public life, including the media. The government will find it hard to stand up to them. Political parties are getting clever at managing the news, so we're ending up with a battle of propaganda, not facts or ideas. Of course, the media controls which side of the story's heard.'

'There's still a place for proper and honest reporting.'

'For those who're thick-skinned enough because people who speak out'll be subjected to personal attacks, believe me. The papers'll dig for dirt, even when it isn't there – anything to discredit anyone who disagrees with them.'

'You mean people like us.'

'Yes. It's what's happening in America.'

'I hope you've got no guilty secrets.'

'Oh, I've got plenty.'

Clive looked at his watch.

'I'll have to go. You did a brilliant job on the Adams murder. You've got my contact details. If anything comes up that looks interesting, give me a ring. I'll do the same.'

'I spoke to Clara about your time at university. She asked me to pass on her best wishes,' Lucy lied. 'When was it you were at university together?'

'Late 60s, and we both finished in June 1968. She's a lovely lady. We got on well. I really like her.'

Clive stood, picked up his book and offered his hand.

'All the best, and I hope we meet again,' he said.

'I'm sure we will.'

Two hours later, Clive left the radio studio, pleased with the way he had handled the interview. It had been important for his confidence because, as he suspected, Smallman had made unkind references to his drinking and public disgrace. He had not been flustered, had forensically critiqued Smallman's novel and stood up to Smallman, who came across as a bigot and a bully. It was late that evening when he arrived home. Ameera had made supper at Clive's house. Nas and Chloe were watching television. Clive tucked into a plate piled with homemade samosas.

'We all listened to you on the radio.'

'All?'

'Yes, at the surgery. I was so proud of you. You made Smallman sound stupid.'

'He is. Why was everyone listening in? Do they know about us?'

'Of course and why shouldn't they? It's been a rumour for months, no, years. Anyhow, I've got more important things to talk about. We've all agreed that Nas and I are moving in,' said Ameera casually. 'Nas will take the spare bedroom and I'm moving in with you.'

'What do you mean, "we've agreed"? Who are you talking about?'

'The three of us – the family – you remember? Obviously, you need to give your assent, but I'm sure it won't be a problem, will it?'

'You're being very domineering. Have I got any choice?'

'Not really. If you don't agree, think what you'll be missing.'

Clive looked up, and Ameera lowered her face to his mouth

for a kiss. Clive who was still eating, drooled, and pieces of vegetable fell from his mouth. She smiled seductively as their lips parted.

'The children want us to get married. I'll arrange it all.'

'You really are bossy.'

Ameera ignored him.

'It would be best if I sold up. We could move to a larger house later, couldn't we?'

'I give up. I'll do whatever you want,' spluttered Clive.

'Whatever?'

'Yes. I give in.'

'Good. That's what I like to hear,' she laughed.

49

MARCUS

Labour won the 1996 election, and Marcus had established himself as a dynamic and controversial editor at the *Echo*. With this had come a degree of fame and media pressure for interviews. He was repeatedly being asked to participate in public discussion and debate, and he had resisted, politely but firmly. Marcus had been avoiding talking to the BBC for weeks.

First, it had been the radio wanting an interview and now television. Jeremy McNeice had tried to make contact, and Marcus had sidestepped talking to him, but McNeice had been insistent.

Reluctantly, he picked up the phone.

'Hello, Marcus.'

'Hello,' replied Marcus, coldly.

'It's good to talk to you, after all this time.'

Marcus remembered the last time he had seen Jeremy, his boyfriend in tow. Jeremy reminisced familiarly about their school days, and Marcus made no reply, waiting for Jeremy to get to the point.

'The *Echo*'s been doing well since you took over.'

'It's been doing better than that, Jeremy. It's become a great newspaper, perhaps more influential than the publicly funded BBC.'

'I couldn't agree more, Marcus.'

I shouldn't have said that. He's going to use my words against me.

'I know you've already been asked to sit on *Question Time*,' Jeremy continued.

'I told them "no". The answer's still the same.'

'The country wants to hear your opinions, Marcus. You said it. You run an influential paper. You're denying the country the opportunity to hear your views.'

'They can buy the paper if they want to know what I've got to say. *Question Time*'s for self-promoting prima donnas, not serious newspaper men. Anyhow, you're nothing to do with *Question Time*.'

'Nobody at the BBC seems to know you, Marcus. At least we had seven good years at school in common.'

'Hmm.'

'We're thinking of developing some new current affairs programmes, something with a bias toward moral and ethical issues. We want to involve opinion formers, like you.'

'I'm not an *opinion former*, whatever that means.'

'Don't you think people have the right to hear what you think? Democracy depends on voters hearing alternative points of view.'

'That's for others to do, not me. If people want different opinions, that's what newspapers are for. The BBC's biased and denigrates what I do. Why'd I participate in a programme that would belittle my paper?'

'If you feel so strongly, come on the television and say it.'

'Sit in front the camera with a group of narcissists, attempting to score points?'

'Your employees and competitors do, all the time.'

'That's their choice, but it's not mine.'

'You attack the BBC in your newspapers, but there's no chance to publicly debate the issues you raise. It's a denial of democracy, don't you think?'

'No, I don't think that at all. I'm not going on TV, full stop! You want to ambush me in some way, but I'm not playing ball. There's no point in continuing this discussion.'

'Marcus, you've got great journalistic instincts and judgement. That's why your paper's so successful.'

'I'm doing my job then, aren't I?'

'But it's easy if nobody challenges you.'

'I get challenged every day.'

'That's not true. You're in total control and nobody dares to contradict you. Come on the television and have your views questioned. It's a great opportunity for you.'

'No!'

'Come on Marcus, you're not frightened of putting yourself in the position where you have to defend…'

Marcus put the phone down.

Jeremy typed an email to colleagues: 'Roache won't do it. He's shit scared.'

Marcus called Simon Howman into his office and indicated, with a wave of his hand, that he shouldn't shut the door. He had been waiting outside whilst Marcus dealt with the phone call.

'That bastard, McNeice,' he muttered.

'Sorry, I didn't catch the gist of conversation,' said Simon.

'Nothing.'

Marcus sat behind his desk, leaning forward intently, and signalled Howman to bring a seat from the table. Howman parked himself bolt upright, facing his boss.

'Simon, I've had an idea. I've been thinking that we need to improve our health coverage,' he said. 'We've had the government telling us lies about BSE, foot and mouth and the safety of vaccinations. Our readers don't trust them anymore. They want an independent opinion, and we'll be the place they come to. I want you to coordinate a campaign. Nothing overcomplicated. I'll expect straight and hard-hitting stuff. It's all too technical and boring at the moment. Too many numbers and not enough bold headlines.'

'I don't know anything about science or medicine,' said Howman.

'You don't need to know anything about science.'

'No,' Howman agreed.

'We've got science experts, and there's never any problem finding someone with letters after his name to provide the ammunition. It's about journalism, not fucking science.'

'Yes, Marcus.'

'We've got the future king involved in alternative medicine. He's got no science qualifications, but everyone listens to him. They're interested in what he's got to say because he challenges the bureaucrats, and people believe him. We've got dangerous foods. We've got the government lying about MMR.'

'There's the spread of MRSA.'

'There's enough evidence of cover-ups to keep things bubbling for years.'

'What if the MMR scare is just that, a scare?' asked Simon, remembering that his children had recently been given the vaccine.

'Kids are getting autism and something must be causing it. I'd never heard of autism when I was a child. Just get on with it, Simon!'

What the hell is that supposed to mean? He's talking garbage!

'I want it in simple terms, backed by boffins in white coats,' Marcus continued. 'Yes, and reports with academic-sounding titles. I want Noreen on the case too. It's always better to get the female touch. It adds weight, and the more public figures we can get to support our campaigns, the better. I want celebrity views, that sort of thing.'

'OK.'

'Look here, Simon!' shouted Marcus, 'Show some enthusiasm. You seem to be forgetting what journalism's all about. I don't want a medical fucking thesis. I don't want educated waffle. I want simple messages put across, explicitly and shockingly, to sell newspapers. I want it personalised. Every reader needs to feel that MRSA could happen to them, or the MMR vaccine could hit their child. I want them worrying that their kids may be starting into class-A drugs by smoking cannabis. Do parents know the tell-tale signs?'

'I don't know. Err... I can find out.'

'That's a rhetorical question. Of course they won't know, but you'll tell them. I want our readers to be annoyed, angry and apoplectic even, writing to our letters page by the sackload. If they don't, you can write some on their behalf. I know that's something you're good at. That's what sells papers.'

'Yes and...'

'If we start writing scientific jargon, nobody'll read it. This paper's circulation is rising, and my intention is to make it number one in the country. More circulation means more profit, which means more pay for you and me and more likelihood that you'll be in a job.'

'I'll get on with it.'

'We'll attract readers with exciting headlines, not dry, unreadable shit. I'm not concerned about a few decimal points on a table in some boffin's thesis. I'm bothered about the impact of the headline. That's why I pay you so well. I pay well, and I expect more. So get stuck into it.'

Perhaps, if I'd said nothing or gone along with him, Marcus would have dropped this idea, and something else would have taken his fancy, like it usually does.

Noreen was on the phone. She beckoned Simon to sit down. Noreen was petite, well into her sixties, dressed in startling colours, immaculately coiffured and displaying one showy piece of jewellery. Today she wore a primrose dress with a gold pin, high on the shoulder. Her small round face was topped with a shiny, dyed, auburn perm. She was from Lancashire, the daughter of a coalman, but her Lanky accent had undergone self-managed reconstructive surgery. Like so many facelifts, it left the beholder wondering why it had been done, whether it could have been done better, and that surely nothing could be worse than what was on show now. It was a travesty of an aristocratic accent.

Simon could not understand what Barry Halstead saw in her. They had been having an affair for over twenty-five years. Everyone at the *Echo* knew – even Marcus. It was common knowledge in the other tabloids, but it had never been made public. She finished her call, turned and looked at Simon over her red-framed glasses.

'Oh. So, we're on the warpath.'

'Yes. We're going to beef up our health reporting. No pun intended.'

'I'm interviewing Kerry Minza. That was her on the phone. She's a completely talentless so-called celebrity, but hurrah for us, she's not going to allow her son to have the MMR jab. The deal is that I'll do a positive piece about her career, and she'll give me the quotes I need on MMR. It's win-win.'

'Marcus wants a headline on MRSA.'

'Recruit someone to work as a hospital cleaner. It's such a shitty job that hospitals will take anybody who applies.' She said 'shitty' as if she could smell the excrement as she spoke, and she screwed up her nose in disgust. 'They might suspect a white person applying, so get one of our Asian or Caribbean cousins. I've been told that it's dead easy to get swabs that are positive for MRSA. Bingo! You've got the headline.'

'GM foods?'

'I'll find a celeb who's against GM and wants publicity. We will have to be careful because this sort of thing attracts the bearded, knit-your-own-trousers, tree-hugging types, and the men are as bad too,' she laughed. 'Can you get some facts against GM?'

'Where from?'

'Talk to the science journalists. Sometimes I think they speak in tongues because I don't understand a word they say, but you can always put a quote into the mouth of some boffin who wants a day in the limelight.'

It was three weeks later when Simon met the young, Asian man who he had planted in the Queen Ann Children's Hospital. He had obtained swabs, but all of them had tested negative.

'A complete waste of time,' Simon said, angrily.

'Not necessarily,' was the reply.

'What do you mean? A negative test's a negative test.'

'Not necessarily.'

'Stop talking in riddles, and get to the point.'

'I've found somewhere that'll always give a positive test.'

'That's nonsense. How can you get a positive test if other labs say there's no MRSA?'

'Look, Mr Howman, this is a proper approved laboratory in Bristol. I've found out that everyone who wants a positive result goes here. Do you want a story or not?'

'Marcus is on the rampage. Get the test results, but I want proof that the lab is up to scratch.'

'Don't worry. The bloke who runs it is called Doctor Finch, and the lab provides data for hospitals all round the world. It's pukka.'

A few days later, Noreen and Simon were seated opposite Marcus, in his office, the display copy in Marcus's hand.

'Fantastic stuff, Simon,' enthused Marcus, 'and a great

headline. "Superbugs infect our filthy hospitals". I like the attack on the hospital management. Can you get the salary of the chief exec? Let's get our readers pissed off at his salary and remind them we need more cleaners and fewer managers.'

'Sure. I'll get on with it. We've stirred up a hornets' nest on MMR,' said the rehabilitated Simon. 'After Noreen's feature with Kerry Minza, we got a full postbag, and thousands of parents are refusing to allow their children to take the jab.'

'Melanie Valliere, the celebrity chef, won't let her children have it,' Noreen added.

'Now she's campaigning against GM foods,' said Simon. 'She says there's medical evidence that they cause cancer. She heard it on a TV documentary.'

'I'll do a "Frankenstein foods" headline, with quotes from the programme, and I'll put in a bit of old stuff from Prince Charles. He's good value,' said Noreen.

'That's just what I'm after,' said Marcus.

'A quack was interviewed on the programme,' added Simon. 'He claimed that rats fed with GM had developed cancer, but the report hasn't been published yet.'

'Did this boffin say there's a link?' asked Marcus.

'Yes.'

'Has he got a PhD?'

'Yes.'

'That's all we need. Give me a simple headline. Nobody'll check the detail.'

'OK.'

'This'll drag the politicians in. With a bit of luck, we can turn the whole issue on them,' said Marcus with a smile. 'They've lied to us before.'

The following morning, in a formal statement, the Queen Ann Hospital denied that they had an MRSA problem and questioned the laboratory results that had been published. They requested samples that they could check for themselves.

A week later, an article by Lucy Kwame appeared in the *Sentinel*. It challenged the MRSA results, the qualifications of the doctor that had provided them, the capability of the laboratory to do the testing and the motives and morality of the *Echo* story. It supported the hospital's stance and was heavily critical of the *Echo*. The article also questioned the validity of the tests that purportedly proved that GM foods cause cancer in animals.

It was also scathing about the campaign against the MMR vaccination. This was the motivation Simon needed, and he redoubled his efforts. With the *Sentinel* on the warpath, questioning his integrity, he became a convert to the cause of honesty about health cover-ups. If the *Sentinel* was in the opposite camp, it proved that the *Echo*'s line of enquiry was right.

'What do you think about the stuff in the *Sentinel*?' Simon asked Noreen.

'Brilliant,' she replied. 'It'll keep the story running. I've a queue of celebrities who want to back us on the MMR and autism scandal. I've done an interview with a mother of an autistic child. It's heart-rending. We'll drip-feed it over the next week.'

'This morning, the health minister gave his support to the Queen Ann and quoted the *Sentinel* story. It's a godsend. We can turn the whole thing on the government. I'm getting an interview with Dr Finch, the man who runs the testing company. He says that the government is trying to put the frighteners on him.'

'We can turn it into a victim story. Dr Finch – a lone, brave voice standing out against the establishment.'

'Remind the readers about thalidomide,' said Simon.

THE VOICE AND THE ECHO

'Who do you think they'll believe, the *Sentinel*, the overpaid chief executive of the hospital, the health secretary or us?'

Simon scribbled Noreen's words into his notepad.

Noreen leaned back in her chair and continued.

'Nobody reads the *Sentinel*. We're in control of the story. It's hit the TV news, it's on the radio, and now it's in the other papers. They're quoting us, not the *Sentinel*.'

'It started here,' Simon said, proudly.

Later that day, Simon's headline lay across Marcus's desk.

'What's this lousy government got to hide?' it bellowed. Marcus read the article to himself:

"We have a health service in crisis and filthy hospitals.

Fortunately we have honest citizens who are prepared to stand up to the faceless bureaucrats. Our pathetic government is more bothered about hiding the truth than protecting the people.

Dr Finch is one of Britain's most prominent experts on MRSA. His ground-breaking research on the testing of MRSA puts him at the forefront of the battle against this killer bug. He is respected, and his advice is sought worldwide.

We should be grateful for Dr Finch and other whistle-blowers that stand up to the government-appointed commissars. Instead, what do we get? Government boot-boys try to prevent him from speaking out.

Do you believe him or the Health Minister? No contest!"

'It's not often that I can say this, but I couldn't have done better myself,' said Marcus.

It was two days later that the *Echo* received a letter from four microbiologists that had visited Dr Finch's laboratory. They used words that Simon did not understand, but the gist was clear. They believed the methodology used by the good doctor was flawed, and his results were not to be trusted. They demanded a correction in the newspaper. Simon ripped up the letter and threw it in the wastepaper basket.

Simon was already looking at his next project. He was in the pub with Ewan Ware, the science correspondent, who looked a little nervous as Simon started his pitch. Simon had briefed Ewan a week before, and he had come prepared.

'There are some scary figures on cannabis strength. That right?' asked Simon.

'It's not as simple as that.'

'There's a twenty-five-fold increase in the strength of cannabis.'

'Who says that?'

'Look, no smartarse stuff.'

'Cannabis has got stronger year on year. It's mainly due to growing it indoors. The data's available from the government. There hasn't been a sudden increase in strength.'

'Get to the point. What does all that crap mean?'

'Well, this twenty-five-fold increase is nonsense. If the average potency of cannabis was four per cent ten years ago, let's say it's ten per cent or twelve per cent now. That's two or three times the strength. Even that's debatable because cannabis strength has fluctuated, so it depends when you do your comparison and whether you compare like with like. If you took the weakest cannabis, say ten years or twenty years ago, perhaps at one per cent, and the strongest now, then the argument might stack up, but it's not true in general.'

'Let's not look at it in general then,' said Simon, angrily.

'What do you mean?'

'I'll do the story based on what you've said, and I'll put the right slant on the specifics. We can't let the detail spoil the story.'

'What the hell do you mean by that? The detail *is* the story.'

'Just get this clear. You do what I ask, not what you want. If I want a story about how bad cannabis is, then you get the facts to support it. If you can't, then I'll find someone who can. Understand?'

Bullying bastard, but I need the work.

'What about this cocaine story?' Simon asked.

'That cocaine use has doubled in a year? It's not true.'

'Don't start that shit again'

'Although the headline figures show increased usage in schoolchildren up from one to two per cent, as soon as you remove rounding and the way the data was collected, the statistics don't show any increase. That's why the report says that there's no increase in drug use.'

'So the numbers show an increase from one per cent to two per cent?'

'Yes, but...'

'That's all I need to know. Drink up!'

'It's totally misleading to use those two figures.'

'Let me be the judge of that.'

Simon decided that the report needed to be harder hitting. Back in his office, he asked a junior reporter to search for all murder cases where the killing had been associated with cannabis use. It was getting close to the afternoon deadline when Simon leaned over the young man's shoulders and asked to see how far he had progressed.

'I haven't found any case where cannabis has been directly implicated in a murder. I could do with a little more time.'

'For fuck's sake, this is a newspaper. You're not doing a PhD!' Simon yelled. Heads were swivelled to see who was getting it in the neck, but eyes quickly returned to tasks when the office realised that it was only a junior.

'What've you got?'

'There are cases where murders have been committed and the murderer has taken cannabis or has a previous offence relating to cannabis.'

'Pictures?'

Simon selected four murders, attached the scariest pictures of the villains and sat back, admiring his handiwork and smiling to himself. Three were black.

'Perfect.'

By now, Simon's qualms had evaporated, and he realised how fertile this field of activity had become, ripe with stories to be harvested. There would be more to come.

50

CLIVE

Clive had been meeting Jeremy to discuss future work. He had already been involved in three projects since the start of the new millennium. When he arrived back from London, Ameera was watching television. Nas and Chloe had both caught the bus into town with friends.

'Hi, Ameera,' Clive shouted from the hall.

'The food's in the oven. You might want to microwave it,' she shouted back. 'I'm just watching the end of *Corrie*.'

Clive peeked through the living room door, and Ameera shooed him away.

'I'll be in the kitchen in five minutes.'

Clive put the kettle on, 'nuked' his dinner, made a pot of tea and sat in front of a steaming plate of sausages in mashed potatoes, with spinach and thick, dark gravy. It was, as far as Clive was concerned, a classic supper. Ameera came in, put her hands on Clive's shoulders and gave him a quick peck.

'Sorry, love, but it was getting exciting.'

'I'm sure it was.'

The tea was poured, and Ameera sat down opposite Clive.

'How did it go?'

'I got another commission. They want me to look at the treatment of suspected terrorists in the justice system. I hadn't realised how many people have been held since 9/11.'

'How's Jeremy.'

Clive sighed. He and Jeremy had become friends over the years. Jeremy was the main source of work for Clive, and they met up almost every month, often going out to eat together. Clive found him to be a charming and straightforward man, and they had something in common. They both knew Marcus Roache.

'He was a bit of a loner at school, with a massive chip on his shoulder,' Jeremy had told Clive. 'He didn't have any spark and couldn't think things out for himself. Underneath the bluster, I don't reckon he's very confident.'

Jeremy told Clive about offers he made for Marcus to appear on TV and radio, all of which he'd turned down. He had concluded that Marcus was worried that he would not be able to handle anyone publicly questioning his views.

'Jeremy's having more treatment,' said Clive to Ameera. 'He looks knackered. I guess the chemotherapy takes a lot out of him, but he won't stop working.'

'Did you find out what it is?'

'He hasn't said, and it's not the sort of subject you can casually introduce in conversation.'

'It could be prostate.'

'He's optimistic, and he's talking about the future, so he thinks he can crack it. I've had some other bad news though.'

Ameera had been blowing the top of her mug to cool her drink, and she looked up.

'Clara Tomlin's died.' Clive took a deep breath. 'She's the same age as me. It was in the *Standard*.'

'Oh no!'

'She had multiple sclerosis. When I last met her, it must be over ten years now, she had a walking stick and a slight shake, which she tried to hide. I'd no idea what it was and how serious it had got. I should've kept in touch.'

'But *she* didn't want to, did she?'

'No, but *I* could have. I feel guilty, and it was only by chance that I read it.'

'It'll be in the *Sentinel*.'

'It didn't say anything about family or a funeral. I don't know what to do.'

'Ring the *Sentinel*. I'm sure someone'll tell you.'

'I'd like to go to her funeral. Clara was, well, it's hard to describe really. She was like a sister, but we were closer than that, much closer.'

Ameera took his hand and smiled.

'I'm an odd bloke, I suppose,' he said wistfully. 'It's women who've been most important in my life; my mum, Marie, you, Chloe and Clara too. I don't make friends with blokes too easily. I've got plenty of mates and business contacts, but not men I'm really close to, not even Jeremy.'

'She never married?'

'No. I guess there's no family because she didn't have brothers or sisters. It sounds lonely and quite sad. I think her job became everything. She was the best.'

Clive rang the *Sentinel* the following morning. He was told that detailed arrangements had not been made, but Clara would be cremated, and it would be a private affair. Clive explained that he was an old friend and would like to attend.

'Her daughter's organising things and has been very clear about it, Mr Parkhouse. Clara left explicit instructions. I'm sorry, but you're not the first person to have made enquiries, and I've had to give the same answer.'

'Perhaps I could speak to Clara's daughter?'

'I don't think that's a good idea.'

'Yes, you're right. Thanks.'

Clive was surprised that Clara had a daughter, and over the following days, he scoured the obituary columns. The *Sentinel* was most comprehensive and focussed on her career, but there were passing references to the fact that she had never married and to her daughter, Lucy. Clive wondered. He thought he should find out more about Lucy, but never got round to doing anything, and life moved on.

At first, it seemed as if Jeremy would fully recover. Clive frequently visited him at home and met his partner, James Halloran, who devoted much of his time to caring for Jeremy. For almost two years, he was like his old self, but then he cancelled a meeting because he had to go to hospital.

Clive did not push for details, but Jeremy said it felt like the 'old trouble'. The BBC provided Clive with another contact and he kept in touch with Jeremy, by phone, on a weekly basis. Then he received an emotional message on his voicemail. Jeremy had been told that his cancer had returned and spread. He did not know what to say to James, who was out of the country for a few days. He did not want to tell him on the phone, but he did not want to lie. He sounded frantic, and Clive phoned him straight back.

Jeremy was tearful, anxious, despairing and irrational. Finally, he decided that if James phoned, he would tell him that the results were inconclusive, and more tests needed to be undertaken. He would break the news when James returned. Clive promised to tell nobody. Clive sensed that Jeremy was not going to recover and was determined to give him as much of his time as he could offer and Jeremy could bear. Things did not work out as planned because the *Echo* reported the news of his cancer before Jeremy could talk to his partner. Jeremy blamed Clive for being indiscrete, accused him on the phone, and they never spoke again.

51

MARCUS

Marcus did not like to make much of birthdays, but today he was sixty. As usual, Mary had made breakfast. The driver had picked him up at the normal time, before the arrival of the postman. Marcus would have to open the cards in the evening.

There would be a quiet family party that night, and later in the week, he would attend the annual lecture of the Editor's Forum. He would receive public and private acclaim, which he normally shunned, but which would be welcome in this auspicious week.

Marcus had read the various reports about his sixtieth birthday in the weekend papers, some speculating on imminent retirement, others analysing his accomplishments. Even those papers critical of the *Echo* and its editorial stance admired the success he had brought, and all said that he was at the peak of his powers.

He had laughed with Mary at some of the older pictures that his competitors had sifted from the archives. He may have put on weight, and he had suffered a heart scare, but he had lost little hair, and age had generally been kind.

'There's talk of a knighthood,' said Mary.

'That'd be nice. Lord and Lady Roache. How does that sound?'

'Good, yes, it sounds good. I thought John Major might have given you something.'

'I'd have refused it from that spineless, sleazy lot. At the first sign of trouble, they ditched Margaret Thatcher.'

'Or Blair?' she laughed.

'That would have been ironic, an honour from the revolting Blair government. Mind you, he was more like Maggie than Major. I want to make this a week to remember for the news I'm going to generate; not for the toadying my birthday's encouraging.'

Stephen Glazier phoned Marcus on his way to work. He told Marcus that a story he had been working on was turning out to be a major scoop. He said that it would run for days, if not weeks.

Marcus felt a little tired in the car and asked his driver to turn on the air conditioning. He had slept badly for the previous two nights. During those early morning hours of half-wakening and half-sleeping, dreams and mad, negative thoughts, jumbled and fantastic, crammed into his semi-consciousness. He saw faces from the past, some recognised and others not, in situations, unreal and surreal. When he was fully awake, the dreams were often unremembered but left a portentous feeling, unwarranted and unwanted, at the back of his mind.

The morning meeting gathered in the usual format, and Marcus opened proceedings as soon as everyone had taken a seat. He stood up and leaned forward over the table, scanning his troops as if assessing whether or not they were ready for battle. Barry, Kevin, Simon, Stephen and Peter were amongst the respectful listeners.

'We're on the attack this week, not just reporting the news, but we'll be creating it. You're going to make this a week to remember, each and every one of you.'

The index finger of his right hand jabbed the air in front of him. It seemed to be in charge, the finger lunging forward

and dragging his arm with it. Only the formidable presence of
Marcus was holding back the wayward digit and preventing it
from poking out the eyes of each of the seated audience.

'We're going to stir things up like never before. Stephen
says he's got something big, but we'll come to that. Is it true
that Jeremy McNeice's died?' asked Marcus. He wiped his
sweating forehead with a crisp, white, folded handkerchief.

'Yes,' said Simon. 'When we heard he'd been ill and was
taking time off work, we put an investigator on his case. He
managed to get into McNeice's messages. McNeice was
working with Clive Parkhouse, and we got into his phone too.
You remember the story?'

'Yes, he told Parkhouse that he'd just been diagnosed with
cancer.'

'He whined to us when we broke the story and then to
the Press Complaints Committee. He wanted to know how
we'd found out. We told him that it was widely known that
he'd been ill before, and we'd been given the story about the
cancer by an impeccable source we couldn't disclose. There's
a rumour that the cancer's linked to AIDS.'

'Find out what you can,' said Marcus, briskly.

'It's a story for Noreen,' added Barry. 'She'll enjoy getting
her teeth into it.'

'Yes, and anything to slant the story against the BBC will
help the TV side of the business,' said Marcus. 'I'd already
thought of a full page, later in the week, on the waste of
taxpayers' money on BBC celebrities.'

Marcus was poking his index finger on the desk as he
spoke, as if the table was one of the celebrities he disliked.

'There's that shit, Jimmy Reade, on mega-millions,
and it looks like Kenny Stamp will get top money too,' he
continued. 'I want figures. What do these big names cost
every licence payer? Find out how much of the licence fee

goes to pay the senior managers, that sort of stuff. What else have you got?'

'We're digging up gold with our Reader's Challenge to find the craziest examples of political correctness. We've had thousands of responses,' said Barry.

'Any gems?' asked Marcus.

'A government department's issued a list of banned words. 'They've included the word "blackball" because it's racist. They've told all their staff to use the word "exclude" instead,' said Barry.

'Great. Let's fill page five with the best examples. Get quotes from insiders if you can. If not, then make some up.'

'We've got plenty to work with.'

'What else, Barry?'

Barry went through a list of potential stories and leads.

'Over to you, Stephen,' said Marcus when Barry had finished.

'I've been working on this for a few weeks now,' said Stephen. 'A reader's been getting angry about one of our politicians.'

'That's what we like to hear,' said Marcus, smiling. 'Angry people get things done.'

'He's worked in a bank for forty years, and he's just retired,' said Stephen, unhurriedly. 'He made contact some weeks ago. He said that a public figure has got a skeleton in his cupboard. This person had made a payment, on every Christmas Eve, into the account of a young lady.'

'Come on Stephen, get to the point,' said Marcus.

'The payments stopped, and money was withdrawn some years ago, on the lady's twenty-first birthday. He found out who was making the payments and sat on the information until he retired. The bank employee wouldn't give me the details until we agreed to pay for the story.'

'I cleared payment last week,' said Marcus.

'The informant's on a small bank pension,' Stephen continued, unflustered, 'and he says he can't risk his name getting out. He's been quite difficult to handle because he wants a large sum of money, and I mean it when I say it's a large sum. I negotiated the final figure last Friday, and that's when I got all the details.'

'I hope it was worth it,' said Marcus.

'I spent Friday and the weekend crosschecking the information. The names and dates all stack up.'

Stephen had spoken slowly throughout. His Yorkshire accent resounded with confidence, and he had a broad smile. It was like the spider and the fly. No need to rush because the fly was caught, and it was a moment to savour. The instant the victim was dead, the pleasure would be gone, and it was just another meal.

'Dave Shearman's the benefactor, and he'd been paying into a special account in the name of Miss Lucy Tomlin. Our informant did a little more research in bank records, and he found out that Lucy Tomlin is Clara Tomlin's daughter.'

There was silence, broken by Marcus. For the first time in front of his subordinates, he looked shocked.

'Fucking hell, we've got to be sure about this.'

He hesitated, deep in thought, and his acolytes knew not to interrupt him. 'We're using highly confidential information, without any documents to prove it, and we can't let on where we got it from.'

'The beauty,' Stephen responded, 'is that all we need to do is to check out the birth certificate. Nobody'll have the slightest inkling about our source.'

'Well?'

'It doesn't say who the father is, but you've already told us that Tomlin and Shearman were living together at university.'

'Sure,' said Marcus, regaining his composure.

'Lucy Tomlin was born on 23rd December 1968,' said Stephen, 'which means that she was conceived round about the end of March, when Shearman was living with Tomlin. It all checks. He married his first wife in October 1968.'

'That means that Shearman got married when Tomlin was seven months pregnant,' said Marcus, looking shaken by the revelation.

'Call me old-fashioned,' said Stephen, 'but even by sixties standards, what Shearman has done seems a little… surprising.'

'He must have known she was pregnant because of the payment, but he still married this other woman,' Marcus mused, rubbing his chin.

'If we corner Shearman and put him under pressure, maybe he'll admit everything,' said Simon.

'But it doesn't matter, does it? How's he going to wriggle on the dates and the fact that he lived with Tomlin?' Stephen continued.

'We're supposed to have had investigators onto Shearman. What've they been doing, not picking this up?' asked Marcus, indignantly.

'They've been into his phone for years,' said Simon, 'but there's been nothing. We know everybody he's been talking to, but there's been no contact with Lucy Tomlin and no mention of her. We've paid the police thousands. They've found nothing, not even a parking ticket, but this'll nail him. He's getting wise though, and he's recently become more careful with his phone and answering machine.'

There was silence as Marcus considered the facts.

'Yes, we run with the story, no matter what,' said Marcus, with renewed confidence.

'The other interesting thing,' Stephen continued, 'is that Lucy Tomlin is actually Lucy Kwame, the *Sentinel* journalist. I did a quick check through marriage records. She's hitched to someone called Victor.'

'Fucking hell!' exclaimed Marcus. 'Are you sure about that?'

'No doubt at all.'

'You need to work on this today, Stephen,' said Marcus, excitedly. 'It'll be on our front page tomorrow. Get an interview with Shearman. Go through Mike Boddington, his PR man. He'll know the story's true because he knows what Shearman's like. Mike was Editor of my university paper, and Tomlin and Shearman worked for him when I started there. Yes, before we go to print, we should confront Shearman with the detail. Try to contact the daughter. See what she's got to say.'

'I wonder how Shearman will play it,' said Peter.

'Under pressure, he's likely to admit to everything,' said Marcus. 'He's no backbone. There's a lot to do, so let's get started.'

Marcus ushered the attendees out of the office.

'Hang on a second, Peter. Close the door.'

Peter took the seat Marcus offered him.

'I've heard that your wife has to go into hospital next week.'

'Yes, she needs an operation.'

'You don't need to explain. I know it's quite serious. You've the children to think of too. It'll take a few weeks for her to get her strength back. You've worked your socks off for the paper. I want you to take a month off, all on full pay. You can start from Friday. It'll give you a breather.'

'Marcus, I don't know what to say. I'm just… My God, the whole thing's got to me. Jennifer's been so ill.' Peter started to cry.

'Peter, take your time. Take however long you need. I won't be back until this afternoon. Look after yourself.'

'Thank you, Marcus.'

Marcus self-consciously patted Peter on the back, left him in the office and told his PA that he should not be disturbed. Peter had been a long-serving stalwart at the *Echo*, a proud and attentive family man, often sacrificing family arrangements for the paper. It was something they had all done in their time, but Peter was in trouble, and it was only honourable that the paper should do its duty. Marcus had made his mind up on the matter, without hesitation.

'We've got that bastard Shearman, and I'm going to turn the screw,' he said to himself as he took the lift to the next floor.

52

MIKE

Stephen Glazier met Mike Boddington at a bar in the city. It was 1.30 and the two men were standing in a quiet corner. Mike was leaning on a raised table, nervously picking at a half-eaten sandwich. His body was at an angle to Stephen, who was relaxed and confident, square on to Mike and feet planted firmly.

'So, what's this all about?' asked Mike, picking up and munching a piece of lettuce from his sandwich. 'You said it was to do with Dave and Clara's relationship at university. It's a fact that they lived together, so I'm not sure what you're after.'

'When did you leave university, Mike?'

Mike thought for a moment.

'Sixty-eight.'

'Did you know that she never married?'

'I had no idea, either one way or the other.'

'Did you know she had a daughter?'

'Not then. Why should I? But I found out later. It was in the obituary.'

'Did you know that she was pregnant when she was at university?'

'No.'

'The daughter was born in December 1968. I've got a birth certificate to prove it.'

'So?'

'Well, work it out. Whose child has it got to be?'

'Quite the Hercule Poirot. You tell me.'

'It's Dave Shearman's child.'

Mike remained silent.

'You heard what I said. Lucy Tomlin, Lucy Kwame if you prefer, is Shearman's daughter.'

'Well, I don't know what… I can't possibly… I mean, you can't expect me to comment on what you've just said. How do you know it's his child?'

'You mean that Clara Tomlin was sleeping around with lots of other men?'

'You unpleasant and spiteful little shit. Clara wasn't like that.'

'I need to speak to Shearman. If I don't speak to him, we'll break the story tomorrow morning.'

'If you do speak to him?'

'Depends what he's got to say.'

'He's in a Select Committee meeting, and I can't make contact until later this afternoon. He'll be finished by about 4.30. Then he'll come back to his office to pick up mail, respond to letters, that sort of stuff. Perhaps he'll see you, but he may refuse.'

'I'll expect to see Shearman at 5.00 tonight. No later.'

'Don't give me orders.'

'5.00.'

Mike nodded and turned to leave.

'You haven't finished your drink, Mike, or your sandwich. Lost your appetite?'

'Fuck off, you bastard.'

Mike Boddington had other business to attend to that afternoon, and Dave Shearman was at his computer when Mike returned at 4.45. Dave had a rim of hair running round the back of his head, from ear to ear and parallel with his collar.

His chin rested on his open left palm, his elbow anchored to the table. Dave was concentrating on the screen while his right hand chattered on the keyboard.

'Hi, Mike,' he murmured, eyes glued to the screen.

'Dave, something important's cropped up, and you need to listen.'

'OK. I'll just be a few more minutes.'

'No. Now,' replied Mike. He strode purposefully to the edge of the desk. 'I've met a guy called Stephen Glazier.'

'Bastard, he's an ugly, vile, bastard; one of Roache's Rottweilers at the *Echo*.'

'You're probably not going to think any better of him when you've heard what I've got to say.'

Shearman stopped typing and looked at Mike. It was the look of a schoolboy caught pinching the pornographic magazine from the top shelf at the newsagent. Theft is bad enough, but the nature of the prize makes it worse.

'I won't beat around the bush. I haven't got time. Is Lucy Tomlin your daughter?'

Shearman's face turned a deep crimson.

'What sort of question's that?' he blurted.

'It's quite straightforward. If the answer's "yes", then you left Clara Tomlin, aware she was pregnant, you know, when you finished university. Then you married another woman and hid the secret. If the answer's "no"...' Mike hesitated, 'but it's not, is it?'

Dave dropped his head. He was quiet for a while.

'Anybody else got the story?'

'Not that I know of, and Glazier's due to arrive here in less than ten minutes.'

'I can't talk to him.'

'You can't avoid him. He says he's got the birth certificate that proves when she was born. They've checked it out.'

'How the hell've they dug this up? Who's told 'em?
They've been out to get me for years.'

'It's true, though?'

'Yes, it's true, but not your insinuations. I didn't find out
she was pregnant till after the wedding had been planned.'

'You must have known.'

'Clara was invited to my wedding. Emma was crazy, and
she wanted Clara to be there. It was spiteful, I suppose,
to show that she'd won. Clara sent a card. It said that she
couldn't come; too busy at the *Sentinel*. I tried to make
contact, for old time's sake, but she kept fobbing me off. I
sensed something was wrong. I was working in the north
east, but I was sent on a training course in London. I went
to her flat. She was very, very pregnant. She refused to speak
to me.'

'She was pregnant and hadn't told you, the father?'

'Yes. We had a row at the door to the flat. She started
yelling. She didn't want anything to do with me and told me
that Emma and I should get married. There was nothing I
could do.'

'You could've stopped the wedding.'

'I wrote to her and told her that I would accept paternity,
but she didn't answer. I tried to delay the marriage, but
everything was arranged. I had to make a decision. After the
baby was born, I went to see her again, and she wouldn't let
me see the child.'

'Why not? She must have had a reason.'

'Reason? She'd lost all sense of reason. She said the child
wasn't mine, it was hers, and she wouldn't share her. She
wasn't talking sense. I couldn't do anything. She wouldn't
budge. We stayed friends until she died, but we went our own
separate ways. It was her choice not mine'

'That's not like Clara.'

'I paid money into a bank account each year until Lucy was twenty-one. I suppose it was a sort of pathetic penance.'

'What did Clara think about that?'

'She didn't know. I put it into an account under Lucy's name and I told Clara when Lucy turned twenty-one. I left it to Clara to explain away the money.'

'Shit. Look, Dave, I'll handle the Minister and the Prime Minister.'

'What the hell will you say?'

'It's a personal matter between you and your family.'

'Well that's true.'

'I guess the PM will play a straight bat and resist resignation cries from the usual quarters. You're lucky that the opposition parties will say nothing because they've got their own skeletons in cupboards. You need to contact your wife. The press will try to get to her.'

'Right.'

'You've got a few minutes, that's all, before Glazier's here. They'll publish, whether you talk to them or not. Does Lucy know you're her father?'

'No. I promised Clara to say nothing to Lucy or anyone else. She was insistent.'

'I'll send Glazier through when he arrives.'

53

DAVE

Dave sat for a few moments, clearing his mind of competing thoughts and emotions.

Almost immediately, the phone buzzed.

'Mr Glazier of the *Echo*'s here. He's coming straight in.'

'Right.'

Stephen Glazier entered the room, and Dave remained seated, attention focussed on his computer screen. Glazier shuffled uncomfortably and coughed. Dave looked up and indicated toward the Chesterfield opposite his desk. He slouched in his own chair, adopting an air of unconcern.

'Yes?'

'I assume that Boddington has briefed you.'

The adversaries had never met, and Shearman was surprised at the northern accent. It was usually an excuse to enquire where the other came from, share anecdotes and complain about the south. Shearman was disappointed that he was about to be sunk by this fellow northerner. The newspaperman held a recording machine.

'Yes. You've dragged up some gossip, I hear.'

'It's not gossip. Have you any comments to make? By the way, I'm recording.'

'Turn it off.'

'No.'

'Turn it off.'

Stephen shrugged and turned the machine off.

'You know what this is about because Boddington's briefed you. What have you got to say?'

'What do you want me to say? My private business is none of your concern.'

'A politician having a child with someone who is, in effect, an unmarried mother, is of huge public interest.'

'It's interesting to you, but it's also private.'

'You married another woman whilst Clara Tomlin was seven months pregnant with your child. How do you explain that?'

'I don't have to explain anything to you.'

'But you accept that you're the father?'

'I didn't say that. I'm refusing to discuss something that's none of your business.'

'If not, you'd have denied it, sent me packing and told me that you'd sue.'

'Whatever I say, you're determined to twist my words.'

'Look, Mr Shearman, we know you were living with Clara Tomlin when the child was conceived. There was nobody else on the scene, so it's your child. I've seen the date on the birth certificate. If you don't like us saying that in tomorrow's newspaper, then you can sue.'

'I might just do that.'

'It'll cost you, and you know you haven't got a leg to stand on.'

'We'll see.'

'You'd never win in court, if it ever comes to that. There are questions to answer. Did you financially support your daughter when she was growing up?'

Shearman hesitated. There was no escape. It was true, and they could prove it.

'Well, did you? You'd better tell the truth because it's all going to come out in the end.'

There was still no reply.

'Are you listening?'

'Yes, I put money aside for her. It was held in an account in Lucy's name.'

As he crossed the Rubicon, he remembered his promise to Clara. He thought about Lucy, the ending of his career and his public humiliation, but there could be no escape. Lying would only make matters worse.

'Does she know you're her father?'

'I can't go into that.'

'So you've met her then?'

Dave tried to speak. He was thinking the words but could not make his mouth say them.

'Sorry,' was all he could manage.

'In your own time.'

'No, I've never met her. Clara brought her up on her own. I can't go on with this. Could you please leave?'

Stephen Glazier left and phoned the *Sentinel*. He asked to speak to Lucy Kwame.

Dave sat motionless.

It's the end, they'll twist things and I'll have to step down. It's the end of everything. Lucy. I should be with Lucy. How will she handle it? What a fuck-up.

54

MARCUS

It was later than usual when Marcus began orchestrating the Tuesday paper. The team had gathered around the large desk in the main office, on which sat a wide computer screen. The desk was strewn with papers and photographs.

'Good headline, "Shearman's secret love child", and the front page looks complete. The picture of the daughter's recent?' he asked.

'Should be,' replied Stephen. 'I've got the techies to lift it from the internet.'

'Page two's got good background to Shearman, Tomlin and her daughter,' Marcus said. 'Yes, the Shearman story's just about right. Good. What about the political correctness article? I can't see it anywhere.'

'There's a bit of a problem on the blackball,' said Barry nervously. 'We went back to get more information, and I don't know whether they had wind of it, but the story's changed. They said that the word hasn't been banned, it's been replaced by a more appropriate word.'

'What sort of shit is that? Banned, replaced, I couldn't care a politically correct fuck.'

'They say that "exclude" is a more modern and better understood word than "blackball".'

'Come on, Barry. Don't confuse the issue with facts,' said Marcus, with no hint of irony. 'Is this a good story?'

'Yes.'

'Making an important point?'

'Of course it is.'

'Do our readers care about the details?'

'No.'

'Is the Department of Whoever going to say anything, and if they do, will anyone take any notice?'

'No.'

'We'll run the story.'

'OK.'

'If it's not completely true, it could be, and most likely is somewhere else. What about Jeremy McNeice?'

'There's a short factual piece on page five, but Noreen picks it up in her column.'

Marcus fingered through the pages and found what he wanted.

'BBC chief dies from AIDS cancer – symbol of a promiscuous age.'

'It's a great headline. Yes, I like the gay lifestyle stuff. The readers will squirm when they see the hand-in-hand photograph with his boyfriend, and the fact that civil partnerships will give the green light to this sort of lifestyle. We need to follow up tomorrow. Let's get moving.'

Marcus went back to his office. A sweat started, and he felt exhausted. He had experienced these symptoms some years before and remembered what had happened last time.

55

CLIVE

That same Monday morning, Clive heard on the radio that a miner in a nearby pit village had been beaten to death by an ex-colleague, the result of a feud that had its roots in the miners' strike.

'It's an interesting story, this murder. I'll find out a bit more about it,' he said to nobody in particular. He looked up from the morning paper, over his metal-rimmed glasses, but Ameera was finishing off a piece of toast and did not reply.

For over a year, Clive had been mulling over writing a book about the miners' strike. He was unsure about the story he wanted to tell, and he needed an angle. He was looking for something out of the ordinary. He had started to write on numerous occasions, but the evidence of his efforts had disappeared into his computer's recycle bin. He knew that something would come up if he waited.

Nas had popped in on his way to work, to pick up his car. The previous evening, he had been to the pub with friends and had left it in the drive. He had grown tall and slim. Although he was in his sombre suit, ready for work, he appeared wild-eyed and mischievous.

'Sounds horrible,' he said. 'Have you ever seen a dead body that's been, you know, battered?'

'Nas!' exclaimed his mother.

'I'm just asking.'

'It's over twenty years since the strike, the right time for a proper perspective,' said Clive studiously.

'Nobody'll be interested,' said Nas.

'I'm after a real life story, seen from the eyes of normal people. This could be the key. I'm going to…'

'It's not exciting enough. People've forgotten about it, and nobody cares,' Nas interrupted.

Clive rolled his eyes.

'Nas,' said his mother, 'stop annoying Clive. Your collar's up and your tie's not straight.'

'Doesn't matter.'

'Doesn't matter? I wouldn't employ a solicitor looking as scruffy as you.'

'I'm not qualified yet, and anyhow, most of our clients don't care. They aren't finicky like you, thank goodness.'

'I'll do a little bit of ferreting about and see where it takes me,' said Clive.

'I thought you were winding down,' replied Ameera, packing her case for surgery.

'This isn't work. It's fun. It'll keep me ticking over on dark winter nights.'

Ameera kissed Clive on the side of the face. She vainly attempted to straighten his full head of hair as she crossed the kitchen to get her coat and depart for work. Three great harbingers of age – hair loss, weight gain and deteriorating complexion – had passed them by. It was true that the back of Clive's neck was a nest of unruly white hair, but he was slim and clear skinned. Ameera's shoulder length hair was flecked with grey, and her shape was a little more rounded than when she had met Clive, but time had been as kind to them as they had been to each other.

'Off you go,' she said to her son.

Nas was quickly out of the door, followed by his mum.

Clive was talking to an ex-miner at the murder scene when he received an unexpected call from James Halloran. They had not spoken for a number of years because of the article in the *Echo* about Jeremy's illness. James told Clive that Jeremy had died early that morning.

'It was expected, but it's a shock just the same. I'd like to see you if you can come down. We've a lot to talk about, and I don't want bad memories for either of us.'

James made no mention of the *Echo*, reflecting only on the times Jeremy and James had enjoyed, and Clive said he would be down the following day. That evening, in a solemn mood, he told Ameera that he would be away for a couple of days.

'You, Chloe, Clara and Jeremy have all been a part of my rehabilitation. Jeremy was a good friend, despite how it ended up.'

Later that evening, Chloe popped in to tell them that she was applying for a job at a large comprehensive school in Leeds. They were seated at the kitchen table.

'It's a good school, good headmaster,' Chloe said.

'And Nick's in Leeds too,' said Clive.

'Yes, and it'll get me away from the two of you,' she smiled. 'I think we're going to get married.'

'Think?' asked Ameera.

'Well it's not official, but we'd said we would, you know, when we got jobs in the same town. We'll get a house in Leeds, if we can, and perhaps marry next year.'

'That's all a bit vague,' said her dad.

'You're telling *me* that *I'm* a bit vague?'

'OK, OK. We'll save up,' he sighed. 'It's something to look forward to.'

'Who said you're invited?' she laughed. 'A cheque will do.'

Clive smiled. He often wondered if it was just his fatherly pride, but Chloe seemed so like her mum; the same willowy looks, her mischievous charm and the way she effortlessly drew people's attention. Chloe had kept the photograph of her mother, that she had taken from her parents' bedroom, in her purse. Chloe had turned out like the photograph, and perhaps it was Chloe's way of keeping Marie alive.

The house phone rang. It was in the hall, behind the kitchen door, and Clive went out and picked it up. It was Lucy Kwame. She had kept Clive's home phone number from the time they had worked together on the Grinderton murder. Clive was surprised to get the call, and Lucy sounded agitated.

They exchanged brief pleasantries, but Lucy quickly got to the point.

'Clive, I need your help. I've just been contacted by the *Echo*. You said you knew Clara Tomlin at university.'

'Yes,' replied Clive.

'And Dave Shearman?' she hurried.

'Yes, we worked on the student newspaper. What's all this about?'

'How well did you know Clara?'

'Very well. Clara and I were good friends.'

'What about Shearman and Clara?'

'What about them?'

'You know what I'm on about.'

'Not unless you tell me.'

'Did they live together?'

'What sort of question's that? I don't want to sound rude, but what's it got to do with you, or the *Echo*, for that matter?'

'Tomorrow, a story's going to break about Clara and Dave Shearman. The *Echo* says that they conceived a child when they were at university.'

'No, it's not true. I don't believe it. Who do they say is the child?' There was no reply. Clive broke the silence. 'It's you, isn't it?'

Clive waited for a reply, but Lucy said nothing.

'It's you. I should have known.'

'Yes, it's me, Clive.'

'Oh my God! I knew that Clara had a daughter called Lucy. It was in her obituary. I sort of wondered then. I should have contacted you. Why didn't you say anything all those years ago, you know, in Grinderton, or when we met in London?'

'Clive, there's too much to explain. I can't do it over the phone.'

'I'm sorry about Clara, your mother, I mean. I wish we could have spoken about her when she died. It's my fault.'

'It's nobody's fault.'

'How did they find out?'

'So it's true, isn't it?'

'Hold on, hold on. I don't know.'

'You must know, Clive. You were there.'

'Who's told you all this?'

'Somebody called Glazier from the *Echo*. Dave Shearman's as good as admitted it.'

'What did your mother tell you?'

'She wouldn't speak about it. I thought you might be my father.'

'What?'

'When we were in Grinderton, and I found out you were on the student paper with my mum, I thought, well I thought you and her... Anyhow, she wouldn't tell me anything, and now I know it's not true.'

'This is a nightmare.'

'Who's that?' shouted Ameera from the kitchen.

Clive covered the mouthpiece.

'It's someone from the *Sentinel*.'

'Glazier got hold of me at work. He told me that Dave Shearman and my mum lived together through university, and I was born a few months after they split. The dates stack up. Shearman's admitted to Glazier that he's my father, and that he put money into a bank account for me. It's got to be true because I got a cheque from a so-called distant relative on my twenty-first, just as Glazier said. Mother never properly explained it.'

'Yes,' Clive whispered, 'Dave and your mum were together. I don't know if he's your father, but if he says he is…'

'I've never met him.' Lucy started crying down the phone. 'I don't know what he's like. It's scary, Clive. I don't know what to do.'

'Look, I need to think about what you've said. It's just, I dunno, it's unbelievable.'

'I had to talk to someone, Clive, I had to. You knew them both. I'll try to get hold of Dave,' she hesitated, 'I mean my father. I don't know if he wants to speak to me.'

'Of course he does, and he'll get in touch with you, I'm sure.'

'Everything OK, love?' asked Ameera, poking her head around the kitchen door. Clive shoed her away with his free hand and pushed the door shut with his foot.

'Look, I can't talk now. Let's meet up. I'm down in London on other business, tomorrow and Wednesday. We can meet up and have a natter. I'll give you a ring, on Tuesday evening or Wednesday morning. We've got lots to talk about.'

Lucy gave Clive her address and home and mobile numbers and then hung up.

'Why didn't she tell me?' Clive whispered to himself. 'Why didn't Clara tell me? She lied to me. Hell, if I'd have known back then, *I'd* have married her.'

Clive poked his head round the kitchen door and told Ameera and Chloe that a problem had cropped up, to do with some work he had done for the *Sentinel*. Ameera looked surprised because she thought that Clive had done nothing for them for many years.

'Is everything alright? You seem a bit flustered.'

'Yes, yes. Everything's fine,' said Clive, annoyed. 'I'll see you before you go, Chloe,' he added.

He went upstairs to the spare room that he used as his office. He picked up his mobile from the desk and tried to contact Marcus Roache, to get him to pull the story, but Clive could not get past the switchboard at the *Echo*. Marcus was in some bolthole for the night.

He tried to get hold of Dave Shearman, and after many dead ends, and telling a few lies, he reached Shearman's office in the House of Commons.

'Hello. I'd like to speak to Dave Shearman, please.'

'He's not taking calls. Sorry.'

'Look, I need to talk to Dave about a story breaking tomorrow.'

'You mean the Minister, don't you?'

'Yes, yes.'

'What story's that?'

'It's private, but I know Dave will want to talk to me. I'm an old friend.'

'Who's speaking?'

'My name's Clive Parkhouse. I...'

'Hell, Clive. It's Mike Boddington here.'

'Mike?'

'I work for Dave. I'm his press secretary.'

'Mike. I'd no idea. You, working for Dave, well bugger me, that's a turn out for the books. Things must've got bad at the *Comet*.'

'Now, now.'

'Sorry. I'd love to chat, but I haven't got time. You must realise what I'm phoning about.'

'No.'

'Don't give me that crap. You know what I'm talking about. Clara and Dave.'

'What d'you know?'

'I picked it up from Lucy Kwame. She's a colleague of mine from the nineties. I never knew she was Clara's daughter. The *Echo* told her about tomorrow's front page, and she contacted me. We can't talk on the phone. I need to see you both. It's got to be tomorrow evening.'

'I can't make the Minister meet you. He'll tell me where to get off.'

'Let *me* speak to him then.'

'He can't talk at the moment. The shit's hitting the fan, and he'll be tied up for a while.'

'Tell Dave I must see him. Here's my mobile. You can text a time and place.'

Clive recited his number.

'You got that Mike?'

'Yes, but…'

'Listen Mike, don't mess me about. It's important,' said Clive, angrily.

'What's the rush?'

'It's got to be tomorrow because that's when I'm in London. I'm seeing Lucy and I need to know… I need to know everything before I meet her.'

'Has Dave contacted her?'

'Don't think so.'

'I think he should phone her. Tell him that when I spoke to Lucy, she was confused, upset and emotional. She needs him to call.'

Clive gave Mike her number and then rang off.

56

MIKE

As Clive was speaking to Mike Boddington, Dave Shearman was in his office, talking to his wife over the phone. Mike heard raised voices and assumed that Dave was explaining the story about to hit the front page of the *Echo*. When Dave had finished his call, Mike knocked and went into his office.

'I've got something for your diary for tomorrow night,' said Mike.

'What's that?'

'We're having a jolly reunion.'

'Stop playing games.'

'Seriously, we're meeting up with Clive Parkhouse.'

'Don't be stupid. My career's on the line, and you're arranging a get-together.'

'Clive phoned a few minutes ago. He'd like to speak to you.'

'What the fuck does he want?'

Mike explained what Clive had said over the phone, and Dave suggested a rendezvous.

'And he's given me your daughter's home and mobile numbers. Clive thought you might want to talk to her. It's the least you can do.'

57

MARCUS

Marcus's feeling of exhaustion had not dissipated by the time he left for home on Monday evening. He decided that he would say nothing to Mary. She would only fret or change her plan to visit friends in Washington, a trip she had been planning for months.

He was worried, and he was not sure why. He felt under the weather, but he was not suffering any of the pains he had experienced before his previous heart attack. He had already arranged to see the specialist, later in the week, whilst Mary was away. It was a precautionary measure, and there was no need to be unnecessarily concerned. It had been an exciting day, a great day, and he had been on the go since early morning. He was sure that the tiredness was due to the effort he was putting into this momentous week. The family celebrations were a quiet affair, and he slept a little better that night.

It was 6.30 the following morning, and Marcus and Mary were at breakfast. Mary's suitcase was in the hall. As he did each morning, Marcus's driver had dropped off a copy of every national newspaper, and he was waiting for Marcus in the car. Marcus, who had been looking through a rival newspaper, picked up and showed Mary the front page of the *Echo*.

'Any qualms, Marcus? They were your friends.'

'I've thought a lot about it. There were moments when

I've felt uncomfortable, but it's my job, and they've brought it on themselves.'

'I don't think I could do it.'

'It's a cut-throat business.'

'It would have been nice if you'd have come to America with me, Marcus.'

'I'm too busy.'

'Come off it, Marcus. You can take time off whenever you choose, but you don't want to.'

Mary was dressed for her journey, with a light, cotton, long-sleeved blouse and loose fitting chinos. She had tossed a fleece over the back of a kitchen chair. Marcus was uncomfortable with the level of casualness that would have been expected of him, and that was enough of a reason to stay at home. Her hair was snow white and close-cropped. She had added a few pounds over the years, but her complexion was ruddy, and her routine was energetic.

'I've got a paper to run, and it's an important week.'

'Yes,' said Mary, 'it's the only thing that interests you.'

'That's not true. Last night, we had a pleasant evening with the family. It's nice to know how they're getting on at work and how the grandchildren are doing at school.'

'You arrived back late, you were so tired that you barely spoke, and you were in bed before ten. That's why they've never been close to you and why you don't understand what's *really* going on in their lives.'

'Rubbish. It's done them no harm. Look how successful they are.'

'How d'you know whether it's done them any harm? They'd never tell you. The only measure, as far as you're concerned, is a job,' she paused. 'Oh, and not getting caught doing anything embarrassing.'

'I don't want to go through this again. It's the umpteenth

time. You were here when they were little, so they've had a good upbringing. Now, they're both successful and happy.'

'Do you think so? Do you think Giles and Michelle are a happy couple?'

'Well they are, aren't they? They look happy.'

'You've no idea, have you?'

'Well, is there a problem?'

'Giles is working every hour he can. He gets home after the children have gone to bed and leaves before they get up. He's permanently shattered, and Michelle is at breaking point. Sound familiar?'

'Yes, and we worked it out. They'll do the same.'

'We didn't work it out Marcus. I did. I had to accept my lot because it made you happy, and it provided a comfortable life. Michelle isn't me, and she won't take it.'

'What's does that mean?'

'I'll find out when I get back. She's been at her mother's for the past few weeks, with the children, leaving Giles to look after himself. Michelle told me not to tell you.'

'Well, have a word with her, or with him. I don't know. Tell them to sort it out.'

'Why don't you?'

'Don't be silly. You're better at dealing with this sort of thing.'

'That's what I'm talking about. Why's it for me? Why can't you talk to them, you know, find out what makes them tick. You've no idea. You won't because if you do, they might say something you don't like. You deal with them as if they're a work problem, not people.'

'Gail seems happy enough.'

'Don't you think she's a bit thin?'

'She trains hard.'

'That's all there is to it?' asked Mary.

'Of course. Give your daughter credit.'

'The hours, the travelling, the pressure, and she doesn't seem to socialise with friends.'

'It isn't the right time for this conversation. Let's have a proper talk when you're back.'

Mary rolled her eyes because Marcus was paying more attention to the paper than to her. Within minutes, he was in the car, his mind focussed on the day ahead.

Tuesday was a display of Marcus at the peak of his powers. As events moved, he adjusted, orchestrated and controlled. It was difficult for his subordinates not to be intoxicated by his drive. The Shearman story moved from the *Echo* to the national news, and then it went worldwide, with complimentary references to the *Echo* and the scandal it had uncovered.

Shearman was reported to be 'considering his position' and Lucy Kwame and her family were not talking to the press. The political consequences kept the story alive, and sales of the paper looked like they would finally overtake the *Globe*. Some competitors criticised the *Echo*, but the censure came from quarters where praise would have been more hurtful.

'We could find out what his daughter's up to, perhaps pick up phone messages,' said Barry.

'Don't get caught, but do whatever you need to.'

'I'll get the investigators moving on it. Shearman's bound to try to make contact with her. If they arrange to meet, we could make sure we're there.'

Barry knew what had to be done, and he had started the ball rolling the previous evening. The money was a good investment and the investigators could be disowned if necessary. As well as accessing her phone, the investigators would call in favours from the police and use contacts in local government, the DVLA and utility companies to track down where she lived. It was accepted practice, and Barry thought nothing of it. Everything was at arm's length and payments hidden amongst the plethora of expense claims. Nobody at the paper could be held responsible, and anyhow, the police had too much to lose and would avoid poking their noses into the paper's business.

Jeremy McNeice's partner had complained that Jeremy did not have AIDS and demanded a retraction. He was put through to Noreen Parfitte. She pointed out that the *Echo* had never said he had AIDS but that he had died from an AIDS cancer. He was not placated by this explanation, so she politely told him to 'fuck off and grow up' and referred to him as a 'little weasel'.

By that evening, the paper had gathered photographs of a stream of men visiting McNeice's partner, and Marcus gleefully fingered through them. He picked one out and thought he recognised the face. He called Kevin Smallman into his office, and Smallman confirmed that it was Clive Parkhouse. The photographs were used with a mischievous headline which said: 'McNeice's partner – getting back to normal'.

On Tuesday night, Barry and Marcus sat opposite each other in Marcus's office, each working his way through a copy of the following day's paper.

'It's everything I'd expect from the *Echo*, Barry. Front to back, it's something to be proud of; campaigning, exciting, provoking, anti-establishment.'

'And more of the same tomorrow,' added Barry.

Then, as Barry left, the sweats and the feeling of anxiety started. Marcus sat quietly in his office, waiting for them to go.

58

CLIVE

Clive checked into his hotel in London after lunch on Tuesday, and it was late in the afternoon when he took the Tube. His first call was at Jeremy McNeice's house. Clive was nervous about how James Halloran would receive him, despite the warmth of James's invitation. Clive had not expected to see two press photographers outside James and Jeremy's house. He felt an urge to turn back and hesitated.

'Sod it,' he mumbled as he strode forward. They photographed him entering the flat.

Since early morning, the press had hounded James. They wanted pictures and a story, but James wanted peace and quiet. James spoke lovingly about his partner, and how, for nearly thirty years, they had lived quietly together. Jeremy had been wild when he was younger, but they had maintained a close and faithful relationship for all of their time together. James explained that the cancer had nothing to do with AIDS, and Clive could sense that James had tended his partner with care and dignity, right to the end.

'It's horrible what they're implying. It's so unkind.' James started to cry. 'I don't know what to do. It's making me feel that,' he paused and wiped his eyes with a handkerchief, 'that there's no point going on.'

'Don't say that. It's not what Jeremy would have wanted.'

'I'm not used to the limelight. I don't know how to

handle the papers. I thought I'd be able to correct what they'd said. I phoned the *Echo*, and this woman, she... she abused me. It was as if she thought it was a joke, as if we didn't matter.'

James explained what Noreen Parfitte had said and started to cry again.

'They make out he had lots of boyfriends, but he only cared for me. They wouldn't dare say anything like that if we were straight.'

Clive sat beside James on the settee and put an arm round him.

'Clive, I'm so sad that Jeremy died without making up with you. He was unhappy about it, too. He wanted to, but he just couldn't, I suppose. Whoever spoke to them, it doesn't matter. You said it wasn't you, and I believe you.'

Friends came and went, offering condolences to a quiet, caring man, distraught at his loss. Later that evening, when Clive charged through the camera flashes, he checked that nobody was following him. He doubted that the cameramen would know who he was. He could barely contain his anger at the way his friends had been treated, and he decided that he would confront the perpetrator of this injustice.

He travelled by Tube to his appointment with Dave Shearman. Mike had texted a time and location. Clive's mood was still sour when he met his ex-boss at Dave's club. They shook hands and exchanged brief and business-like pleasantries.

'Dave's on his way. He'll be here in ten minutes. Still friends?' asked Mike.

'Still friends,' confirmed Clive.

They moved into a private and sumptuously furnished lounge area, and Mike offered Clive a drink. He declined, and Mike poured himself a large malt whisky from a decanter on the table. Clive surveyed the scene. How different from his own lifestyle.

'So what have you been doing for the past twenty, no, nearer twenty-five years?' he asked.

'I was going nowhere at the *Comet*, and to be frank, the *Comet* was going nowhere. You were right what you said, you know, when you left the *Comet*. I *was* being leaned on.'

'Surprise, surprise.'

'I had a big bust up with the owners and was desperate for work, so I took a job at the *Globe*, as News Editor.'

'That must've been worse than working for Dave.'

'Ha ha. I was prepared to take anything they offered. I'd a young family and needed the cash. I bumped into Dave at a conference, kept in touch, and a few years later, he offered me this job. I couldn't wait to get out. Anyhow, until now, I've managed to keep him out of bother.'

'I bet that's taken some doing, knowing Dave.'

'He's calmed down a fair bit.'

'That's not what I heard. He had a string of affairs, and then he fell out with his daughter, didn't he?'

'You should know better than to believe what you read in the papers.'

'We all should,' Clive laughed.

'He didn't see Becky, that's his daughter, for years, and she didn't want to see him. To his credit, Dave stuck at it and eventually made contact. They've made up.'

'She got some bad headlines too.'

'Dave and his wife, Christine, are close to Becky and the grandchildren, and they helped her through a sticky period in her marriage. Of course, a story like that's not headline news.'

'That's not the Dave I knew.'

'Underneath all the bullshit, he's a good bloke.'

'You would say that, wouldn't you?'

'But it's true.'

'You would say that too. It's your job.'

'Hold on a minute. My job's to provide balance. Everyone out there's hostile, and without people like me, everything would get misrepresented.'

'But spin-doctors have made it impossible to work out what's true and what's a lie. That's why the public don't trust the newspapers or the government.'

'Don't exaggerate, Clive. Presentation's important if you want to win elections.'

'You could be brave. You could face them up and put forward your case.'

'Don't lecture me. *You're* not squeaky clean, are you?'

'No I'm not, but you'll recall that I'm not prepared to misrepresent things, just because the people I disagree with do.'

'I thought we were still friends.'

'We are. That's why we can talk like this.'

The door opened and Dave rushed in, flustered and glum.

'Sorry, sorry, Clive, I'm late. Whew! What a day. Well it's good to see you... I think!'

They shook hands. Mike remained standing, and Clive and Dave took seats opposite each other.

'Can't recollect how many years,' he mumbled. 'Drink, Mike. I need a drink. How long is it? It must be over twenty years. It's really good to see you. Not very auspicious circumstances though. Hell, I wish I had as much hair as you've got. You must have lived a good life.'

'Yes, it's well over twenty years – during the miners' strike. I think the hair's hereditary.'

Mike filled Dave's glass, dutifully.

'What you grinning at, Clive?' asked Dave.

'How the tables are turned. When we first met, you were the underdog, fetching and carrying for our master.'

'Ignore him,' said Mike. 'He's stirring, just like he always did.'

Dave downed the neat whisky in one. He gasped and held out the glass for another drink.

'Mike says that you've something to say about Clara and me.'

'Have you spoken to Lucy?'

'Yes, I phoned her on her mobile. It was difficult because the newspapers have got hold of her number, and she was reluctant to take the call. We only spoke for a few seconds. I'm meeting up with her, tomorrow, at Becky's house. I just hope she turns up, and I told her to be careful that she's not followed.'

'Look, Dave,' said Clive, 'I want to piece together what happened. I need to understand why Clara didn't tell me the truth. After you split up with her, she told me she thought she was pregnant. I was close to her, very, very close, and I knew she was worried.'

'She never told me. I'd have married her if I'd have known she was pregnant. I said I'd marry her when I found out.'

'The two of you weren't in love. She may have felt something for you in the early days, but that'd worn thin.'

'When she moved out that last Easter,' Dave nodded toward Clive, 'you're right, things weren't working out. The spark had gone.'

'You'd become convenient for each other. She was glad that you were splitting up, but something happened when she came off the pill. She was uptight because of splitting up, exams and thinking she was pregnant. She wanted someone to talk to… me. She said her periods had got messed up. She didn't know what to do. She refused to think about having an abortion. I'd always had a thing about Clara – you know what I mean, it was that aura she had – and I talked seriously about marrying her, if she *was* pregnant.'

'Marry you? You're kidding.'

'Anyhow, just before her finals, she told me that everything was OK. I could see a change come over her, you know, a weight lifted.'

'She must've lied. The baby was born in December. Work out the dates. She'll have told you that she wasn't pregnant, I don't know, to get you off her back,' said Dave.

'Get me off her back?'

'I'm sorry. I didn't mean it like that.'

'When did you find out?'

Dave explained the circumstances of his meeting with Clara.

'She refused to talk, and I had to leave. When she had the baby, I went to see her again, in January. Lucy would have been a couple of weeks old. Clara wouldn't let me see her. She made me promise to tell nobody, and I was never to make contact with Lucy.'

'And you've never met Lucy?'

'No. Clara refused to let me anywhere near her.'

'It's starting to make sense,' Clive sighed. 'When Clara had time to weigh things up, I guess she decided that she wanted the baby. Perhaps it was the Catholic in her, who knows? Clara never followed convention. At first, she needed someone to talk to, and when she realised that I was prepared to marry her, she lied. She was in love with neither of us and was left with only one option.'

'Have the baby and bring it up on her own,' said Dave, sadly. 'But why didn't she tell Lucy I was the father?'

'Perhaps she intended to, who knows? As time passed, it would have become more difficult. Perhaps she was frightened that this might happen.'

'Well, it's all come out in the end, hasn't it? In a way, it's a relief. I'm going to try to make things up with Lucy. I seem to have the knack for screwing things up with my kids.'

'Give me a ring when you've sorted things with Lucy,' said Clive. 'She's a lovely woman, like her mum. You'll be proud of her. I'll phone her tonight. I'll probably see her on Thursday.'

'I'd like you to meet me at Becky's, tomorrow afternoon,' said Dave, scribbling her address on the top sheet of a pad of headed notepaper lying on the table. 'I'm going to stay there tonight, away from the press. She's off the radar and the press don't know where she lives. It'd be good to catch up, but not now. There's too much to do, you know, politics.'

'I've got things planned for tomorrow. I'll probably not be able to make it.'

'I'd like to talk some more, Clive, just you and me,' pleaded Dave.

'I'll see.'

'Be careful what messages you leave,' said Mike. 'The papers will have mobilised their private investigators. Some policemen will talk for money, and investigators will be into your phone messages before you know it. Make sure nobody's following you. Change the PIN on your phone. Tell Lucy too.'

'You think they may be picking up my phone messages?'

'Of course. I've been told they're doing it at the *Globe*. I pick up whispers about what's going, so don't take risks. I even heard a pissed hack brag about it. If they've worked out your mobile PIN, they'll be into your messages.'

'Why would they bother with me?'

'You may not be of interest, but people you deal with could be. They'll trace you through them and get at them through you. That's how it works.'

Clive thought for a moment.

'Jeremy McNeice, for example, would he have been on the radar?'

'I'd bet my house on it.'

'Shit!'

When Clive returned to his hotel, he changed Tube twice and doubled back on himself to check for followers. As soon as he was back to his room, he rang Lucy's mobile.

'Clive.'

'Lucy, how are you?'

'It's awful. They've got my phone number. I'm only picking up calls from people I know. Photographers and reporters, they're outside the house. I can't leave without having a camera stuck in my face, and it's the same for Victor and the children. How do they know where I live and my phone numbers? My house phone number is ex-directory.'

'It's a long story. Be careful on the phone. Assume messages are being picked up. Change all your PINs.'

'What?'

'Yes, I know it sounds crazy. I've seen Dave, and I know what the score is. We've a lot to talk about. I'm staying over till Thursday morning. I'll ring then, and we can meet up. Don't worry, it'll blow over quickly. I'm sorry it's happened like this.'

59

MARCUS

On Tuesday night, Marcus stayed at his flat in London. He endured another restless sleep. His driver picked him up early on Wednesday morning and drove him to a nearby hotel where he regularly took breakfast. He was eating in the main breakfast area and had read most of the daily press. He was, by nature, a quiet man who did not court recognition or celebrity. Today, however, he was happy to be acknowledged, and he was enjoying the sound of his name.

'Coffee or tea, Mr Roache?'

'Would you like more toast, Mr Roache?'

He was aware other breakfasters had recognised him, and he was luxuriating in it.

He was to be disappointed when he settled the bill and was addressed as 'Sir'. However this was more than compensated for when the concierge asked, 'Your car is waiting outside, Mr Roache. Shall I take your case?'

Marcus was in a contemplative mood as he sat in the car. Restless nights seeded his thoughts. He was not much taken to philosophising, preferring the immediacy and personal discipline of action to the self-indulgence and waste of reflection and introspection. Although his paper offered a daily diet of medical and psychological advice and administered regular doses of self-help, he thought it was all gobbledygook.

There was too much to be done on a day-to-day basis to

worry about oneself or to be spent navel-gazing. However, something was different about this week. One event had removed a burden he had felt for more than forty years. He could admit it to nobody, not even Mary.

Jeremy had been right. Marcus was plagued by the fear of being made to look foolish by others. He was frightened of not being in control. His imagined nemesis was the smooth-tongued Jeremy McNeice, and his death had lifted a great weight. Marcus felt invincible and saw no reason why he should not continue at the *Echo* for years to come, despite the suggestions in the press that he might decide to retire.

During the morning, Marcus was involved in a meeting with the finance director, preparing for a forthcoming Board Meeting. The trusted Barry was managing the preparation of the following day's paper. Marcus had asked not to be interrupted, except in an emergency. It was late morning, and the finance director had left. Marcus was rewriting his report for the Board Meeting, and Barry knocked and entered.

'A guy's been pestering switchboard all morning, and now he's in reception. I've just been told it's Clive Parkhouse, and he says he wants to see you. They've told him you're not available. He won't leave. D'you want to speak to him?'

'No, and get security to remove him if he doesn't go.'

'There's a story breaking in the States about Sam Reilly at the *Globe*. He's been having an affair with an American woman. Reilly filed for divorce a few weeks ago, but it's been going on for years. They've stayed in hotels in America and the Far East, and there's witnesses and photographs.'

'None of the other British papers will run with it. We'll stick to our policy on the competition. We can't afford to start a sleaze war with them, particularly not the *Globe*. It's a good story, but it's not for us. I don't want their hounds sniffing out stories about us. They'd hang us out to dry.'

Barry blushed and Marcus continued.

'We don't print this sort of story about them, and they won't do anything about us. They're the unwritten rules. We've got the only story in town that matters. Let's not dilute *that* scoop with a pointless pop at the *Globe*.'

Barry left with a shrug of acceptance and a smile. Within a minute he was back in the office.

'It's being leaked that Shearman's going to resign, either later on today or tomorrow. Wants to spend more time with his family, he says, and doesn't want to cause any embarrassment to the government.'

'Bit late for that,' said Marcus. 'Labour won't want him around. He's finished. I wish he'd hung on for a bit longer. Hounding him out would have filled a few more column inches and sold a few more papers. It's a shame, but never mind.'

He looked at Barry and asked him draw up a seat.

Barry nodded, sat down. Something was afoot. Perhaps, as suggested in other papers, Marcus had been considering his future, and Barry would be the first to know.

'It's a big week for me. The papers are covering my career, but I don't really care what *they* say,' he said, untruthfully. 'What do *you* think we've achieved over the years at the *Echo*?'

Barry hesitated.

'That's a big question.'

'Come on. You must have an opinion.'

'Our circulation. As a newspaper man, that's the most important thing.'

'More than that?'

'Nobody in power can ignore us. We may not run the country, but no party will get elected without carrying our readers. The *Echo* keeps the politicians in line.'

Marcus had formed his hands into the praying position in front of his chin, his elbows on the desk.

'Yes, Barry, I like that. It'd make a good epitaph. It's alright; I'm not dying or thinking of retiring. Not yet anyhow.'

Barry watched Marcus scan the paintings of his predecessors on the office wall, and Marcus turned away, embarrassed, when he caught Barry's eye.

'Yes, thanks Barry. Err. You've been a great support. Thanks again.'

Barry left the room with a 'Phew!'

Unusually for Marcus, he found it hard to concentrate that afternoon, thinking more about past events than producing the following day's paper. He was unassailable, but there was something making him anxious. He'd felt this way before his previous heart attack but pushed the memory to the back of his mind.

Marcus left the Editors' Forum at the Dorchester at 9.30 that evening. He jumped into his car, which his driver had drawn up. As the car pulled away, and Marcus headed to his London flat, he reflected on a momentous evening. He had expected some formal recognition from his peers, but the warmth and sincerity took him by surprise.

There had been a speech in his honour, which had been well researched, and it listed his achievements in glowing terms. Afterwards he had been assaulted by warm handshakes and kind words. He was not foolish enough to believe that many of his peers liked him, but he knew that they all respected him and his success. It was with an effort that Marcus banished these reflections because Thursday was another day, and the *Echo* had to improve to stay ahead of the pack. His mind focussed on what the paper would be delivering tomorrow and the next day. It was an exciting prospect.

Not long afterwards, his car pulled into the entrance of the underground car park that serviced the Georgian terrace where he had his flat. He got out of the car and started to walk back the way he had come, toward the front door of the flat. He glanced across at a taxi that had pulled up suddenly. As he strode quickly past, he caught a brief glimpse of the male passenger inside. It was dark, and perhaps he was mistaken, but the man's features were familiar. Marcus's heart missed a beat. He started sweating and continued onwards, the face firmly in his mind.

He sensed that the man in the taxi had paid the driver and was walking quickly, trying to catch Marcus up. It was the past returning to haunt his present, and he did not want to confront this ghost, whoever he was. He tried, unsuccessfully, to expel these tired and silly thoughts from his consciousness. The key entered the lock.

60

CLIVE

Clive lay on his bed in the hotel on Tuesday evening, thinking about how he could correct the unkind slurs about his two friends and the damage it had caused. He could write a letter to the *Echo*, respond online or write an article that would put out the other side of the story. None of these options were satisfactory. He was sure that the *Echo* had discovered Jeremy's cancer from the message left on his phone. He must have been hacked, and he took Mike's advice and changed his PIN.

He had to find a way to confront Marcus. Marcus had destroyed his friendship with Jeremy, and Jeremy had died thinking that Clive had betrayed him. It was a personal matter, and he needed to confront Marcus face-to-face.

On Wednesday morning, straight after breakfast, Clive returned to James Halloran's house, and the paparazzi had gone. He rang the bell, and a man that Clive had not seen before opened the door. When Clive explained who he was, the man let him in. His name was Alan, and he explained that James had taken an overdose. Alan had been staying the night. He had been sleeping in the spare room, but he had been worried about James and had checked on him after he had gone to bed. He had seen empty pill bottles on the bedside table and had acted quickly. James was now asleep, and the doctor had said that he could not see visitors that day.

Clive tried to phone Marcus Roache and was told that he

was not taking calls, so he took a taxi to the *Echo*'s offices. He pleaded with reception, and then he argued. Exasperated, he walked into the offices, only for security to chase and stop him. Clive had lost none of his determination, and he had to find another way to meet Marcus. For the moment, there was nothing more he could do, and he decided to make his rendezvous with Dave, checking he was not being followed.

Clive arrived at the address, and a woman, who introduced herself as Becky, opened the door. Clive could see Dave behind her, in the hallway.

'Come in,' said Dave. 'Have a coffee.'

'If you're busy, I don't want to intrude. I've got lots to do.'

'Nonsense! You can spare a few minutes,' said Dave, ushering Clive into the living room. 'I'm a granddad you know,' he continued proudly.

'Congratulations. I can't stay long, Dave.'

'Have you got kids?'

'Yes. Grown up.'

'Grandchildren?'

'No.'

'The children are at Mum's house,' said Becky. 'I thought it'd be best while Dad's here.'

Clive had remembered Becky Shearman from pictures taken when she had been at the height of her music career and during her meteoric fall. Now she was dressed in well-worn jeans and a loose and comfortable sweatshirt, the same as millions of other middle-aged mothers.

She made coffee as the men talked about the years since university. Becky listened and smiled at reminiscences of this far-off world. Dave told Clive that he had met Lucy that morning. He described it as business-like, not warm. Lucy had wanted to know about Dave's relationship with her mother, and he had told her how they had met, lived together and finally split up. He had then explained to Lucy how he had found out that Clara was pregnant, offered to marry her, but that she would not consider it. Clara had not allowed him to see his daughter, but she and Dave had maintained contact for a number of years afterwards.

He had told her how sorry he was about her mother's death. He had been in Hong Kong and had only found out on his return. He had kept the promise he had made to Clara that he would not contact Lucy. Lucy had asked about the bequest, and he had told her that he had kept it a secret from Clara. When Lucy had got up to go, he had wanted to hug her, but she had avoided contact and said she needed to think things over. Dave said she had looked confused and had not appeared completely satisfied with his answers. Perhaps she had not trusted him.

As he finished his explanation of Lucy's visit, Dave's mobile phone rang. It was Mike Boddington, and Dave went into a bedroom for privacy.

The conversation continued between Clive and Becky. She talked with affection about her dad.

'It was a shock when my mum left him, and he went off the rails for a bit. It was hardly surprising, you know, a married man having his wife run off with another woman. It was acrimonious.'

'You were very young.'

'I can't remember much, but my mum didn't want Dad to have access, and she kept us apart. She'd heard about the other women, and I think she used it against him. I didn't see Dad for years. It wasn't nice, you know.'

'Didn't he try to see you?'

'Mum was difficult. Then Dad married Christine, and his politics started to take up more time. He sent me a Christmas card every year, with a letter. He made contact when my marriage got into trouble.'

'I read about it in the newspapers.'

'I'd had my first baby and became depressed. Lots of things got on top of me. My career was, well, to be honest, it fell off a cliff edge. Danny was transferred, and he lived up north in the week. There were rumours about him being out on the town. I started partying too. It was a sort of revenge. It all hit the headlines.'

'I remember some unflattering photographs.'

'They said I was leaving the baby alone, at home. It wasn't true because Mum was always there if I was out. They said I was drinking and having an affair. None of that was true either. A few times, I got brought home late, but that was all.'

'That's not the image you'd have got from the papers.'

'Anyhow, out of the blue, my dad turned up at the door. He was just so lovely to me. I cried a bit, and he comforted me, and then we talked, and he made it a regular thing, once or twice a week.'

'What about your mum?'

'I didn't tell her. He only came when they weren't around. Then I met Christine and she was so nice to me too. Things settled down for me when Danny was transferred back to London. He wanted to be here with his family. It cost him a lot of money.'

'I remember that. He never played in the top flight again.'

'Then Mum and Dad made up, not lovey-dovey, but you know, alright. We meet up most weeks. Danny gets Dad tickets for the football.'

'What do you do now? Still in the music business?'

'This probably sounds a bit of nonsense, but I am a music therapist.'

'What's that?' asked Clive.

'Children with some disabilities can benefit from music

therapy, like autistic children. Danny got involved with a charity because his brother is autistic. It wasn't diagnosed properly at the time. Anyhow, I got interested in it; it seemed something I could do.'

'I've never heard of it.'

'I studied for a music degree and then my postgraduate qualification. One of the benefits of being married to a footballer is that he's got enough spare time to share the workload at home.'

'So, who do you work for?'

'I work in a hospital, in something called a child development centre.'

Becky explained how she worked with youngsters, using music to help children and young adults with behavioural problems to develop social and communication skills.

'It sounds a fantastic job.'

'It is, but I still keep in touch with the music scene. I play with my band at pubs and small venues, at weekends, if anyone'll have me. It's my bit of fun.'

'Do you miss the glamour?'

'I'm glad I did it, but I'm glad I'm out. You have to be lucky to make a career and stay normal at the end of it. Too many people are destroyed by the pressure and become tabloid fodder.'

'It's not quite as glamorous as it seems, is it?'

'I'm lucky that I left showbiz, or to be honest, I got the push, and that I've a strong family.'

Dave burst into the room.

'I'm out of government. The rumours aren't helping the PM, so I'm about to fall on my sword.'

'I'm sorry it's ended like this,' Clive said. 'It's for the best, Dave, for everybody.'

'Now it's happened, and I'm out of it, it's a blessed relief.'

'You'll be able to give Christine the time she deserves, Dad,' Becky added.

Clive explained what had happened that morning. He still had a busy day ahead, and he had to leave. He offered his hand, which Dave shook vigorously. Dave showed him to the door.

'I'm going to talk to Marcus if it's the last thing I do,' Clive said, as he was leaving. 'I'll try to track him down tonight, and I'll keep in touch. You've got a lovely daughter,' and then on reflection, he added, 'two lovely daughters. You're a lucky man, yes, a very lucky man.'

Clive returned to his hotel and switched on his laptop. A quick search informed him that Marcus would be attending the Editors' Forum at The Dorchester that night. Twenty minutes more and he learned that Marcus lived in a village in the country but also had a flat in London that he often used in the week.

Clive could not find out where the flat was located but hoped that Marcus would sleep there. If not, then Clive would have a hefty taxi fare to pay. He found the most up-to-date photograph of Marcus on the internet. He had changed, but Clive recognised him.

Clive left for central London. He had everything he needed for the evening.

'Let's hear what Marcus Roache has got to say for himself,' he murmured.

61

CLIVE

Clive stopped a taxi and kept it waiting on the meter for fifteen minutes, just off Park Lane. The Dorchester disgorged the first of the press grandees, and Marcus jumped into his car. Clive pointed out the prey to the driver, and they pulled away in pursuit. It was only ten minutes later that Marcus Roache's car pulled off the main road, along a wide side street and then into the entry of an underground car park. Marcus stepped out and started to walk back the way he had come. His car drove away down the road. As he strolled past Clive's taxi, which had pulled quickly into the side of the road, he seemed to glance toward Clive. Clive was distracted when a car behind sounded its horn.

'Car behind nearly hit me,' said the taxi driver. 'Woman driver… not bleedin' concentrating.'

Clive paid no attention as he pulled a note from his wallet and turned to keep an eye on Marcus. He paid the driver, jumped out and followed Marcus up the street, some fifty yards behind him.

Marcus stood at the front door of a house in a Georgian terrace. Each door led to two flats. Marcus was scratching a key against the brass barrel of the lock. Clive heard the satisfying noise of the key making a perfect union with the locking mechanism, and after a vigorous turn, the door opened. Marcus removed the key, and his hand snaked inwards, switching on the hall lights. He entered the hallway and turned to shut the door.

'Hello, Marcus.'

Clive greeted Marcus in a friendly voice, and Marcus peered warily into the dim light at the figure who was addressing him from the pavement.

Clive realised that he had not been recognised. Perhaps the face was familiar but Marcus had failed to make the connections.

'Long time, no see,' said Clive.

'It's Clive, isn't it? Clive Parkhouse?'

Marcus sounded relieved.

'Yes,' replied Clive, offering a hand. 'You ought to recognise me. I've just been in your paper.'

'Really?'

Marcus did not reciprocate because his hands were soaked in sweat, and he made out he had not seen the greeting being offered.

'What the hell are you doing here?' he asked. 'It's a long way from home, isn't it? You've not come looking for me, have you?' he laughed, nervously.

'I've been in London to see friends from way back.'

'How extraordinary bumping into you like this,' he replied, apparently satisfied with the reply and regaining his confident demeanour. 'This isn't a chance meeting, is it?'

'I wanted to see you, Marcus. I couldn't get past your gatekeepers at the *Echo*, so I thought I'd ambush you.'

'It's not the photograph. You're not angry about that are you?'

'Not really. No, I've got other things to talk about. Perhaps it would be better if we didn't chat out here.'

'Yes, yes. Come in.'

Clive made a mental note of the flat number. The door

opened into a wide hallway. On the left was a stairway to the first floor flat, and Clive followed Marcus upstairs to a second door, which Marcus unlocked.

The flat was large and functionally decorated. Marcus offered Clive a seat on a large, brown leather settee, which had no creases or scuffs to show that it had ever been sat on. Marcus had stopped perspiring, and he went into the kitchen to dry his hands and face on a tea towel. He returned to the living room and offered his hand, which Clive accepted, and then a drink, which he declined. Marcus poured himself a whisky from a decanter. He spoke as he poured.

'You still working?'

'Yes, I'm doing bits and pieces, but I'm winding down.'

Marcus sat in a leather chair and slid his whisky glass onto the coffee table, which was between him and Clive. Marcus had recovered his poise and displayed a jaunty superiority. He recounted their first meeting at university, friends they had known and incidents that had occurred. He talked about when they had last seen each other, and he asked what Clive was doing and where he lived.

Clive was clipped in his response.

'You're not your usual talkative self, Clive. You didn't come here for a social visit, did you? You've clearly got a chip on your shoulder about something. If it's not the picture in the paper, is it the stuff on Dave and Clara, your two old buddies?'

'*Your* two old buddies, Marcus.'

'Ah, I get it now. It's Dave and Clara. You're going to tell me that, for old time's sake, I shouldn't have run the story. I'm in the business of telling my readers the truth. I can't let emotion get in the way of that, can I? There are principles at stake here. You were always the one who insisted on reporting the facts.'

'I didn't come to London to criticise you for what you've

written about Clara and Dave. God, how much I'd like to, but it's not my business.'

'Well, it's clearly not a social call.'

'I've met up with Dave and Mike, and I'll be seeing Lucy Kwame, but I came to London to give my support to Jeremy McNeice's partner.'

'Jeremy McNeice?'

'I've known Jeremy and James Halloran for years. Clara and Jeremy helped me get my career back on the rails. He was a kind man, Jeremy McNeice, and so is James.'

'You're not gay, are you?'

'What's that got to do with you? I'm a friend of James and Jeremy. That photograph was a crude attempt to suggest that I'm gay. You tried to embarrass me, but the only problem is… I don't care.'

'You're gay, aren't you?'

'Don't mess me about, Marcus. I remember your campaigning days. Do you? You seemed to have different views about homosexuality back then.'

'I'm not prejudiced against homosexuals. I'm against promiscuity. It's the lifestyle they adopt.'

'They were close, James and Jeremy. Just because they're gay doesn't mean they're promiscuous.'

'Hmm.'

'How did you find out about Jeremy's cancer?'

'I don't reveal sources. Do you?'

'Only three people knew. There was the doctor, Jeremy and me. It wasn't me, I doubt it was the doctor, and it certainly wasn't Jeremy.'

'Well one of you must have blabbed.'

'Jeremy died blaming me. We didn't speak for his last years because he thought it must have been me. But it wasn't, and that leaves only one other possibility. Your people hacked my phone. Jeremy left a message that told me everything about his illness. That's how you found out.'

'You're clutching at straws.'

'You know that's what happened, and so do I.'

'Prove it.'

'Just think, Marcus, you ruined the friendship I had with a sick and dying man, just for your circulation.'

'I've had enough of your libellous accusations.'

'Jeremy's death was tough enough, but the way your newspaper handled it was sickening,' said Clive, pointing angrily.

'Well he chose his lifestyle,' Marcus replied, quietly.

'What the hell does that mean? Jeremy and James didn't choose to be gay. It's what they are, not what they've chosen. Can't you remember? That's what you believed, once.'

'Don't preach to me.'

'The *Echo* didn't report the truth. It told the readers what they wanted to hear. They were a faithful couple, and his cancer had nothing to do AIDS.'

'We never said it was caused by AIDS.'

'The implication's clear. Why mention AIDS unless you want your readers to make the connection? What you said hurt an innocent and loving man.'

'It's a big leap from accepting homosexuality to all this talk of *gay love*, isn't it?'

'James Halloran asked the *Echo* for a retraction, and one of your staff told him to fuck off.'

'Our job's to report, not to pander to someone who feels a bit hurt.'

'This morning you've printed photos of men going to Jeremy and James's house, including me, with the headline, "McNeice's partner – getting back to normal". What's that about?' barked Clive.

'Well, it was light-hearted. Anyhow, who were all those people?'

'You bastard. What do you mean by light-hearted? A man's bereaved and you have fun at his expense, all for a titter from your millions of readers, and if it means heartbreak for a gay man, so what?'

'Heartbreak? Keep things in perspective.' Marcus's voice was beginning to betray annoyance.

Clive thought for a moment about mentioning the suicide attempt, but he realised that Marcus might use this information in the *Echo*.

'It was a vindictive swipe at someone you didn't like. As for those visitors, well they were Jeremy's friends. You know what friends are? They're people who liked him, liked him a lot. You smeared them too!' shouted Clive.

'You can fuck off. Don't talk to me like that. I'm not some stupid oik!'

'And all because of a personal vendetta against Jeremy that goes back to school.'

'What *are* you talking about? I've no personal vendetta. I couldn't care less about the man.'

'Jeremy told me that you'd expected to get to Cambridge, but you ended up with us instead because you weren't good enough. You weren't good enough and he was. Forty years holding a grudge. How pathetic is that?'

Clive smiled. A strange sensation was enveloping him. He was enjoying provoking Marcus. His temper had subsided and he was taking pleasure from needling his adversary. Clive was beginning to experience what he imagined Marcus felt when he launched one of his moralising campaigns – unconcerned about whomever he hurt because they deserved it. Along with the pleasure, there was a little guilt.

'That's a lie,' shouted Marcus. 'I didn't like him because

he was a pompous toff. I earned my place at that school. I got a scholarship. His family has owned half of East Anglia since the Norman Conquest. That's what I hated.'

'And he achieved what you couldn't. He got the grades and the degree, and you didn't. He went to the BBC, and you got the short straw: the *Echo*.'

'You're just like him, sneering at the *Echo*. He was a smug bastard. He thought he was superior. Anyhow, I achieved what I wanted.'

'And the BBC?'

'It's populated by thousands of Jeremy McNeice's, a bastion of permissive attitudes and socialist politics.'

'So you'll print an apology, now you know the facts, will you, for the AIDS smear and the suggestion that James is promiscuous?'

Marcus ignored the taunt.

'Noreen Parfitte will offer a separate apology about the way she treated him.'

'Fuck off.'

'You can apologise to me privately – your insinuation about my sexuality. I don't need anything public.'

'Go to hell.'

'And hacking my phone to get the story on Jeremy's cancer. He died thinking I'd been disloyal to him when it was you.'

'You're making that up. It's a lie and I'll take you to court if you say that in public.'

Clive was distracted when his mobile phone buzzed in his trouser pocket. He stood up and pulled it out, and as he did so, a crumpled piece of paper fell onto the table. It was a press cutting. Clive was about to grab it when Marcus snatched it.

Clive glanced at his mobile. It was a text from Lucy Kwame. He did not read it and put the mobile back.

The crumpled page, which was from *Student Voice*,

displayed a listing of up-and-coming entertainments at the students union. Marcus turned it over and saw that his own column was on the other side. It was headlined 'Prejudice toward homosexuals', a fierce polemic in favour of dropping the age of consent for consenting adults from twenty-one to eighteen. Marcus scanned it. He had penned it shortly after the change in the law that decriminalised homosexuality.

'Trying to be clever?'

'No. I brought my file of memorabilia with me, you know, to reminisce with old friends. It was in a bottom drawer at home, and I hadn't looked at it for forty years, but I rummaged through it last night, at the hotel. I'd kept that,' he said, pointing, 'because I thought it was the sort of writing I should aspire to. I'm sure it was something you were proud to have written.'

'Don't you start moralising. You were on the radio, drunk, incapable of doing your job. You should be fucking ashamed.'

'You've no idea how ashamed I was, of that and worse things I did. Are you ashamed?'

'Fuck off!'

'You've never thought for yourself, have you? At university you copied Dave Shearman, because you couldn't work things out for yourself.'

'You're really off your head. Shearman's a twat who can't keep his zip done up. He's getting what he deserves, and the country will be better for it.'

'You're the best editor around.'

'Thank you,' said Marcus, sarcastically.

'But you haven't quite got it up there,' said Clive, tapping the side if his head and looking Marcus directly in the eyes.

'Where do you get all this crap from, you pompous prick? If you were so damned smart, you wouldn't be scraping a living at the arse end of the business.'

'When you haven't the brains to work things out, you just

revert to your prejudices, don't you? At the end of the day you're second-rate, and your whole life has been spent trying to prove you're not.'

Marcus attempted to interrupt, but Clive continued, talking over Marcus.

'That's why you despised Jeremy McNeice, because he was first-rate, and that's why you get such pleasure from demeaning others.'

'How dare you talk to me like that? Are you pissed? You're the one that's second-rate, not me. Just look at yourself and what you've achieved. Fuck all.'

'Do you remember that party, in the last term of your first year?' asked Clive calmly.

'What?'

'You said you wanted one thing. You wanted to run the number one paper in the country.'

'Yes… vaguely. Yes I do, and I've achieved what I set out to do, haven't I?'

'Yes, and you talked about how you'd go about it, didn't you?'

'I've no idea.'

'Well you did. You talked about what a paper should be. You told Clara and me how you'd achieve it with no compromise on your ideals. Remember? You used words like "honesty", "integrity", "objectivity".'

'That's what the *Echo* stands for. I'm proud of it. I'm proud I've achieved my ambition.'

'You talked about standing up to bigots. You said all of that stuff, Marcus. It was a promise, and you meant it.'

'I did. I still do.'

'Your words inspired me and influenced the way I've tried to behave in my career, to follow your example. What do you think, Marcus, forty years on?'

'I'm glad I've been an inspiration to you Clive,' Marcus scoffed, 'but you've no business questioning my standards. I've lived up to them, and you've turned into a drunken, unprofessional hack, the like of which I cleared out of the *Echo* years ago. Perhaps one of the missing words from my list of values was sobriety.'

'No regrets, not even about the way you've misrepresented Jeremy McNeice?'

'No.'

'How your staff treated his partner, James?'

'You must be joking. I run a successful newspaper and that's a rare commodity.'

'Remember those principled days at university? Remember your promise, Marcus?'

'I've no regrets. I've earned my success through hard work. There's nothing to apologise for. I'm running an adult newspaper, read by millions every day. If any individual has a gripe, they can write to the Press Complaints Committee.'

'Don't joke. That's there to protect the newspapers, not the public. No regrets about hacking my phone?'

Marcus shrugged and smiled.

'That's a lie. You can't prove anything.'

Clive's phone buzzed and indicated another text message. He pulled it out of his pocket and read the first:

'Am nearby. Followed U from hotel. Need to talk. Which house? Lucy K'

Then he read the second.

'Know you R here. What number. Will ring every bell till I get answer. Lucy.'

'Sorry, Marcus. I've got to text back,' said Clive

Marcus rolled his eyes impatiently.

'53b. Down in a few mins. WAIT AT DOOR C.'

My God, thought Clive. *What the hell's she up to? She must have been following me.*

62

LUCY

Lucy was wary of meeting Dave Shearman and had not slept. He was her father, but she did not know him. She thought about how to greet him and behave toward him. How would he treat her? Why had her mother and father split, and why, if he had known Lucy was her daughter, had he not made contact before? She managed to avoid the press outside her house. She took a path at the bottom of the garden where the dustbins were stored, and came out on another street. Nervously, she looked around making sure nobody was following her.

As soon as she saw her father, she realised that he was as anxious as she was. Nothing felt right about the meeting. She was embarrassed throughout, and he seemed the same. He was not telling lies, but something about what he said suggested there was more that she did not know, or perhaps that Dave or Clive had not told her. She was glad when it was all over.

That evening, Lucy spotted Clive outside the Dorchester. It was not what she had planned or wanted. He was looking at his watch and waiting. Lucy drove past in her car and completed a circuit. She pulled over to the side of the road, about a hundred yards from the hotel. Clive was talking to a taxi driver. The taxi zoomed off, and after about three minutes, it reappeared and pulled in about thirty metres in front of her. There was nowhere to park legally, but it was not long before she saw her quarry in the flesh. He was with a group of dinner-jacketed men, laughing and backslapping at the hotel entrance. Cars were arriving and Marcus jumped into one, and it pulled away, followed by Clive in his taxi.

She tailed the taxi, which was following its prey, and she had to jump lights on more than one occasion to maintain contact. Twice she lost sight of them, only to catch up at a later set of lights. Once, she even got in front of the two cars and slowed to let them pass. She had no idea where they were going.

Suddenly, the taxi stopped, and Lucy hit the brakes. Her tyres squealed, and she pulled halfway past to avoid crashing into it from behind. She was now blocking the narrow road, and a car behind her was pipping its horn and flashing its lights. She saw Marcus walk back along the street and peer into the taxi, and then he looked straight at her. He walked on, and a few seconds later, Clive jumped out of the taxi and followed Marcus up the street.

She was unsure what to do, but there was nowhere to park, and she was blocking the road. She followed the taxi and looked in her mirror to establish which house the two men had gone into. She could not see either of them. There were no spaces, with vehicles nose to tail on both sides of the road.

It was ten minutes before she had found a space, parked the car and walked back to where the taxi had stopped. She looked for clues on the doors, but there was nothing to identify the whereabouts of the two men. She decided to text Clive. She walked up and down the street impatiently, but there was no reply and she texted again. If he did not respond soon, she would start ringing doorbells. Then there was a reply. He would be out in a few minutes. She rummaged in her handbag, and what she was feeling for was there. She was reassured.

63

MARCUS

'I've had enough of you. You've overstayed your welcome,' said Marcus.

Clive finished his text, and Marcus moved to the door, opened it and stood on the landing, waiting for Clive to leave.

'No apology, then?' Clive asked.

'Get out. I don't want to see you for another forty years.'

Clive made a resigned shrug.

The bell rang.

'What the... Who's that?' Marcus bellowed.

'Shit,' said Clive to himself. 'I'll go,' he shouted, but Marcus was already on his way.

Marcus peered through the door viewer but could only see the top of someone's head. He opened the door and was surprised by the elfin apparition, bathed in the warm glow of the outdoor light. At first, he thought that it was a young boy, but realised that he was looking at a woman of about forty, casually but neatly dressed in Levis and a long-sleeved, hooped rugby top. Her hands were tucked into the side pockets of her jeans with the thumbs showing, and a bag swung freely from her shoulder. Marcus recovered from his shock and addressed this fragile and vulnerable looking woman.

She stared back at him, penetratingly. Marcus kept the half-open door between himself and the apparition.

64

LUCY

Lucy had decided to ignore Clive's instruction to wait. She had hung around long enough and pressed the doorbell of 53b. She heard someone descending a flight of stairs. There was a hesitation as she was scrutinised through the brass door viewer, and then she heard the turn of the night latch. Marcus opened the door, and she could see the surprised look on his face.

'It's a bit late to be knocking on people's doors, isn't it?'

Lucy lifted her right arm and peered at her green Swatch in the glow of the street light.

'Yes, it's gone 10.00.'

'Are you looking for someone?'

'Yes… that's right, I *am* looking for somebody.'

Lucy could not take her eyes off the man she was facing. He was above her on the step but gave the impression of hiding behind the door.

Why are people so frightened of him?

'Clive. You're looking for Clive?' asked Marcus, suspiciously.

'Clive?'

'Someone else? Got an address?' asked Marcus.

'Yes, I'm looking for Clive, and I'm looking for you too, Mr Roache.'

The voice was quiet but assured.

'Sorry, do I know you?' he asked, nervously.

'No, we've never met, but you know *about* me. Because of you, the whole world seems to know about me.'

'What are you on about?'

'I'm Lucy Kwame.'

'What the hell are you doing here? Have you been following me? You've been put up to this by Clive Parkhouse, haven't you?'

Marcus's voice was loud and angry.

'Nobody's put me up to anything,' said Lucy quietly.

'So it's a coincidence, Clive being here?'

'What did Clive want?'

'Oh, it was some nonsense about Jeremy McNeice. Anyhow, more to the point, what do you want?'

'It might be better if I come in, Mr Roache. We don't want to disturb the neighbours, do we?'

'If you've come about...' Marcus hesitated, 'about your mother and Dave Shearman, then I've nothing to say, and you'd better go.'

Marcus was maintaining his position inside the doorway, left hand on the door as he cast a nervous glance down the street.

'Yes, it's about my father. Please let me in. It's important.'

Marcus looked directly at Lucy, hesitated for a moment and opened the door. She stepped past him and heard it close behind her. The solid clunk seemed to represent the solidity and security of the house and the man.

'You'd better come upstairs,' said Marcus.

Clive stood facing her as she entered the room, and she acknowledged him with the slightest of nods. Marcus invited Lucy to sit on the leather settee, and Marcus sat in the leather armchair.

'I thought you were going,' said Marcus, brusquely, to Clive.

'No, he *must* stay. I want him here. I want you both here.'

'Well get on with it. I'm telling you though; you'll not get an apology. Get that from your father, not from me.'

'Perhaps I will.'

Clive was leaning against a sideboard behind Marcus, and Lucy glanced at him and then at a photograph on a bookcase. It was Marcus's wife and family, taken some years earlier, perfectly posed. For a few seconds, Lucy's eyes rested on the two children and then returned to Marcus.

'Get on with it. I've got to be up early in the morning. What do you want?' asked Marcus.

'Why did you print the story about Dave Shearman and my mother?' asked Lucy, her manner composed, as she adjusted to the man and the place.

'It's a public interest story. They've covered the whole thing up for years, and my job's to expose it. It's what my readers expect. It's what a good paper's all about.'

'You'd do the same to anyone in the public eye, would you?'

'Of course,' said Marcus, 'Why shouldn't I?'

'What about Noreen Parfitte and Barry Halstead? They're in the public eye, and they've been having an affair for… how long?'

'Who says?'

'Come on! Shouldn't that be reported?' she asked and raised her arms from her lap, palms upward, imploringly. 'There must be others.'

'They're not public figures. Anyhow, it's not true.'

'You know it's true. Why don't you treat everyone's private affairs the same way? Doesn't private mean private?'

'Not if you're in the public eye it doesn't. The public should know what their holier-than-thou politicians have been up to.'

'What about the pain and hurt it causes? Doesn't that bother you?'

Lucy stood up and walked over to the bookcase, Clive and Marcus's eyes following her intently. She picked up the family photograph, looked at it and turned to Marcus.

'What if it was your family? What if they were smeared across the front pages?'

'But it isn't, and it wouldn't be. Anyhow, other papers wouldn't publish...'

'No,' Lucy interrupted, 'because there's an unwritten rule in the tabloids. Never tell tales about each other.'

Lucy put the photograph down and walked slowly back to her seat. She adopted a relaxed position, back and shoulders sunk into the soft leather.

'I'm not doing this to cause pain,' said Marcus, 'I'm doing it to tell the truth. Your mother and Dave Shearman made their decisions, and now Shearman has to live with it. If you've got a problem with what he did, speak to him, not me.'

'I have.'

'Look, I don't want to hurt you, but what we've reported is a public interest story.'

'What did you think when you first heard the details? Did it... did it concern you at all?'

'I don't know what you mean. Once the dates stacked up, I knew it was a good story. I was at university with them, and everyone knew that Dave and Clara were living together.'

'But just for a while, before the dates checked out, did you have any qualms... any at all?'

'I don't know what you're getting at.'

'Did it bring back memories?'

'Not really.'

'Would you have printed it if the father had not been Dave? Say, if it had been Clive.'

'That wouldn't have surprised me. Yes, I would have enjoyed publishing, if it was Clive.'

Lucy watched Marcus turn and smile fleetingly at him.

'What if it'd have been someone else, someone like you, perhaps?' she continued.

'Don't be stupid.'

'We all know about students in the swinging sixties, don't we?'

'Don't talk rubbish.'

'You know Clive had a thing for my mother, don't you?'

Lucy glanced at Clive, who lowered his head.

'Yes, everybody knew. It wouldn't have surprised me if...'

Lucy interrupted.

'It wouldn't have surprised me too. Did you find out anything more about my birth, you know, when you had the story checked out?'

'I've no idea what you're talking about.'

Suddenly, Lucy sat forward.

'Perhaps you should have done some more research. Perhaps you're not as smart as you think.'

Lucy looked directly and intently at Marcus as she spoke, as if trying to read his mind, or to pick up some minute change in his demeanour.

'I was eight weeks premature.'

'So what?'

'You know what that means don't you?'

'It means nothing.'

'Dave Shearman and my mum split up before I was conceived. Perhaps Clive's my father, after all.'

Her accusing stare turned to Clive, rested on him for a moment and then settled back on Marcus.

'Look, I've had enough of these riddles, and you'd better leave,' said Marcus. He stood up and gestured Lucy toward the door. She remained in her seat.

'I could leave and tell what I know to someone else. Would you prefer that?' Lucy was maintaining the intensity of her gaze.

'Are you threatening me?' asked Marcus, with a menace of his own.

There was a silence for a few moments, which Lucy broke.

'Who else could be my father?'

He said nothing.

'Who else do you *think* could be my father?'

'I don't know. Clive Parkhouse.' Marcus pointed. 'Is it Clive? Is that why he's here?'

'Yes, it all fits, doesn't it? Clive could well be my father. Anyone else?'

'I don't know how many people Clara slept with.'

'Are you sure you don't know anyone else she slept with?' Marcus shook his head.

'*I* do.'

'Really?'

'Could it be you?' she asked, almost in a whisper.

'What?' screamed Marcus.

'Did my mother sleep with you?'

'How dare you...'

'Could you be my father?' Lucy interrupted, firmly, quietly, but intently.

'Get out. Get out of this house!'

Marcus leant across to grab Lucy's arm, but she pulled away. She edged along the settee to increase the distance from Marcus.

'Could it? Could it be you, all those years ago? Could you be my father?'

'Don't you talk to me like that.'

'Could it be you? Did you sleep with Clara Tomlin? That's all I want to know. I'll leave then.'

Her tone had become measured and confident, and it seemed like a taunt to Marcus.

'Who do you think you are? Smearing me; you've got no proof of anything.'

Marcus was becoming increasingly agitated, like a wounded beast, with a slowly pacing predator, circling and waiting for its moment.

'But could it be you. You know the answer, don't you? I just want to know if it *could* be.'

Lucy stood up and stepped nearer to Clive, as if declaring her allegiance. There was a silence. Marcus glared and screwed up his face in anger and frustration.

'You're lying about being premature,' he snarled.

'Maybe, yes, I could be lying, but I'm not. You know whether you slept with my mother. You're the only person alive who knows for sure.'

'What did *she* tell you?' asked Marcus angrily

'You haven't said that you *didn't* sleep with her.'

Marcus stood, rooted, at one side of the coffee table. He had a distant look in his eyes. Anger was melting into disbelief. Lucy looked penetratingly at him, but Marcus resolutely avoided her gaze. Lucy broke the silence.

'You don't get it do you? I don't want a paternity test. I don't want to go to court. All I want to know is if it could be you. Tell me, could you be my father?'

'Leave,' whispered Marcus.

'You know what'll happen if I don't get an answer, and you wouldn't want that.'

'What are you going to do?' Marcus asked, quietly.

'Tell me first. Could you be my father?'

'I'm not going to tell you anything. There's nothing to tell.'

There was a minute's silence. Marcus's face was contorted,

444

as if one Marcus wanted to speak, and the other was screaming for him to stay quiet.

'Could it be you? It'll be a burden lifted. You'll see things in a different light. It's your chance.'

Then more silence. Lucy Kwame was immoveable, stock still and piercing gaze. A minute passed, then two. Marcus looked away. He wanted desperately to keep quiet but she was willing him to speak. Then he turned and looked at her with hatred in his eyes.

'Yes, I could be your father,' he gasped and fell back into the chair, 'but I'm not, am I? I'll deny it if you say I am.'

'If you could be my father, then you are,' she sighed. 'I know you are. Now you know too, don't you?'

Marcus did not answer. Lucy waited for a response that was not forthcoming. Marcus stared groundward.

'Look at me. I'm your daughter. Doesn't that mean anything to you?'

Marcus kept his silence. Lucy walked up to him, her head bent over his.

'Can't you look at me? I *am* your daughter. You've a chance to make up for all these lost years. It's in your hands.'

Marcus shook his head. Lucy walked round the table. She put her hand into her handbag and leaned over her prey, threateningly.

'Lucy!' Clive shouted.

Marcus froze, prepared to accept his fate.

65

MARCUS

Lucy pulled out a small photograph and dropped it on the table in front of her adversary.

'That's my husband, Victor. He's a Nigerian refugee. We met at university.' Lucy was struggling to hold back tears as she pointed out the three figures on the photograph, one by one.

'That's Emily. She's at secondary school. Adam, he's still at junior. They're your grandchildren. Clara loved them so much, yes, so very much. They miss her too.'

Marcus glanced sidelong at the photograph, in numb bewilderment, a white woman with a black family.

'They're your family, your grandchildren.'

'No, they're not mine.'

'Look at them. Look, look, look,' she shouted as she picked up the photograph and held it in front of him. 'You may not want it, but it's true.'

'You can't prove it.'

'I don't need to because you know, and I know, and that's all that really matters.'

'What are you going to do?' he asked.

'What do you want me to do?'

Marcus was silent, and Lucy continued.

'You want me to go away and say nothing.'

'But you won't, will you?'

'I could destroy you. That's what you'd do in my position, isn't it?'

She dropped the photograph back on the table.

'Do whatever you want. It doesn't matter,' he lied.

'Look at me. I'm your daughter. Come on, what are you ashamed of – me, Clara, yourself, my family? They're your family, too. Well?'

Marcus glanced sidelong at Lucy.

'Don't taunt me. Just tell me what you're going to do.'

'What do you feel when you look at me?'

'I don't know you. I don't feel anything.'

'Do you want to see your grandchildren?'

Marcus leaned forward and fingered the photograph dispassionately.

'No, I couldn't. They mean nothing to me. They're just faces,' he sighed.

'Do you want to see me again?'

'No.'

'You'd just like me to get out of your life, wouldn't you? You'd like me to take my story away and bury it?'

'Yes, but it's too late.'

'After all you've said and done, do you expect me to just forget? Marcus Roache, the man who's sat in judgement on the British nation, who's condemned, criticised, vilified… and in the end you're no better yourself,' she said with contempt. 'You sicken me so much. I can't… I can't even bring myself to think of you as my father.'

The room went silent. Marcus looked toward the photograph of his family on the bookcase, and a tear appeared in his eye.

'I didn't know that Clara was pregnant. She never said. I'm sorry.'

'Perhaps she kept her pregnancy secret to protect you. She

would *never* have married you,' said Lucy spitefully, 'and you'd have regretted it if you'd married her. She's allowed you the life you wanted.'

'It was just one moment of drunken madness, that's all. I can barely remember. You're going to ruin me, just because of it – my work, my reputation and my family.'

'You don't understand do you? Sleeping with my mum wasn't a crime. Young people, you know, have moments of madness. We all make mistakes. That's what happens when you're young.' Lucy shrugged. 'You made your mistake quietly and secretly, and then you forgot about it, but it still happened.'

Lucy began to pace, restlessly, across the room in front of Clive.

'I didn't know.'

'No. That's a lie,' she shouted. 'You knew what you'd done. I don't mean having a child, but sleeping with my mum. You've spent a lifetime vilifying people like her. You've made a living out of it.'

'One mistake. I'm sorry, truly sorry.'

'You didn't let all those others you've maligned make their one mistake, did you?'

'It's my job.'

'You're no different from any of them.'

'You don't understand.'

'You attacked Dave Shearman in your rag, but you'd slept with my mum too.'

'I wasn't like that, but Dave was.'

'What?' she yelled.

'Dave's always been a womaniser. I'm not like him. I'm not.'

'How can you say that? Doesn't my mum count?'

'If I'd have known, I'd have stopped the story.'

'Why?'

Marcus did not reply.

'You'd have only stopped the story because the world would have found out about you.'

Lucy stopped pacing, stood next to Clive and calmly addressed her adversary.

'I'm glad I've found out the truth. I'd hoped that you might show, I don't know, some feeling for me and my children – your grandchildren.'

'I've had no time to...' Marcus started, but Lucy interrupted.

'I've spent so much time thinking about my father. I wanted to meet him, and I wanted him to see his grandchildren.'

'That's not fair...'

'Tonight, I hoped you might be remorseful, not at getting my mum pregnant, but at the way you treated her, Dave Shearman, me and my family and everyone like us.'

'I *am* sorry.'

'What for?'

'I'm sorry for... I'm sorry this has upset you.'

'Upset me! If you're not sorry for what you've done, you're not sorry at all.'

Marcus picked up the family photograph.

'Whatever you do, I understand. You've every right. I've caused enough harm. I don't want to cause any more – not to you,' Marcus looked at the photograph, 'or your children.'

'I'd love to expose you for the hypocrite you are... and if I say nothing about this, it'll be for me and my children, not for you. I'll do it because I don't want anyone to know that you're my father.' Lucy fixed Marcus with fierce and unforgiving eyes. 'I never want to see you again. I don't ever want to hear your voice. I don't want to think about you, and I want to keep you as far away from everyone I love as I can. I won't let you taint my life. Of course, tomorrow, or some other day, I might change my mind,' she smiled. 'Just pray that day doesn't come.'

'How many people know?'

'Victor, but he won't tell anyone.'

'But what about Shearman? He could sink me. And Clive could too.'

'I hope they'll respect my privacy, the privacy you've tried to destroy.'

'Including Shearman?'

'Dave? He doesn't know you're my father, but I'll have to tell him. You've wrecked his career, so who knows what he'll do?'

She turned and walked through the door, down the stairs and waited in the street. Clive looked at Marcus, hunched in his chair.

66

CLIVE

'If I see anything in the *Echo* that's not complimentary to Dave,' said Clive, 'then watch out because your secret *will* hit the headlines. I'll make sure of that. Say something nice about him and perhaps I can persuade him to keep quiet. I'm not as forgiving as your daughter. Bye Marcus. Sleep well.'

Clive smiled and winked at Marcus. He left the flat and followed Lucy as she walked to her car. She took her seat behind the driver's wheel, and Clive sat in the passenger seat. She turned to him.

'Thanks, Clive.'

'I didn't do anything.'

'You were there. That's what fathers are for, aren't they… to be there?'

She turned the ignition.

'I'm not your father.'

'No, but you'll do. What did you say to Marcus?'

'Nothing much.'

'Perhaps this'll change him.'

Clive did not reply.

67

MARCUS

As Lucy was speaking to Clive, Marcus picked up the photograph she had left.

He stared at the incriminating evidence. It was undeniable, and his future was in the hands of people he did not trust; people who hated him. If they wanted to, his enemies could destroy him. Marcus thought about Mary and the children. They must not find out. He placed the photograph back on the table and sat down.

Even though it was late in the evening, and he was in the comfort of his London flat, he was still in his suit jacket. He had not wished the unwanted guests, who had just left, to see the sweat that had soaked his shirt and the yellow stain under his armpits. He picked up the photograph and was about to tear at it. He did not start the task.

A sense of doom, a feeling he had experienced intermittently for the past few days, swept over him, and he found his thoughts shifting between the problem at hand and his darkest thoughts. The sweats started again, and the fear became panic. It was a sheer and irresistible terror. He felt numb and sick, and he could not concentrate on the act of destroying the photograph. He thought he was choking, and his hands were trembling.

He was reaching for the phone when the chest pain smashed into him, mercilessly. He was being crushed, his own ribcage squeezing the life out of him. He could not raise his left arm, and he tried to swing round to pick up the phone in his right hand, but his body refused to respond. He knew what was happening, and he had been expecting it.

'Oh no. Please, God,' he groaned as he slumped into the leather seat, the photograph crumpled in his hand.

Why, why, why have they done this to me?

He heard knocking at the door, silence and knocking again; then a rattle of keys, but it would be too late, all too late.

68

CONCLUSION

Clive phoned Dave Shearman from the car. He said that he and Lucy would meet him at Becky's house, early the next morning.

Clive arrived at 9.30. Becky was making toast, coffee and tea. Dave was at the kitchen table, a mug of coffee in his hand, and Lucy was next to him, caressing her own cup. Lucy had already told Dave that Marcus was her father, but not the detail of what had happened the previous night.

'Becky,' said Dave, 'a tea for Clive.'

'Have you heard the news about Marcus? It's been on the radio,' said Clive.

'Has he resigned? Joined the Labour Party?' asked Dave.

'He's been rushed into hospital. They say it's a heart attack.'

Lucy turned to Clive.

'Serious?' she asked.

'I don't know, but it doesn't sound good. Apparently, it's his second. He's in intensive care, and he's lucky to be alive. It seems that Marcus's driver realised that he had left some important papers in the car and decided he'd drop them off. He had keys to the flat, and he found Marcus. It couldn't have been long after we left.'

'He's alive, though?' she asked.

'I don't know.'

'We could have killed him, couldn't we?' Lucy murmured.

'He's got a weak heart, so I don't think we should blame ourselves.'

'I wouldn't be able to bear it if I thought it was us,' said Lucy.

'I couldn't care less,' added Dave.

'Dad, that's a horrid thing to say,' said Becky. 'You shouldn't wish that on anyone.'

'I know, but he's been so spiteful. He's hurt you and your family, me, Clive, Lucy and… and Clara.'

'Becky's right,' said Lucy. 'It's not just Marcus. Think of his family and what they're going through.'

Becky walked into the living room, turned on the television and scoured text for any news.

'It's here,' she shouted through the door. 'It says… he's in a critical condition… stable… more tests… I'm scrolling down.' Becky paused. 'Wife's flying back from the States, children at bedside. That's all.'

Lucy sighed.

'OK, OK. There's nothing we can do about Marcus,' said Dave. 'I still don't know everything that happened last night.'

'I'm sorry I was so short with you yesterday,' said Lucy.

'It wasn't easy for either of us.'

'When you spoke about my mum, I was confused. You told me you'd split at the end of March. Since I was a kid, I'd known I'd been in an incubator after I was born. I was two months premature. I must've been conceived in May, so you couldn't have been be my father. I was trying to work out what it all meant. When I got home, I tried to piece it all together.'

Lucy took a sip of her coffee and continued.

'I remembered when I'd met Clive in Grinderton, and he told me he was at university with my mum…'

'You thought I was your father?' Clive interrupted.

'I wished. The dates stacked up, but I knew that couldn't be true either.'

'How?' asked Clive.

'Mum told me, when I was seven or eight, that my father was married and had children of his own. I did some research on the internet. You weren't married back then, and you didn't have a family, not for nine or ten years. There was no need for Mum to lie. She may have concealed the truth, but no, she'd never lie.'

'Why didn't you tell me Clara was your mum was when we were in Grinderton? You had the chance.'

'It came out of the blue, and I didn't have time to think. I was surprised that you knew my mum, and I was thinking that you could be my father.'

'Or when we met in London?'

'I'd have had to explain why I'd not told you before, and you'd ask questions, questions that would lead you back to Mum, and she didn't want that. Her health was on the slide, and there was no point upsetting her. Anyway, I suppose I wanted to be treated on my own merits, not because I was Clara Tomlin's daughter.'

'So how did you work out that Marcus was your father?' asked Clive.

'Dave put Marcus in the frame. He told me about the last time he'd seen Mum at university. He'd left her, you and Marcus together at a party. I guessed what might have happened. The dates were right. If it wasn't Marcus, then I'd never find who my father was.'

'So you weren't sure,' said Clive.

'No, but something else made sense too. If Marcus *was* my father, then Mum would never have told him. She wouldn't have put him in the position of thinking he had to marry her, never jeopardised his ambition and never, ever, considered marrying him. There was no reason *to* tell him, and she didn't tell me because she would've been frightened what I'd say, or do.'

'So you acted on a hunch,' said Dave.

'That's why I had to confront Roache. If I was right, he was the only person alive who knew. I had to make him admit it. If he hadn't, I'd have felt stupid, and I'd never have known, but it was worth the risk.'

'You were... you were sensational.'

'Thanks, but it was scary. I didn't expect to see you though. We were both looking for Marcus.'

'Google,' they said at the same time and laughed.

Clive and Lucy explained how the evening had unfolded, what had been said and Marcus's reaction. Clive didn't mention his final words to Marcus. They discussed what should be made public. If Marcus did not recover, it was agreed that they would say nothing. It was more difficult to decide what to do if he pulled through and went back to work.

Dave was prepared to expose Marcus and wanted him to endure the condemnation he had meted out to others. If Lucy needed legal proof, she could demand a paternity test. Lucy didn't want further press intrusion and the disruption it would cause to her family. She made it clear that she had no intention of having a test.

'He's my father,' said Lucy. 'As soon as I met him, I knew. It was a scary feeling. I can't say how, but it was so obvious to me. I don't need the law to tell me what I already know. I want this to be kept to ourselves.'

'What about the whole world thinking that I'm Lucy's father?' Dave asked.

'That's how I want it to stay,' said Lucy. 'Other than us, Victor and Marcus, nobody else knows the truth, or needs to know. I hope you don't mind.'

'If it's what you want,' Dave shrugged. 'What about Christine?'

'Tell her the truth, of course,' Lucy replied.

'But I don't want him to get away with it.'

'Come on, Dad. It would just be spiteful, and it's not what Lucy wants,' said Becky.

Clive nodded.

'OK, OK.' Dave said. 'I'll go along with it. I've been outvoted. I don't know what I'll do with myself. That bastard has ruined my career.'

'You could write your memoirs, Dad,' said Becky. 'That'll keep you busy.'

The conversation meandered. They talked about their families, and Dave and Clive filled in some of the gaps from the previous forty years. They checked the news for any update on Marcus, but there was none.

'What about meeting up?' Dave asked. 'We could bring husbands and wives and have a weekend away. It'd be a forty year reunion.'

'Invite Mike,' said Clive.

'Becky and Lucy too. Lucy should arrange it,' said Dave, enthusiastically.

Early the following week, Dave phoned Clive. It was the day that Marcus left hospital.

'Have you seen the papers for the past few days? Not the papers in general – I mean the *Echo*.'

'It's not the first thing I do after shaving.'

'No follow up on me and Lucy, well not much. I got a call from Peter Kellock at the *Echo*. He's after an interview. He sounded very… well, very conciliatory. He said they'd take a positive view. I detect Marcus behind it. Why the sudden interest?'

'Change of heart. Close-to-death experience. How do I know?'

'It's something to do with you, isn't it?'

'I told him to be nice to you. I sent him a get well card with, what shall I call it, a reminder and a few suggestions. I never thought I'd end up editing the *Echo*.'

Clive and Lucy had separately sent get well cards to Marcus. They were each unaware of the other's actions.

When Marcus had come round in hospital, a nurse had been taking his blood pressure.

'How you feelin', Mr Roache?'

Marcus had been disorientated and had taken a few moments to piece together what had happened.

'You're in good hands here. No need to talk. I'll get you some water.'

He had remembered the photograph he had clasped so tightly. His hands had been on top of the blanket and the photograph had not been there. Had it been left in his flat? What if Mary found it? The nurse had seen his actions.

'Don't worry. I got that photograph. Couldn't get it out your hand, and it's really crumpled. It's in there,' she had said, pointing toward the bedside table. 'I'll get it out for you. Family?'

He had shaken his head. She had opened a drawer in the cupboard and had handed him the photograph.

'OK? Your wife'll be here in a few hours.'

When the nurse had gone, he had finished the task that had been uncompleted in his flat, and the evidence had fallen into the plastic rubbish bag at the side of the bed.

It was three days later when Marcus had read Lucy's message.

'Wishing you a speedy recovery.' He had placed the card flat on the top of the bedside cabinet and had opened Clive's. A note had slipped from it, reminding Marcus of his threat and a few editorial suggestions.

He had placed the card on top of Lucy's and then had picked them up together. He had torn them into small pieces, slowly and silently, before dropping them into the rubbish bag.

Many months later, the reunion took place. It was at a large London hotel, and Mike, Lucy, Clive, Becky and Dave attended, with their spouses.

'Did you send Marcus an invite?' Clive asked Lucy.

'Oh yes, of course I did.'

'What?' exclaimed Dave.

'It's a reunion, after all,' replied Lucy. 'I knew I wouldn't get a reply, but it was a reminder. I don't want him ever to forget. It is the least I can do for Mum... for all of us.'

Marcus had recognised Lucy's handwriting on the envelope, and with barely a glance at the contents, he had shredded the invitation. The shredder gave out a reassuring noise as well as providing a satisfying conclusion. The invitation to receive his knighthood, for his services to journalism, proudly adorned his desk at the *Echo*.

ABOUT THE AUTHOR

BJ Bulckley is a self-taught writer. He grew up in the Midlands and currently lives in the South East.